The Girl Who Tempted God

Daniel Basil Lyle

LylePublishing

Sulphur, Oklahoma

The Girl Who Tempted God

Copyright © 2015 by Daniel Basil Lyle

ISBN 978-0-9794101-6-1

Published by LylePublishing
505 W. 12th Street, Sulphur, OK 73086
(www.LylePublishing.com)

Printed by CreateSpace, an Amazon.com company. Available from Amazon.com and other retail outlets. Also available as an ebook on Kindle and other devices.

LCED10292018

DISCLAIMER and FORWARD

Although this book draws heavily from the author's experiences, all characters are fictitious. Any resemblance to real contemporary persons, living or dead, is purely coincidental. Although the heroine of this story is depicted as interacting with the historical Jesus, his words and behavior, plus other historical figures, are fictionalized. This book is a sequel to *"The Girl Who Played with Fate,"* beginning where that book left off.

Chapter 1

<u>**LAST CHANCE**</u>

Hurry don't dawdle

With the horses at the gate

Huffing and snorting, wild-eyed

With everything set to begin the race

The gatekeeper with gun in hand, pointed up

Run as fast as you can to throw down your Bet

On which of the beasts you favor to win

Or which of them merely to place high

And which to lose and come in last

The money's there to be made

Or tossed away with a sigh

Your last feeble excuse

"At least I tried."

The Luminary Chronicles, 1:123-128

Sally returned to consciousness lying sprawled on a hot rock in a blistering desert.

Her back hurt terribly. She feared it was broken.

And she was being *baked* by a relentlessly blazing sun! It hung high in a cloudless sky, nearly blinding the rapidly blinking Sally.

A strong *hot wind* continually blew against her body, slamming her face and eyes with biting sand.

Also, her clothes felt uncomfortably loose.

"Where am I?" she gasped through cracked lips. "And how long...have I been...lying here?"

1

Close around her she saw only sand, rugged yellow cliffs, and rocky hills.

Looking further, she saw she was in a wide gully between two high peaks that look to her blurred sight like *giant upturned fangs!* Some ancient cataclysm had scooped out the middle of an existing mountain, leaving two sharp cliffs protruding upward on each side.

The only vegetation was a few dried-up shrubs also blasted by the merciless wind.

But off at a distance in the wide gully, lying on its side, Sally glimpsed the *red Obelisk!*

She managed to roll over from lying on her back. Then she painfully crawled in the direction of the huge, rectangular, red-glass structure. She noted that it was quickly being covered up by wind-blown sand.

It should have been shimmering and glowing, but it wasn't. She and her scientists had come up with intricate algorithms and mechanisms to control the transport device originally made by an extinct Martian race. The ancient artifact, once activated, was able to tap-into that rarest form of dispersed energy: *Time* itself! Having traveled in time more than 2,000 years into the past, it should be brimming with energy, fully charged up! It was supposed to be her base of operations once she arrived. Then, she'd use its incredible power incisively, altering the distant past to set mankind upon a new, better timeline.

But it just lay there like a giant, dead, rectangular rock.

It took a long time for her to finally drag her hurting, weak body up to its towering side. Then she *slammed* a weak fist into its red, glassy side...

"You were supposed to be how I take control of the primitive civilizations of the first century!" she screamed at it.

She half-expected it to reply.

Instead, it did nothing. It was just a useless piece of *dead rock,* oblivious to her outrage.

The only thing that moved was the brutally hot desert wind whipping hot sand into her eyes.

"Water...I need *water*," she gasped, trying to open up a panel set into the side of the Obelisk to get at stored supplies—but finding it fused shut.

She *banged* on it futilely with her fists.

Indeed, the structure being buried in the blowing sand was *completely inert*. Sally could see areas inside the translucent material where there appeared to be dark shafts of burnt material. The powerful Dark Energy generator inside, which triggered its flight back in time, had apparently been destroyed by the passage. And she'd ended up...who knew when or where?

The Obelisk was now just a big slab of useless, fused red rock.

Sally came to the horrifying realization that she was marooned, helpless, and without supplies.

"I've...*got*...to find...water!" she angrily told herself, struggling to stand upright.

It hurt her injured back terribly, but she ignored the pain.

Tottering on her feet, she tore off her now-smothering robe, tossing it angrily to the side.

"How did that get so large?" she asked herself, looking at what seemed like a huge pile of white cloth.

But that wasn't all—even her underclothes were too big, so baggy that they just slid down off her squirming body!

Shaking her head in confusion, she leaned back against the hot red glass, totally naked.

It was then that Sally caught sight of her reflection in the looming side of the Obelisk.

She had no breasts. She had no pubic hair. On her head was just short fuzz. The magnificent *tattoos* that had covered most of her body were completely gone. Her skin was tender and pink—though now reddened by the blazing sun.

The reflection looking back at her was that of a young child no more than five years old.

I'm a little girl!—she marveled.

"It worked..." she ruefully gasped out loud, understanding the magnitude of her transformation.

The entire bottle filled with Optimmune pills that she'd swallowed—a huge dosage to take all at once—by rights should have killed her. Instead, she'd hoped it would regenerate her cells as they were subjected to incredible forces as she was flung back against the flow of time. Yes, the DE-generator encased the Obelisk in a force field, but her calculations showed it would weaken trying to contain such a gigantic, active structure. Gulping the entire bottle was her only hope to arrive atop the Obelisk intact. Her strategy worked even better than anticipated. As she traveled back in time atop the Obelisk...the pills had caused her entire *eighty-seven year-old body* to revert to that of a child!

"Huh...how about that?" she weakly laughed to herself. "But maybe it's better this way."

As an old woman she would never be able to sway Jesus from becoming the Founder of a great religion. The only way to stop him would be to kill him.

But as a contemporary little girl, might she find a way to *tempt him* away from his preferred path?

By insinuating into his Presence as an innocent-appearing, harmless little girl—she just might have a chance to save mankind from the looming Wrath of God!

At least, that was her desperate plan.

Though she was now a child, her memories remained intact. She remembered the horrific reality of seeing God's Judgment Day, when a *solar super-storm* burned off the surface of planet Earth! And that occurred because scientists discovered a means to routinely and easily access concentrated Dark Energy—part of the underlying fabric of the Universe—setting off a "cosmic flare" bringing wicked mankind to God's full attention: to be judged and found wanting.

In the linked Dimension in which she'd been born, judicious measured usage of Dark Energy was assured via brutal, dictatorial Empires. It was the norm of her civilization since, for whatever reasons, Jesus was never there to start his great religion. But in *this* parallel Dimension, the casual future usage of Dark Energy became a way of life: even fueling spaceships colonizing the moon and Mars. Vast amounts of Dark Energy were being contemplated to power prototype craft capable of traveling at near light-speed to the stars.

Here, mankind proceeded *not* under the careful but cruel oversight of strict Elites, but in the supposed benevolence of "democratic" permissive governments. And it was the teachings of this "Jesus of Nazareth" that infected the psyches of this world's societies—fostering experimentation and liberalism—which allowed things to get so out of hand.

So to push off the Day of Judgment, Sally embarked on a terrible mission: to go back in time and *erase this Jesus* from history!

But now that Mission seemed far away, distant.

Sally's immediate reality was just a *burning sun, suffocating heat,* and *no water*.

She wouldn't survive long in this barren desert.

So she determined to climb up the highest close peak and see if she could spy water. Surely there must be a river somewhere, or even just a stream. The entire world that she landed in could not be composed of sand, could it?

"I'm...getting...delirious," she gasped, swallowing hard, realizing that even her saliva was drying up.

She managed to rip out sections of her white robe and wrap it loosely around her small body, belt it securely, and flip up over her head a shielding white hood.

"My gun—where's my gun?" she frantically gasped-out, remembering the energy-weapon she'd had cradled on her chest when she lay flat onto the top of the Obelisk for her journey back in time.

She floundered around the Obelisk, searching.

"I need a *weapon!*" she screamed into the dry, hot air.

She didn't know what was out there in the desert. She could be stopped dead in her in her tracks by a poisonous snake, wild animals, or even bandits.

"Damn!" she cursed, leaning wearily against the hot Obelisk.

The gun was nowhere to be found.

She was defenseless.

Even her white tennis shoes were conspiring against her. They were now much too large for her feet, hindering her movement. So she impulsively kicked them to the side and stubbornly proceeded barefoot across the hot sand.

"Gotta find water...gotta find water," she mumbled to herself as she began climbing up the nearest hill, angrily persisting—handhold by handhold, one foot after the other, inch by inch.

Until, as the blazing sun was mercifully descending on the horizon, she finally topped a ledge and stood precariously on top of the peak. It was one of the twin upturned "fangs" she'd seen from below. From its top, she looked out over a shadowed expanse of low hills.

No green was visible.

"*Damn!*" Sally weakly swore again, swaying back and forth in the strong hot wind. "I'm doomed..."

Wait!

There off in the distance, just behind the hills on the horizon. Was that a hint of blue? Was it water? Was it, perhaps, an oasis or even a lake?

Yes! There was no doubt. It was a line of gorgeous *deep blue!*

As the sun sank beneath the horizon and the blistering heat paradoxically plummeted into a chill that made Sally shiver, she determined to reach that *sparkling, blue water.*

"I'm not stopping until I get there," she encouraged herself, slipping and sliding back down the rocky slope.

It would take most of the night to get there.

Or, she'd just drop dead in her tracks.

Whatever!

At least she'd die with the satisfaction that she *tried...*

Dave found himself crouched behind garbage cans in a smelly alley.

How he'd gotten there, he had no idea.

The last thing he remembered was hugging his friends tightly as raiders from a galactic Harvester spaceship swooped downward to destroy the town of Edmond, Oklahoma—leveling the city with devastating laser weapons!

"You ok, David?" a man at his elbow asked him.

Dave looked over to see a man in a torn military uniform crouched beside him. He was a burly man sporting a messed-up blond crewcut. He wore dark eyeglasses.

It was the FBI agent, Arthur Anderson.

Dave gaped at him, speechless with surprise and shock.

"*What?*" Arthur said, hefting his handgun, sticking its black muzzle up above the garbage cans. "Is there something on my face—a leach or something?"

"You're *alive!*"

"Well, hell—I hope so," the Agent laughed. "But we may not be for much longer if you don't shut up. Those Reapers are close enough to hear us."

"But...?"

"*Quiet!*" Arthur said, pulling Dave down lower behind the garbage cans.

Dave heard an ominous "CLOMP, CLOMP, CLOMP" coming along the street outside the alleyway.

Then the sounds stopped...

—as a twenty-foot tall *Robot* peered into the alley!

"Keep down!" Arthur harshly whispered, pulling Dave's head back as he tried to get a better view of the behemoth.

But what he'd seen when he'd peeked up was enough. It was a bipedal robot with a swiveling top—sporting what looked to be five camera-lenses, its "eyes", arranged in a circle, giving it total 360-degree vision. In the place of arms were three writhing, metallic-looking tentacles that seemed able to extend out to any desired length.

Also, a dozen mobile gun barrels were aligned along the swiveling top of the killer robot, right below the five "eyes"—thick and lethal-looking, independently taking careful aim at any possible threats.

It was a walking death machine. And Dave could hear it *advancing* into the alley!

Dave, eyes stretched wide in fear, saw an *extended metallic tentacle* creep past the garbage cans, as if "sniffing" the air...

Dave instinctively held his breath, not making a sound.

Slowly, as if satisfied, the gleaming tentacle tip withdrew.

The looming robot then exited the alley and continued away on the street outside the alley.

CLOMP! CLOMP! CLOMP!—the heavy steps retreated off into the distance.

"Close one, that..." Arthur grimly stated, relaxing with his back to a crumbling brick wall. "It must have heard us talking from a distance. Lucky it didn't get a good bead on us. We've got a reprieve, maybe twenty minutes before the next patrol-bot goes by. After that, we're in the clear for maybe an hour. Perhaps we'll live to complete this mission after all."

Arthur began quietly humming to himself as he happily stood up, stretched, brushed dirt off his pants, and started pawing through the nearest garbage can.

"What...is...going...on...here?" Dave said through clenched teeth.

"Hey! We've hit the jackpot, David. What's going on here is— *breakfast!*"

Arthur jubilantly withdrew from the garbage can the stiffened corpse of a big fat, dead *rat*.

It smelled awful.

Agent Anderson began ripping tattered fur off the animal, exposing rotting flesh.

Tearing off one of the legs and handing it to Dave, Arthur heartily bit into the side of the rat, gobbling down both bone and flesh.

Dave gingerly accepted the leg before carefully setting it to the side. It stank horribly.

"This is going to sound strange..." Dave tentatively began.

"What?" Arthur said around a mouthful of dead rat meat.

"I seem to be having...a memory lapse, I guess...and I can't recall some things."

"Hey, must be that blow to your skull you caught yesterday," Arthur said, expressing concern. "You said you were alright. I knew I should have made you stay at the camp today and rest. But no, you insisted on coming hunting with me. Soon as we get back you're..."

"Sure, sure, whatever," Dave said, feeling tentatively at a swollen lump he discovered on the side of his head. "But for right now I just need to get oriented, so..."

"Fine! Fine! Ask away! We can't move until the next Reaper's passed by, anyway. What do you need to know?" Arthur asked as he slid down again behind the concealing garbage cans, still munching on his dead rat.

"The last I remember...of *you*...is when we attacked Aberdeen to snag the Device. Do you remember that?"

"Damn right, David! We almost got our asses handed to us on a platter. We were lucky to abort the mission just as we were flying into the base, Sally catching chatter on your laptop of prowling attack 'copters that were waiting to ambush us."

"And what happened after that?" Dave eagerly asked, as Arthur went back to chomping on the tough flesh of the dead rat.

An emaciated alley cat stalked warily past Dave, eyeing their meal greedily.

Arthur scared it off with an abrupt wave of his hand.

"You know full well what happened, kiddo—you playin' a game with me?"

"Humor me. What happened next?"

Overhead Dave could hear the sound of a flying vehicle—but it wasn't a jet or propeller sound, more like a loud *vibration* in the sky.

It was ominous.

It seemed to be hovering at a high altitude, searching...

Arthur shrugged as if this were a big waste of time: "We landed back in Vermont where elite commandos were waiting for us. They grabbed us before we could do anything. You, Sally, and your old Professor were taken away and forced to work on the new power-generator. Fortunately our aborted incursion at least got them to postpone their initial test. You guys then figured out how to make it function without destroying half the world—and I got sent away to a military prison. Surely you remember some of this?"

"It's all fuzzy..." Dave diverted the question. "So why aren't you still there, in prison?"

"Because before they could figure out that I wasn't just a renegade FBI agent with fancy eyewear, my friends got me out."

"And me—and Sally?"

"You both eventually escaped. The Professor and his wife we don't know exactly what happened to them. There's a rumor they're still at a hidden underground research facility that the Reapers ain't found yet, working on new weapons against the invaders. Hell, David, don't tell me you can't remember *any* of this?"

"Well...maybe it's coming back now," he lied, furiously thinking that he'd better not reveal his cards until he knew better how this new game was played.

He was obviously in a *whole new timeline!*

The possibility of different timelines was quite disturbing. He'd only just been informed of it by the Dinosapien, George. And now he was experiencing it!

Somehow he'd been sent into the mind of a new version of himself.

But where were *his* Sally, the two Dinosapiens—George and his wife Alice—plus the man-sized dinosaur Breep and the android-child Tommy?

Were they tossed into this new timeline with him? If so, where were they? Were they also in the heads of prior versions of themselves? Or did they go into George's evolved dinosaur Dimension version of Earth...or...?

This was all way too confusing.

Dave shook his head and tried to force himself to concentrate on his immediate situation.

He definitely had a headache. And it wasn't just the tender lump on his head. This was all happening too fast! And the stench in the alley was revolting.

"But," he said, trying to focus his jumbled thoughts, "then, when was it that the Harvesters arrived?"

"Man, you really *did* get banged up, didn't you—not to remember that?" Arthur said, sounding more sympathetic. "It was just after I escaped prison, right when the U.S. Military announced a working Dark Energy Generator, which they said they'd lease out to cooperative nations that..."

"Makes sense," Dave interrupted him. "They'd want to keep such a mammoth power source under tight control."

"Except that they couldn't."

"What?"

"Scientists all across the world figured out the key principles. Before the allied nations even got their central Dark Energy power generators up and running, small sealed versions popped up everywhere. The cat was out of the bag. Nobody knows for sure, but we figure that tapping into Dark Energy wuz what attracted the alien invaders in the first place."

"So...it really *is* my fault, then—that the whole world's been destroyed?" Dave gulped, overwhelmed with crushing guilt.

"Ah, don't feel so bad," Arthur tried to encourage him. "You damn scientists want to figure everything out, no matter the consequences. If it wasn't you and Sally getting it to work and then letting the cat out of the bag, some other researchers would have done the same."

"Maybe...maybe not..."

"It's just the way the world is, friend," Anderson flatly stated. "There's no stopping Science—particularly in our loose, individualistic societies. No sense in blaming yourself."

"But didn't the militaries of the world fight against the invaders? Couldn't our nuclear missiles stop those Harvester spaceships?"

"David, our non-nuclear jets and missiles were gnats against elephants. The Harvesters hardly took notice of them—just swatted them away. And our nukes were somehow neutralized. We didn't get a single one of them to detonate against those spaceships. The nuclear-tipped missiles just bounced off. The military claims the invaders have some sort of energy-fields or whatnot."

"Like ants in a construction zone," Dave sighed sadly, "Not even a nuisance to the builders."

It was scorching. Dave realized that he was sweating profusely. His legs were cramped from crouching behind the garbage cans for so long. He was dizzy from the putrid smell. He wiped salty sweat out of his eyes.

"So why don't we just give up?" Dave whispered. He was drained of energy.

"Not in our nature," Arthur gruffly stated. "But I'm here at your side, David. I believe in your idea of linking up DE-generators all across the world to produce a planetary shield. Once that's in place—and we've walled-off Earth from the orbiting Harvesters—then we'll *kick the butts* of these damn alien robots prowling the surface!"

"That's my idea?" Dave frowned, wiping more sweat off his forehead with a grimy hand. "When Dark Energy generation caused so much trouble, I wanted to do even more of it? Really?"

"*Right*," Anderson emphatically stated. "Don't you remember? The military rejected your idea of a planetary shield in favor of trying to build controlled-release DE-bombs. But you said that was too dangerous, more likely to destroy the entire planet than the invaders. That's why you escaped, to enlist the help of hundreds of Resistance cells who were subsisting off of small, sealed DE-generators. Once you figure out how to cloak their signatures and link them all together, then we've got a fighting chance to..."

Dave stopped listening to Arthur prattling on. His thoughts were jumbled. The entire hot, stinking alley seemed to be spinning around him. Had he really experienced what Arthur claimed? Perhaps his own memory of a previous, distinctly different life was itself just a fantasy caused by that blow to his head? Did they really extract from a dying Arthur's brain a super-evolved computer intelligence embedded into a neurological-sponge? Were he and Victor really thrown into the past by their Device to fight off cavemen and giant woolly mammoths? And did they really make it to the United Nations Assembly Chamber to announce to the entire world the specifications of his Dark Energy-generating Device?

But according to Arthur, *none* of that happened.

Dave knew he couldn't resolve the discrepancies. It was all too jumbled. The possible "real" timeline was "mushed-up" with this "new" one. So he decided to concentrate on the present moment's dangers.

"But...Arthur... Don't the Alien Harvester Ships work off of Dark Energy? If so, they must be far ahead of us in their technological mastery. Wouldn't our primitive use of DE be like cavemen waving torches at an invading army that's using machine guns?"

The burly man shrugged before answering: "Who the bloody hell knows, kiddo? But we can't just give up because they have more advanced technology. The more you experiment with Dark Energy, I say the better. After all, you're the *Leader of the Resistance*. If you stop, then the few remaining humans scattered across the world will give up on DE and just focus on day-to-day survival. That's a prescription for complete defeat. It'll be the end of humanity."

"I'm...what? The *Leader* of the world's Resistance fighting the invaders? Really?"

"Damn right! It's you that's kept us going, David—given us a purpose beyond hiding in holes waiting to get snatched up by the next prowling Reaper Bot. Cranking up and linking our small DE-generators is our only hope to stop the invaders. If we can somehow defeat these Aliens then our shattered world could rebound. It could eventually become a paradise! We were well on the way to making this place heaven-on-earth before the Alien Starships showed up. The more DE-generators we get going, the better chance we'll have to survive and maybe even win."

Dave frowned, trying to believe Anderson's pep-talk but failing. Something was fundamentally wrong with Arthur's argument— something that Dave couldn't quite put his finger on...

"Hey, buddy, I'm with you," Arthur encouraged him, putting a big hand firmly on Dave's shoulder. "Now don't start second-guessing yourself. We've got a plan. Let's execute it. If we can find the original-model generator that we picked up a weak signal from yesterday, you may have what you need for your research, right?"

"I...I guess..."

Dave still had trouble thinking of himself as a "freedom-fighter"— let alone the *Leader* of the "Resistance"!

This was just too fantastic...like some low budget science fiction movie.

He knew that he sure didn't look like a world-wide leader.

He noticed that he had on raggedy blue jeans and a long-sleeved, thick shirt. A heavy knapsack was slung over his back. To his side sat a classic military assault rifle. Presumably he knew how to use it?

"How come you just have a pistol and I have this big rifle?" Dave absently asked.

"You know full well this ain't just a pistol," Arthur huffed. "This is one of that religious nut-job High Priestess lady's inventions. My colleagues got their hands on a few of them before the Alien Invasion started. Beside the Resistance, her female army's the only world-wide organizing force left. But those 'Priestesses' are all nuts—won't let anyone outside their new religion have any of these guns or their 'tame' energizer 'artificial-suns' that suck energy from the atmosphere and ground. They say that Dark Energy is from the devil and anyone who uses it should be summarily executed. But I've gotta admit their guns are useful. They're nowhere near as powerful as a DE generator—but when charged up they pack a hell of a punch!"

"Well, that's good to know, I guess," Dave sighed, putting a hand to his throbbing head as Anderson withdrew his own hand from Dave's shoulder.

"Hey, I'm getting really worried about you, David. You're talking like you haven't even been here post-invasion. That has to be one *serious* head injury you got."

"I'm...just dizzy. I'll be ok."

"You gonna eat that?" Arthur mildly asked, pointing to the bloody stump of the dead rat's leg lying beside Dave.

Dave distastefully handed it to him: "Not too hungry, I guess."

"Your loss," Arthur laughed, happily gnawing at the rotten meat.

Dave felt a vibration through the pavement beneath him, then another...

"It's the next patrolling Reaper," Arthur said, dropping the now-bare bone and hunching lower behind the garbage cans. "Quiet!"

Dave barely breathed as this next giant robot "*clomped*" on past the alleyway.

Fortunately, this one didn't pause to inspect the space.

In a few minutes the sound of its ponderous steps faded off into the distance.

"Let's get going," Arthur said, spryly hopping up to his feet, slinging his own backpack up over his shoulder, and holding his black pistol out in front of him as he headed for the street.

Dave followed along behind, his rifle also at-ready, nestled in both of his hands.

Yes, it felt quite natural. It was as if his body instinctively knew how to use the gun. In fact, he vaguely recalled that it was an "AK-47" Kalashnikov. It wouldn't do much against a Reaper, of course—but it might serve to distract those devilish machines enough to allow Dave and Anderson to escape an attack.

The worn, wooden stock of the rifle was smooth, the trigger taut, and the curve of the hanging magazine of bullets comforting.

Dave instinctively knew its real value was to kill fellow marauding *human* bandits.

Yes, there were memories in this new version of him that he was starting to access.

They snuck out onto the street.

Actually, there was no street. Instead, there was simply *total destruction*.

The "alley" they'd been hiding in was, in fact, merely two partially-standing walls of once-adjacent buildings. In all directions around them the city buildings were leveled or torn to pieces!

As far as Dave could see, there were only bombed-out, burned remnants. Heavy debris covered up what used to be streets, making walking difficult. However, the devastation did offer many crumbling piles of building-materials which they hid behind as they ducked from spot to spot.

"What city is this?" Dave gasped to Arthur as they slid into a dark hole beneath a collapsed roof. They were apparently in what once was a hardware store, judging from the few remaining items scattered around.

"City?" Arthur looked at Dave worriedly. "Jesus, your poor brain's fried, isn't it? You still remember how to use that rifle?" he worriedly asked.

"Uhm...point and pull the trigger?"

"That's a start—but this is Washington D.C., or what remains of it. It was one of the first cities leveled in the initial attack. The alien bastards immediately took out our major cities and military installations to make us easy pickings. Over there used to be the Mall."

Dave looked in the direction that Arthur pointed.

Sure enough, among the rubble Dave could make out the white rectangular side of the fallen Washington Monument. And...over there...he could see part of the curved dome of the crushed Capitol Building. They must be standing near where Pennsylvania Avenue once ran.

"And...the President...the members of Congress?" Dave tentatively asked.

"Long dead and gone," Arthur flatly stated. "It's pretty much anarchy now, the few of us remaining. There are small cooperative groups, but they can't congregate or the Reapers find them, grab them, and deliver them up to the orbiting Harvesters. We even have to run our DE-generators sparingly. The Reapers catch the signature radiation and swoop in. I sure hope you get your 'cloaking' thing working, David. Otherwise, we won't even have our energy generators. The regular electrical grid is long gone. Our portable DE-generators are our last hope—both for us and for the planet."

"What do the Reapers do with us when they catch us?" Dave asked as they dug deeper into the smashed store.

"Who knows," Arthur shrugged, "—maybe use us for slaves, pets, food, or biological components...no one's come back from a Harvester to tell us, even though millions have been snagged. But it's not just us humans they want. They're grabbing up our processed materials. They're like salvage ships on the sea—anything is fair game for them, the bastards!"

"Anyone ever try and negotiate with them?" Dave quietly asked.

"Oh, sure—at first," Arthur shrugged again as he pawed through the contents of the store under the smashed-in ceiling. He ducked into a particularly-jumbled corner, tossing things out to dig deeper. "But the 'negotiators' either got fried or grabbed. Nothing ever came of it. Hey, gimme a hand here. I think I found something."

Dave got to his knees and crawled into the alcove where Arthur was struggling with something heavy.

"Grab onto that side and pull," Arthur directed him.

Dave set his rifle to the side and grabbed a hunk of metal, painfully rocking it out from beneath the collapsed ceiling beams.

It "screeched" as they pulled it free.

"Ah! We got it! We got it!" Arthur happily exclaimed.

Dave was amazed.

What sat there in front of him and Arthur was a near-duplicate of his and Victor's original "Device"!

"Wow, it's an antique, isn't it?" Arthur smiled triumphantly. "The units manufactured later were sealed pods that self-destruct if you dig into them. This one's got the open framework where you can access the equipment inside. It's just what you needed to experiment on, isn't it?"

"It's...great, Arthur...but how?"

"Bootleg tech, my man," Arthur grinned, as they dragged the bathtub-sized contraption out into a relatively clear space in the collapsed store. "When you smuggled out and published your initial specs on the web, smart guys here and there got it working. Companies started to mass-produce the small, sealed units. That's why you had to escape. Your military 'masters' found out you were the 'spy' that 'spread the word', so to speak. It was you that 'let the cat out of the bag' for DE-generators outside of the few giant, officially-sanctioned governmental power plants. Hah! You're a hero, my man! You were on the run but world-famous. At least, that's up until the Invasion—when now it only matters if a person survives from one day to the next. But this gadget is priceless, isn't it? You can..."

"Put your hands *up!*" a snide voice suddenly yelled at them.

Spinning around in the tight confines, Dave grabbed at his rifle, whipped it up at the intruders, and pulled the trigger...

—*nothing!*

What? Was there a safety or something...?

As he fumbled at it, the rifle was *kicked* to the side and a fist *slammed* into his jaw!

He dropped like a stone, vaguely aware that three shabbily-dressed, grubby-looking females wielding guns were also busily pummeling Arthur.

Anderson was thrown to the floor beside Dave, his black pistol kicked off to the side.

"Well...what kinda crap we got here?" a dark-skinned woman with a dirty baseball cap on her head leered down at them.

"Listen!" Arthur earnestly yelled up from the floor. "This guy with me is the Leader, and we're..."

"Shut the hell up!" the woman said, kicking Arthur square in his face. "We don't follow no 'leader'. We're just lookin' to grab some smack, that's it!"

"Leader?" another, younger lady queried, leaning over Dave to grab him by his hair and peer closely at his face. He grimaced from her foul breath and red scar slashed across a blind eye. "Hey, it *is* him! The High Priestess will pay a pretty penny for this one. We've hit the jackpot, ladies!"

"And early tech, too," a squat, short-haired female said, pawing at the bathtub-sized apparatus.

"Yep, they's real good tradin'...heh," the dark-skinned woman grinned. Her upper three central teeth were entirely missing. "Should we keeps the blond guy to help haul the goods, or jist kill him?"

"Too dangerous to let him live, I guess," the first one mused. "The two of you can haul our prize tech. Tie up the 'Leader' and shoot the older guy..."

"No!" Dave desperately yelled, jerking away from the scarred lady to cover the fallen Arthur with his own body...

—as *darting metallic tentacles* wrapped themselves around the necks of the three standing females and *yanked* them away!

Abbreviated screams echoed back into the smashed store from the "street" as the attacking females were efficiently stuffed into storage chambers in the Patrol-Bots' wide torsos.

Then Dave heard the heavy "*clomps*" as the robots continued on their prowl.

"Well...first time I've been happy to see a pack of Reapers," Arthur weakly laughed from the floor. He wiped blood from his broken nose as he pushed out from beneath Dave and started hunting for his pistol on the floor.

"They sure snuck up on us," Dave gasped, levering himself up on his elbows, looking around for his Kalashnikov.

"Here you go, David," Arthur said, handing Dave his rifle while helping him up off the floor. "We'll wait until it is good and dark tonight before trying to move our prize. Those local Reapers will be happy with their catches. Meanwhile, we'll hunker down here."

"Sounds good," Dave gulped, trembling from exhaustion and fear.

"Both the marauders and those 'Bots must have heard us wrenching that equipment out from under those beams," Arthur calmly observed. "They came up to us on 'tippy-toes', both of them. Hah! Well, we'll carry it back to camp *real* quiet later tonight."

"Right," Dave raggedly whispered. He found a block of cement to sit on, hands on the shaft of his rifle with its butt on the floor below him. He closed his eyes and wished this horrible day was finished.

"Hey, thanks for the assist, there," Arthur said as he calmly lay down on the floor with his head leaned back against his pack.

"Assist?"

"That dame almost shot me. You jumped on me and stopped her. Thanks buddy!"

"Uh...happy to help," Dave mumbled.

He rubbed his bruised, throbbing jaw.

Now his jaw hurt as much as his head.

He supposed he should be grateful he was still alive—and had some grand "plan", at least according to Arthur.

But he wasn't.

It just didn't make any sense. Nothing made sense anymore. It was as if he couldn't discern fantasy from reality.

What was next—a flying elephant?

He knew he should cherish this second chance. In his previous life—just a few minutes ago, it seemed—he and his friends were about to be incinerated by immense laser beams from descending alien spaceships...and now here he was, intact and alive!

But he just *hurt*.

He wanted it all to be finished.

Sally staggered forward barely able to put one foot in front of the other.

Her bare feet hurt terribly.

It was a long, long way to walk—and her short legs just increased the distance!

After all, she was now physically only a five-year-old little girl—lost in a huge desert.

She'd been walking through cold hills and gullies all throughout the night. In one way it was a hypnotically beautiful trek—so silent she could hear snakes slithering in the sand around her. The sky was the blackest she'd ever seen in her life. The stars were brilliant diamonds piercing the blackness, a vast cloud of sparkling points hanging majestically high above her.

But jagged rocks tore her feet mercilessly. Then she stumbled and fell down several hard-to-discern slopes, bruising and bloodying herself. Her ragged robe and hood did little to keep out the icy chill. She was shivering uncontrollably. Her vision was blurry. He tongue was so swollen from thirst that she couldn't fully close her mouth.

But she knew she had kept on going—one excruciating step after the other—certain that she wouldn't survive another day under the blistering desert sun.

And though she couldn't plot her course exactly through the meandering hills, she knew the direction of the water.

She could *smell* it.

It drew her forward.

And just as the sun began peeking above the low, rocky hills she saw it...

—a glistening, shining, beckoning BLUR OF RIPPLING WATER!

"Water! Water! Water! Water! *Water!*" she called-out through cracked lips as she staggered toward it, arms outstretched...

—and with one last burst of energy *ran* toward its shimmering, wide expanse...

—to *fall* into its welcoming embrace...

—then *bouncing* unexpectedly up to its surface as she simultaneously *drank deeply* of its cool substance...

"Auuugggghhh!" she shrieked in horror as she stood up and in a blind panic splashed back to the shoreline.

She collapsed down on the rocky shore, unbelievingly spitting-out *foul* liquid.

She gagged—afraid she was going to vomit.

The "water" was *disgusting, oily,* and *intensely salty.*

It enflamed Sally's thirst even further as she slumped flat, twisting-about in agony...

And as she lay there on the sloped, bare rocks looking to her side at the morning sun lighting up an incredibly-beautiful panorama of deep emerald-blue water, she knew she was going to die.

Well, she had certainly tried her best.

But her quest to stop Jesus from radically influencing the future of all societies of this doomed Earth was at an end.

"*God...*" she gasped, looking blearily up at the brightening sky as her fevered field of vision shrank steadily narrower and narrower. "Help us stupid humans...appreciate your Jesus—or please just take him away from us. We're not worthy. We deserve our fate..."

She had no tears left to cry.

So she just closed her eyes and surrendered, drifting peacefully away.

Chapter 2

INTROSPECTION

Get away, demons of the night

Who come to hold my eyelids open

When I'd rather drift away into sleep

Grateful for the respite from the day's trials

Retreating happily into blessed unconsciousness

Kept at bay by the waking, pain-filled nightmares

Puzzled, contorted, played-again, and keenly analyzed

What I did right or wrong or intermediate or lost

Choices made, chances dashed, options unrealized

Paths pursued or closed by fearful hesitation

Played again and again in rerun mode

How to understand motivation

The driving force within...

What, then, is 'me'?

The Luminary Chronicles, 2:54-57

Sally stood on a high hill looking out over Paradise.

At least, it seemed such—a lush green valley with a peaceful river meandering through it. A forest was set-off on the side—with *long-necked, giant dinosaurs* stretching far up to munch on tasty high leaves.

"Let's go play with them!" Tommy grinned up at Sally, his blond curls bouncing as he hopped gleefully in a circle.

She reached down and took his small hand in hers, preventing him from running down into the valley and being trampled by sixty-ton behemoths. Even though he was an android, he was still just a little boy.

21

"So how do you like our world, Sally?" George asked.

He and his wife Alice stood beside Sally, paw in paw. They were Dinosapiens, evolved intelligent bipedal dinosaurs. Each of them stood upright on two wide, strong legs. Their arms were free, their hands sporting three nimble fingers each, ending with sharp claws. Their heads were large and reptilian, but mobile with strong expressions. Their oblong heads were supported by longish thick necks. Their big eyes were luminous orange. They each stood nine feet high, looming above Sally.

"It's peaceful," Sally enthusiastically replied. "Is your entire world like this?"

"It is much like your Earth with the same surface features—mountains and deserts and plains and seas—but unspoiled by our sapient activities," Alice said, her voice sounding like a clear, high musical instrument. "Almost all of our cities are subterranean so as not to despoil the surface. Plus our population density is far less than on your Earth. There are only several tens of millions of us—versus the billions swamping and destroying your own ecology. Fortunately, our superficially primitive surface isn't attractive to those terrible Alien ships, from which we narrowly escaped in your world."

Sally breathed deeply, enjoying the fresh, warm breeze blowing up the valley. The gentle wind was rustling her fluffy brown-red hair.

"I like your world a lot," Sally smiled.

It was tempting to just stay in this wonderful place to which her Turtle Tattoo had somehow transported both her and her friends. Apparently the Harvesters hadn't come here...yet. But this magnificent world was headed towards Judgment Day as inexorably as was her Earth.

The verdant surface was doomed to be *burned away*—because of what she and Dave invented.

And just where was Dave, anyway? He should have been here with her and the others. But he didn't make it across. For whatever unknown reason, he'd been left behind as his home town was incinerated by the descending alien Harvesters.

She'd just been warming up to him. Now he was dead.

So the guilt of dooming all the Earth Dimensions fell on her alone. It was beyond bearing.

"You understand Dark Energy much better than us, don't you?" Sally said, resolutely turning to face the two Dinosapiens.

They looked at each other worriedly.

"We do..." George hesitantly admitted. "But in that understanding is also an acute awareness of the unpredictability and danger to its usage. As in your other human Dimension—from which your poor Sanako lady came—we've been sparing in our usage of Dark Energy. But, in your defense, we've had the time and latitude to experiment carefully. Our species has been sapient for ten million years—yours for a mere two or three million years. Plus we've had time to learn how to blend with nature while carefully controlling our numbers. Your greedy mammalian race has devoured your planet with uncontrolled population explosions—and stands on the brink of disaster. To you, Dark Energy seems a solution that you must pounce upon without delay to save yourselves from your own excesses. For us, it is a luxury, not a necessity."

"Yes, I see," Sally nodded.

"So whereas we've stayed 'under-the-radar' your race has just sent up a *cosmic flare* to the Creator—and thereby provoking Judgment Day," Alice sadly stated, shaking her big reptilian head in dismay. "George and I were sent to your world, disguised as humans, to help key individuals—such as you and David—to learn how to moderate your natural selfishness and greed. But now with those Alien Ships looking to grab whatever of value they can before God burns off your planet, we..."

"Sanako said that *you* were doomed too," Sally interrupted her.

"Yes, that's true. All the linked Dimensions—the two human ones plus reptilian ones like ours—are doomed to be incinerated by a massive solar flare in just ten years."

"But I just don't understand," Sally grimaced, "how could God destroy your Earth along with ours? If it's the fault of humans like me, then shouldn't *we* be the ones judged—then punished if found 'unworthy'—*not* you?"

George snorted, the sharp teeth in his snout glittering with nervous saliva.

"We don't know the ways of the Creator," he sighed, his large head sagging downward. "Our strength has never been in theological inquiry. But we've seen the future and there's no denying our fate. Our Earth is inexorably linked to your Earth. When your planet is consumed by fire, we shall likewise be destroyed."

Sally looked up into the deep blue sky, thinking furiously.

"Can't we do *anything* to...?"

"That's why we brought you here, dear," Alice gently but firmly stated, laying a cool paw upon Sally's arm. "For whatever reason, *you* occupy a key *fulcrum-point* about which a timeline can tilt in unpredictable directions. We need you to *save* us."

Sally, unable to believe what she was hearing, continued to stare upward into the sky.

"But *how?*" she whispered.

"We don't know," George quietly answered, taking the scaly arm of Alice in his own. "But we, like you, don't want our world to come to an end. Somehow—with your help—we must find a way to escape the implacable *Wrath of God.*"

She saw a flock of *giant Pterodactyl* web-winged lizards floating lazily high above her. A cold chill went through her heart. One of the dots seemed to be descending.

Sally gripped Tommy's little hand tighter lest he dash away to play and be snatched up by one of the circling predators.

Plus, the Turtle Tattoo on her right wrist was again warming up, even becoming *painful.*

She grimaced, looking down at her wrist.

"Did *you* do this to me?" she accused her hosts, rotating her left wrist so that the dinosapiens could see it *glowing.*

They both glanced at each other in apparent concern.

"No, we did not," George hurriedly answered, his big orange eyes blinking rapidly. "But we know of it. Your Turtle Tattoo was given to you by another reptilian race, far more ancient than us, from yet another of the nonhuman Earth Dimensions. We know of them but have little direct contact with them. To them, *we* are too young of a race to offer them much of value. We revere them greatly, however, and observe their activities from afar."

"*Another* reptilian race, older than you?" Sally dumbly repeated.

"Yes, Sally. In fact your friend 'Snake' who inked that tattoo was one of them—similarly disguised as us to look like you humans. The

Turtle Tattoo is made with pigments that resonate with the Dark Energy of the Universe. And Snake directly controlled your tattoo, helping to direct your movements."

Sally stared in disbelief at the undeniably active, glowing Turtle Tattoo on her wrist.

"But he's dead!" Sally gasped. "He was killed by that oriental guy from the other human Dimension who was trying to stop me. How is it then that my Turtle Tattoo is *still* directing me? Is it warning me *not* to listen to you? I don't know what is happening!"

Sally was gasping for breath, her face scrunched up in dismay, starting to panic...

"Mommy, Mommy!" Tommy smiled up at her, squeezing her hand tightly. "It's ok. Mr. Snake wasn't really killed. He just pretended to get shot. He's back in his home. He's still looking after us."

"But how do you...?" Sally began.

Then she moaned in pain as the Turtle Tattoo glowed *brightly!*

The George and Alice dinosapiens looked at each other in concern, their long tails slashing the surrounding vegetation as they whipped-about in fear.

"We've got to get below ground—right *now!*" George said, slinging Sally up onto the thick green hide of his back as Alice did the same with Tommy.

Sally clung on tightly, her arms around George's stocky, scaly neck, as he scampered along beside Alice, heading back down the long hill they'd just climbed. They zipped into a thick forest where tree trunks flashing past just inches to Sally's side...

—when she saw that the sunlight flooding down through the forest was suddenly *blocked out*, throwing everything into deep *shadow!*

She looked up through the overhanging branches and gasped.

"They're here!" Tommy called-out enthusiastically. Tightly clinging onto Alice's neck he looked upward also, his little body bounced up-and-down on Alice's undulating back.

Glimpsed through the leaves above Sally saw descending overhead a gigantic, rectangular *Harvester spaceship*—blocking out the sun!

Sally groaned, looking away from the horrible sight above.

Then she saw they were about to smash head-on into a high, rocky cliff!

"Watch out!" she shouted...

—as a *disguised barrier* snapped open and they galloped full-tilt into a welcoming darkness.

Dave and Arthur limped out of the starlit night of the apocalyptic Washington D.C. panorama into the even greater darkness of a buried, underground parking structure.

Arthur switched on a small penlight set right below the barrel of his pistol. It was located right in front of the trigger, apparently drawing energy from the gun itself.

The dim light was barely enough to see where they were going.

The downward-slanted entrance ramp was still intact though the building above had been "smushed" over onto its side. Several crushed cars blocked further progress.

They had to lift the heavy Device carefully over the crumpled hoods to get it past.

"Any cars left running?" Dave said as they staggered on down the ramp lugging the bathtub-sized Device between them.

"Ain't no oil wells left, David—no refineries, no gas pumps, and no navigable streets. So what do you think?" Arthur humorlessly stated.

"Uhm...electric cars?"

"Ok, there's a few of those left," Arthur conceded as they trudged on down the tunnel. "But we use them as batteries, basically. We charge them with quick bursts from the DE-generators and then run most of our remaining lights and such off them in the interim."

"Stop!" a command was barked at them from further down in the collapsed structure.

Dave heard a number of guns being cocked.

"Don't shot!" Arthur called back. "It's just me and Dave. We found an original Device. Come give us a hand."

"Password?" the hidden voice loudly insisted.

"Introspection," Arthur barked back.

A group of fighters emerged from the darkness below, breaking into grins at the sight of Arthur and Dave. They took the Device out of Arthur and Dave's weary arms, rushing it reverently away.

Stepping out of the darkness behind the fighters was an irate female.

She stalked out of the gloom and *slapped Dave hard on his face!*

"Ow!" he groaned. His jaw was still tender from the female marauder's blow. "What did you do that for?"

Hey, wait, it was *Sally!*

"It's so good to see you, we're..." Dave started to say.

"You two were gone for a day longer than in your mission plan!" she angrily confronted them, her pert face turned up at them, her hands balled on her hips. "I thought you were both *dead!* We concluded that the signal you were tracking was a *decoy.* You being dead meant we wouldn't get our hands on an original prototype. How dare you make me think I'd not be able to proceed with my research?"

Her hair swung in loose, brown-red waves. Her bright green eyes were fierce. She had on faded blue denim overalls, wearing a rumpled white blouse under the suspenders.

To Dave she looked absolutely gorgeous.

"We, uh, we had to hide from..." Dave tried to protest.

"But you got it!" she suddenly grinned, her face lighting up with excitement.

She started to turn away as Dave impulsively reached out and grabbed her arm...

"Let go of me!" she shouted, jerking away from him.

"Come on now, you two lovers," Arthur laughed. "Be nice."

"He's *not* my boyfriend," she huffed as she turned and raced away down the ramp, in the direction the Device had been carried.

"Girls, huh?" Arthur sighed at Dave's side. "What can you do? You can't live with them and you can't live without them. Hah!"

It was getting cooler as they continued walking down the long ramp. Though it was night outside, it was still miserably hot on the devastated surface. It must be the middle of summer.

Even before the apocalypse, summer in Washington D.C. was no picnic.

Dave was feverish, bruised, and weary to his bones—but relieved. At least they were safe...for now.

"Why is she so mad at me?" he asked Arthur, genuinely puzzled by this new version of Sally.

"Oh, she's mad at everyone," Arthur shrugged.

"What do you mean?"

"Well, for one—you amnesiac, you—I guess you don't remember that when you escaped from the military research facility you had to conk her out and carry her to get her to go with you?"

"Say what?"

"Yep," he said, his deep voice starting to echo in the dark tunnel, "She liked it there with their fancy gismos and such. They treated her as a celebrity—nice quarters, the best food, respect, all that sort of crap. You knew if you left her there she'd just help them get their DE-weapons up and running—then probably blow up the entire planet. So you brought her along, whether she wanted to come or not."

"Oh...alright...so she's not just mad at me, but...?"

"She's a royal pain, for sure. She blames all of us, especially since..." his voice trailed off.

"What?"

"Her own Mother went over to the CPH," he sighed. "The old lady bought the teachings of the High Priestess hook, line, and sinker. I guess that's not so surprising since that new medication of the CPH *cured* her from dying of lung cancer. But before regular communications stopped, Sally's mother publically renounced her 'devil' daughter for her key part in DE research. Sally took that hard, blaming us for being 'subversive' rebels instead of true patriots."

"So why is she helping us now?"

"Revenge on the Harvesters, one way or another."

"Revenge?"

"A Reaper raid got her Mom along with a troop of Priestesses."

"Oh..."

"Yep, it was a bad scene all around when it happened. Sally had a tough time keeping at her research with us, until she came out of her funk. So we tolerate Sally's bad behavior. And you've told us time and again how you can't link up the DE-generators around the world without her mathematical genius in the mix."

"Really?"

"Hey, find a way to do it without her—and we'd be happy to toss her fine little rump out to fend for itself on the surface."

"She's that bad?"

"Wait and see," Arthur sighed. "Where do you think you got that lump on your skull?"

"No...really?"

"Yep. You tried to sneak a kiss from her and she banged you on your head with a loose computer terminal."

"I tried to kiss her?"

"Everyone knows you have the hots for her," Arthur leered at him.

"I do?"

"But she ain't givin' you or anybody else the time of day," Arthur observed. "She just plays with her damn computers in her 'lab'—like none the rest of us matter in the slightest. She's the weirdest girl I've ever seen."

"She's weird, that's for sure."

And she definitely *wasn't* Dave's Sally!

Where had his Sally gone, anyway? Was she even alive? Or had she been *erased* in the flux of Time?

It was damn hard to love someone who might not even exist, or who was split into too many versions to keep up with!

"So we gotta keep her?" Arthur asked, seemingly hoping for a negative response.

"I suppose," Dave sighed, shrugging his shoulders.

After going through a few more checkpoints, Dave and Arthur trudged wearily into a well-lit lower floor of the subterranean parking structure.

Up ahead was a series of tents and work-areas where people were bustling about doing things.

It was an entire, underground rebel base.

Well, things were looking up. It wasn't arriving to visit his Mother in Sulphur, Oklahoma in a pre-invasion world—as he'd expected to do only a day ago in the other timeline—but it was close enough.

For better or worse, he was home.

Ivanna was quite worried about Victor.

Her husband had been working way too many hours for a man in his nineties. But she knew not to bother him when he was in one of his "research" frenzies.

So she sat sedately on the balcony looking out over the wide cavern.

High above, a mobile heat/light source moved across the ceiling to simulate yellow sunlight. It was quite realistic if you didn't look too close. The cavern ceiling was painted blue to simulate the sky, with the mobile light looking just like the sun.

Their apartment was set-into the surrounding rock on one of the top levels, so Ivanna could see everything. Closest to her was the lake. It was their central reservoir for water. It was over two hundred feet deep, a healthy blue-green color. Along one of its edges a shallow area permitted people to even go for a swim. Banks of oxygen-generating trees were planted in soil chambers along its sides. Further away were the dome-shaped laboratories, studding the floor of the cavern like concrete mushrooms.

At the far edge of the cavern sat *ten large missiles*, each on its own launching pad.

The rockets were ICBMs, capable of leaving Earth's atmosphere. They were pointed at the high ceiling, a portion of which could roll back on command, allowing them to exit the cavern via long, large tubes whenever they were fired. Explosives at the top of the exit tubes would shatter the cap of melted mountain rock to allow them to proceed on into the sky.

Doing so, of course, would reveal the existence and location of the secret military research facility to the Harvesters and ensure the quick death of all inside.

Their devastating laser beams, if targeting the site long enough, could melt the mountain into a smoking caldera.

Ivanna was certain the rockets would only be launched when everything was tested and ready. They'd have only one shot at disrupting the operations of the alien spaceships in orbit around Earth.

Victor and his team were not preparing nuclear bombs, which had proved useless against the Harvesters. Rather, the scientists were frantically perfecting Dark Energy weapons to load onto the tips of those missiles. Hopefully the DE-bombs would unleash sufficient raw energy to penetrate even the force fields of the Harvesters, *destroying* the alien spaceships.

It was, indeed, mankind's last, desperate hope.

But even if the missiles succeeded, only a handful of the thousands of Harvesters circling or hovering over the planet would be blown up.

It would hardly be a victory—just a final defiant gasp of thoroughly decimated humanity.

"Am I interrupting?" a voice came from behind Ivanna, breaking her increasingly fatalistic thoughts.

Ivanna looked around to see a tall, grey-haired woman with a pert nose, dark eyebrows, and heavily lined face.

"Not at all, Madam President, please come in," Ivanna graciously nodded, starting to get up from her webbed garden chair.

"Oh don't get up," the President told her, slowly walking over to sink into a rigid chair to Ivanna's side. "I just wanted to see how you were holding up."

Ivanna was touched. Since having the job of *President of the United States of America* thrust upon her, the woman had worked nonstop. Julia Swartz was attending a National Parks summit in Colorado when the Harvesters first descended and leveled Washington D.C. Her job in the President's Cabinet was that of Secretary of the Interior. She was a retired Director of the federal Bureau of Land Management. She held a Ph.D. in biology and served as a Professor of Wildlife Management at the University of California, Riverside before being appointed as Secretary of the Interior.

Although her job in Washington D.C. as Secretary of the Interior was substantial, it certainly had *not* prepared Julia to be a wartime President fighting off an alien invasion! But the surprise attack by the Alien Armada killed off virtually everyone in the capital, including the President and other officials. In the presidential line of succession, Julia was about all that remained—safely isolated on Pikes Peak with a small gathering of National Park directors. Still, when whisked up by secret service agents and taken to the Cheyenne Mountain Nuclear Bunker near Colorado Springs, Colorado, Secretary Swartz calmly accepted the post with a determined, "can do" attitude.

Since the conclusion of the Cold War with the Soviet Union back in the 20th Century, the Cheyenne Mountain retreat had been largely mothballed. But everything was still maintained on a ready basis for quick reactivation. Now it held a small contingent of soldiers, politicians, and scientists. They were completely self-sufficient, sealed off from the outer world. Even communications had been cut off to off-base facilities. Nothing could be allowed to alert the orbiting Harvesters of their presence until they were ready to respond in kind to the alien's savage invasion.

Fortunately, a small nuclear reactor supplied plenty of power for life-support functions. Thus they didn't have to activate a DE-generator that would likely signal their location. Stored food sources would last the limited number of personnel for years. Extensive banks of hydro-cultured plants provided additional food plus critical oxygen. The water supply was more than adequate, supplied by deep artesian springs. The ICBM missiles were old but functional. And fortunately it was on a now-destroyed higher level that Victor's Device was originally perfected into a working Dark Energy generator. So once the Aliens appeared, Ivanna found herself and Victor taken down to the secure lowest levels. Then the massive doors leading into the interior of the mountain were sealed and they were safe for the moment.

The hardened bunker had originally been constructed to withstand a thirty megaton nuclear explosion. But it nearly didn't survive the immense laser beams from the attack ships deployed by the orbiting Harvesters. Ivanna and Victor were deep inside when the attack upon the base began. The entire mountain shuddered as its top was sheared off, melted down, and methodically punctured. Ivanna feared that even deep within the mountain's lowest level they'd be killed!

Indeed, the top layers of the bunker complex were destroyed. But, fortunately, the lowest, newest-constructed manufacturing cavern had survived. It was large and deep in case any Dark Energy generators constructed there malfunctioned, thus hopefully containing any unanticipated, immense explosion. So after the alien bombardment concluded, the military decided to treat it as a secure site for trying to perfect a Dark Energy bomb. Its occupants figured that the Harvesters thought the complex completely dead. And if the occupants did not broadcast their presence, they might yet survive long enough to launch their handful of missiles.

Even if they succeeded, though, the effort would likely be futile. But they had to try. They couldn't just exist. It wasn't in their nature.

They had to *fight!*

"I am doing as well as can be expected of a stranded sociologist," Ivanna gamely smiled to the President. "I try not to think of myself as a prisoner here, only as a grateful guest."

Julia sighed deeply in response, briefly smiling as she looked down below at a few children splashing in the water at the edge of the artificial lake.

"Well said, Dr. Petrovich," Julia replied. "I could say the same for myself. We are both survivors by merit of military intervention. I was here at a *conference* when I got dragged into this prison. I thought I'd do some skiing in my free time while I was out here in Colorado. Some vacation!"

They both sat in silence for a minute.

"Any news of the outside world?" Ivanna tentatively asked.

Julia sadly shook her head in the negative.

"As you know, Ivanna, all our sensor arrays—antennas and the like—were melted into slag by the initial attack on the base," she explained. "But our clever guys and gals managed to drill narrow holes up through the solidified magma," she grimaced. "But the small antennas we've managed to get up to the surface picked up nothing informative—just static on all frequencies. And of course we can't broadcast anything. We keep listening, but so far we've gotten nothing to indicate any technologically competent groups out there beside ourselves survived the initial assault on the planet."

"But wouldn't they be just like us, afraid to broadcast anything for fear of being targeted by the aliens?" Ivanna observed. "Or, they might be using encrypted bursts that without precise timing and coding information we'd perceive as mere static. At least that's what Victor tells me."

"Yes, that is indeed possible—that other groups similar to us are deliberately keeping silent. Or they are using secured communications from group to group."

"So..."

"Regardless, we have to assume that the United States—probably the entire world—is thrown back to the Stone Age," Julia quietly stated. "There are likely other small pockets of survivors. Maybe they'll even raise their heads if conditions warrant it. But I've no doubt things on the surface are going from bad to worse."

Ivanna reached for a nearby pitcher of lemonade sitting on a lawn table.

"At least a small slice of civilization still exists down here," Ivanna said, filling a glass and handing it to Julia. "We've even got lemonade, from stored powder concentrate of course."

The President gratefully accepted it, drinking deeply before continuing.

"I've been in meetings all day—didn't even have time for lunch, not that the dehydrated food packets are much of a treat," she said. "I hope the hydroponics gardens will get something growing beside potatoes and tomatoes—I'm sick of those."

Ivanna nodded in agreement, feeling cheered by the President's visit. But then she sobered.

"I'm sure you didn't come here just to discuss our food resources," Ivanna astutely observed. "How can I help, Madam President?"

The grey-haired woman sighed deeply.

"You read me too well, Dr. Petrovich," she quietly and formally replied, her expression serious. "Well, the military folks are happy for me to make the final decisions. And I've a big one in my lap right now. *When* to launch the missiles is definitely an executive decision, now that the DE-bombs are nearly ready."

"We're that close?" Ivanna gasped. "I had no idea! Victor usually keeps me informed, but..."

"Oh, it's not tomorrow," Julia sighed, breathing deeply as she tilted her head back and looked up at the blue-painted concrete dome above them. "But it's soon."

"Do you think they have a chance to succeed?"

"A chance?" Julia pondered. "Sure, everything has a chance, doesn't it? But a *good* chance...I doubt it."

"Why not?"

"Even forgetting our tiny number of missiles against their vast armada, we're still fighting fire with fire," Julia frowned. "In the case of a forest fire—which I've successfully dealt with before at the Bureau of Land Management—that makes sense. You do a controlled burn to strip away fuel that the uncontrolled forest fire needs to keep going. A back-fire can stop an inferno dead in its tracks. But what we're up against now..." her voice trailed off.

Sensing that Julia wanted her response, Ivanna mentally put on her historical/sociological Professor cap.

"Our nuclear bombs didn't do any good against them, correct?" Ivanna stated.

"True, but now...I don't know...this is in the 'Hail Mary' mode— just *try* something," Julia shook her head sadly. "The game's about over, it looks like we've lost anyway, so why not toss in the kitchen sink? I'm just not sure that we should be content with making a final gesture of defiance. With all the brainpower in this place we should be able to do something better than just hitting for one homerun in an already hopelessly lost game."

Ivanna allowed herself a mental, hysterical giggle. English was not Ivanna's first language, so she could stand back and be clinical about its usage. That was a lot of allegories by Julia to mix into one paragraph!

"But if not this...then what?" Ivanna asked, happy for the President to utilize her as an intelligent sounding board.

Julia looked away from the high domed ceiling, put her head in her hands and *groaned*.

"Something...is...not...right," Julia grated, hammering out each word.

"Like what?" Ivanna patiently replied.

"We're *missing* something," Julia sighed, standing up stiffly from the comfortable chair and pacing back and forth on the short balcony. "We don't know enough. Things are going on that are too big for us to understand. And I'm about to commit everything on a toss of dice with unknown symbols on a table I can't see with opponents I can't even imagine."

Yes, definitely mixing a lot of different allegories there...

"So, you need...?"

"Information!" Julia yelled out over the balcony. "I've got to know more—and quickly."

Ivanna was shocked by the outburst, but realized it was only a symptom of the incredible stress under which the President was operating.

"But how—and from where?"

"Ivanna, I know this is asking a lot, but you're the only person I can spare who has the expertise to even understand any answers that might be out there waiting to be found."

"Julia, just what are you asking?" Ivanna frowned, now aware that this meeting was much more than just her providing a helpful sounding-board.

"There's a top secret tunnel leading out of this research facility that ends in a basement located in Colorado Springs. I want you to take a small squad of commandos and go there to find whatever you can, out on the surface. I know I'm risking exposing our entire operation to the enemy by allowing even this small break in our absolute seclusion. But I can't make a decision that will use up our last resources against our enemy without trying to get more information! You're just to do a quick look-around, mind you. Talk to anyone you may find. Then report back within a couple days at most. For instance, if there's a viable Resistance effort out there—I've got to know it. What if launching our missiles provokes a devastating reaction that destroys an effective guerilla effort? We've just no idea of the situation up there on the surface."

Ivanna was following the logic, but not the commission. Things were moving a bit too fast for her to keep up.

"What, go *now*—without even telling Victor?"

"You'll just distract him from the work he and his team are doing," Julia said. "As I understand it, they are at a critical stage in their preparations. They're working around the clock to iron out the fine details for controlling the Dark Energy explosions. They tell me if they are off by even a microsecond then not just a Harvester, but the *entire planet* could be disintegrated!"

"Yes...he's told me how delicate it is—how great the uncertainties..."

"So you understand," Julia grimaced. "I wouldn't ask you to do this if we weren't right up against the wall. Your commando team is quite good. I know that you are a civilian and I as Commander In

Chief can't order you to do this. I can only ask for you to do this, Ivanna. I'm sure you'll be kept as safe as possible, but..."

"There are no guarantees," Ivanna nodded grimly, standing up also, speaking with resolve. "My answer is 'yes', Madam President. I will do it. In fact, I'm glad finally to have an active role. Besides patting my old hubby on his cheek each morning and sending him off to his lab, I've done nothing of note. When do I leave?"

"I have a backpack for you to take a few items with you. Your team is waiting in the hallway. They have military jurisdiction, of course—but you have operational command. Your mission must come first, even above their efforts to keep both you and them safe. Do you understand?"

"I do, Madam President."

Julia took Ivanna's thin hands in her own. "I'd go myself if I could, but..."

"—you are needed here," Ivanna firmly nodded, finishing her sentence. "Plus, I am the only qualified sociologist. I have been thinking of this Alien Invasion a lot. And I agree with you. It doesn't make sense. Perhaps I can discover a few answers while reconnoitering the 'lay of the land'."

The door of the small apartment opened and five camouflage-uniformed soldiers walked in, carrying a knapsack for Ivanna.

"Then God be with you," Julia said, releasing Ivanna's hand and quickly departing.

Ivanna felt the urge to throw up all over the carpeting. But terrified vomiting wouldn't engender much confidence by these fine young soldiers in their new 'leader', would it?

She forced down the bile and smiled at them.

"I'll be with you in a moment," she said, heading for the bathroom to pack a toothbrush and a few other essentials.

She was already dressed in the civilian "uniform" of their habitat: featureless grey coveralls and tennis shoes. She was ready for some exercise!

But she had a terrible feeling that this short "fieldtrip" was *not* going to be much fun.

She was going to get a look not just outside but inside. As a student of the psychology of traumatized societies, she knew that both the best and worst came out in times of national crises. What would she find out there? Would it be ravaging cannibals sunk to the depths of human despair? Or would she discover courageous "freedom fighters" of an organized Resistance—waging principled war on an implacable foe?

Regardless, there had to be a way to defeat these vicious aliens! Or, at least to understand not just *what* they were, but *why* they were here—and why *now?*

She knew she had to be ready for anything, no matter how strange or bizarre. She wasn't a religious person, but she felt an irrational need for prayer.

Though not active in the religion, her Catholic upbringing gave her the knowledge of how to word an acceptable prayer, which she silently verbalized as she gathered the last few items to take with her: *"Dear Lord. Please help me. Give me strength to do that which needs to be done. Give me the answers you know that I need. Help me to understand Your Will. Tell me what to do. In Jesus' name I ask this, Amen."*

The standard doctrine from devout Believers was that God allowed terrible things to happen to good people in order to test them, train them, or refine them. But to Ivanna those "apologetic" arguments always fell short.

It was hard to believe in a God that would allow this to happen to Earth. The entire world was being savaged. The fate of humanity hung in the balance.

This was a time for miracles, not silence.

"Well?" she asked, looking up hopefully at the low ceiling.

God did not answer her prayer.

It was as if He weren't there at all.

Chapter 3

EXPANSION

Would that I could

Grow as big as an elephant

Then become a cloud, a moon, a sun

Merging into the death throes of a supernova

Blasting my innards out to the limits of space-time

My heavy atoms made the stuff of new planets and stars

Where everything begins anew in a wondrous stew

Organic molecules roasting, toasting, and cooking

Conjuring up fresh forms of delicious life

Clashing and fighting, ever growing

Until I with them reach our limits

And, not content, want more

Always grasping up

Until we die

Happy!

The Luminary Chronicles, 3:152-156

Sally became aware of a gentle voice. It soothed her.

It *sang* to her in a foreign language, using a simple melody with much repetition.

Clearly, it was a lullaby.

Before attempting her journey back in time to the 1st Century, Sally as the *High Priestess* of the *Church of Perpetual Health* had mastered many languages. Chief amongst them, in preparation for her trip, were the Biblical languages of Hebrew, Aramaic, and Greek.

Now she allowed her brain to take in whatever words were spoken and translate them into their English equivalents. In the same way, she spoke in her brain in English then allowed her mouth to utter the equivalent sounds best suited to the understanding of those around her.

"W-where...am I?" she managed to croak out through cracked, swollen lips, speaking the language of the person singing to her.

Sally blearily saw a friendly looking young woman wearing rough robes. A shawl went around and over her head. Her hair was a luxurious deep brown, her skin light brown. She had large brown eyes. And she was dabbing at Sally's swollen lips with a moist rag.

Off to the side, a placid donkey was standing.

"Don't try to talk, child," the woman kindly ordered her in a soft, sweet voice. "You are lucky we came upon you in this desolate place. We will take you with us when we depart on the morrow. You are safe now."

"Where...to?" Sally managed to croak out around her grotesquely swollen tongue.

The woman put a warm finger to Sally's lips as Sally lay upon a soft blanket, looking up at twinkling stars. Sally heard waves lapping up nearby. She smelled salty air. She realized that was still beside the seashore where she'd fallen.

"Do not try to talk, dear child," the woman gently continued. "You were near death when we found you. You must take time to recover. But if you must know, I and my family are traveling off the main trade routes. We come from Egypt. We are returning to our home country in Galilee. We had intended to go to Judea, which is closer, via a direct route. But a cruel king is ruling there. We dared not take the regular road, but lucky for you decided to travel along the shore of the Dead Sea. The cruel king is known to tax heavily, kidnap, and even kill travelers. But do not be concerned, child. Our homeland is now ruled by a much calmer king. You will be safe with us."

Sally desperately struggled to clear her throat, get more words out: "And...what is his name...this King?"

"Do not fear, child," the woman repeated, gently wiping away sand, dirt, and dried salt from Sally's forehead. "His name is Herod Antipas. He welcomes refugees. But our true home is there as well.

We have many friends and relatives among the Nazarenes in Galilee. But what are *you* doing out here, all by yourself in the desert? Was it slavers? Did you escape from them?"

Memories of her appearance in the 12th Century flickered into Sally's brain. Yes, what a convenient excuse! It would do here as well—around one thousand two hundred years earlier—as it did when she'd spent fourteen years in the Convent of Hildegard von Bingen in Germany.

"Y-yes," Sally stammered, barely able to stay conscious.

"Do not worry, child," the woman firmly stated. "You are safe from those horrible slavers. We will not let them hurt you any further. The Lord has brought us to your aid, to deny those foul beasts their prey."

"Thank you," Sally whispered, her eyes starting to roll back in her head...her breathing becoming labored.

"Jesus, quick—bring the water jug," the woman called out.

Jesus?

A young boy about two years old tottered into Sally's blurred field of vision. He was lugging a big jug, almost as tall as he. He had a prominent nose, thick brown curls on his head, a light brown boyish face, and the large brown eyes of his mother.

"Here, Mother," he cheerfully said, setting the jar down in the sand. He curiously examined the supine, apparently five-year-old Sally.

"Thank you, Son," she smiled at the boy, laying a gentle hand upon his head.

"How is the girl, Mary?" a rough voice sounded from behind Sally. Moving into view was a tough-looking, robed man with a prominent nose and a longish brown beard. He was carrying dried shrubbery likely gathered from nearby hills.

"She will live, Joseph," Mary stated firmly, starting to drip cool water into Sally's parched mouth. "I believe that God has brought us here to rescue her. She could become the fine servant girl I've told you that I need. Would you like to do that, dear?" she asked Sally.

Sally could only nod her head weakly in the affirmative. The cool water dribbling down her throat was like nectar from the gods. It was the most delicious thing she'd ever tasted.

"Don't drink too much," Mary kindly said, carefully rationing the drips. "Too much will make you sick. And this one jug must last our whole family until we're out of this desert."

"Please...m-more," Sally stammered.

"I don't trust her," the two-year-old Jesus frowned. He peered suspiciously down at Sally. "We should leave her here."

"Jesus!" Joseph sharply admonished him. "Why do you say such an awful thing?"

Mary also seemed shocked by the boy's brutal assertion, looking at him with concern.

He knows me!—Sally thought, starting to panic, realizing that she might well be left behind to die in the desert. *How is this possible?*

The boy picked up one of Sally's limp hands and held it firmly while peering deeply into her green eyes.

"The Devil is in her," he flatly stated, his boyish tones belying the wisdom behind his words. Even in her feverish delirium, Sally noted that for a two-year-old his words were remarkably mature, "...but maybe we can teach her?"

He let her trembling hand drop with a small "thud" to her side.

Joseph crouched down, putting his strong arms around the boy's shoulders while looking sternly into his eyes.

"Yes, Jesus, I agree that this young girl we've come across out here in the wilderness is scary," he said in a deep, husky voice. "But we must help even those people who are not of our family, especially travelers who are hurt. This is the way of our people. Do you understand?"

"Yes, Father," he nodded, stepping back from Sally. "But I still don't like her."

Sally was relieved that at least she wasn't going to be left behind to die.

As the family went about their camping duties, Sally looked up at a full moon floating high above in the night sky. It was so quiet out here. It was *too* quiet. And the moon above—to her fevered gaze— seemed to be turning *red*.

Joseph was lighting a fire to get them through the cold night.

Jesus strode over with short steps, crouching down beside the supine five-year-old girl.

"I am watching you," the little boy whispered in her ear such that his parents couldn't hear. "So you be nice!"

Then he stood up straight and cheerfully walked back to his mother who was putting flat bread to warm in a pan on the crackling fire.

Sally closed her eyes and thankfully drifted back toward unconsciousness.

I guess...I won't...be tempting him much—she thought to herself. *It's going to be hard to kill him.*

The commandos were placing the last charges in the solid brick wall in front of them.

Their trip through the ten-mile-long narrow tunnel had been swift.

They rode in a wheeled, enclosed vehicle that just fit within the rounded tunnel. It barely accommodated the dozen soldiers, their gear, and Ivanna.

She found the trip stifling and distressing. There was no light outside the vehicle. They were traveling inside a dark, dismal dungeon.

It had been many years since she'd been on a "subway" commute, let alone a military mission.

After what seemed like an eternity but in actuality lasted less than an hour they arrived at a rusted, solid steel barrier. It was an impenetrable blast door. It took the commandos another hour to get it open, necessitating triggering small explosive bolts around its sides before they could slide it back into an alcove set into the wall to its side, unblocking their progress forward. Then it took another ten minutes to arrive at their present destination.

Their only remaining barrier was a thick brick wall.

"Are we at a safe distance?" Ivanna gulped, fearful of the impending explosion. She strained to see the work being done just yards up ahead by the light of dim flashlight beams.

A young, tough-sounding female soldier reassured her: "We're fine, Ma'am. They're taking their time to plant multiple small charges. They don't want to blow up that brick wall, just fracture it so that we can move the big pieces to the side. We're perfectly safe."

"Fire in the hole!" someone yelled from up ahead as the four men hastily withdrew.

WHUMMPPPP!—Ivanna heard the sound of a muffled explosion.

A cloud of dust rushed back at the vehicle, obscuring Ivanna's view of the operations and making her cough.

Then there came the sound of people hurriedly clearing away bricks and rubble.

"What do you think we'll find on the other side?" Ivanna asked the calm female soldier next to her. "When this whole terrible invasion began giant robots emerged from landing craft into the streets. They were grabbing people right and left for who knows what purpose."

"Not to worry, Ma'am," the efficient-sounding female soldier reassured her. "This secret tunnel was dug back in the cold war period, ending in a sub-basement of the then-*Broadmoor World Arena* in Colorado Springs. So we're not marching out onto an open street. We should have plenty of cover to figure out the dangers before trying to get any actionable Intel."

"That's good to know," Ivanna sighed, suddenly feeling woozy. The adrenalin rush of going on a secret mission outside of Cheyenne Mountain was plunging rapidly. She felt every one of her *eighty-four* years of age.

"And if there are any of those robots lurking about, we'll take care of them," the woman confidently concluded.

Ivanna hoped that the strong young woman was right. But from what she'd briefly seen on the initial TV broadcasts of those alien robots...

—well, it could get ugly.

"So, what's your name? How long have you been in the military?" Ivanna asked, trying to make a solid connection with the young woman.

"I'm Sergeant Murphy, Ma'am, special forces," she answered while keeping a careful eye on the progress in clearing the tunnel exit up in front of their vehicle. "I've been in the army for ten years. My specialty is in communications. If we can make contact with other groups, I'll be the one to do it. I've got gear with me for transmitting or picking up whatever signal we need. I'll be hiding our signals so that the aliens think it's just static."

"Oh, that's excellent," Ivanna answered. "So you're a Ranger?"

"Yes, Ma'am," the lady answered with pride. "You're familiar with us?"

"Why of course," Ivanna replied. "I've studied American history extensively. The Rangers go back to before the Revolutionary War. They originate in the 1700's, fighting during the French and Indian Wars. They have a proud history of being hardy frontiersmen who got the job done whatever the task."

"That's us, Ma'am," the woman said with pride.

Ivanna took a good look at the young lady sitting next to her. She looked to be in her mid-twenties. The short-haired Ranger was clad in gray camouflage. Her uniform was adorned with many filled pockets, weapons, and spare ammunition. Across her lap she had a large assault rifle that looked capable of blowing holes right through that brick wall ahead of them.

"I'm glad to have you protecting me," Ivanna said with sincerity.

"We'll keep you safe, Ma'am," she curtly replied.

Up ahead, the other soldiers were returning to the vehicle. Ivanna could see a glimmer of light filtering through the cloud of dust. The tunnel was open.

"Please call me 'Ivanna'. And, if you don't mind, Sergeant—what's your name?"

"My name is Sergeant Murphy."

"I mean your first name."

"Oh..." she grinned shyly, "it's 'Shirley'. But please don't call me that in front of the guys. My tag with them is 'deadeye'."

"Deadeye?"

"In addition to communications, I'm the team's best shot."

"Wow, good to know," Ivanna grinned back.

The team leader stuck his helmeted head into the vehicle. "We've got to go by foot from here, Ma'am. The stadium is collapsed down upon the sublevels. There's no way our vehicle can go onward. Are you up to walking or should we rig up a sling?"

"I'm up to it," Ivanna gamely stated. He reached in with a strong hand, supporting her thin arm, helping her exit the vehicle. She didn't know if she'd be able to keep up with these super-fit soldiers. But even though she was in her eighties she regularly worked out at the small gym in the Cheyenne Mountain complex. She was damned if she'd slow her comrades down by them having to lug her along.

"You get tired, you just let me know and we'll take a break," Shirley whispered to her. "You're the reason we're out here, so don't burn yourself out."

Ivanna gratefully nodded.

They were silent as they slipped past the breached brick wall...

—when all *hell* broke loose!

Dave strolled into the "computer lab" to see what was being done with the counterfeit "original" Device.

The lab was a tent lit by a lone, flickering light bulb—powered by a car battery off in the corner.

It was a far cry from the real laboratories at Yale University where he and Professor Volodymyr had developed the palladium matrix which allowed deuterium ions not just to trigger cold fusion, but to make a tiny slice into Subspace—from which Dark Energy poured out!

But then again, the tent reminded him of his garage where he'd gotten the damn Device to work "well enough" to *explode*.

So maybe they'd just blow themselves to hell?

But he'd just gotten a good night's sleep and a hearty breakfast. He almost felt back to his pre-apocalyptic self. He didn't like being pessimistic.

Sally, along with several technicians, was busily at work carefully lifting out the guts of the bootleg Device.

"You didn't wait for me?" Dave said as he walked up to them, trying to joke but finding himself genuinely a bit annoyed.

"You're *bothering* me—*leave!*" Sally loudly and curtly dismissed him, grunting as she struggled to lift out the heavy central control unit.

Dave pushed aside a technician to grab onto the other end, helping Sally lay it gently down onto the concrete floor.

"You know you love me," he joked at her.

She fixed him with a cold stare, saying nothing.

"Look, you'll never get this unit to link up world-wide with the other still-functioning units without me optimizing the vibrational modes of the matrix," he seriously stated, putting aside his joking manner of a few seconds before. "I want to get those bastards as much as you do. You lost your mother, sure. I lost my whole world. We *all* hate those damn monsters. You don't have a monopoly on despising them."

She sighed, sinking onto the floor in a lotus position. Then she put her forehead dejectedly forward onto the central control unit's top. Her fluffy red-brown hair drifted around it as if protecting it.

She raised her head and fixed Dave with an unblinking stare from her vividly green eyes.

Dave noticed that the Turtle Tattoo on her wrist seemed to be faintly glowing. Was that a good omen or bad?

"You seem different since you got back," she observed, while still glowering at him. "Before, you hated the military apparatus even more than you hated the aliens. Now you don't even seem to care that you and I were held captive doing research at their bidding for over a year. Don't you even remember what happened to us at Cheyenne Mountain? Before it got destroyed by the Aliens, you were eager to escape."

He didn't know what to say. So he just shrugged.

"You hit me on the head with a computer terminal," he desperately tried to change the discussion. He wasn't yet willing to admit he was from a whole different timeline, plopped into this new version of his body.

"Because you were being an *ass*," she snapped at him. "You were *yelling* at me and even *slapping* me when I couldn't get the remnant of my newly evolved computer intelligence to propagate and grow in these *pieces of junk* that you and Arthur haul in for me to try and work miracles on!"

Dave looked at the technicians for support.

But they wouldn't meet his eyes.

What? Was it really true? Did the period of enforced servitude in the military—which he'd never experienced in his own timeline—turn him here into a jerk?

"I'm...I'm sorry—really, Sally. I'm ashamed of being so stupid," he stumbled through an apology as she ignored him and started probing into the control unit.

"I don't like being slapped," she sniffed.

"And you shouldn't," he firmly agreed with her. "Actually, I think maybe you knocked some sense into my thick skull by bashing me with that computer terminal. Also, you gave me amnesia at the same time. I can't even remember most of the things that you're telling me. Honest! Ask Arthur. I almost got us both killed out there when I couldn't even remember how to use my rifle. *Ask* him!"

She abruptly motioned for the other people to leave. They gladly beat a hasty retreat from the "domestic" squabble.

She was the genius mathematician. He was the physicist promising to save the world. Plus he was the respected Leader of the Resistance. The other people didn't want any part of *their* high-powered arguments.

"So then...truce, Sally?" he asked, squatting down beside her.

"I'll—give you a chance to prove you've turned over a new leaf," she grudgingly said. "But if you try and slap me again I'll *bash* your head completely off your neck, not just dent it a bit."

"Fair enough," he nodded. "So do you see any hope for replicating your remnant in this programmable model?" he hastily moved on to a more neutral subject.

She squinted, obviously relieved to focus on a more agreeable subject.

"Well...the memory is more pliable than in the standard fixed units—which tend to self-destruct when we try to access their guts. So there's hope."

"Good," he gently smiled at her.

He felt he was making some progress with this sulking, angry Sally. But he was careful not to touch her.

He didn't want another computer terminal "denting" his already-aching skull.

Arthur, standing outside the tent entrance, was pleased.

Soon the DE-units scattered across the world would be linked together. That—regardless of Dave and Sally's expectations—would *not* stop the alien armada's rape of planet Earth. But the combined "cosmic flare" of that many DE-generators continually running would ensure the rapid advent of Judgment Day.

Praise the Lord! Hallelujah!

That Day could not come soon enough when the entire human species would merge with its Creator.

And all that *he* had to do was to keep helping Dave and Sally "do *their* thing."

God would not be deterred from His Righteous Wrath.

Chapter 4

JUST DO SOMETHING

Don't just sit there
Do something
Says the village idiot
Cackling at the gate
While invaders gather
Surrounding you
Ready to plunder and kill
And desperation grows
No good plan apparent
You panic and cry
Echoing the plea
"Just do something!"
Afraid to die
You give it a try
Ending worse than before
Wishing that you'd
Not done something
But just sat there...
And thought!
The Luminary Chronicles, 4:58-64

Sally heard the heavy barrier "SLAM" down behind her...
—as George slowed to a trot, then a stumble, and then to a gasping waddle; and she slid off his back onto the ground.
Beside her—hopping up and down with glee—was Tommy.

51

"Again! Again! Again!" he exclaimed, clapping his small hands together repeatedly.

Alice flopped down beside Sally, her scaly chest heaving, her long tongue hanging out across the sharp teeth in her muzzle, her thick reptilian legs trembling.

"We escaped," Alice gasped.

George, still breathing hard himself, reached out a clawed hand to help both Alice and Sally back to their feet.

A big-wheeled, flat granite platform was rolling up to them, with other concerned Dinosapiens jumping off to confer excitedly with George and Alice.

Their "speech" was a rapid series of melodious whistles and clicks, plus interspersed guttural grunts. It was impossible for Sally to follow or understand. High tones alternated with deep rumbles. The deeper tones were apparent only by the vibration they induced in Sally's skin. The squeals rose above Sally's range of hearing.

Tommy was fascinated by the reptilian speech, hanging onto their every whistle or grunt.

"Can you understand what they are saying?" Sally asked the little robot-boy, bending over to speak with him privately.

His big blue eyes looked up innocently.

"It is hard to follow them, they talk so fast. But yes, Mommy, I can understand."

"What are they saying?"

He cocked his cute head of blond curls to the side, listening intently.

"They say if those bad aliens didn't see us running away, they might not bother us down here underground."

"Oh, that's good."

"Uh oh," he frowned.

"What?" she urgently asked him.

"They *did* see us."

Sally felt the entire, smooth tunnel around her *quiver*.

"What's happening?" Sally gasped.

Tommy frowned.

"A bad, bad thing," he said, furrowing his little brow.

"Well, what...*what* is happening?" Sally said again, wanting to know their exact predicament.

George walked over to her and put an arm around her shoulders. His big orange eyes were blinking rapidly as if to drive back tears.

"They are firing on us, Sally," he said in English, his voice quavering.

"Those laser beams that destroyed Edmond, Oklahoma? The aliens followed us here?"

"Yes to both," he sighed, shaking his head sadly as yet another blast from above shook the tunnel. "We must descend into our city-proper. This tunnel will soon collapse. Come! Come quickly!"

The Dinosapiens all jumped onto the black granite platform. Sally and Tommy climbed up also. Then they began an agonizingly slow roll down a gentle slope.

The tunnel wall was made of clear glass within which sparkled a symphony of incredibly-intense colors and images. Many of them made no sense to Sally except to stimulate her senses. It was a kaleidoscope of wondrous fantasies playing out all around her.

But the images were flickering, the colors blurring, as distant loud "BANGS" interrupted their intricate sequencing.

Small pieces of fractured glass rained down on Sally and the other occupants on the open platform, causing them to cringe.

Then, as they traveled deeper and deeper, the BLASTS lessened in intensity—and the platform rolled out of the tunnel into a large, underground city-complex.

"Oh, how pretty!" Tommy exclaimed as he excitedly clung to Sally's hand, looking around with avid interest.

It was a series of darkened caverns only lit by the inward glow of thousands of rounded structures, each displaying distinctive colors and patterns.

There was not one straight line to be seen anywhere. Sally was amazed by the non-angular structures that sloped and melted into each other, towering up to about ten stories high.

"This is where you live?" Sally asked George as he stood placidly balanced on his two legs and long tail on the rolling platform.

"Yes, Sally," he answered, still blinking rapidly.

"Are they still firing on your city?"

"The surface of the land overhead has been burned down to the bedrock. And the rock that's still protecting us is being gradually melted away. They're attempting to penetrate to the city."

"But that's awful!" Sally gasped. "Will they be able to do so?"

He paused, calculating.

"Yes," he sadly stated. "In approximately one hour their gigantic laser weapon, fired from their Mother Ship, will breach our upper levels. At that time, thousands of us will die. Our atmosphere will be superheated, killing any survivors. By this time tomorrow, our city will be erased. We will all be dead."

Sally gasped in horror.

"But can't you shoot back?" she urgently asked him. "I thought you said your species has been intelligent for millions of years. Surely you have weapons to stop these invaders?"

He sighed, his big reptilian head hanging down in dejection, as he led Sally and Tommy off the now-stopped platform through an open doorway into an adjacent structure.

"We don't have weapons," he said. "We haven't had any crime or war for over five million years. It is a concept we not only can't deal with, we no longer understand it."

"But...?" Sally began but stopped in confusion.

They were in George and Alice's home.

"Eat and drink," George commanded. "Then we will talk further."

Alice brought over a platter of fruit-like objects that Sally and Tommy greedily devoured. Rounded cups held a frothy, gold-colored liquid. It tasted like sweet nectar. Sally hadn't realized she was so hungry and thirsty.

Square cubes tasted like meat, though Sally suspected they were artificially produced protein. Alice had previously told her they were all vegetarians, long since evolving past the point of needing to kill and harvest fellow animals.

"I still can't believe you don't understand conflict," Sally said after quickly finishing the welcomed meal. "Surely you observe fighting on the surface of your world out in Nature. You yourself evolved from those animals up there, didn't you? Fighting has to be part of your DNA!"

"Oh, Sally," George sighed, settling on all fours upon the floor as a strange, soothing music filtered from the rounded ceiling above, more "whistles" and "clicks" to something that sounded like violin strings. "It is in *your* DNA. You humans are still close to your savage, ape ancestry. We have evolved far beyond such nonsense. Our genetic imperatives are completely different from yours. Have you never thought how stupid it is that your species kills, rapes, abuses, and tortures *itself*? Before the aliens arrived, your ills did *not* come from a higher predator attacking you. You did all of that 'evil' to *yourselves*, right?"

Alice settled onto the warm floor next to her husband, laying her longish neck tenderly over his back.

"Well...yes—our philosophers and religious teachers have noted such," Sally reluctantly acknowledged. "But my point still stands, George. You know of this evil from all the less-evolved animals out there on the surface. It shouldn't come as a surprise."

"Oh, Sally," George sighed. "Those animals don't know any better. So it's not evil. But you and I *do* know better. That which is mere survival behavior for the lower animals for us *becomes* evil."

"So are you saying that from the perspective of the aliens attacking us, they're not doing anything bad?"

"Perhaps...who knows? They may think that they're actually doing a good thing ridding this world of us higher, 'polluting' lifeforms."

"Regardless, what could be wrong with defending ourselves? Why don't you have any *weapons* you can use?"

Alice sadly interjected: "We're not arguing with you, Sally. Please don't be mad at us. We've just long ago moved beyond such primitive things. And, yes, that may well be our undoing, so..."

"—the reality is that we, in this version of Earth, simply don't know how to deal with technologically superior invaders," George concluded for her. "For us to attack them is simply to repeat their barbarism. It is illogical. Even if we were to agree to such horror, we don't have the slightest idea how to begin."

"Then don't attack them!" Sally exclaimed in exasperation, standing up and pacing around the room in frustration. "All you have to do is just *defend* yourself! You understand Dark Energy far more than my people. Can't you erect a shield to stop the attacker's beams?

How is that a difficult thing? In our terms it's called 'passive' aggression!"

George sighed, leaning his head against his wife's neck for comfort.

"It is not difficult," he admitted. "We could do it. But it would be illogical because it would be futile. We've assessed the level of technology of the invaders and it is far above our own mastery. Any barriers we might erect they'd quickly breach. As such, we have already elected throughout this city to each enjoy our last few minutes in the peace of our own homes and..."

"But you *can't* just give up!" Sally interrupted him, throwing up her hands in exasperation. She paused in her nervous pacing to directly confront him. "You have to *do* something."

"What?" Alice said. "We brought you here because your species' low level of maturity has a certain primitive brilliance. We *welcome* your guidance, Sally. Please tell us what to do. How can we 'do something' that will not be just a futile, brief delay of our destruction?"

Oh, great. These overgrown lizards were looking to *her* to save them. What could she possibly do for them except sit on the warm floor and wait to be cooked by the relentlessly descending giant laser beam?

But...

"Wait just a minute," Sally said, grabbing her long red-brown hair to each side of her head and pulling downward in fierce concentration. "Have any of your other cities been attacked?"

"No..."

"Only this one?"

"Yes..."

"Then maybe *I'm* the reason that they are attacking you. Maybe they've detected that I, a human, am amongst you. Otherwise, they might have left you entirely alone. You don't seem to have much advanced tech here other than glass, music, and lights—am I right?"

"Well, yes...we have little need for other things."

"Then why not just give them *me?*"

George surged up to his feet, looming a full four feet above the still-standing Sally.

"Never! We would never give up a guest just to save ourselves, even if that were possible."

"George is right, Sally," Alice added, getting slowly back to her feet as well. "We cannot communicate with this 'Harvester' spaceship. They've not answered any of our broadband hails. We have no idea what they want or how they'd respond to what you suggest."

"*How much longer* will it be until your underground city is breached?" Sally demanded to know.

"Well...maybe thirty minutes."

"Then that's it," Sally insisted. "I'll give *myself* up. You've got nothing to lose. Call that roller platform back. Is there an exit by which I can return to the surface?"

"Well, yes, we have an alternative to the route we came in. That first tunnel is now collapsed, melted to slag. But the other is still open."

"Great! But I'll need something I can use for offense. Surely you have something that generates force or heat or power? What can you give me to take with me?"

"No, nothing," George said, shaking his big reptilian head in the negative. "Our systems are distributed throughout the city as integrated parts of the cooperative materials of our buildings. We don't have separate, portable power units."

"Wait...I think I may have something," Alice said, scampering away into another room, her tail lashing about in excitement.

She returned with a small blue sphere plus a large rectangular, black box.

"What does this do?" Sally said, accepting the sphere.

It looked like an old-fashioned "crystal ball" that witches could supposedly use to do magic. It was warm to the touch, with strange patterns floating through it—now a blue sky, then a frog, then a flower, on and on.

"It generates images. You need only hold it tight while visualizing what you want. Then you will be *surrounded* by the thing that you desire."

Oh, great. It was a holographic projector, like in the glass walls of the tunnel they'd traveled through. How in the world would that stop an invading super-starship? Well, it was better than nothing.

Sally didn't have a pocket large enough for it. So she thought to put it into the large black box, which came up to her waist. The top was latched, which she opened. It was empty inside. She started to place the sphere inside...

"No, Sally!" Alice stopped her. "You must carry the globe with you. Don't put it into the box."

"Why not?"

"It might disappear."

"Just *what* does this box do?" Sally frowned, puzzled.

"It is a transporter," Alice said. "I need only think of where I want to send fruit, say, to a friend—and it appears in their home in a similar box. Or, I can send a message, or whatever. Also, our waste materials are returned by it to the outer earth's substrate as fertilizer."

Great. She had a music box and a super-toilet. Maybe she could sing or "stink" those aliens to death?

Probably not...

"Wait, I have one more thing for you," Alice said as she ran back into her room.

She emerged with a bright-red knapsack-like carrying garment. She adjusted the straps so it hung snugly over Sally's much-smaller shoulder.

Sally gratefully slid the globe into it.

But, regardless of her "weapons", if she could just stop the attack on the city by giving herself up to the aliens—then that would be worth her sacrifice. These gentle, wise Dinosapiens would be safe. That would be victory enough.

"Ok, then," she grimly summarized. "I'd rather have a big gun, mind you, but I guess these will have to do. Take me back to the platform."

"Take *us*, Mommy, don't you mean?" Tommy said, jumping forward and tightly grabbing onto Sally's hand.

"No, Tommy," she sternly ordered him. "You stay with...*Aunt and Uncle* Alice and George. There's nothing you could do if you came with me. So I want you to be safe here with them. That's the best way you can help me."

"But Mommy...?" he whined.

"That's an order, Mister!" she again sternly ordered him, placing his little hand into Alice's paw.

Tears welled up in his android eyes as he did as directed, sullenly staying with the kindly lady Dinosapien.

Sally resolutely turned her back and strode out of the rounded, opened doorway onto the street.

There, a crowd had gathered.

The T-rex-looking reptiles were silent.

Then they began chanting together in perfect English: "Sally! Sally! Sally! Sally!"

She was touched by their support, but knew that time was fast ticking down to the entire city being destroyed. She had to move!

As the black granite platform again rolled up to the house, Sally climbed up on it and accepted the big black box from George. It was a light as a feather. She sat it next to her on the platform.

Absently she wondered what powered the platform. It didn't have any external motor. Ah well, what did it matter?

She waved goodbye to the crowd of big lizards who were still gratefully chanting her name—as she rolled away back toward the surface.

Then it was only her, the black box, and the sphere in her knapsack speeding along through the curved streets.

She felt queasy, the alien fruit having upset her stomach. The protein cubes were tasty. But the fruit was too tart. She considered throwing up into the black box. But she was still within sight of the lizard-people peeking out of doorways. She forced back the bile and continued smiling and waving as she departed the "magical" underground city.

Great, a hero's departure...

Maybe someday one of these intelligent lizards would write a song about her, to waft gently from their delicate glass walls. That is, if their species survived.

She certainly didn't think she had any chance of defeating a giant Harvester starship. Giving herself up was probably just a futile gesture. She knew that not only this city, but the entire planet of naive, too-smart, defenseless Dinosapiens was probably doomed.

How sad that, once again, the advent of a mammal would herald their reptilian demise.

Ivanna was immediately surrounded by a barrage of ear-splitting *blasts* and *explosions!*

"Get down! Get down!" Shirley shouted in her ears, throwing Ivanna bodily to the hard floor before dragging her backward into the tunnel.

All around, *barrages* of bullets were smashing into the tunnel walls, showering Ivanna and Shirley with rock fragments.

The other commandos were crouched just outside the tunnel's mouth, hiding behind slabs of fallen cement, popping up with their rifles to spit out short bursts.

One of them was thrown back into the tunnel, covered in blood, dead.

"Oh my God!" Ivanna gasped.

"We've got to retreat to our vehicle," Shirley said, pulling on Ivanna's arm...

—as yet another *loud explosion* outside the tunnel deafened Ivanna, blinding her with a huge flash of white light!

Everything seemed to be moving in slow motion.

Lit by weak light coming out the vehicle's windows behind her, Ivanna's returning sight registered dim figures leaping over the concrete slabs and approaching the stunned soldiers.

"We're overrun!" Shirley snarled into Ivanna's ear while jamming her big assault rifle into Ivanna's hands. "You've got to give me a few seconds. Shoot them. Shoot *all* of them!"

Shirley was grabbing a flat device from a pocket, flicking open a lid, punching in commands...

Ivanna knew how to use a gun. She'd gone deer hunting with Victor on multiple occasions. To her trained hands, the assault rifle was just a large deer-rifle.

As she pulled the trigger on the rifle she let its butt nestle against her shoulder, absorbing its kick.

It wasn't near as "thudding" as she'd anticipated.

The attackers were caught by surprise by the blazing gun shooting up at them from the floor.

In the roiling black smoke the attackers reeled backward, shouting commands to retreat.

But many more voices outside the tunnel answered them. It seemed there was a whole *army* out there!

A couple of the surviving commandos were just raising their helmeted heads when Shirley grabbed Ivanna by the pits of her arms and dragged her, while still clutching the smoking assault rifle, out of the tunnel to flop beside the surviving commandos.

"You're ready to seal the tunnel?" one of the men croaked through the thick smoke.

"Yes, Sir!" Shirley replied, holding the flat device firmly. On it, a red light was blinking.

"Let's get off to the side—then hit the switch," he ordered.

"Sir!" she responded, again grabbing Ivanna and dragging her off into the smoky darkness, following the two surviving commandos.

They flopped down behind more overlapping, partially fallen concrete beams.

Ivanna still had a tight grip on the heavy assault rifle, keeping it aimed out into the darkness—where she saw many more forms approaching.

They all lay on their faces in the narrow space, partially hidden from the attackers.

"Now, Sergeant," Ivanna heard the man whisper.

The tunnel opening *erupted* into a red column of solid fire that swept out like a *blowtorch*, engulfing everyone and everything in front of it!

A gigantic "THUD" shook the remains of the building as the tunnel they'd just traveled through collapsed.

Ivanna was afraid the remains of the building above them were also going to fall upon them, squashing them flat!

But aside from a searing heat that instantly faded—plus screams of attackers thrashing wildly as they burned to death—the surroundings remained stable.

She heard a few additional "thuds" as large pieces of the debris above her broke loose, but the main structure stayed intact.

"Sorry we had to do that, Professor," the man sadly grated-out next to Ivanna. "But we couldn't risk any invaders getting into the Mountain complex. Standing orders, Ma'am."

"But," Ivanna gasped, trying to blink the soot and debris out of her eyes to see out into the darkness. One of the soldier's flashlights was still on, lying a short distance away. It allowed Ivanna to see things dimly in outline. "How will we get back?"

"We won't," the man flatly stated. "But with Murphy here, we can still report back any significant findings. Right, Murphy?"

They both looked over at Shirley.

She was staring to the side, silently.

Ivanna locked eyes with the woman, *willing* her to reply.

But it was not to be.

"Murphy?" the man whispered, nudging her with his rifle butt.

The top half of her body slid away from them, riding on an underlying pool of blood.

A concrete block from higher up had crushed the back half of her prone body, severing it from her front half.

She was dead.

"Oh, Jesus," Ivanna gasped—her hands to her mouth in horror.

"We're cross-trained," the commando grimly stated, reaching over to grab equipment out of the dead woman's upper pockets. "We can still send a signal when we're ready. We've got to move!"

The other man gently took the rifle from Ivanna, slung it around his shoulder, and helped her to her feet.

Though they had to crouch to get under jumbles of still-overhanging debris, they could move forward.

Ivanna heard shouting off in the darkness.

They headed in the opposite direction.

"We've still got a mission to complete, Ma'am," the commando harshly whispered into her ear as he guided her along with a strong hand on her arm.

"But...but...how did they...?" she gasped as she stumbled along.

"It was clearly an ambush," he said, whispering directly into her ear. "Somehow they knew we were coming and were waiting for us. They probably wanted to wipe us out with one quick blow, and then proceed onward into the secret tunnel to attack the base. Murphy's quick actions saved us, plus the base. Also, that was real nice shooting back there, Ma'am. Your quick reactions saved me and Zeke."

"Yes—but the other men and Shirley...?"

Her voice choked off, realizing the awful slaughter she'd just witnessed.

"We'll grieve for them later," he whispered back to her. "For now we've got to find a safe place, away from here!"

"Yes," she agreed, stunned by the recent violent events and quite willing to let him direct her.

Actions and reactions—she involuntarily mused as they crept along. *Sequences and consequences, yin and yang, positives and negatives—everything is connected. Everything has already happened in one form or another.*

Ivanna was surprised to realize that she was philosophizing in the midst of battle.

She'd always believed that war was merely primal instinct, to kill or be killed. You just did what you had to do in order to protect yourself and your comrades.

It wasn't evil, it was just self-preservation.

But now she knew better.

Murphy's glazed-over eyes would haunt Ivanna forever.

Chapter 5

MESSIAH

Hold me tight and close
Away from the rampaging hordes
Tucked snugly into a warm bed
Protected by Mommy and Daddy
With nothing to fear or distrust
Cradled in the Arms of the Lord
Comforted by Almighty God Himself
We all rest secure, safe, and happy
Until the Creator decides differently
Bringing us not peace and tranquility
But purging fires of instructive hate!
The Luminary Chronicles, 5:94-98

Lower Galilee was as close to paradise on Earth as one could get.

Sally was enthralled with both the lush landscape and its hard-working people. Versus the toxic Dead Sea, the nearby Sea of Galilee was fresh and nourishing. Also, an abundant water table furnished water from wells to the small villages that dotted the verdant farm land. Low mountain ranges protected the valley. The soil was rich, allowing productive farming and ranching.

Sally soon discovered that the people in Galilee were mainly devout Jews of the Essene sect. Jesus' family, in particular, was part of the Essene group called the Nazarenes. Joseph, Mary, and Jesus lived in a cooperative village where people shared much in common, looking after one another's needs. The Nazarenes were a deeply devout people who strove not just to live up to the "letter" of Moses' Law but first and foremost to the *spirit* of the Holy Writings.

The Nazarenes fervently opposed several things, including slavery, sacrificing animals, and eating of flesh. Their highest aim as individuals was to be the true temple of God, expressing their faith through actively helping and healing one another. As such they strove to be angels of heaven set upon the earth: rejecting criminal or immoral acts, concentrating on dedicated service to others, while espousing a strong belief in immortality—life after death.

Theirs was a religion firmly embedded in sacred texts and tradition, but not bound by stifling rules and regulations. Indeed, daily life for them was a privilege and joy rather than a painfully restrictive duty.

It could have been an idyllic existence...

—except for the Roman occupiers, who insisted on turning Paradise into a living hell!

Joseph worked as a tenant farmer, growing enough food to feed his family, plus selling what was left over. But the Romans brutally taxed the people. Sally learned from Mary about Herod the Great, a king appointed by Rome to rule all of Judea. The cruel King almost succeeded in killing baby Jesus when he ordered the execution of the prophesied would-be "Messiah" babies in Bethlehem. That was when Joseph fled with his young family to Egypt, escaping the purge. After the death of Herod the Great, though, they returned—fortuitously discovering Sally on the shoreline of the Dead Sea.

It was Herod the Great that started the vicious taxation which was still crippling the people of Galilee. In his zeal to build huge monuments to his own prestige, he insisted on imposing an extra tax. The people already paid 10% of their earnings to the Jewish Temple plus up to another 15% to Rome. Herod demanded another 20% on top of the two other taxes! As Palestine had no gold or other mineral wealth, the tax came from the one resource of the area: farming.

The farmers in Galilee were crushed by the three different taxations. It was unsustainable. But if they didn't pay, Roman soldiers confiscated their lands, sent the delinquent farmers into slavery, or even abducted and raped the young women. Consequently, the people hated the Roman occupiers—and their puppet regimes—with a fierce loathing. Many of the farmers went into crippling debt trying to save their farms, a downward spiral from which they only rarely recovered.

Mary and the other women had to take in whatever extra work they could find to earn enough not only to scrape by, but also to help their husbands pay the crushing taxes and debts. When manual labor was available outside the farms, many of the men took on second jobs themselves. It was for this reason that the growing boy, Jesus, went with his father Joseph to the nearby cosmopolitan town of Sepphoris to work on construction projects. This was possible because a son of Herod the Great, Herold Antipas, the present ruler of Galilee, took on Sepphoris as his own personal construction project, creating many new jobs.

It was here that the young boy Jesus was exposed to travelers from other countries, particularly Greece, who brought with them strange new viewpoints and perspectives. In this way Jesus talked with travelers educated in the ways of Socrates and Plato. Other traders came from even further lands, particularly the orient. He eagerly devoured the teachings of the Hindus and the Buddhists.

This was all fascinating to Jesus. He had a bottomless intellectual curiosity. Thus he accomplished two goals—expanding his worldview and helping the finances of his dad—as he did manual labor in Sepphoris. The negative of these new part-time jobs, however, was that Herod Antipas needed even more abusive taxations to pay for the new construction!

It was an escalating cycle of harder, longer, back-breaking toil.

Sally saw that the young Jesus definitely did not live a life of relaxed philosophical pursuit as she'd imagined when she lived in the far future. He stole time for such pursuits from a life of heavy labor from sunrise to sunset. Such it was for everyone, a few moments of pleasure stolen within a framework of increasingly hard labor.

And even then the fruits of their hard work were often cavalierly stolen by corrupt officials and power brokers. The peasants of Galilee could not suffer this life without protest. Indeed, several revolts occurred, which Joseph, Mary, and their extended household studiously avoided. They knew the consequences of being identified as a rebel. Indeed, Roman troops swept in on several occasions—savagely crushing uprisings, burning houses, torching fields, and killing all those who'd dared participate in the revolts.

And so it was a time of great turmoil and struggles.

Though the young Jesus was still overtly suspicious of Sally—rarely even acknowledging her presence in the household—she could see that he did appreciate her helping his mother Mary in her daily struggles. In addition, Sally always tried to be friendly towards the growing boy even as his own peers and many of the adults ostracized him. Sally knew, as did everyone else in the small village, that Jesus was conceived before Joseph and Mary were officially wed. Though Mary steadfastly insisted that a miracle of God caused her conception of Jesus, many people talked behind her back. So Jesus, despite his mistrust of the older but relentlessly supportive Sally, began acknowledging her more and more—eventually accepting her not only as a servant in the household but even as a friend.

And as the intellectually restless Jesus grew he talked with Sally from time to time concerning religious matters. He recognized her "foreign" viewpoint, her willingness to discuss religious and philosophical teachings often heretical to a good Jew boy. She, in turn, encouraged his great curiosity and keen intelligence. She'd bring him a late-night snack as he stayed up late studying holy texts by candlelight.

Though the local religious leaders still held the boy at arm's length, they were flattered by his persistent and polite questions—grudgingly willing to "share their wisdom" with the eager young man. Sally, though, was his only real confidant—and steadily lowered his defenses...

—until she finally had the chance to *kill* him!

With Mary out of the house doing a late-night job at another household and the others deep in exhausted slumber—she crept to his bedside with a knife. She stood there poised to cut his throat.

She looked down at the young man, his tense face relaxed in fitful sleep. His eyes were closed tightly. His brown hair lay limply over a pillow. His powerful hands were clenched into the pillow. A rough woolen blanket was pulled up to his shoulders. But his neck was exposed. Thick blood vessels pulsed rhythmically in the dim light.

She knew that one brutal action would prevent the budding religious scholar from ever becoming the Messiah. Thus he'd be stopped
from not only rocking the local power structure, but altering the entire Roman Empire with his radical teachings.

Sally held the knife tightly in her hand, determined to stop a great
Religion from spreading across the entire world. Christianity would
never flourish. Although modulating the excesses of governments, in
the abstract, did seem a worthy goal for Jesus to pursue—Sally knew
the eventual result of Jesus' new, "loving" religion would be to allow
widespread access to Dark Energy. That, in turn, would fully alert the
Creator to the activities of *Homo sapiens*—who would be judged
harshly on their immense failures.

Mankind would be justifiably condemned and erased from the
Universe by a solar-superstorm.

A quick slash with her knife and she could prevent all of that from
happening!

She steeled herself to make the deep cut in his throat...

But she couldn't do it.

With a sigh, she dropped her hand holding the knife and quietly
returned to her small room.

She knew Jesus had to be stopped—but not in such an ugly fashion. He did not deserve to be brutally murdered, by Sally or anyone
else. Sally had to find a way of preventing him from achieving fame
that was subtler and kinder than slitting his throat.

Sally reluctantly admitted to herself that whatever the truth of his
conception, he was a remarkable individual—one whom Sally had
grown to deeply love...

He had the gift of gentleness embedded within an iron will. He
tended a flock as if the lambs were his own children. Upon seeing a
beautiful sunrise, Sally several times caught him weeping with joy.
Yet he could stand in the road and be whipped to the ground by a
passing Roman soldier insisting on a clear path for his horse—then
without protest rise to be whipped to the side yet again! And his
mind was a whirlpool: engaged and fascinated with all the many fac-
ets of reality. And rather than become stuck in the trappings of his
inherited religion, the boy Jesus untangled the knots and wove new,
ever more-meaningful spiritual patterns.

So Sally saw firsthand the young Jesus working all day then studying late into the night, determined not to be dragged down by the abuses of his day. But every time it seemed the family was starting to get ahead, they were thrown back into poverty and oppression.

And it all came to a head when Joseph died.

Jesus was only fourteen when a terrible construction accident occurred. His father, Joseph, was crushed to death by falling masonry as he labored in the city of Sepphoris. Jesus rightly blamed Herod Antipas—both for his ruthless building spree and for his heavy taxes that forced Joseph to work outside the village. The awful accident left the young Jesus in charge of the family—now responsible for his mother, his siblings, and the household servants.

Immediately following his father's funeral—apparently in a deep depression—Jesus walked off into the fields to be by himself.

Mary and the other mourners let him go, knowing the heavy burdens he faced—which he now needed to sort out on his own.

But Sally followed him at a discrete distance, discovering him sitting on a boulder staring off into the distance.

The setting sun lighted up the tops of the surrounding hills. A random ray struck him as he sat there, turning the white-robed Jesus for a few moments into a golden young man, a motionless heavenly statue.

Sally settled upon the green grass of the meadow right next to him, quietly sharing his time of grief.

Next to them was a still pond, above which a few dragonflies hovered.

"You've been a good friend and servant, Sahlee," he said after a long silence. His voice was measured and resonant. "I want you to know that I was wrong about you when we first found you in the desert, there beside the Dead Sea. You've been a hard worker and a loyal servant. And now as the new head of the family I want you to know you are no longer bound to us. If you wish to go your way, make a life for yourself or start your own family—you are free to do so. My sisters and brothers are old enough to take on more duties around the household, making up for your absence. But if you should wish to stay with us, I would be grateful. This is a hard time for us...for me."

Sally was greatly touched by his concern and compassion.

She had indeed worked hard for the past fourteen years with Jesus' family. But it wasn't back-breaking slavery. She cooked, cleaned, toiled in the fields, carried water jugs, milked the goats, and did sewing. Then, in the late evenings, there was time for quiet contemplation and study of the ancient texts by candlelight. And, increasingly frequently, she'd been privileged to discuss the teachings of the Essenes with Jesus while he did his own studies after a full day of physical work. It actually wasn't too different from her time spent in the Convent under Hildegard von Bingen more than a thousand years in the future. There she also labored during the day in the Convent, to in the evenings discuss wonderful things with the Magistra. And so it was again, except this time her intellectual friend was the young Jesus! It was not a bad life...

—if it weren't for the *crushing burden* of living under the *iron fist* of the Roman occupiers!

Her strategy of blending into the background—studiously avoiding soldiers, officials, and townsfolks—had until now kept her out of trouble. But the maturing Jesus was another matter entirely. To this point his father had shielded the boy from the heavy hand of the Romans. Now, as the new head of the family, he was fully exposed.

He was poised to begin a growth-spurt, both physically and spiritually.

"That is kind of you to say, Jesus," Sally properly replied. "But your family saved me. I don't turn my back on my friends. In this time of uncertainty and pain, I am happy to help you in any fashion that I can. Perhaps I can take on more outside work, to help pay the taxes?"

Jesus' young face twisted up into an ugly snarl as he struggled to control his emotions.

"It is...*hard*...to keep the love of our God in our hearts in the face of such wanton *evil*," he said through clenched teeth. "Their cruel hold on us must be loosened—by whatever means necessary."

"Direct opposition is met with the sword," Sally sadly stated. "What can we do?"

For a moment he was silent. Then he spoke.

"There is a *Teacher of Light* prophesied," he softly observed, looking up at the sun still lighting the peaks of the hills, "who will lead the people out of darkness."

"Do you mean the Teacher of Righteousness?" Sally asked, "Did he not already come a couple hundred years ago?"

"No, Sahlee," he said as he firmly shook his head in denial. "That great Teacher only told us of Israel's many faults. The coming Teacher will proclaim *the Way* out of our earthly trials. He will show us the *Light of God* in a new and awesome way. And he will enlist *everyone* on earth to his Cause."

"Not just us Jews?"

"*Everyone*, Sahlee," he said again in a firm, loud voice. "Mark my words, the time of cruel Dictators and evil Emperors is coming to an end. People all over the world will no longer be slaves to the whims of godless monsters. The *Kingdom of God* will rise up and subsume *all* of those perverse earthly kingdoms!"

Sally sucked in her breath. Where had these grandiose thoughts come from? He'd never before spoken in such an overtly subversive manner.

"It sounds like you are talking of the Messiah who will lead us Jews into our own new Kingdom," she tentatively observed.

"Perhaps, perhaps not," he mused, looking up at the fading blue sky. "But even *more* than just Israel's Messiah..." he cryptically stated, his voice trailing off.

"So are we Jews to look for a new King?" she prodded him. "Are we to look for a *King of the Jews*—who will *also* be the King of the whole world?"

He laughed, brushing aside the seriousness of his previous words. To utter such statements was to risk being hauled up on trial for sedition.

"Oh, that would just get this new 'Messiah' killed, wouldn't it?" Jesus ruefully sighed. "I doubt the Emperor would care much for such an ambitious Jew."

"It hardly seems worth the effort if he just gets killed for his efforts," Sally reasonably agreed.

They were both quiet for a bit, luxuriating in the warm evening breeze.

She was dressed in the full robes and concealing shawl of the times. Indeed, Jesus had not seen her full head for years. Now, in the warmth of the evening, alone with Jesus at last, she took it as an opportunity to stand up and stretch, slipping her shapeless outer robe to the side and removing her concealing shawl. Doing so revealed her lean, supple body and youthful head.

She shook out her long, flowing red-brown hair.

"What are you doing, Sahlee?" Jesus mildly asked.

She sighed, sitting back down beside him. She put her hands flat to the earth behind her and prettily looked skyward.

"I want you to see me as more than just a servant," she said, now looking at him seriously—straight into his face. "I want you to know that I am here for you in *any* way that you please."

Perhaps this was her chance. He was vulnerable. His father had just died. He was coming to terms with being thrust into his new role as head of the family. It was more than obvious where his messianic conclusions were leading him. It was a goal to which he would sacrifice anything and everything! But also he'd just recently come into his puberty. His hormones had to be boiling in his young body. And what better way would there be to stop him from becoming a celibate crusading preacher bent on dying on the Cross to save all humanity—than to marry him? She was now nineteen years old in 1st Century years. Mary had only been around fourteen years old when she'd married Joseph. Maybe Jesus was still a bit young himself, but if she planted seeds might they not germinate, if not now then in later years?

"Are you trying to *tempt* me?" Jesus softly queried.

A flock of doves flapped leisurely past. Their spectral white feathers set them apart from the green-brown fields. It seemed to Sally an encouraging omen.

"Of course not," Sally promptly and properly replied, while still continuing to shake out her long, fluffy hair. She then took a large comb from a pocket and started casually combing out her locks. "But surely you've thought of having a family of your own—even taking a wife? And what other woman in this village is your intellectual equal than me?"

He was silent, so she assumed she had his consent to continue.

"What female here knows more than just rote repetition of the chants, superficial execution of the ceremonies, or unquestioned acceptance of the traditional rituals?" she reasonably and softly asked him. "I come from a far land where females are valued not just for their bodies but for their minds. Before I was...*kidnapped* to this land, I was in a *royal* family. I never told anyone of this before because I didn't want to seem haughty or ungrateful. But what I remember from my younger days is far more than the simple folks here could ever comprehend."

Unexpectedly, Jesus laughed.

"You want me to believe that you are *Princess*, Sahlee? Fit for a King?"

"Why not?" she casually laughed back at him, pretending she was just playing with him. "Aren't I pretty enough to be a Princess?"

"You are indeed a lovely young lady, that is true," Jesus nodded thoughtfully. "But Sahlee, you are only a child."

"A child? But I'm..." Sally began to argue until she caught a glimpse of herself reflected in the pond.

It was true.

In the last fourteen years she'd barely aged! Now she appeared to be a young girl of no more than nine or ten years old. Those damn pills that'd returned her youth were now preventing her from aging properly! She'd gulped a whole bottle of the retroviral DNA-optimizer interactive sequences. A bottle of the booster pills was normally spread across an entire lifetime for the Elites of her Dimension. Her blood must still be swarming with the little buggers. That massive dose should have killed her, but instead turned her into a perpetual child.

Jesus didn't see her as a seductive candidate wife—just as a silly younger sister.

He stood up and held out both hands to her.

Ruefully, she placed her own small hands into his calloused, work-hardened, larger ones.

"I do love you Sahlee," he gently smiled at her. "You already give me great pleasure, especially in our 'intellectual' conversations. But now please put your beautiful long hair back under its proper covering so as not to shock the good folks back at the house. And don your outer robe. Let us return to our friends and family. *They* need both of us."

"Yes, I suppose so," Sally sighed, reluctantly doing as directed while Jesus turned back towards the village and began walking slowly away from her. "But Jesus...?"

"Yes?" he said, pausing to turn back toward her.

She saw his strong, upright body clad in rough robes, the tough sandals on his feet, the glint of deep awareness in his large eyes, the tangle of long brown hair falling to his shoulders, and the fuzz of a beard just starting to grow out on his chin.

He was no longer a young boy.

"Oh...nothing," she gulped, looking down at the ground.

"Stay as long as you wish," he kindly said, walking away. "It is a beautiful evening."

She sighed again, sitting dejectedly down upon the hard boulder where Jesus had just been.

His destiny was set. How could she possibly sway him from his path? It seemed impossible.

And yet—she knew she had to find a way.

Dave cursed like a sailor, letting his anger spew out his lips in foul doses.

"*Why* doesn't it work?" he snarled.

He was getting increasingly frustrated and angry.

The bootleg original Device was scattered about the "lab" in pieces. He'd been trying to adjust the vibrational interfaces of the matrix into opposing planes, hopefully to cancel out signals propagating into subspace.

Trying to realign the matrix just caused it to crumble into dust.

His "technicians" were silent. They were as dejected as he. And they certainly weren't scientists or even graduate students. One, in the pre-invasion world, had been a computer repairman. Another was a high school science teacher. And the remaining lady used to be a plumber by trade—hardly qualified to even help move things around in a real research lab.

Dave was exhausted, not having slept for two days, barely able to keep his eyes open.

It looked hopeless.

"Hey there, David," Arthur cheerfully said as he hurried into the large tent through the front flap. "I heard you swearing. In fact, the entire personnel heard you all throughout this level. So I take it things aren't going well?"

"I'm...beginning to think...it just isn't possible," Dave groaned, staggering over to drop wearily into a chair, burying his head in his arms.

"What's not possible, David?" Arthur said, sitting next to him and laying a big arm across Dave's shoulders.

Dave felt somewhat comforted by Arthur's fatherly presence, though no closer to a solution than before.

"Shielding the generator from detection!" Dave exclaimed in exasperation. "You know as well as me that the instant we turn a DE-generator on, the Reapers converge upon us. Liberating Dark Energy is like banging on a bell that rings throughout subspace. Ergo, all over the world we can only use DE-generators in short bursts—either at a safe distance from our hideouts or right before having to pull up stakes and run for our lives. And if we can't have sustained activation, then we'll never get a worldwide net into place to stop the Harvesters."

"Yep, that's what you and Sally are trying to fix, for sure—shielding the generators from detection," Arthur reiterated, withdrawing his arm and adjusting his big dark eyeglasses. "Where is that snotty little girl, anyway?"

"Ah, she conked out a few hours ago," Dave sighed, wincing. "I thought I was onto something so I kept on. But it all came to crap. All I accomplished was destroying a precious sample of the crystalline matrix. *Damn* it!"

"Exactly what were you trying to do?" Anderson supportively asked.

"Oh, just to make the deuterium ions run in parallel but opposite tracks through the crystalline matrix, that's all! Sounds simple, right? The little fractures in subspace would then run in opposite directions with the 'sound' waves theoretically cancelling each other out."

"Ok..." Arthur cautiously encouraged Dave to continue.

"But I can't even get those tracks into place," Dave groaned, slamming a fist onto his own leg. "When I tamper with the crystalline structure that's critical to getting the deuterium ions to trigger cold fusion—everything stops dead."

"So it's just a technological manufacturing problem?" Arthur cautiously ventured.

"Hell no! That's the *heart* of the problem!" Dave yelled, jumping up from the chair and pacing through the piled heaps of old, "liberated" equipment.

"What do you mean?"

"In pre-invasion times figuring how to accomplish this step—assuming it's even possible—might take *years* of research in a fully-equipped materials lab. And all I have here to work with is salvaged *junk!*"

"But...?"

"And that's not the worst of it, Arthur," Dave continued on without a break.

"You mean...?"

"It may not even be a *quantitative* problem, of just adjusting existing components in new ways."

"So...?"

"It may require a *qualitative* solution, meaning *brand new stuff!*" he shouted loudly in frustration, not caring who heard him. "How the *hell* can I figure out novel modalities working in a *damn tent* with a bunch of *refugees* hiding in an underground parking garage?"

Dave sank back into the chair, put his head in his hands, and started sobbing.

Arthur sat quietly by his side.

Outside the tent there were no sounds. Everyone had certainly heard Dave yelling. Before, they'd all been working together to achieve a defined objective—with a ray of hope to keep them going. Now, he realized that he was announcing to them that their Leader was giving up.

"Dave!" Arthur's curt sharp voice cut through Dave's funk.

Dave lifted his head, angrily wiping away tears from his cheeks.

"*What?*" he combatively replied, looking Arthur square into his dark eyeglasses.

"What can I do to help?"

"Nothing!" Dave snapped. "You don't have the capacity to even understand the situation, let alone offer any meaningful help. Sally's the only one who understands this stuff—and she hardly even talks to me anymore. She's just as lost as me."

"You said you need a new direction—maybe new technology, a whole new approach, right?"

"Yes," Dave suspiciously agreed.

"So how do those damn robots prowling the streets communicate?"

"How the hell should I know?"

"They immediately react in unison when the Harvesters give them directions. They all congregate instantly to a 'hot' area."

"So?"

"Are they communicating by radio waves, microwaves, laser beams, or what?"

"Well..." Dave paused, furrowing his brow, engaging with the new problem brought up by Arthur. "Sally told me that before our technological centers were destroyed, our scientists tried to figure it out but didn't detect any of the normal modalities of communication between the Reapers, the shuttlecrafts, and the Mother "Harvester" Ships up in orbit."

"Your memory hasn't yet fully returned?" Arthur worriedly interjected.

"It's still hazy," Dave ducked the question, still not sure what was real or not—or what he should reveal to the ex-FBI agent about the previous timeline.

"Well, what did Sally say the officials concluded about the Alien communications?" Arthur pressed him.

"Uhm...they only had days before everything went to hell, so they didn't have much time. But from what Sally told me—they figured maybe neutrinos? But that was just reaching for straws, not even possible as far as we know."

"And what powers their spaceships, Dave?" Arthur calmly asked him.

Dave sat up straight, frowning.

"It has to be Dark Energy, of course. Nothing else explains how they could appear around earth undetected—somehow using Dark Energy to travel through subspace to..."

"And their communications?"

"*Damn*, Arthur," Dave said, jumping up to start frantically pacing back-and-forth yet again, "you're a *genius!*"

"I'll leave that title to you and your grouchy little girlfriend," Anderson modestly stated. "But I'm not stupid."

A whole set of new ideas was racing through Dave's head.

"If those robots communicate with their ship by vibrational modalities through subspace," Dave hurriedly continued, "then they must have the physical means to generate and control those vibrations."

"Sounds logical."

"And if I could get my hands on that equipment, I might be able to..."

"—figure out how it works and adapt it to our own DE-generators?" Arthur concluded.

"We need one of those robots," Dave grated, grabbing Arthur by his shirt collar and shaking him for emphasis.

"Now *that's* the Leader I know who can save both us and the entire world," Arthur grinned as he gently removed Dave's clawed hands from his shirt.

"Let's go catch us a robot!" Dave yelled triumphantly, grabbing up his assault rifle that'd been leaning in a corner before running headlong out of the tent.

Where before he was defeated, now he had an achievable objective! It was a rather foolish, *dangerous* objective—but it was something to latch onto.

"Right," Arthur sighed, standing up and following the eager "warrior" out into the sub-basement.

Just catch a killer Reaper robot—easier said than done.

But Arthur knew everything hinged on Dave and Sally getting the DE-generators fired up and continuously running across the world.

Without lighting up subspace, the *Day of the Lord* might never arrive.

And Arthur, if nothing else, was a true Servant of the Lord: willing to do *anything* to bring humanity into the *full, glorious gaze* of the Creator!

—no matter the consequences.

Chapter 6

<u>PHOENIX</u>

From the ashes of defeat
Often arises a brand new thing
Leaving behind the old rust and wear
Creaky repairs no longer even a consideration
When the strong, forged, pure components gleam
Failure, indeed, is consumed by victory
Totally unexpected by one's enemies
Your burnt remains crumble away
As you arise reborn and fresh
Ready to strike viciously
Doing so with blind rage
Unhindered by the past
Liberated by the present
Expanding into the far future...

The Luminary Chronicles, 6:158-163

Sally stood on a high hill overlooking a *huge smoking caldron* that was being melted ever-deeper by *mammoth red laser beams* flashing down from the sky!

The THUNDERING from the relentless bombardment was deafening.

The granite rolling platform had just exited from a tunnel on the opposite side of the underground city from which she'd first entered. This platform had moved quickly, unlike the sedate descent of the other one. Within only a few minutes she'd been deposited out of the tunnel onto a meadow on the far side of a low mountain. Grabbing the black box in both of her arms she trudged up to the peak of that hill.

81

"Here I am!" she shouted up into the sky, trying to be heard over the constant *"thrumming"* of the gigantic laser blasts. "I surrender! Come get me!"

Nothing happened.

The laser blasts kept *SLAMMING* into the bubbling pit where a low mountain had been just an hour before.

The noise was unbelievably intense. The ground beneath Sally's feet vibrated. The smell of scorched earth was acrid. Around her in the forests and plains packs of long-necked dinosaurs were fleeing in panic as fires swept out from the deepening pit.

Desperate to end the attack on the underground city, Sally reached into her bag and pulled out the blue globe.

It's a holosphere projector...for images and music and light—she thought to herself. *Maybe if I think hard enough, grab it tight enough?*

She closed her eyes and clutched it tightly to her chest.

In her mind she constructed an idealized vivid image of herself standing *a thousand feet* up into the air: LONG, FLOWING RED HAIR; FIERCE GREEN EYES; FISTS CLENCHED AT HER SIDES; BLUE PANTS AND WHITE BLOUSE.; LIFTING UP A GLITTERING LIGHTNING BOLT LIKE THE NORSE GOD THOR; A RAINBOW BURSTING FROM HER HANDS TO SWEEP UP ACROSS THE SKY; plus A HUGE CHORUS OF ANGELS SINGING AROUND HER!

Hah! Take that, you stupid Aliens!—she congratulated herself.

The blue sphere was vibrating in her hands as if struggling to accommodate her instructions.

Opening her eyes, she looked up and saw what indeed appeared to be a thousand foot-high idealized replica of her, towering up into the clouds at the center of a kaleidoscope of light and music!

The laser bombardment abruptly stopped.

Her holo-image celestial concert faded away—the blue sphere turning dark and cold in her hands as if drained of energy—as she glumly observed a craft descending out of the sky.

It looked like a "flying saucer" of the old twentieth century science fiction movies.

White lights dotted its underside. And in the center of its bottom was a *blazing spiral of white energy*, clearly its thrusting mechanism.

It was as big as a small house, silvery in color, making no noise, and drifted down to land lightly on the top of the hill just a few yards away from her.

A hatch slid up into its side as if welcoming her aboard.

She put the blue sphere into her backpack, lifted up the black box in both her arms, and resolutely strode forward to enter the spacecraft.

"This is spooky," she whispered to herself as the hatch slid closed with a "snap" and a faint red light came on.

It was chilly inside, the air stale and musty.

On both sides of her, secured by metallic harnesses, were silent unmoving *robots!* There were a dozen of them...

And each of them stood around twenty feet tall. They were bipedal. They had swivel-tops inset with five "eyes" arranged in a circle around each "head". Below the eyes on each robot were arranged a dozen thick, lethal-looking gun barrels. In place of arms were three metallic-looking stocky tentacles that wrapped several times around each of their large metal chests.

They were lined up in a row, suspended from the ceiling.

In the dim red light they looked *demonic*.

"Hey, how's it going?" she said, forcing herself to address the inert creatures with bravado.

But they didn't reply.

She felt the flooring pushing up at her and knew they were lifting up off the surface of the planet, zipping up into the clouds!

Indeed, as if for her review, a viewing panel slid out of the ceiling in front of the robots, showing her the ground dwindling away far below.

She made out the outlines of the North American continent. Then she saw the edges of the rounded planet, the thin blue line of atmosphere standing out against the blackness of space.

And just that fast they were up in orbit.

Wow! That was quick—Sally thought to herself.

Off in the distance in space—rapidly growing ever larger—Sally saw a huge rectangular spaceship.

It was a *Harvester*.

As they drew near, Sally looked around frantically for a weapon. If she was to meet the masters of that gigantic spaceship, it would be nice if she had a defense better than a musical sphere and a portable toilet!

But other than the suspended, gently-swaying giant robots, there was nothing else in the cramped space within the shuttlecraft.

Starting to panic, Sally set the black box on the floor and grabbed ahold of one of the cold tentacles of a robot, clambering up onto its chest.

She tried to loosen one of the thick gun barrels, to drag it out of the robot.

It wouldn't budge.

"Can I help?" she heard a boyish voice and looked down in surprise.

Pushing the lid up of the black box and poking his curly blond-haired head out was...Tommy!

She dropped back to the floor, astonished.

"But...but...that box was as light as a feather! You weren't hiding inside, were you?"

"Oh, no, Mommy! You said for me to stay with Aunt Alice and I did. But when the shuttlecraft took you they knew you might need me so they sent me through another black box into this one. Are you glad to see me?"

He grinned happily up at her.

"You...you *bad* little boy—you just *go back* the way you came!" she sternly admonished him as she saw the Harvester ship looming in the viewscreen against the blackness of outer space, filling up the screen. "We're about to be taken in by one of the Mother Ships. I don't want you to get hurt...and I don't have anything here to use to defend you."

"But I'm just a robot, like these big guys," he continued grinning happily as he hopped out of the box and walked over to one of them.

He ran his small hand along a large metallic leg.

"Careful, they're dangerous!"

"Yep, and they're *slick*," he marveled. "Maybe I should look like them?"

"You're *not* just a robot," Sally insisted, grabbing his warm little hand and pulling him away from the swaying, suspended monsters. "You're an *android* with an evolved intelligent computer program put in you by my future 'High Priestess' self. Or at least, that's what the High Priestess told Ivanna when they thought I was dozing off below the Throne back on Mars."

"Yep, that's me," he giggled. "I'm a little *robot*—but a *nice* one. Yay!"

"Oh...you!"

A slight jar told Sally that they'd arrived.

"You won't go back?" she implored him. "You could still hop back into that box and be safe with the Dinosapiens, couldn't you? The monsters are after me, not you."

"Nope—I'm staying with you, Mommy. You might need me to help you."

"Well, ok...but I sure wished you'd brought me a weapon. It's nice to talk to you, Tommy, but I'd rather have a nice big gun."

"I'm tougher than I look," the boy bragged, puffing out his chest grandly.

"I'm sure you are," Sally sighed. She was actually glad to have him with her, but fearful he'd just be sacrificed needlessly.

The viewscreen showed that they were inside a huge hanger, where hundreds of the saucer-like transports were housed. Also, more sinister, were black square ships that each sported huge cannons poking out of their sides. Sally guessed that they were mobile laser-beaming attack ships. Still other ships were towering and cylindrical. Sally guessed that they were transports for looted materials. Indeed, she saw even more-gigantic robots unloading several of the big cylinders, pouring out what looked to be debris of crushed buildings into a huge hopper.

Large and small cables dangled from the heights above, some attached to various ships, others hanging free.

It was a lively, active working site. It reminded Sally of a busy seaport with cargo being continually loaded and offloaded.

Several of the large craft were being guided by squat robots toward ejection slides, preparing to depart the hanger.

"Well, what now?" Tommy cheerfully asked.

As if in answer, the hatch slid open.

A transparent rectangular cabinet sat there, with a plastic-looking tunnel attached between it and the hatch. The clear container looked just big enough to hold Sally, her possessions, and Tommy.

"I guess we get into that thing," she sighed, now doubly-concerned that she had no weapons—just a silly android, a toilet, and a musical projection-sphere tucked inside her backpack.

Dragging her possessions behind her she went through the tunnel and entered the cabinet. The door sealed behind her. The air inside was fresher than in the saucer-transport. Something was circulating the air. Clearly, the Aliens didn't want her immediately dying of asphyxiation.

The entire transparent container rose up off the floor and floated up toward a large yellow light set into the ceiling of the huge hanger.

"We're off to see the Wizard!" Tommy said gleefully, clapping his small hands together.

"Ah yes, the 'yellow brick road'," Sally gulped, fearful of what awaited her up above. Maybe the Alien masters were going to dissect her and Tommy. That wouldn't be much fun. "So do you like movies, Tommy?"

"I *love* them," he cheered.

"So what did Dorothy find in the Land of Oz?" she seriously asked him, looking down at him.

"She found *herself*," Tommy grinned up at her.

"You're awful smart for being 'just' a little robot," she snorted at him.

"Well, I *am* forty eight years old," he giggled.

"Oh, that's right," Sally idly replied. Her eyes fixed on the yellow light above to which their transparent cage was fast approaching. "I forgot about..."

"Lots of people don't think I'm too smart 'cause I'm so small," he impishly grinned as he balled up his small fist and SMASHED it through the glass-like wall in front of him.

Sally was stunned by his unexpected violence, finding herself *gasping* as the air rushed out!

"Put the box over your head," he cheerfully ordered her.

She grabbed it and did so, astonished to see the black box extending and collapsing at her neck to cover her entire head, before clarifying into a protective helmet.

What a versatile 'toilet'!

"Come on," Tommy cheerfully yelled at her, taking her hand and jerking her out into the *empty expanse!*

—where they fell for a terrifying few seconds in the weak gravity outside the box...

—Tommy grabbing onto several cables which they were falling past to slow their fall and guide their descent, to land with a faint "thud" back onto the oddly flexible surface of the hanger.

Around her, Sally saw a couple of the larger lifting robots slowing in their work, turning towards them...

—as from the transport vehicle, Sally saw several of the twenty-foot-tall, tentacle-sporting robots emerging!

"But...how did you...?" Sally gasped at Tommy who was tugging her rapidly towards one of the big black squared crafts.

She vaguely noticed that it had a large, protruding laser-beam "cannon" on it.

"Get in! Get in!" he urged her as a panel slid opened on its side.

"What are you...?"

"I'm just a smart computer program, remember?" he cheerfully explained as they clambered inside an empty hold, closing the panel behind them. Then he led her up a short, sloping tunnel into a control room.

Clearly, the control room had not been used by living beings for a long time. Metallic-looking, glittering dust covered the exposed surfaces. The same dim red light as outside glowed from the materials.

"In this hanger, they 'talk' to each other with point-to-point microwaves," he quickly continued. "I just figured it out, Mommy—and got us a ride."

"Well, aren't you clever?" she marveled, sliding into a central command chair. It was built for a creature twice her size, but by leaning forward she could grab onto a joystick.

Her "helmet" was fogging up from her breath so she lifted it up—feeling it loosening from around her neck—and dropped it to the side.

It immediately turned back into a black box.

Fresh air began flowing around her. It was thick, probably meant for a living being different from her. But luckily it contained enough oxygen to keep her alive.

Suddenly a viewscreen with blinking lights appeared in front of her.

Laid out in exquisite detail as pictograms, were the entire contents of the hanger.

A circle with inset crosshairs sat off to the side on the screen, blinking on and off.

"You said you wanted a weapon, Mommy," Tommy smiled up from her side. "So I got you one."

For the first time in a long while, Sally *smiled*.

"I've got control of this ship?" she asked him, "—*plus* the laser cannon?"

Several large robots were stomping menacingly towards her on the screen...

"I hacked into it," he giggled, hopping up-and-down with excitement. "It's just regular RF-transmissions. That's easy for me. So I stopped it from talking with the Big Ship. Now you've got it all for yourself!"

"That's just what I wanted to hear," she said as she swung the crosshairs with her joystick onto an approaching robot and pushed the top button.

The robot vanished in a blaze of exploding pieces!

A wheel and other intuitive controls on a panel before her controlled the movement of the entire ship so that she could quickly swing the cannon around in a complete circle.

As each hostile target came up on her screen she repeatedly pressed the trigger, *incinerating* them with the powerful laser-cannon!

It seemed that she and Tommy had caught the Mother Ship by surprise. In just a few seconds she decimated the entire contents of the huge hanger.

All around them now were only smoking, ruined, blown-apart spaceships and smashed, lifeless robots.

In addition, a number of the blasts had blown gaping holes into the innards of the ship.

A strange green smoke was wafting out of the laser-melted breaches from the interior of the Mother Ship.

It was as if the ship was *bleeding.*

"Can we *kill* the entire Mother Ship?" she eagerly asked Tommy, searching for new targets.

"Oh...you better not," he gulped, looking chagrinned.

"What...?"

The walls around Sally in the control room suddenly *twisted and contorted* before *snapping* back into place!

"What the hell?" she gasped, feeling like she'd just been turned inside-out. "What just happened to us?"

"Oh, something *bad,*" he frowned, reaching up to grab her hand for support.

She let loose of the joystick and put her other hand onto his soft-haired, blond head.

"It's ok, Tommy, don't worry," she comforted him. "You've done great. We stopped this entire giant spaceship from attacking the Dinosapiens' Earth. So...are we crashing? Is that what's happening?"

"No..." he said in a hesitant small voice.

"Then what?" she asked again, this time more earnestly. "I'm not mad at you, Tommy. I just need to know."

"We're no longer in Uncle George and Aunt Alice's dinosaur Dimension."

"The Harvester jumped?"

"Yep. We're back in our own Dimension."

"Then...that's good, right?"

"Well...that's not all," he glumly replied.

"*Tell* me!" she yelled at him. Then, more softly, she continued, "Please, Tommy. Just tell me what happened when we got back into our own Dimension!"

"It went on 'automatic retrieval'," he said. "It knew bad things were happening to it, so it got away."

"And that means...?"

"It got *all* the way away. It's taking its present cargo back to where it came from."

Oh, hell! Where in the Universe did this thing come from, anyway? Sally didn't mind dying, if necessary, to save dinosaur-Earth—but she hadn't bargained on being lost in space.

"Ok, Tommy..." she paused, trying to get her racing thoughts together.

"Yes, Mommy?"

"Can you find out where the ship is taking us?"

"Yes."

He squinted, pursing his little lips.

"And that is...?" she urged him.

"It's a *big black hole,*" he unexpectedly laughed, releasing her hand to dance-about the cramped control room, stirring up the diamond-glittering dust that layered the floor.

It was pretty but distractive.

"A 'big black hole'?" Sally dully repeated.

"Yes! Doesn't that sound like *fun?*" he laughed, clapping his little hands together.

Sally knew that astronomers had documented the presence of a massive Black Hole at the center of Earth's galaxy, the Milky Way. The Black Hole contained the mass of four million suns. Gravity in it was so powerful that not even light could escape its interior, hence its name. Anything falling into it was lost forever. And it was *26,000 light-years* away from earth!

Even traveling at the speed of light, Sally would still be long dead by the time they reached their destination.

"How long until we arrive there?" Sally gasped, trying to wrap her head around the implications.

Tommy put his little fists up against the sides of his head, closing his eyes entirely in fierce concentration.

"It's...hard to make contact. The ship isn't letting me read it unopposed anymore. It's blocking its systems, keeping me out. But I think..." he paused and then slipped to a sitting position with his back to the wall.

His eyes glazed over.

"Are you ok, Tommy?" Sally asked, concerned.

"I don't know," he weakly replied, blinking while putting his small fists to the side of his cute head. "My head hurts."

"Don't try it again, then," she ordered him. "But did you find out anything?"

"I don't know," he repeated himself.

"You don't know what?" she asked, starting to feel irritated in addition to her amazement at what was happening.

"I don't know—how long till we get there," he whispered. "I'm kind of tired."

He looked like he was falling asleep. Maybe he had the mental capacity of several super-computers, but physically he was limited to being just a little boy—except of course when he was hardening his hand to punch a hole through a transparent wall!

Regardless, he did seem drained of energy.

"Then tell me *how* we are traveling through space," she urged him. "Tommy, please concentrate! Does the Mother Ship go at lightspeed or by some sort of warp drive?"

"Uhm..." he mused, tilting his small head to the side. "I think that...we're in—*subspace?*"

"Oh, Jesus," she sighed, climbing out of the oversized command chair to slump next to Tommy, placing her own back also to the wall.

"Is that bad, Mommy?" he innocently asked, taking one of her larger hands in both of his smaller ones.

"Well," she sighed, exhausted, the adrenalin of the last few minutes draining rapidly from her own body, "it could mean we'll be traveling a few minutes...or *thousands* of years. And if we do manage to arrive safely, we've no idea what we're going to find there."

"But we're ok for now?" he asked hopefully.

"I suppose—nothing is attacking us anymore—but we've no idea about the condition of the rest of the ship. I was shooting it up pretty fiercely when..."

"So maybe we should go exploring?" he weakly asked.

"Sure," she said, pulling his head over onto her lap. "But first let's take a little nap."

"Good idea," he yawned. "I'm all tuckered out."

She leaned back and closed her eyes. Sally had no idea what awaited them at the Galactic Core. But at least they were still alive.

Ivanna was tiring rapidly. But she was determined to keep up with her two remaining comrades.

Their "secret" exit from the Cheyenne Mountain complex had been a disaster. But at least she and some of her team were still alive.

"Could we...rest for just a bit?" she tentatively asked, afraid she was about to collapse. She was breathing hard. She could barely move her arms and legs. And her vision was blurring.

"Of course, Ma'am," the man in front of her whispered back, pushing aside burnt timbers to reveal an alcove off to the side.

He helped her to crawl into it, huddling beside her, as the soldier at the rear blocked the entrance with his own body—quietly pulling debris up onto himself to camouflage their position.

They'd been crawling under a series of large, collapsed supporting concrete beams. The commando beside Ivanna was Major Sidney Cotrell, a tough-looking middle-aged, crew-cut warrior. He was of African-American heritage, with deep black skin. The only other survivor of the initial ambush, Staff Sergeant Zeke Grant, lay at the entrance to their small hiding place. Untypical of a stereotypically tanned Ranger, he had skin the opposite color of the Major, a pale white. This was likely due to his Irish heritage, which he'd mentioned to her when he took his helmet off to show her his bright orange, crew-cut hair. She'd found out their names during another rest an hour previously as they lay hidden in another small "cave" of rubble while a band of searching marauders hurried past.

Now they were nearing an exit out of the top basement level onto the ground floor of the crushed stadium.

"Major, could I have a sip of water, please?" she gasped as she lay curled up on the flooring.

She was shivering. The thin jacket she had on didn't warm her much. Her coveralls were ripped at the knees. Her thin hands were spotted with small cuts from the rubble she'd crawled over.

He uncapped a canteen and held it to her lips.

"Not too much, Ma'am," he cautioned her. "That's all we've got left. The ambushers succeeded in destroying most of our supplies."

She gratefully took a slow drink out of it before recapping and returning the canteen.

"Thanks," she whispered. "That's a lot better."

Her throat felt raw. She could barely draw air in through her nostrils. She'd been breathing smoke, dust, and dirt for several hours as they struggled to escape the smashed lower basement levels and get up into the city proper.

There were areas clear of rubble where they could have made better progress if they'd gone through them, but they were swarming with ragged, searching bandits.

Ivanna could hear them not far off, trudging through the opened spaces, still searching.

They'd known that Ivanna and her team were coming! How was that possible?

"Ma'am, once we're free of this building we can try to make contact with any local resistance leaders," the Major whispered to her. "Unlike the riff-raff hunting us here, they should be civil. They have at least a rudimentary command-structure. I don't know for sure that they exist, but if I'd survived the initial attack out there I'd have formed up a local unit. So just hang in there and it's likely we'll get you to reasonable people. Then you can assess the ground situation for the President."

She nodded, stealing herself up for another hard trek forward. But it felt so good just to lie still...

"Why do you think they ambushed us?" she softly queried, trying to come to grips with their predicament.

"There's probably a bounty that's been put on us," he quietly replied. "There are only so many spots where secret tunnels out of the Cheyenne complex could exit successfully. Whoever it is that wants to put a stop to our program in the complex would have them staked out, waiting for us to emerge. Unfortunately for us, they must have heard us through the brick wall when we got that blast-door opened. The few 'watchers' then had time to call in reinforcements as we worked on the final barrier."

Suddenly everything outside their hiding space got quiet. There were no more "thudding" boots or barked orders.

Ivanna felt a chill go down her spine. She was afraid that something terrible was about to happen...

"WE KNOW YOU'RE IN THERE!" a loud, amplified female voice echoed in the cleared areas of the basement. "COME ON OUT AND

YOU WON'T BE HURT. I CAN FLOOD THIS SECTION WITH ELECTRICITY. IT WILL KNOCK YOU OUT. I DON'T WANT TO DO THAT BECAUSE IT MIGHT ALSO TRIGGER ANY EXPLOSIVES YOU MAY BE CARRYING AND KILL YOU. I WANT TO TALK TO YOU. THESE OVER-EAGER BOUNTY HUNTERS WEREN'T SUPPOSED TO ATTACK YOU, JUST CAPTURE YOU. SURRENDER NOW OR I'LL RELEASE THE ELECTRICITY. I'M GIVING YOU FIVE MINUTES, NO MORE. MAKE THE RIGHT DECISION. WE'VE GOT YOU COMPLETELY SURROUNDED ON THIS LEVEL. EVEN IF YOU MADE IT OUT OF THE STADIUM, THE STREETS ARE SWARMING WITH REAPER ROBOTS. IN EXCHANGE FOR INFORMATION I WILL GIVE YOU SACTUARY. THE BOUNTY HUNTERS WORK FOR ME. SURRENDER AND YOU'LL NOT BE HURT!"

In the dim light, Major Cotrell and Sergeant Grant looked at each other knowingly.

"Do we have a chance to escape?" Ivanna whispered.

Both of them shook their heads in the negative.

"Then we must surrender," she said. "Perhaps they'll have the information that *we* are seeking. That voice certainly isn't an alien. It is the voice of a fellow human. We don't have to give them any classified information. They already know a military presence still exists in Cheyenne Mountain. But, then again, that doesn't sound like someone from a local resistance," she frowned.

"I'm certain it's not," the Major whispered back to her. "It's an independent group. We can still try to make a break for it—attempt to shoot our way out—but after all the noise we've already made down here they've got dozens of their people out there."

He shrugged in resignation.

"And that woman, whoever she is, is probably telling us the truth," the young Sergeant reluctantly concluded the thought. "From what I saw of the Reapers before the base was sealed, we've got no chance against the robots. They can't get down here into the basement areas because there's just not enough room for their huge bodies—they're like self-directed, walking tanks—but up on the ground level...?"

"—they're probably all over the place," the Major grimly nodded.

"So we're in agreement?" Ivanna asked them both.

Both soldiers nodded in the affirmative.

"Don't shoot!" Ivanna yelled at the top of her lungs. "We're coming out!"

Wearily, she followed the Major and Sergeant as they wormed their way out of the maze of overlain, fallen concrete beams. They emerged with their hands held above their heads.

In front of Ivanna she saw more of the dirty, rag-tag scavengers—who were pointing an assortment of deadly weapons at her!

One of them even held a heavy grenade-launcher.

But behind those stood a small group of neatly-dressed, white-hooded females. Each of the hooded females was armed with just a single black pistol. And around their necks, each of them wore a *gold medallion* sporting *outward-poking spikes* like little golden suns.

And behind them was a small woman also with a hood and a spiked gold medallion—but of obvious great authority. She carried no weapons, fixing the emerging trio with an unblinking, fierce STARE...

—who suddenly came dashing forward, grabbed Ivanna up in a strong bear hug, and *swung* her around in a circle!

"Professor Petrovich, it's so *good* to see you again!" the woman exclaimed, a big smile on her face.

"Do...do I know you?" Ivanna gulped, nonplussed by this unexpected, friendly greeting.

The middle-aged woman held Ivanna off at arm's length, still grinning widely.

"In a prior life, Ivanna, you were nice to me," she replied. "You baked me some *mean* brownies."

Ivanna frowned, trying to remember having seen this middle-aged woman before, but failing.

"I'm sorry—I don't recognize you. Should I?"

The woman pushed back the white hood.

Beneath the concealing hood she had long, fluffed-out bright red hair. Her eyes were deep green. Her face was rounded, showing that she was a bit overweight. She had prominent age-wrinkles at the corners of her mouth and eyes.

"I'm a...relative of Sally Smith. My name is, oh, *Linda Powers*. You probably know me as the *High Priestess* of the *Church of Perpet-*

ual Health. A long time ago I was accused in the news as a so-called 'terrorist' who..."

"—and you say that you are related to that sweet young girl Sally...how?"

"I'll explain later," she grinned, supporting an arm of the now-staggering Ivanna. "You gentlemen, please come with us," she gallantly said to the two commandos. "You can put your guns down," she spoke to the rag-tag female marauders.

Reluctantly, the crowd of searchers lowered their various weapons.

"And what about *their* guns?" one of the other, gun-toting white-hooded women grimly asked, pointing to the three assault rifles held by the two Rangers.

"I'm sure they will be much more comfortable keeping them, won't you gentlemen?" Linda sweetly said to them.

The two soldiers hesitantly nodded, suspiciously lowering their hands. Then each cradled one of their assault rifles that'd been slung over their shoulders.

"And what about *us?*" a raggedly clad, heavy-set woman standing off to the side amongst a larger group yelled loudly. "We found them. So where's our promised bounty?"

"Oh, yes—you 'found' them," the High Priestess nodded, pausing. "And in 'finding' them you *killed* most of them, despite my strict orders to the contrary. And *then* you allowed them destroy the access tunnel, which was my primary objective, didn't you? *Not* such good work, I'd say."

"They resisted us. You promised us a reward!"

"No matter!" she said, holding up a hand to silence them. "You are, indeed, due your 'reward.' Priestesses, please give them all they deserve."

The white-hooded women surrounding Sally jerked up their pistols and *fired* on the gathered vigilantes...

—who crumpled, covered and permeated by a *cloud of crackling electricity!*

Fortunately, no explosions of ammo resulted from the knockout jolts. Apparently the "dosage" was less then would have been required to saturate the entire basement levels.

"Jesus!" Sergeant Grant grunted admiringly.

"Your reward," the High Priestess solemnly intoned, gesturing grandly at the fallen, unconscious bandits, "is to wake up in an hour or so, still alive."

The spastically quivering vigilantes did not reply.

"Shall we leave, gentlemen and lady?" she grinned at them, indicating a cleared path up to the surface.

"Affirmative!" the Major barked, striding over to join the Priestesses, with Sergeant Grant right behind him.

"It is such a pleasure to find you with the expeditionary party," the High Priestess said, patting Ivanna's arm affectionately as she helped the elderly woman along. "I'd hoped to march into the base and terminate its evil directly. Unfortunately your soldier friends cut off that direct approach. But with you here, Professor Petrovich, there's still hope. I just have to be more articulate than forceful. I assume you are able to get a message into the sealed base?"

"Uhm...I think so, Linda," Ivanna cautiously replied.

"Good," Linda said as they reached the surface where they could hear loud "CLOMPS" of a large group of passing Reaper robots. "As soon as we evade these idiot machines, we'll have a long conversation. I'm sure you will come to agree with me that your DE-bomb missiles should never be launched. In fact, I hope to convince you that our Salvation is not in offensive measures, nor active defense, but in passive *surrender*."

"That's...I'm sure—a theological, not a practical argument?" Ivanna tentatively disagreed.

"Oh, no," the High Priestess laughed in a shrill, faintly maniacal manner that made Ivanna cringe. "It is *not* 'theological' and it *is* imminently practical. Oh, we're going to have a *great* time discussing this and many other critical ideas."

Ivanna saw that this "Linda" person was not to be trifled with.

"And in we go," Linda said, helping Ivanna climb a few steps into an ancient, battered school bus. "Welcome, Professor, to our local academy's glorious transportation."

The sliding door closed on the five hooded women, the two soldiers, the High Priestess, and Ivanna.

Linda motioned to a driver up front.

Thrusters fired along the bottom of the bus as it jerkily rose up into the air.

"We won't be shot at," Linda curtly explained to the occupants. "I've a simple cloaking device in place around the bus. Other than visual detection, we're too small and slow for the Harvesters or their Laser Weapons to take note of us."

In a few moments they'd zoomed up a thousand feet into the air and were cruising above what remained of Colorado Springs. Looking through her side window, Ivanna expected to see moderately tall skyscrapers at the heart of a bustling city nestled in a fertile valley, beside low mountains. Instead, there were only the blackened remains of a shattered civilization.

Ivanna continued looking down in horror, only now realizing the vast desolation that the orbiting Alien Armada had caused.

Even the mountains were scarred.

Ivanna could see Cheyenne Mountain coming up below them—a melted-down slag-heap! It looked like a volcano had erupted there, leaving behind a lifeless caldera crater.

"We can't defeat the aliens by just surrendering to them," Ivanna stated to the High Priestess. The woman was calmly sitting next to Ivanna and happily humming.

"I *thought* you were an *expert* sociologist?" Linda suddenly snapped at Ivanna, making the Professor jerk back in fear.

Ivanna saw her two soldiers eye each other worriedly, fingering their rifles. They were keeping a cautious eye on the surrounding, armed, white-hooded Priestesses.

"Well...I like to think so," Ivanna gasped back. She was still horrified by everything she'd just viewed on the ground far beneath their flying yellow bus.

"And yet you have no concept of underlying, fundamental *causes* to historical, 'unprecedented' upheavals?"

"Well, of course I do, but..."

"—but when faced with your own personal Armageddon, you fall back automatically to the stupid response of 'kill the enemy'?"

Ivanna was confused by the woman's intimidating and disrespectful language. Who was she, anyway? Ivanna had certainly heard of this new religion with its reclusive woman leader, a 'Linda Powers'.

But nothing much was known about her except that she'd supposedly *resurrected* Sally's mother, Samantha Smith—then offered two fantastic new inventions to anyone that agreed to her strict terms. Was that the connection this woman claimed to Sally? Or was she indeed a relative of Sally's? She certainly looked like Sally, but much older. Was she perhaps an aunt?

Well, regardless of the truth to her relationship to Sally, Ivanna felt that this woman might indeed have Answers—exactly what the President had sent Ivanna out to discover!

"I am...eager...to learn better," Ivanna firmly stated, staring unblinkingly into the wide green eyes of the obvious zealot sitting next to her.

"Ah...that's good then," the High Priestess smiled, settling back in her seat, abruptly relaxed and peaceful-appearing. "We'll be landing shortly. But if you'd like, I have in-flight refreshments. My sweet ladies baked you cookies. Plus there's milk—as much as you want. Don't be hesitant to ask for more. Now isn't that a wonderful treat?"

One of the hooded ladies reached into a compartment and pulled out a tray. It held delicious-looking, steaming-fresh chocolate-chip cookies—plus bottles of thin-looking milk, probably reconstituted from powder.

How amazingly hospitable—Ivanna thought, deeply impressed with the gesture.

"See?" the High Priestess said, leaning over to whisper in Ivanna's ear, "I learned this from *you*."

"From me?" Ivanna repeated, confused. She was now even *more* puzzled by the High Priestess' odd words.

Ivanna saw that the Major and Sergeant gratefully accepted the treats.

Ivanna politely took one of the big cookies and started nibbling on it. She greedily guzzled a bottle of the thin milk. Then she turned back to the cookies and happily scarfed down two of them.

But she wasn't so much hungry for *food* as she was *starved* for Answers.

"Where are we going?" she quietly asked the High Priestess, setting her half-eaten cookie to the side. She saw the two commandos settle back into their seats, happily munching and slurping their goodies.

"*Pike's Peak*, of course," Linda laughed, "where else?"

Where else, indeed?

Ivanna had been there years before with Victor. It offered an amazing vista. It was a major tourist site for the state of Colorado, located close to Colorado Springs.

They were going from the depths of utter despair buried beneath a mountain to the heights of exhilaration on one of the mountain range's highest peaks.

For the first time in a long while, Ivanna felt a hint of possible hope.

She was reasonably sure it wasn't just a sugar high from the cookies she'd just gobbled down. She was also sure it wasn't a brief elation of escaping the "frying pan" before falling into the surrounding fire. No, it was contacting a highly organized, still-existing surface group of humans who had some sort of a "plan."

Ivanna was certain this was just what the President had in mind when she'd commissioned the expedition.

Regardless, Ivanna knew she had to remain on her guard. This "Linda Powers" was obviously highly intelligent, though clearly insane. Getting the information Ivanna needed from her was likely going to require delicate negotiation.

Chapter 7

INTRANSIGENCE

How rude to insist
It must be my way or nothing
Not even minor concessions
Given to assuage the loser's pride
"I win and you lose"
It's so simple and direct
"Get out of my face, you 'reject'
While I scamper ahead in victory
You vile people left behind
Eating my delightful dust"
What a wonderful way to live
Alone in my intolerance
Salvation at the point of a sword
I find, instead, a slice of regret
Thinking we both played soldiers
At least up to our sudden deaths...

The Luminary Chronicles, 7:78-85

Dave and Arthur crept cautiously through the rubble of Pennsylvania Avenue.

The sun was low on the horizon, casting everything into stark relief. The tops of the few remaining upright structures were still brightly illuminated, but everything lower was cast into dark shadow.

Approaching Reapers would stand out like sore thumbs above the rubble.

Normally, humans would be trying to get away from any prowling Reapers.

Now, they were *hunting* one.

101

It was insane, but necessary. Dave was convinced that the key to shielding their DE-generators was right there in front of them, contained within their most vicious and implacable enemy.

And I'm going to get it!—he snarled to himself.

"Are we set at the Art Museum?" Dave asked Arthur for the umpteenth time.

Arthur nodded with a sly grin of satisfaction.

"Yep, we are indeed, my dear Dr. King," he replied yet again. "It's all arranged. I saw to the details myself. It was a clever idea of yours on how to isolate and trap one of those monsters."

"If it works..."

Dave was getting more and more nervous about his plan. If it didn't work, the heart of the Resistance would be crushed.

"Out here in the open we'd just attract a herd of those killer robots," Arthur happily stated, reaching up to adjust his black eyeglasses. "We have to trap it out of sight in order to operate on its ugly guts."

"Yes, we've got to wound it, not kill it," Dave cautioned Anderson, looking pointedly at the black gun held in the FBI agent's hand.

"Oh, I'll be delicate," Arthur reassured him.

Then the Agent held a finger to his lips.

The two of them were crouched behind a burnt mound of timber, peeking out at the somewhat-cleared area in the middle of the wide street.

In the distance the both of them could hear the faint "clomp, clomp, clomp" of an approaching patrol-bot.

"So who did you get to volunteer to be the bait?" Dave whispered to Arthur.

"Someone small, fast, and highly motivated," Arthur quietly replied.

The "clomping" was getting louder.

The "head" of the twenty foot-high robot appeared above fallen columns of the crushed buildings, swiveling rapidly to scan the area around it. It was lit by the setting sun like a Greek statue, a modern-day metallic Colossus. In a perverted sort of way, Dave found it beautiful.

"There she goes," Arthur said.

"But, that's...!" Dave gasped, gripping his assault rifle tighter as he surged up to his feet.

"She's got its attention," Arthur said as he rose up beside Dave. "Quick, we've got to keep up!"

Dave was aghast. He couldn't believe his eyes.

Yes, it was *Sally*. She didn't even have a helmet on. Her long fluffy red-brown hair was bouncing around as a seductive lure, a tempting target for the five guns of the Reaper!

She was darting from spot to spot not even trying to hide.

In fact, she was yelling back at the Robot, taunting it!

"Come *get* me! Come *get* me! You stupid big tin can, you can't catch me! Hah! I'm too *fast* for you!"

She waved her gun-free hands up in the air, apparently defenseless.

As if intrigued, the twenty foot-high robot strode after her, using both its thudding legs and three writhing tentacles to scamper and leap over the ruins of the city. It was a giant-squid mechanical monster!

Dave could see Sally's head of flopping red hair appearing above the rubble here and there as she darted along, running full-out.

Rapidly closing in behind her was the flailing monster. But it wasn't firing its guns. Seeing that its prey had no weapons, it apparently wanted to catch her alive. Then it would stuff her into its belly to deliver to an orbiting Harvester.

Behind the robot, Dave and Arthur were fast on its tail, not caring if they were exposed.

Almost out of breath, his chest heaving, Dave felt Arthur's arm pull him up short.

"She's almost got it," he whispered, making sure that he and Arthur were concealed as they crept closer. "Let's not draw its attention away."

Sally was now on the top of a high pile of a wrecked building, standing stock still, her hands firmly on her hips, defiantly staring back at the fast-approaching giant robot, her green eyes glaring at it!

"You *want* me?" she defiantly yelled at it. "Then *grab* me, if you can!"

As if angry at the prancing little human, the tentacles "whizzed" through the air right at her as the Reaper hurtled on forward...

—and she *dropped downward* out of sight!

—as the robot, propelled forward by its momentum, continued forward to CRASH through an overlying grillwork into a *dark cavern* hidden beneath...

Dave skidded to a stop at the edge of the hidden pit, looking frantically around for Sally.

"Give me a hand!" Dave heard a voice calling up from below. He looked down through wide, interwoven beams to see Sally dangling, holding on with both arms...

Dave grabbed one of her arms tightly as Arthur surged past, falling flat upon a beam, and aimed his gun into the depths below.

WHUMP!—the gun barked as it discharged.

The cavern below the dangling Sally lit up as if a *giant light bulb* had exploded within it!

Dave saw the banged-up but still-moving colossal robot struggling to get up from where it had fallen several stories down, illuminated by an *enveloping cocoon* of crackling, yellow electricity!

Dave dragged Sally back up safely to the top of the beam.

"Are you *trying* to get yourself killed?" Dave angrily barked at her, shaking her hard. "Any of the others could have led the Reaper into the trap. What the hell were you thinking, Sally? You can't be replaced! No one else has your mathematical genius."

She jerked free of his grasp, glaring at him while still gasping for breath from her hard run.

"You don't tell me what to do!" she spat back at him. "Those things took my Mother—and if there's a chance to hurt them back then I'm just the girl to do it!"

A large "thud" sounded from below as in the flickering, fading electrical glow Dave saw the robot struggling to stand up before falling flat upon the hard concrete floor.

"Children, children," Arthur admonished Dave and Sally. "Play nice! We've only a few minutes until the other Reapers miss our friend and come searching for him. Come on, the ladder's over here."

Sally angrily turned away from Dave to hop nimbly over beside Arthur as he started climbing down a dangling rope-ladder. As soon as he was out of the way she quickly followed him.

"But I just saved your life," Dave peevishly whispered to himself before following Sally down the precarious ropes.

They descended into the crushed but still intact *Kogod Courtyard* of the *Smithsonian American Art Museum*.

Dave knew that long before the Alien Invasion occurred, the now-crushed structure was praised by Walt Whitman as the "noblest of Washington Buildings." It was built in a Greek Revival style. Abraham Lincoln's inaugural ball was held there in 1865. The Robert and Arlene Kogod Courtyard, illuminated by a giant glass canopy, gave the Art Museum a contemporary flare. Many great performances and special events were held in the large courtyard. Now, though, it was just a big deep hole beneath a barely-intact giant grillwork whose glass had long-since shattered or been melted-away.

Arthur landed first, running over to the still-twitching robot which was now recovering, jerkily trying to sit upright...

—surrounded by a dozen of Arthur's fellow Resistance fighters, their conventional guns pointed at its head.

Arthur waved them back while pointing his energy-gun pointblank at the Reaper's head and BLASTED it with another burst of crackling electricity!

It fell backward with a "CLANK" and lay entirely motionless.

Sally raced up to it and began kicking its inert, badly-dented body.

"Take *that*, you stupid robot! Take *that!*" she screamed at it, tears running down her face as she kept kicking its metallic side.

One of the surrounding fighters gently took hold of her arms and moved her backward, away from the inert beast.

"Oh, no," Dave gasped, running up to stand beside Arthur and Sally. "You weren't supposed to *kill* it. A bunch of fried components is *worthless* to us!"

"Who says it's dead?" Arthur mildly retorted.

He readjusted the nozzle of his handgun and aimed from a few inches away an *intense red laser beam* directly into the circular upper region of the robot.

Sputtering metal droplets flew around as the intense beam neatly severed the head of the robot.

"*Now* it's dead," Arthur laughed.

"You mean that just the robot is dead, right—*not* the components?" Dave hopefully observed.

"Well, dead or alive, there's your intact 'components'," Arthur gestured at the severed head-region of the giant robot. "It was impossible to do that from a distance. But up close with my gun, it's a piece of cake. You happy, Dr. King?"

Dave ran forward and scooped up the large, still-glowing, severed head.

"It's great—just what I wanted," Dave grinned widely as he staggered under the heavy load. It easily weighed in at over one hundred pounds.

Sally just glared at him, crossing her arms and refusing to help.

A couple other fighters ran up with a net for Dave to drop the severed head into. Several more fighters grabbed the edges so they could easily run with it dangling between them.

"There's a bunch more of the Reapers coming," another fighter called down from the grillwork high above. "They know something's up. They're massing against us. You've got to *move!*"

"Then let's get out of here via the tunnel," Arthur said to the others around him down in the pit, looking up furtively at the still-sunlit grillwork high above. "It'll take too long to climb back out. Plant the charges and let's run. We'll give those damn robots something other than just the corpse of their friend."

"Two birds with one stone," Dave nodded in satisfaction.

"Yep," Arthur grunted. "Instead of just one sliced-off head, I want a heap of them. Let's see if they're dumb enough to come climbing down into a 'booby-trap'!"

The others quickly took from their knapsacks packages of plastic explosives. They ripped out cables and gears from the open neck region of the felled robot. Then they jammed the explosives deep into the still-smoking neck of the monster.

Dave saw that the resistance fighters had brought a *lot* of explosives. It was going to be a big surprise for whatever 'bots came searching for their comrade—plus, regrettably, to whatever remained of the already-destroyed museum complex.

"Five minutes," one of them said, giving the "thumbs-up" sign. "Then it explodes."

The resistance fighters hastily grabbed up surrounding debris and covered the top half of the mutilated robot, hiding the ticking bomb.

"Good," Arthur said as they hastily exited through a still-standing, intact doorway into the remains of the Art Museum. "Hopefully its friends won't notice that we took the head until they get close—and they're all *blown to robot hell!* Hah!"

Arthur switched on the penlight set beneath the barrel of his handgun. In the dark interior of the smashed museum, it gave an eerie yellow glow.

This was once the heart and soul of our human civilization— Dave sadly observed to himself. *Now it's just leftover trash.*

It seemed to Dave as he ran along through the escape tunnel that'd been hewn through the guts of the collapsed museum that they were saying goodbye to a fallen civilization.

In the jumbled debris of the walls of the tunnel he caught glimpses of proud-looking Presidents of the United States, headdress-sporting noble Indians, abstract art, and forever-frozen dainty ladies.

The torn and dangling paintings were glimpses of a lost past. So many talented artists had tried to conjure upon themselves a type of immortality. Now, that lie was revealed as sad delusion. Nothing lasts forever. Everything comes to an end...

"Stop!" Sally suddenly yelled, startling everyone.

They all skidded to a stop, looking about warily for whatever threat she'd seen!

—as Sally yanked a knife out of her waistband, approached a cracked picture frame hanging lopsided off to the side of the crude tunnel, and sliced out its canvas. She rolled it up, stuffing it under her arm.

"Ok, we can go," she said as she dashed off.

Dave was at her elbow as they continued ducking and dodging their way through the rough tunnel.

"What was that?" he said to her. "Why'd you stop us?"

"I couldn't let all of this be destroyed. I had to save something."

He grabbed the canvas from her and unfurled it as they kept jogging through the tunnel.

By the dancing light from Arthur's penlight Dave saw that the picture was a painting of a rocky seashore set beside a blue, rippling ocean. A lady in a white dress sat primly on a boulder. She wore a big straw hat. She was looking out over a peaceful sea. The lady was elegant, even regal. An attached label said: "Childe Hassam, *The South Ledges, Appledore*, 1913."

Sally angrily grabbed the canvas back from him, curling it up back under her armpit as they lurched along.

"You risked our lives for some stupid seascape?" he huffed at her unbelievingly.

She glared at him.

Then he realized how unfeeling that sounded and tried to correct his mistake.

"So what's it about?" he gasped at her, breathing heavily.

She glared at him again. Then she seemed to relent.

"It's of a civilized, privileged woman right before World War I broke out," she explained as they hurried along behind Arthur and the others who were lugging the heavy, netted robot head. "It's what life used to be—and what we want it to be again. It's sitting and sipping iced tea as long as you want out in the open. I never saw the painting in real life, only on the web. But I always liked it. So when I glimpsed it in the wreckage I..."

Dave's fragile patience dissolved.

"It's dumb," Dave dismissed it, interrupting her. "We can't live in the past! We have to..."

"I said I *liked* it!" she snarled back at him, deliberately poking him sharply in his side with an elbow while surging on ahead and past him...

Dave grunted, falling back...

—as behind them a huge EXPLOSION deafened Dave...and an *earthquake* swept through the tunnel, threatening to bring the entire, unstable mass down around their heads!

Dave staggered, holding his rifle up over his head to block raining-down debris...

—as an overhanging *concrete block* broke free and SMASHED down into the tunnel, right in front of Dave!

He jerked to a wavering stop, surrounded by suffocating dust and smoke.

Another BLAST from behind knocked him to his knees.

Crawling, he pawed forward, encountering the big block of cement, trying to find a way around it...

—and his hands touched the *legs* of a body *crushed* beneath the big, fallen block.

"Sally?" he whispered, frozen in place.

Big hands grabbed him and dragged him forward, squeezing him around and past the obstruction.

"She's gone...she's gone," Arthur coughed in the acrid smoke. "We've got to escape—we've still got the robot's head for you to work on, and we..."

"No!" Dave shouted, jerking free and stumbling back.

One of her arms jutted forward from beneath the concrete block. Its limp hand still held the curled-up canvas.

Dave gently freed it from her slack grasp.

"We've got to *go*, David," Arthur coughed at him through the smoke, roughly grabbing him again and pulling him away.

Behind them, Dave could hear the *crackling roar* of a fast-approaching raging fire.

Thick black smoke roiled around them.

"Goodbye, Sally," Dave whispered, peering back into the expanding inferno behind him. "It was actually a nice painting—I was just messing with you."

He knew what he had to do.

He must inherit her *hatred!*

Jesus grew in wisdom, strength, and influence.

Where he might have become bitter and withdrawn following the death of his father Joseph, he instead chose to simultaneously focus and widen his efforts. Although his contemporary youngsters and town folks still regarded him with suspicion, he used the connections he'd made with the intellectual religious elite in Sepphoris to expand his growing fame and influence. Since the time he'd been taken by his family to Jerusalem when he was twelve years old—when he'd stayed behind after the Feast of the Passover to discuss sophisticated questions with the Priests in the Temple—he'd been regarded amongst the religious elite as a child prodigy.

So he continued to study the books of the Essene, plus any other Holy Texts he could get his hands on, devouring religious precepts: analyzing, deconstructing, and recombining them in new ways that were both insightful and inspirational. Since he was always careful to be polite and respectful to all his Teachers, they loved him! Sally knew that this mutual admiration would soon change, however— when the smart young man sitting at their "exalted" feet would instead be labelled as a dangerous heretic.

But for now he still received their admiration and support. And as long as he kept to the accepted Teachings, the proper Rituals, and the time-honored Traditions he was their darling prodigy. They even let the young man stand up in the gatherings and give short lectures— which amazed and invigorated his audiences.

Accustomed to sitting through long boring sermons on well-worn subjects, Jesus' fresh approach brought in many visitors, plus greater revenues. Where the solemn Priests were content spouting accepted doctrine, Jesus enlivened the crowds with clever stories and interesting thought-questions. He even invited questions from his audience, whether publically or in private small groups. Plus he took the ancient teachings and made them relevant to the individuals he was teaching.

So Jesus was both entertaining and helpful.

Sally noted these things, comparing his methods favorably to Mother Hildegard from more than a thousand years in the future. She longed to share these observations with the young Jesus. She knew he'd be intrigued and amazed about what happened in her past timeline in regards to his innovative teachings. But she knew to keep quiet, sticking to her "origin" story. The last things she needed now was to get herself be kicked out of Jesus' family as an insane heretic.

But Jesus went beyond Hildegard von Bingen's tactics. She sought to mold the existing religious hierarchy around higher Ideals. He sought to use people's cherished hatreds to drive them closer to God...

Yes, Jesus found subtle ways to voice the people's great societal, cultural, and religious hatreds.   More and more he held "tent-meetings" sponsored by wealthy Jewish business people—often his admiring older women—in which his theme was the "Kingdom of God."   Everything he taught was couched in religious terms—particularly in regards to personal transformation of one's heart into a true Temple for God—but the people welcomed the veiled validation of their deepest desires: to *cast off* the brutal hand of the Romans and forge their own Jewish Kingdom!

It was a rage-infused, justified hatred wanting nothing more than revenge, war, and reversal of fortunes: to lift the boot off their own necks and SLAM it down upon the Occupiers and their lackeys.

So Jesus learned how to mobilize people, inspire them, and give them a sense of hope—all built upon their own worst instincts.

Sally saw him rapidly growing into Jesus the Messiah.

All the stars were aligning behind Jesus, making Sally's mission more and more unlikely to succeed...

Once he matured into his twenties, Jesus no longer needed to toil at a daily, common job. His financial backers in Sepphoris saw that he had sufficient money to devote himself fully to his charismatic teachings. In fact, they were talking of sending him on missionary journeys far beyond the local region. His family benefited as well. His mother and younger siblings were well cared for, indeed increasingly serving vital roles in Jesus' growing political-religious machine.

The Romans to this point had taken little note of him. To them he was just another moderately successful Jewish lay-preacher. As long as he didn't advocate revolt against the King or the Emperor, he was on safe religious ground. However, he was attracting increasingly larger crowds to his local events. Though spies reported back to the authorities that Jesus was only a particularly interesting and dynamic religious teacher, the government was now keeping a close eye on him.

Just as ominously, Jesus was falling out of favor with the local and extended Jewish Hierarchy. Where they had seen value in draw-ing more people to the local synagogue, they now suspected he was drawing people not to the establishment but to himself. Even more unsettling to the established leadership, wealthy secular-minded Jews were supporting him over the politically correct power-brokers at the Temple in Jerusalem.

Jesus was preaching passionately of a new spiritual Kingdom—while the anointed religious hierarchy studiously and boringly insisted on maintaining the painful but stable *status quo*. The Pharisees and Sadducees in particular—the other two major sects of the Jews in addition to the Essenes—were growing increasingly unhappy with this upstart lay preacher. Whereas the Pharisees derived great personal prestige and power by legislating the supposed details of "God's Will", Jesus proclaimed a disconcerting *freedom of the Spirit!* The rapidly-maturing Jesus never quite "walked over the line" of Jewish rules and regulations, but often tip-toed right up to their edge...

The Sadducees, on the other hand, had a strong doctrine of there being no life after death, which Jesus directly affirmed. Also, the Sadducees controlled the office of the High Priest in Jerusalem. They were the privileged elite of the Jewish religion, few in numbers but great in power. To them Jesus was a common man of the people, claiming no power via inherited lineage. So he resonated with the common man, not the pandered elite.

However, many of Jesus backers still came from the Jewish elite of the business community. As such, they particularly chaffed at being crushed under the greedy hands of the Romans. Although a few truly admired and supported Jesus for his amazing religious insights, most considered Jesus to be their convenient pawn. In clever and non-confrontational ways—or so they thought—he "kept up the pressure" on the local rulers: to be as lenient as possible to the commercial barons while they paid due homage to the Emperor.

But they knew that their pawn could not be allowed to stir the people up to actual revolt. They wanted to keep him on a tight leash.

Sally—content to stay in the background as a mere servant girl in Jesus' extended family—watched everything evolving around the young Jesus with increasing fascination and dread.

She, of course, well-knew the possible future for this young man whose local fame was growing by leaps and bounds. She knew that in her own Dimension this Jesus-movement never became Christianity. For whatever reason, her Jesus failed to make an impact upon the history of her Earth. Consequently, she believed, authoritative regimes from the 1st Century onward lacked the "brakes" of Christian love, tolerance, and deep outrage against naked injustice.

So when scientists in her Dimension discovered how to crack open subspace and release Dark Energy, it was done cautiously at only a few highly controlled governmental centers. However, in the parallel Dimension from which Dave and this boy-Jesus came, DE-generation was *not* a carefully-protected State Secret—but eventually produced even routine household devices! This massive overuse of Dark Energy caught the full attention of the Intelligent Creator of the Universe, labelled by many as "God".

Sitting in judgement on the technologically-advanced race of *Homo sapiens* upon Dave's planet Earth, God found them falling far short of species maturity. Consequently, they were scheduled to be erased! Sally knew that a massive solar super-storm would sterilize the surface of Earth. Yet not only Dave's world would be destroyed, but also the linked parallel Dimensions—including Sally's world and even the Dinosapien Earths!

To save the dimensionally linked Earths from God's Wrath, Sally was determined that Dave's Jesus should join the Jesus on her Earth in being *lost* to history! If Christianity on Dave's Earth could be stopped—despite its many positive features—then perhaps all the Earths could avoid God's full attention long enough to—in some future millennium—reach an acceptable level of intelligent-species maturity.

Sally knew this was an "unholy" mission to stop Jesus, to save mankind from God's Wrath—delaying the Day of Judgment long enough for *Homo sapiens* to rise above being just another smart animal.

She didn't relish her task, but knew it was possible to achieve because of the example of her own "Jesus-less" Earth. And she knew without any doubt it was necessary, since she'd been to the far future several times to view with her own eyes the awful result.

This wonderful, powerful, and magnificent person called "Jesus" had to be *stopped!* But it was a terrible and lonely assignment. Sally, from the future, was the only one who knew why it must be so...

—except, of course, for Jesus himself.

She increasingly loved and feared him at the same time. Every day she saw him grow more powerful: extending further and further beyond the norms of his time.

Clearly, he was more than just a mere human.

"What are you thinking, Sahlee?" he asked her one day as she sat by a well, resting after she'd pulled up a heavy bucket of water.

It was one of the rare occasions he happened to be home and not tied up with business meetings and rallies. He was taking a much-deserved short break from his many duties and responsibilities.

She wanted to tell him that he and the other strong males should *help her* pull up heavy water up out of the well! She had fond memories of turning on spigots in the distant future where water just flowed out at one's command. But to get a drink of water now was a chore, often left to the women.

But she couldn't be cross with Jesus.

He was now twenty-nine years old. He was just one year away from beginning his massive three-year crusade for religious transformation, culminating with his death upon the cross. He was a handsome, youthful, and powerful-looking man. From his years laboring in the fields plus heavy construction work he was an imposing figure—with wide shoulders, a slim waist, and large biceps. He now sported a full beard plus carefully manicured flowing long hair dropping to his shoulders. His large brown eyes perpetually glowed with intensity, revealing both a tender love and a compelling confidence.

If he'd had the proper familial connections, he could have easily been a wildly popular politician. But instead of elegant finery, he was clad in a "uniform" of plain brown sandals, long white robe, extendable scarf he could flip up over his head to block the sun, and plain rope-belt at his waist.

In the warm morning sun he looked exactly like the pictures Sally had seen in the future that depicted "Jesus the Messiah." Clearly he was now on the brink of occupying the role that both his passions and the Jewish business community were pushing him toward: a *sacrificial lamb* whose execution would change the entire world.

"Oh, Jesus," she said, smiling warmly at him. "I didn't know you were back from your meeting in Sepphoris. I was just thinking what a nice day it is today."

"You are a poor liar, Sahlee," he grinned at her, sitting on a boulder next to both her and the well.

He wiped sweat from his brow and politely asked her: "May I have some water, please?"

Nearby, a flock of sheep was grazing in a wide green meadow. A young boy and girl ran past the well, chasing a prancing kid goat.

Other than that, Sally and Jesus were by themselves—beyond earshout of any passersby out on the main road.

She immediately stood up, dipped water out of the bucket and handed the ladle to Jesus.

He gratefully accepted it, first bowing his head in silent prayer, and then lustily guzzling the cool contents.

"All, that was *most* delicious—the *water of life*," he smiled in satisfaction, wiping glistening moisture from his full lips and upper beard.

"You are welcome," Sally answered, taking back the ladle and sitting back down beside Jesus. "Oh, by the way, that's a wonderful allegory you just made—perhaps you might use that in one of your sermons? Precious water soothes the thirst not only of the flesh but also the spirit?"

After her near-death in the desert and immersion in the foul waters of the Dead Sea PURE, CLEAR WATER was still an obsession for Sally.

"Hmmm...good idea, Sahlee," he sincerely congratulated her. "I note your enthusiasm and appreciate your insight."

Overhead, the sun was pleasantly warm, the air fresh. It was a great day to be alive. And it was a great day to make yet another attempt to sway Jesus from his life-path...

"And you are *also* right," she smiled back, fixing him with her intense green-eyed gaze, "that I wasn't thinking of the weather. I was actually thinking of you and me."

"Oh?"

"We haven't talked of personal matters since that day fifteen years ago in this very same meadow. You have esteemed religious scholars with whom to debate every detail of the Law. And I'm no longer a little girl. And you, my dear Jesus, are now *long* past the required age that males should marry."

He laughed good-naturedly.

"I have not ignored you, little Sahlee," he factually stated. "We still talk and joke from time to time. And I have well-compensated you for the work you do helping my mother and our family. Since you spend little, you must be quite wealthy by now. Plus you occupy a place of prestige in this community. No one thinks ill of you anymore. You are one of us, no longer a strange escaped slave from a far land. You could have your pick of any of the wealthy men or young heirs around us. Any of them would make you a much more stable and devoted husband than me."

She was excited. He was actually speaking of marriage. She had a chance to engage his attention, draw his Ideals away from his terrible Quest.

She seemingly shyly twirled the ends of her long brown hair with a stray finger. Her scarf, however, remained firmly over her head, the picture of a proper woman of the time.

"I've always wished only the best for you, Jesus. You know that," she stated truthfully. "And *you* must know that *I'm* the absolute best for *you*. There is no one else in this entire world that would be a more faithful, more supportive, more enjoyable, and more engaging wife for you than me."

He nodded agreeably.

"That is true, Sahlee—but *you* know I must remain celibate."

"Even though the Holy Scriptures teach differently?" she shot back at him.

"Oh, I am sure you can quote to me the relevant passages—you who my Mother has so pampered through the years to allow access to all the Holy Writings that I brought home for study," he mildly replied, leaning back on his hands to let the morning sun warm his deeply tanned face.

She saw that as an invitation to do just that...

"Genesis 1:28—*be fruitful and multiply!* Genesis 2:18—*it is not good for man to be alone!* And..."

"Yes, yes," he dismissed her speech by holding up one of his well-calloused, large hands to silence her. "Those and many more from our Holy Scriptures and texts—I know them well. The old women of the village have chided me for years for not marrying their daughters or other female kinfolk. And *you* also know, Sahlee, that it is accepted practice for a male to postpone marriage to study the Law and..."

"—which you've done to the point of becoming a Master Teacher," she eagerly interrupted him. "The main word that you just used was 'postpone', *not* to 'give up'. You've clearly fulfilled the 'study' objective. And now you are completely free to take on a beloved, loving, attentive, and female companion who..."

"Do *not* presume to lecture me, Sahlee," he quietly admonished her, holding up an index finger of warning. "I enjoy our conversations, but not a debate."

She bit her tongue, forcing herself to look submissively down at her sandals. It was difficult to not fall into the mode of a *High Priestess* of her *own* religion in the distant future, who often lectured without interruptions.

"Oh, I am just having fun with you, Sahlee," he suddenly laughed. "Do not be so serious. What is life if you cannot enjoy it with your friends? You have my permission to say anything you want to me at any time that you wish. Just please be careful not to do so in front of others who will not understand our special friendship. Ok?"

Sally was relieved.

She'd thought she'd gone too far. But Jesus seemed to be enjoying this rare peaceful moment with her—and was apparently going to stay there for a while. Nowadays his time was taken up with endless meetings and events. He was fast maturing beyond the point where she'd be able to speak with him at all.

She had to make the most of this opportunity.

"I am now of age to marry," Sahlee quietly but firmly stated.

Yep, that was certainly true. She'd now been in the 1st Century for twenty-seven years. Adding that to her starting age of five years old, she was now thirty-two years old—an ancient crone for these times when girls were married off as early as twelve years!

But that massive dose of Optimmune that had transformed her into a young girl was *still* slowing her aging process. In fact, she ap-

peared externally to be only a teenager. That was quite old enough to
marry Jesus, if only he'd relent to societal imperatives—or give in,
allowing his normal male physical passions to be expressed.

"You are, indeed, remarkably attractive, Sahlee," Jesus graciously
admitted. "Any man would be honored to be your husband. You are
as pretty now as the day I first saw you as a child on the edge of the
Dead Sea. I knew you were dangerous then and I still know it—
dangerously attractive. Indeed, I would gladly give in to your beauty.
But I serve a larger Lord than the norms of society. I must *transcend*
all Traditions, familial or otherwise. You *know* this to be true."

He fixed her with a piercing gaze that seemed to penetrate to her
innermost soul.

She looked at him suspiciously. A fly was buzzing around his
head, trying to land on his prominent nose. He absently brushed it
away, taking care not to kill it. He certainly didn't look like a Seer
seeing into the thoughts of her brain—but then, who knew with this
man?

She couldn't give up. He admitted she was "dangerous." In many
ways she was his intellectual equal. By appealing to his mind and
body she might still impose her will upon him...

"You *have* broken with Tradition at times," Sally slyly stated. "So
why not break with it yet again? Why must you deny yourself the
physical pleasures of marriage? You can still preach and have a wife.
They are not mutually exclusive! There is precedence for this. In fact,
you could have *multiple* wives if you chose. You could have a nice,
young-looking one like me to pleasure you—and many old fat ones to
cook and do the housework. How about that?"

Jesus threw his head back and heartily laughed. His smile was
genuine and wide, his white teeth gleaming in the sun.

"You know that I don't approve of polygamy," he snickered, apparently contemplating the uncommon arrangement she'd painted.

She continued to press her case, gratified by his easy humor.

"I *would* be a fitting match for you, though," Sally "jokingly" insisted, reaching over to pick a yellow flower from the field and sniff it
seductively. "I'm short where you are tall. I'm fair where you are
dark. I'm a servant, even lower than your already-low social status.
I'm wise where you are wiser. I am pure! I am fertile! I make you

laugh while others just make demands on you for your time and strength. I am suitably submissive in public but wild in private. I can talk with you as an equal on intellectual and religious matters, yet maintain a properly female 'dumb' silence in public. I dress demurely yet still have a great figure under these robes and concealments."

Jesus again nodded in agreement.

But his cheerful expression suddenly turned *icy*.

"And yet if people *really* knew you, Sahlee," he slowly stated in a tightly controlled whisper, "then they would surely *burn* you as a witch—is that not true?"

He fixed her with a sad, regretful stare.

"What...what d-do you m-mean, Jesus?" she stammered, not daring to meet his withering gaze.

"You know *exactly* what I mean," he said, standing up.

She was suddenly frozen in fear, his words having invoked the horror of what she'd already experienced "back" in the 12th Century—more than a thousand years in their future!

As if it had happened yesterday, she felt the flames searing her legs and feet as she writhed at the stake being burned alive...

She shuddered, her skin crawling.

She never wanted that to happen again.

Jesus shook buzzing flies off of his robe, looked around as if seeing the verdant Galilee valley for the first and, perhaps, the last time—and then *looked beyond* with a fierce determination in his blazing eyes.

"I must be about my Father's business," he quietly stated, turning his broad back to her. "Do not approach me again with your sweet *temptations*, Sahlee! If you do, I will sell you back into slavery. And that would break my Mother's heart...and mine as well."

He strode back to the main road, his head held high.

But Sally thought she saw a hesitation in his stride, a hint of deep sadness in his piercing gaze.

She wished she could help him. She wished he'd relent. She wished she could be "Mrs. Jesus"—steering him to a long and happy life as her contented husband.

But that was not going to happen.

She had to find another way to stop him than pleasant seduction.

What she had to do now was far more drastic than mere diversionary tactics.

She had to kill him.

Chapter 8

GALACTIC CORE

Nestled at the heart
Of 400 billion stars
100,000 light-years across
Crowded into the middle
The oldest and wisest lived
Now long extinct or gone
Leaving only faint traces
Amazing, incredible races
Their story-arcs finished
They still strive to survive
If not in fact, then fiction
Echoing a battle cry
Lost to ancient history
Still inaudibly lingering
Trapped in an eternal
Black Hole prison
They lust for resurrection
Whatever the cost...
Defying even God!

The Luminary Chronicles, 8:58-63

Sally knew that she and Tommy had to explore the Harvester. It might give her clues as to what they were going to face at the Galactic Core.

She also knew that she should be terrified, but instead felt oddly invigorated. When she'd volunteered to give herself up to the Harvester she'd expected to be packaged in with the rest of the grabbed-up humans: doomed to be summarily killed, used as slaves, made into biological factories, or whatever other strange purpose the invaders had for humanity.

She certainly hadn't expected a plucky little robot to allow her to mess with the entire alien spaceship!

So she was grateful to be alive, and eager to find out more.

"I don't know how long we've been conked out," she yawned widely, shaking Tommy awake. "But it's time to get up and at 'em!"

Tommy irritably moaned, squinting his eyes shut even tighter.

She slid to the side and gently allowed his blond-haired head to rest upon the floor as she clambered stiffly up, looking at the still-functioning viewscreen.

What she saw was *ominous*.

The huge hanger outside looked considerably *smaller...w*hat the heck? Even as she watched, a few more of the burnt, exploded ships slid off to the side into a dazzling vortex of light—as a few more yards of the hanger vanished!

She realized what was happening. The ship was *extruding* the damaged area and its contents into the surrounding subspace!

If Sally didn't get moving—she and Tommy's cannon-ship might well be next.

"Tommy, wake up!" she yelled at him. "We've got to get out of here right now! Can you still communicate with the Mother Ship?"

"Huh? What?" he said, levering himself up and rubbing his eyes with both hands. "What did you say, Mommy?"

But Sally was leaning far forward in the outsized seat to move the oversized control wheel and levers, experimenting.

Yes! She could make the big, black, squared vehicle float in whatever direction she wanted.

Several of the larger holes she'd blasted into the interior of the Mother Ship in her battle with the hanger's machines were still there—but *rapidly closing* as the ship sealed off the damaged hanger.

"Tommy!" she frantically asked him. "Which of the big gaps should we go into? We've only time to get into one of them!"

He squinted, frowning.

"The...center one...I think...is open to whatever's further inside the ship. The others are just into messed-up guts."

"Center it is!" Sally exclaimed as she pushed a throttle and they flew into the middle of the shrinking hole—just escaping the imploding hanger.

And they were suddenly in total darkness.

"Turn on the lights, Mommy," Tommy said, grabbing onto her arm.

"How? Where?" she said, trying to find something with an "external-light" symbol on the alien control panel.

"There, Mommy, that green button..."

She saw it: a large, rounded knob that both pushed and twisted.

She pushed it in and twisted it as far as it went in a clockwise direction...

Instantly, the viewscreen revealed a *green light* shining from their craft into a *vast storage chamber*: illuminating a small slice of what appeared to be many millions of transparent tubes! The tubes were suspended in stacks that each contained about a hundred tubes. And there were many more stacks receding into the darkness...

"What's *in* those tubes, Mommy?" Tommy asked, squinting at the viewscreen. "I can't access the Mother Ship's files clearly. Can you get us closer?"

"I think so," she said, nudging the controls to drift the cannon-craft over to the closest suspended group of tubes.

Each tube was ten feet long and four feet in width. The inner surfaces were fogged up. But clear patches let one see into the interiors.

Sally gasped, shocked at what she saw!

Looking back at her from inside the closest tube was the *face of an old man*—frozen in fear!

"Oh, Mommy...those are *people* in there," Tommy said in a small voice, his big blue eyes stretched wide in amazement. "Are they sleeping?"

"I don't know if they are asleep or dead," she gasped. "Is there any way you can find out, Tommy?"

He closed his eyes tight, bunching his little fists up as he concentrated.

"I...I...it's *fighting* me, Mommy. But I...*got* something! Oh no, they're hurting me, hurting me, hurting me!" he yelled out...

—as RED LIGHTS suddenly flared on outside across the entire huge storage chamber...

—and Tommy fell flat upon the floor, his eyes rolling back in his head!

Horrified, Sally jumped out of the oversized alien control seat and dropped on her knees, poised over the boy, slapping him sharply on both sides of his cheeks.

"Break it off! Break it off!" she frantically ordered him.

The viewscreen showed that without her at the controls the cannon-ship was drifting downward...

—to SLAM into the storage chamber's floor, tossing Sally and Tommy up into the air...

—then BASHING them both against the wall of the small control room, depositing them in a heap at the base of the control panel's strangely curved table.

"Unggghhh," Sally groaned, feeling fresh bruises along the side of her body where she'd hit the wall. Then she struggled to get to her feet in the still-rocking craft and climb back into the oversized control chair.

"I'm sure getting...lots of training...on guiding this clunky cannon-spaceship," Sally grated as she struggled with the various controls to find a combination that would place the craft stably upon the huge storage chamber's floor.

Then they were finally still, resting solidly on the floor.

Adjusting the viewscreen, Sally could now clearly see in the pervasive outside red glow. The many groups of tubes were fortunately undisturbed by the floundering of the cannon-ship. But she could see that the groups retreated smaller and smaller into the far distance—likewise as she panned the view upward.

"Jesus Christ!" Sally gasped, now that the full extent of what they'd found started to sink in, "there must be *millions* of people in here."

"Actually, it is right around *ten* million people," Tommy said in a weak voice at her elbow.

"Ten million? Really?"

Something must have happened in her transit to the Dinosapien Earth. It would take a long time for one of these ships to collect that many survivors on her Earth, right?   Or perhaps many Harvester ships collected their bounty and transferred it to this one ship?

"Did you *hear* me, Mommy?" Tommy insisted, crawling up and clutching onto one of her legs.

She started, looking down at the mop-haired boy. "Hey, kid, you were in bad shape trying to talk to the ship's command computer. Are you ok now?"

"I put up a firewall in my brain to keep out the Mother Ship's intelligent programs that were defending from my attack," he lopsidedly grinned. "I grabbed a lot before they completely cut off my access. They can't hurt me now, but I can't get at them either."

He was pouting.

"Hey, you did great, Tommy," she said, lifting him up to sit in her lap as they both viewed the vast numbers of tubes in the chamber.

She hugged him tightly.

"I'm sure glad you decided to come with me, despite my orders to the contrary," she softly spoke in his ear. "You're a *very* good little boy."

He snickered happily.

"And Mommy...?" he said.

"Yes, Tommy?"

"Before I had to run away from the Ship's mind, I got something important..." his voice trailed off.

"What's that?"

"I found *your* Mommy," he added.

"Say what?" she said, hardly daring to believe her ears. "Are you sure?"

"They've got DNA profiles on each of the people they captured and put into time-freeze in the capsules," he excitedly continued. "And one of them matches your own Mother. She's my *Granny!* Yay!"

"You...y-you have *my* DNA p-profile...and she's...b-but...?" Sally stammered, struggling to absorb what Tommy had just matter-of-factly revealed to her, holding him at arm's length and looking at him suspiciously.

Yes, she continually needed to remind herself that he was not a real child, but rather an extremely sophisticated android-computer.

"Sure, Mommy," he shrugged. "All I need is a flake of skin or hair strands. It's easy to do. I do it for fun, DNA-profiling things around me...I hope that's ok? I've done it to the Priestesses and *you*...lots of stuff."

"Wow!" she said, hugging him tightly. "You are an *amazingly* clever little boy."

"Thank you, Mommy," he happily smiled, snuggling close in her arms.

Sally was stunned. Was it really true? Was her own mother still "alive", having survived the initial bombardment to be taken for whatever unknown purpose by the Harvester?

After Sally saved Dave and the others from the clutches of that evil time-traveler Sanako—and then helped get the GE-generator schematics out to the general public at the United Nations—Sally was looking forward to finally returning to her still-healing mother, Samantha Smith. But Sally never got there.

Sally was side-tracked from her attempt to get back to her mother by the "little matter" of an Alien Armada descending upon earth—from which Sally, Tommy, the pet dinosaur Breep, and the two Dinosapiens George and Alice had barely escaped.

So what happened to the others? Her Turtle Tattoo swept Sally away to the Dinosapien world—where she tried to save them from the pursuing Harvester, then wound up here. But what happened to the rest of humanity, including her mother?

In the turmoil, Sally hadn't had time to give her mother's fate much thought. She'd just bitterly assumed that her mother plus many others died in the initial attack on Earth. According to her Dinosapien friends, the major cities of her world were all destroyed, left burning and decimated by the alien invaders.

But then again, Samantha Smith was living in the relatively smaller city of Ada, Oklahoma. What if the smaller cities were the major "harvest" points where these gigantic invading spaceships took prizes—their primary hunting ground for human survivors?

It seemed possible that Samantha Smith was indeed in one of those millions of pods hanging out there in the vast storage chamber.

"I've got to find her," Sally said with fierce determination. "Tommy, search the databases you stole from the ship again. Can you tell exactly *where* Granny is located?"

"I can lead you right to her," he replied happily.

She set him on the floor at her side, bending forward to reach the outsized controls.

"So tell me where to go."

"And we've got to hurry!" he suddenly said, looking terrified.

"What?"

"The people in the tubes are going to get *used*," he gulped.

"Used?" she dumbly repeated as she got the square craft to rise jerkily up off the surface...

—when suddenly, as had happened earlier, the walls seemed to *melt:* bent into incomprehensible shapes they then *snapped* back into sharp focus!

Sally felt sick, like she'd again just been turned inside out.

"We're *there*," Tommy ominously announced.

"You mean...?"

"Yes, Mommy," he said, his normally-cheerful, boyish voice low and trembling with fear. "We've *arrived*—at the Big Black Hole."

Pike's Peak was like going off to another world.

Ivanna looked out of the side window of the flying yellow school bus as they rapidly descended. Below them was a jagged mountain, towering 8,000 feet above downtown Colorado Springs. Altogether, it rose more than 14,000 feet above sea level. Ivanna was breathing more quickly than normal due to the reduced oxygen level at that high altitude.

"We'll be landing soon, so fasten your seatbelts if you haven't already," the High Priestess announced in a loud voice, sounding like an airline stewardess. "Landing with our rocket jets can be a bit bumpy."

Ivanna saw they were descending toward white strips of snow laid out on bare rock, alongside two long flat structures.

It was a rapid descent.

Then the rockets cut out and the bus dropped a couple feet to land jarringly. The bus bounced a couple times as its wheels and shocks absorbed their downward momentum.

At the front door of the bus, armed ladies in thick white jackets with white hoods appeared.

"My troops are punctual as always—to escort you, my dear guests, to your quarters."

"Escorts, my ass," the Sergeant muttered, sitting behind Ivanna.

"At least we've still got our weapons," the Major whispered pointedly back to him. Ivanna noted he'd whispered loud enough for her to hear as well.

"Shall we?" the High Priestess invited her "guests"—standing up and grandly gesturing for them to follow.

Ivanna did as directed, exiting out the bus door and carefully going down a couple shaky steps to the ground.

It was freezing.

A strong wind was blowing across the mound of the mountain's top. Ivanna blinked, shivering, looking around at an awesome spectacle. Rugged lower mountains spread out around them. The invasion by the aliens seemed far away. The peak probably looked similar to what Zebulon Pike, Jr. viewed in his exploration of southern Colorado in 1806. The solid rock around them had a pinkish hue to it. Ivanna vaguely recalled from her visit years earlier that the pink color was due to the granite containing potassium.

"This is the *Summit Visitor Center* that we've converted into a local Temple," the High Priestess said to Ivanna as she hustled her towards an entrance to escape the biting cold. It didn't look any different from a regular building, except for sporting a large, new sign on which was painted an image of the *spiked gold medallion* that all the Priestesses wore.

It seemed to be the "holy" symbol of the CPH.

"You'll be our honored guest here," the High Priestess continued. "And you two gentlemen," she indicated with a wave of her hand, "are to accompany our colleagues here to the other building—which prior to the invasion was the United States Army *Pike's Peak Research Laboratory.*"

Standing in the icy wind in thick jackets were three United States Army personnel.

The two commandos' expressions clearly said they were not happy at being separated from Ivanna.

"But don't be alarmed," the regal woman soothed them. "It's just for your housing needs. You are free to come over and join us at the Temple once you get settled. Several of your fellow army soldiers were stranded here when the invasion began, lucky for them."

"Are the facilities still intact?" the Major asked as he was led by Priestesses towards the waiting soldiers.

The High Priestess cheerfully answered him, raising her voice to be heard against the howling wind.

"Due, I suspect, to our few numbers and extreme isolation, none of the laser-ships or Reapers have bothered with us here. Yes, the facilities are intact. We have power both from a small research nuclear reactor that the Army facility luckily had in place, plus our energy-gathering invention—all of which adequately powers both buildings."

"Then you have communications?" Sergeant Grant eagerly asked.

"Indeed, gentlemen, the army's communication equipment here is all up and working," she replied. "When you are ready you should be able to send a short encrypted burst to Cheyenne Mountain without attracting alien attention. Isn't that great? We've insisted on strict radio silence up until now of course, so as not to attract any undue attention from the alien armada—which I must continue to insist upon. But I'm sure at the appropriate time you'll want to report Ivanna's findings. Isn't that correct?" she sweetly concluded.

The two commandos just stared back at her, refusing to confirm the Priestess' observation that they could communicate with the hidden base.

Ivanna waved a quick goodbye to them as they walked away, also not happy to be separated from them—but feeling more at ease than she had for quite a while.

This mysterious "Linda Powers" was growing on her. It was obvious to Ivanna that the High Priestess was at least partially insane. The woman's relentless cheerfulness could become an icy rage at the drop of a hat. But, if handled diplomatically, she might be a wealth of information. What was her agenda? What did she know of the aliens? Did she have ideas on how to defeat them other than launching a token, futile missile attack?

As Ivanna entered the double doors of the Visitor's Center, she was immensely relieved to be out of the blasting, icy wind.

But the wall of warmth hit her hard, causing Ivanna's legs to buckle in relief.

She was barely able to stand upright.

The High Priestess took her by the elbow, supporting her.

"We have a few guest rooms, Professor," the High Priestess told her. "You probably want to get cleaned up, put on fresh clothes we've lain out for you, and maybe take a nap. Then we'll have dinner together—you, my Priestesses, our army friends, and your commandos. You see, you have nothing to fear from us—and everything to gain. Then after our communal meal, you and I will have a long, private talk. Does that sound acceptable? Please, here is your room."

"Thank you...for your kind hospitality," Ivanna nodded weakly, stepping inside.

She was exhausted beyond anything she'd ever felt before. Also, she was filthy from their long crawl through the debris in the lower basement levels trying to evade the bandits. In addition, her jumpsuit was torn and bloodied from her scrapes and minor wounds.

She saw within the room a made-up bed, a dresser, and a closet with its doors hanging open. Inside the closet was an assortment of appropriately-sized clothes. Laid out in a small bathroom next to a sink was a medical kit with ointments and bandages. Also, Ivanna rejoiced at seeing a compact shower.

"Does...the shower...?" Ivanna tentatively asked her host.

"Oh, it works fine. We even have warm water. Please, Professor, take your time. It's still three hours until supper time. Use as much water in your shower as you like. I mandate that our Temples always have extensive stores of water. And if you need anything, just open your door and tell your attendant. One of my Priestesses will be sitting outside to assist you. Please, enjoy our humble accommodations."

The High Priestess graciously left, closing the door behind her.

To Ivanna the room looked no different from a comfortable motel room.

But at the moment it was a palace.

Ivanna sank onto the clean bed, exhausted. She lay there on her back without moving for over an hour, just letting her strained muscles relax.

Her body wanted to drift off into a dreamless slumber. But her brain was racing.

She was furiously thinking, trying to make sense of everything that had taken place in the last few hours. And the main thought she kept returning to was: *Why did this place not have a compact DE-generator?* They were using an archaic, research-class *nuclear* generator for power—plus the High Priestess' weak energy-gathering invention. Although that seemed adequate for the two buildings, it was hardly the energy needed for resisting the aliens.

What was Linda Powers hiding? What was she not telling Ivanna?

It was a mystery.

But Ivanna put it aside, forcing herself up to get up, clean up, and get ready for dinner.

Later, after a good shower, discrete bandages, putting on a freshly ironed pink pant suit, and combing out her blond-dyed hair—Ivanna went to dinner.

All the people of the small commune were there, including Ivanna's two commando comrades. They also looked a lot better, freshly showered with cleaned uniforms.

Ivanna noted that for a High Priestess of a world-wide religion, Linda Powers was decidedly casual. Her "prayer" for the meal was a hearty "thanks for coming and dig in!"

They were seated around a series of smaller tables arranged into one big rectangle, with platters set on a long narrow table in the middle within easy reach.

It was a wonderful buffet.

And each person had a *large glass filled to the brim with water* sitting on the table at their place. After having to ration their water, that luxury was much appreciated by Ivanna.

The food was tasty, considering. Apparently these Priestesses were good at scavenging with their mobile bus, swooping down to grab whatever remained in grocery stores—since hardly any fresh food was being produced anymore. Farm animals were dead. Crops were burnt to the ground. The orbiting aliens apparently preferred the "scorched earth" method of conquest. According to the High Priestess they leveled an entire inhabited region then picked over the remains—concentrating on abducting disoriented, starving survivors. The "well-torched earth" strategy certainly cut down on any meaningful resistance.

The dinner was canned vegetables, canned fruits, canned meats, and rehydrated dried foods. Nonetheless, Ivanna found the steaming-hot spaghetti and meatballs dish quite tasty.

There was little talk except polite comments on the food. Ivanna noted that her two commando friends, sitting at her table, were particularly tight-lipped. They were obviously not being drawn into the High Priestesses' few attempts at casual conversation, unwilling to give up any info on their hidden base located beneath nearby Cheyenne Mountain.

And, yes, the Priestesses all wore their black guns to the table, in holsters at their hips.

Although the occupants of the "Pike's Peak Temple" were polite, it was quite clear to Ivanna and her two companions that they were prisoners.

Ivanna noted that the two commandos were now without their weapons—either by polite choice to not sport combat rifles at the dinner table, or by insistence of their new army "comrades" who were clearly respectful of their generous hostess.

"So—shall we adjourn then?" their hostess cheerfully said after they'd eaten a dessert of canned fried apples.

"As you wish," Ivanna politely replied, standing up. "Can we talk now?"

"Yes, of course," the High Priestess nodded emphatically, leading her away to a private extension of the rectangular building. It obviously was newly constructed since it was made of different materials than the main building. It was a short tunnel that lead out to an enclosed, heated observation "deck". An entire glass wall looked out onto the mountainous expanse gloriously laid-out below.

"So," Ivanna said as she sat in a comfortable armchair beside which a nice cup of hot chocolate was waiting for her on a low, wooden side table, "what are you *hiding* from me, *Linda?*"

"Nothing!" Linda Powers replied as she settled into an armchair on the glass-walled observation deck, looking out with obvious pleasure at the setting evening sun highlighting the magnificent panorama.

The High Priestess had in her hand a large glass of iced tea. She seemed to have a thing about staying well-hydrated.

And it seemed to Ivanna that the *Church of Perpetual Health* had put considerable resources into their Pike's Peak Temple. Although fairly cramped—holding only a dozen Priestesses plus guests—it was still quite comfortable. Ivanna had almost expected after-dinner scotch or wine. But the Priestesses were apparently nonalcoholic. Ivanna had to do with the warm cup of hot chocolate.

But despite the fine hospitality, Ivanna knew that President Swartz was desperately awaiting her report. Ivanna didn't have time for idle chatter. She needed an honest answer from her host straightaway: what she was hiding?

"Nothing at all, Linda?" Ivanna persisted, trying to penetrate the woman's defenses by being overly familiar repeatedly using her first name.

"Well, we do of course have religious secrets—such as the proprietary ingredients of our health pills or the exact mechanisms of our energy-gathering guns and mobile energy sources," Linda Powers shrugged. She wore a simple white dress. Her long red hair flared out around her shoulders. "But as to a 'grand conspiracy' or such, that's all been superseded by the alien invasion, right? All the great schemes of us little humans have been roundly disrupted, haven't they?"

"The decimation of human civilization certainly has taken priority over our prior concerns," Ivanna ruefully admitted. "But our one defense against the invaders that has any promise to work is our newly-acquired mastery of subspace-derived, concentrated Dark Energy. Why on earth don't you support its usage? Before the invasion occurred, compact units were available to the common person, worldwide. So this has been the focus of my people, to figure out how to attack the invaders with our most powerful weapon!"

The middle-aged woman sighed as if exasperated having to an-swer a question she'd dealt with many times from lowly new recruits up to the world's mightiest leaders.

"It's *evil*, Ivanna," she stated simply. "It's too *powerful!* It *de-ludes* us stupid little humans—just out of the jungle from swinging in trees and throwing our droppings at each other—to think we've mas-tered the Universe when we haven't."

Taking a moment to process Linda Powers' fierce reply, Ivanna sipped at her steaming cup of hot chocolate. The Priestesses had even put little marshmallows on top. It was delicious.

Ivanna noticed that the High Priestess had finished her big glass of iced tea, setting the glass off to the side.

"But what's wrong with appreciating our scientific advance-ments?" Ivanna persisted, sincerely trying to understand the crazy Priestess' position. "Dark Energy is powerful enough—or so my fellow scientists tell me—to even power space travel to the stars! I'd think you'd *want* to spread your ideology across the Universe, should that prove possible. Don't all religions, particularly new ones, want to evangelize?"

The High Priestess fixed Ivanna with a withering stare before con-tinuing.

Ivanna again noted that strange, intimidating stare! Ivanna could see why this "High Priestess" had become so powerful.

"We're *different!*" she curtly replied. And then more softly, as if realizing that dictatorial proclamations would not work with Ivanna, "We're a religion of facts, not fiction. We're *practical*. Our new ener-gy-generator, which powers the gun we all carry, is sufficient to meet the entire energy needs of our world. We don't have to explode an atomic bomb just to give us a nice warm fire with which to cook food. Plus, we've no idea what cracking open this 'subspace' means. Our little generators just suck up surrounding energy in the real world, not open up a new Pandora's Box."

Ivanna narrowed her eyes.

"And it's a method that you keep entirely secret. Anyone fooling with your jealously handed-out devices get to see them automatically melt into useless slag if anyone tries to tamper with them."

"Yes, that's true," Linda mildly acknowledged. "But that's so they are used properly, for only their intended purpose. I'm not making the mistake of those who invented previous energy sources, letting them become the means of mass destruction!"

"Ok," Ivanna said, leaning back in the comfortable armchair, willing to concede the point even though she was still skeptical of the woman's argument. "But back to Dark Energy—isn't it man's aspiration to go to the stars? We are defined by our curiosity. Just think what awaits us out there, even in our own Galaxy, if we could build our own starships. As a sociologist, I'd jump at the opportunity to study nonhuman societies. From what expert astronomers have told me, there are likely races in our own galaxy that have been self-aware and intelligent for millions, even billions of years! Why, if we were to go to the Galactic Core where the oldest stars exist, I suspect that we'd..."

The middle-aged Priestess abruptly SLAMMED her hand down on the side table—knocking over the empty glass, scattering ice cubes onto the floor—while shaking her head firmly in the negative.

"You make my point!" the Priestess addressed Ivanna, speaking with alarming intensity. "Who knows what's out amongst the stars that will put our tiny arrogance to shame?"

"Well, to shrink from the unknown isn't..."

"—and the proof of what I say is the Harvesters that orbit our planet!" Linda again interrupted Ivanna. "How is it that they suddenly appeared just as we were given this great 'gift' of Dark Energy from our scientists? I say that tapping into Dark Energy *attracted* them to us! Isn't that logical?"

"Well, since it was my husband that helped make much of it happen I probably should argue with you. But you're right. It's too tiny of a cosmic probability to be coincidence that..."

"Right!" the High Priestess triumphantly concluded, reaching over and grabbing Ivanna's shoulder tightly. "And as such, we need to *fade back* into the shadows and allow this rampaging, irresistible, unstoppable Alien Force to play out. They'll get their fill of us. They'll take what they want. And then, if they think we're destroyed and of no further use to them, they'll depart and leave us alone."

"But that might take centuries, even millennia," Ivanna frowned, carefully loosening Sally's painful grasp on her shoulder and politely moving the hand off her body. "And even if the present fleet does eventually depart, another might take its place. I think that we, as a planet harboring an intelligent species, are *already* exposed to the Galaxy. We can't put the Genie back in the Bottle. Trying to hide now is simply not workable. We've already been revealed to the Universe! I can't tell President Swartz to just hunker down. And even if I did tell her to do that, she'd just ignore such defeatist advice. That's simply not a viable strategy now that we've already been revealed to the technologically superior marauders out there looking for whatever we've got—be that our warm bodies or processed raw materials. We can't just surrender to them."

The High Priestess sat in her armchair for a full minute, silent.

Then she stood up, looking out over the magnificent, sunset-highlighted expanse through the large glass window.

"Alright, then, Ivanna," she sighed, her voice low and carefully controlled. "I suppose I will have to do it—tell you the whole truth. You're too intelligent for me to handle like an easily misdirected and manipulated top politician. I'm going to tell you things that your President hiding next door in Cheyenne Mountain would never believe, except to write me off as a raving lunatic. But for you to believe it, I'm going to have to tell you not just part of it, but *all* of it. Are you willing to at least concede I might be telling you the truth, however fantastic it might seem? And are you willing to sit and listen to my incredible story without interruption?"

Ivanna nodded.

She was taken-aback. The High Priestess *was* hiding something. But from the intensity in her voice, Ivanna was not sure she wanted to know what it was.

Regardless, her mission for the President was to figure out what was really happening on the surface of the planet.

"Go on, Linda," Ivanna urged her, taking another sip of her drink.

Then a deep dread caused Ivanna to suddenly and quietly gag on the hot chocolate, shakily setting it aside. She realized she needed to direct her entire attention at the scary woman next to her.

The High Priestess' big green eyes were somber.

"It all started when my *Turtle Tattoo* started to burn me..."

Chapter 9

<u>REINVIGORATION</u>

As the old saying goes
"Just keep on keeping on"
To stop and sit is stagnation
And from stagnation comes rot
So sad to see the juicy fruit stinking
Its ripe luscious goodness corrupted
Nourishing vitality turned to awful mush
But therein to find the little seeds
Waiting to feed on the supposed waste
Embedded into the "useless" dirt
Invigorating soil recycles "wasted" life
Little crawling leaves pushing upward
Their greedy roots wriggling outward
Giving a fresh start to that which died
New strength to the depleted weary
Finding in the incredible effort
Putting one foot in front of the other
A "second wind" of steadying breath
Beyond exhaustion of the initial effort
Ability to go beyond one's perceived limits
And therein to find a new type of success
Not in terms of the old, limited objectives
But as culmination of fresh perspective
A reward of persistent stubbornness
When we refuse to acknowledge defeat
Given even to the most stupid amongst us

The precious chance of unexpected revival

A regeneration of our very spirits...

Change your staid taste buds and

Savor the stinking "dead" rot!

The Luminary Chronicles, 9:128-135

Dave had been working nonstop in the "lab" for three days and nights.

He was totally exhausted, but also exhilarated!

"So...made any progress?" Dave heard Arthur ask. The Agent was tentatively stepping through the tent's front flap...

Dave appreciated the FBI agent avoiding disturbing him and the other technicians' work on the captured robot head. But now as the equally exhausted techs departed to go collapse on their sleeping bags, Arthur was obviously there for a report. He deserved one, since the expedition had cost them all so much.

Dave felt the loss of Sally like a knife continually twisting in his guts.

He knew he'd liked the spunky girl, but his distress at her death was completely unexpected.

It was more than love. It was an obsession. It was as if his beating heart had been ripped out of his chest—leaving him spent and lifeless.

They had shared a remarkable connection—even though it was often highly charged and adversarial—such that her final shock and brief pain flowed into him like concentrated sulfuric acid injected straight into his veins!

He wanted to just give up and run from the pain and the guilt. If she'd been just a few steps up or back she'd still be alive. It would have been easy for him to urge her forward or hold her back. Intellectually, he knew the best way to honor her death was to figure out the severed robot head's sophisticated technology. But, emotionally, he was a crushed derelict ship sinking into the greedy depths of a black ocean.

"Anything? Anything at all?" the burly, dark eyeglasses-sprouting Agent interrogated Dave.

The large metallic half-orb lay disassembled on the tent's floor. Wires and cables from within stretched out from the bottom of its opened shell—leading to a number of intact components: a few of which still twitched and flopped-about! Yes, its "guts" still lived-on, sufficient to give clues as to their functions. Dave could vaguely recognize some of the robot head's innards, like obvious gear boxes. Other parts were totally alien, their purposes unknown, perhaps unknowable by mere-human minds.

Dave carefully stepped out of the swirl of dissected mechanical and electrical components, walking over to a wooden table to slump into a chair. He put his arms on the rough surface and lay his head down.

"We hunted and hunted amongst the guts of the thing's head," he mumbled, not looking at the Agent. "We finally figured out that the generator powering the robot was probably in its shoulder region. That's where the main power cables lead—right where you cut them away with your concentrated laser beam."

Arthur sat beside the exhausted Dave, silently looking at the mass of parts from the disassembled alien robot head spread out there on the floor.

"So we did this for nothing?" he finally asked. "We lost our genius mathematician in exchange for some useless robot parts?"

"Oh, we got we wanted," Dave said, wearily raising his head.

"What?" Arthur asked, surprised, "Really?"

"Yes," Dave nodded. "The subspace rupture caused by the cold-fusion-like initiator—similar to what I, Sally, and Victor made—extends upward into the head. There, to contain it, are a series of amazingly simple metallic folds running through the metal which cause overlapping electrical waveforms. Effectively, it turns the subspace rupture back on itself, cancelling out rippling outward signals—while effectively amplifying the Dark Energy generation. I suppose that's why the robots utilize this methodology, not to shield their presence, but to use minimum space in the tight structure for the DE-generator. After all, the killer-bots are just glorified weaponized dump trucks that want to maximize their human-cargo transport volume."

"Well...that's quite interesting," Arthur said, scratching his blond crewcut head in puzzlement, "but how does that help shield our own generators?"

"It took us three days and nights of work to figure it out. That's because the answer *wasn't* in the parts we dissected out of the head," Dave ruefully stated. "It actually was so simple that we initially overlooked it and..."

He sighed deeply.

"What? What?" Arthur frowned. "Come on, buddy, speak clearly! Is it something we can use or not?"

"It's nothing we have the technology to duplicate," Dave softly replied. "Even if we had all our pre-Invasion research and industrial capacity, we still couldn't duplicate it. The metals, the alloys, the micro-fabrication, the energy vibrational wave patterns...it would take us decades of research to even understand it fully, let alone replicate it."

"So...we're doomed?"

Dave grinned sadistically.

"No, *Sir!*" he slyly stated. *"That's* the answer!"

He savagely *kicked* the large metallic "head"...causing the half-orb with its jagged laser-melted bottom to *bounce* across the floor!

"The head itself?"

"Yep...the head itself! The inner layers contain everything I just described to you. All we have to do is slap that big 'salad dish' over our rounded, modular DE-generator—and we can run it continually without fear of detection by the aliens."

"Really?" Arthur gasped. "We use the head just as it is?"

"That's right," Dave said, standing stiffly up. "Give it a shot. You'll see that it works. Actually, you don't even have to do that. I already tried it. No problems. I recharged our camp's storage batteries with no detectable DE-signature broadcasting past the overlapping helmet. Signals of our ruptures still propagate through subspace, of course, but not outward into 'regular' space."

"But then...to use this world-wide...we need to..."

"—send out the damn information," Dave curtly cut Arthur off. "From now on *we're* hunting the robots, instead of them hunting us. It's *them* that have what *we* want!"

"But they're almost invulnerable," Arthur protested, shaking his head in denial.

"And how was it that *we* captured a head?" Dave coldly reminded him.

"Well, we isolated and trapped a robot, then used one of the Priestess' captured guns that..."

"Can you get more?"

"I can...through my colleagues...get a few more..."

"But we don't need dozens—rather we've got to have *hundreds*, even *thousands* of the guns at our rebel bases all across the world. If we can slice off enough robot heads to shield our generators on all the continents, then we can create an impenetrable, global shield against the circling armada!"

"But to get the guns...?"

"Yes," Dave soberly nodded, "the Priestesses of the Church of Perpetual Health. It's their jealously guarded proprietary manufacture. And they each carry one."

"But they'd never cooperate with us," Arthur mused, again scratching at his head with one big hand. "For whatever crazy reasons, they think that accessing Dark Energy is a devilish pursuit. They preach against it. They want us to only use their little, weak, energy-suckers based on their gun technology. And they *never* give out their actual guns to anyone outside their sect."

"Then we'll tell our Resistance cells to just *take* the guns," Dave grated. He was quite deliberately channeling his rage at the death of Sally onto the uncooperative new religion.

"So...you're saying...we go to *war* with the High Priestess and her followers?"

"It's about time, don't you think?" Dave said in a flat, controlled voice. "They haven't helped us. They have this ignorant teaching against Dark Energy usage. They use their rocket-buses to beat us to what little food and supplies remain. They've been our *enemies* all along."

Arthur nodded thoughtfully.

"Maybe once they were nice, reasonable fellow citizens," Dave continued, his eyes narrowing in anger. "But now they're nothing more than fanatical, religious terrorists. They're as much a threat to civilized humanity as the aliens."

Arthur nodded in agreement.

"I'll put out the word," he said, abruptly rising to hurry out of the "lab" tent. "And good work, David!" he called back.

Dave just stared straight ahead.

He wished Sally was there with him to share this moment of triumph...but she was dead.

Sally had always been a royal pain—and *continued* to be so! But maybe he could soothe the pain with the blood of his enemies.

The placid painting pinned up on the inside of the tent seemed to silently rebuke him.

It preached peace and tranquility.

But it was poised on the lip of a horrendous world war.

"Don't you look at me like that!" he shouted-out at the painting, the elegant lady's back turned "disdainfully" to him. "You're no better than me!"

Outside in the parking-basement "camp" he heard people gasp with concern at him shouting to himself in an empty tent—their "mighty" Leader.

He didn't care what they thought. To hell with them! They could think he was crazy. They could think he was having a nervous breakdown. They could think he was conversing with a ghost. Whatever! His only concern was with how the lady in the painting regarded him—a lady that might have been an earlier incarnation of Sally herself.

"I know they are fellow human beings, but they are wrong. They are *appeasing* our enemies!" he shouted again at the inert blue painting. "We're *defending* our way of life. Isn't that what you wanted?"

He collapsed onto the cluttered floor, sobbing uncontrollably.

Damn, it was hard to get rid of Sally.

Sally was increasingly excluded from contact with Jesus.

Clearly, the word had been put out that she was to have no direct contact with the Master. She was still honored for her work in the household, but cut off from Jesus. She wasn't even allowed to study the ancient texts in the evenings least Jesus come by to consult them while she was there.

She *was* allowed, though, to accompany Mary and the rest of Jesus' family as they supported his travels and ever-increasing fame. But she was carefully kept in the background. It was fine for her to help serve food, to do chores—but not to do anything beyond being a valued servant.

She grew increasingly frustrated and restless, blaming her isolation on Jesus. She knew the orders were coming from Mary, who certainly knew of Sally's romantic interest in her son. But Sally was sure the Master Teacher put his sweet, nonjudgmental mother up to it.

"I am *not* just a servant," she muttered to herself, ignoring the admiring looks of handsome young men in the village square as she trudged dejectedly along. She was carrying a basket filled with fresh fruit she'd just purchased for Jesus' next expedition.

He was famous for encouraging the talents of people in his expanding organization, both male and female. He now had a core cadre of twelve apostles—mostly common folks like him. Yet he could not be bothered to even *talk* to his oldest and most fervent supporter, Sally.

Her resentment festered and grew.

And her prior admiration for him was steadily turning to rancid *hatred!*

She needed to stop his operation not just to alter future societies, but to *teach him a lesson!*

How dare he reject her advances?

"Ah, Sahlee," a grinning young man hesitantly approached her, shyly holding out a bundle of flowers. "I got these for..."

"Get away from me!" she snapped at him, batting-aside the flowers while trudging onward. "Don't you know not to talk to women in public?"

Chastened, he scampered away.

And these all-enveloping, tent-like *clothes!* They were as bad as the nuns' habits in the 12th Century. It had been ages since she'd felt free in either spirit or body. Would the world really stop spinning on its axis if she were to uncover her hair or show a knee?

God! What a backward society of male chauvinists!

She was *angry*...and began carefully plotting her *revenge* against Jesus, working out every detail in her mind.

She watched for an opportunity to put her plan into action. She saw him being baptized in the Jordan River by his cousin "John the Baptist." Yes, he was joining forces with his "crazy" cousin. John the Baptist ran around in the wilderness "returning to nature," supposedly to get closer to God. Jesus apparently shared in that nonsense, himself disappearing from time to time to wander all alone out in the desert—nearly killing himself from starvation and thirst.

But though his death from dehydration and starvation would have solved Sally's problem, his survival after those horrendous ordeals only heightened his mystique with the common people.

And when he produced gallons of wine where there should have been only water remaining at the end of a marriage feast—the crowds went wild! Suddenly he wasn't just a charismatic preacher, but a miracle-worker! And now the sick, crippled, and hopelessly handicapped people of the region flocked to his faith-healing events. And many of the miserable people did, indeed, get better, further elevating his fame.

But it was a year into his region-wide campaign that he really grabbed the attention of the Jewish commoner at the heart of Jewish life. It was at the Passover celebration in Jerusalem. In one of the large courts of the Temple merchants routinely gouged pilgrims who'd traveled there from afar. The greedy businessmen demanded an inflated exchange rate for foreign currency and sky-high prices to buy animals for the mandated blood-sacrifices. And to make sure a blind eye was turned to their dishonest practices, the merchants paid bribes back to the Temple rulers and officials.

Sally—accompanying the group along with Mary and the other women—saw the look of ferocity glinting in Jesus' deep brown eyes as he stood there with his disciples surveying the scene.

Despite her desire to humble and defeat Jesus, she didn't want someone else to do it. She knew from her knowledge of future history that this explosion of outrage would cement his fate at the hands of the Jewish rulers.

So she brazenly shouldered her way through the surrounding men up to him, supposedly to offer him drink from a small jug of wine which she carried.

"*What* do you want?" he irritably snapped, glaring at her.

"Are you thirsty?" she demurely replied, holding up her jug.

"Go away, Sahlee," he grated. "And take my Mother with you! There's going to be trouble here that..."

"But they aren't worth it," she interrupted him. "And it won't solve *anything*, Jesus. Tomorrow they'll just be back doing their same dishonest practices, no matter what you do to them today. It's always been this way. It's just business!"

Peter grabbed her roughly by the shoulder and pushed her back a step. "Why do speak to the Master so?" he demanded, his voice deep and gravelly.

"Let her be, my friend," Jesus now kindly said, the fury in his eyes diminishing. "Sahlee speaks the truth."

"Then should we leave this place?" Peter asked, confused, but still standing between Sally and Jesus. "Should we just go and have a nice meal together?"

"The people need to be *reminded*, Sahlee," Jesus spoke in a fierce though soft voice to her, which only those closest could hear, "of *Purpose!* They need to *remember* their primary mission—as do *you!*"

She stood stock still, looking up at his normally gentle face which now was twisted with anger. Indeed, his tanned face looked increasingly lined and weary with each passing day.

He was aging rapidly.

"And just what 'purpose' is that, Master?" she respectfully asked, bowing her head in supposed submission while allowing a sharp edge to her voice.

"Do you not remember, Sahlee...the *water of life?*" he whispered to only her, intensely serious.

"But...?" she tried to respond.

"Well—our Purpose here at God's Most Holy Place is certainly *not* to make as much money as possible from poor, honest pilgrims!" he suddenly *shouted* to everyone in the courtyard.

Shocked by the outburst from the famous preacher, all eyes turned to him.

"My Father's house is *not* a money-making, *crooked* business!" he *screamed* in outrage.

He grabbed up a handful of long leather belts from a shocked clothing-merchant and *CHARGED* at the remaining stalls!

Everyone stood or sat in stunned silence as Jesus went *berserk!*

Using every sinewy, powerful muscle in his tall frame, Jesus *whipped*, *hit*, and *kicked* the startled merchants out of the temple courtyard—as sheep and oxen squealed and bleated, stalls came crashing down, freed doves took flight, and the moneychanger's coins clattered onto the pavement stones!

Pilgrims and other visitors scampered about in the tumult, happily grabbing up the scattered money and wares...

—as Peter tried to pull Jesus back, but was powerfully shoved away!

Then Jesus leapt up on a still-standing table and defiantly confronted the arriving, outraged temple Priests and guards.

They were stopped in their tracks by his fierce gaze.

"Who are *you* to commit this outrage?" one of the Priests shouted at him. "Your time in the desert has driven you mad, Jesus of Nazareth! Leave this place or we will have you *arrested*, no matter how many of your followers gather at the gates!"

"I have a zeal for this house because I am the *son* of my Father who is the *Master* of this house!" Jesus screamed back at them.

"How *dare* you claim Divine heritage?" another Priest yelled back at him. "We know your familial background and it is hardly divine. Here and now, once and for all, in front of all these witnesses—*prove* you are the Son of God and we will let you stay and preach. Otherwise, get out of here! Give us a *sign from God* or be gone!"

Jesus drew himself up to his full height, contemptuously throwing the belt-whips down upon the paving stones.

"I *will* give you a sign!" he yelled, his deep voice projecting powerfully.

Everyone paused, listening and watching him intently—totally transfixed at what this maniacal preacher had done, waiting with bated breath for what he'd do next.

"I will *tear down* this entire temple—and then *rebuild* it in three days!" he announced grandly.

After a momentary pause for the words to sink in, Sally heard the Priests break out into uproarious laughter!

"It took forty-six years for this great Temple to be built and you will destroy it then build it back up in three days?" they mocked him. "Surely everyone can see and hear that you are a *madman*. Guards, *arrest* him!"

But Peter had a firm grip on Jesus' arm and was hastily pulling him back into the surrounding, cheering crowd.

Sally stayed glued to Peter's side, afraid that she'd be torn to pieces by the foaming-at-the-mouth Priests if she got separated.

"Why did he say those things?" she gasped to Peter. "He's just asking for them to kill him!"

The rough-hewn Peter, hustling Jesus away through the mob, leaned to her and unexpectedly quoted a passage: "Sahlee, the Messiah is prophesied in the writings of the Holy Scriptures to *'have a consuming zeal for the House of the Lord'*."

"He has a *death-wish*," she dejectedly replied. "Can't you calm him down, Peter—get him to be less confrontational? He has incredible talent—but can't he be more diplomatic? He doesn't need to get *publicly executed* to be famous and successful, does he?"

Peter laughed gruffly.

"You can't tell him what to do," he mildly observed to her, speaking into her ear to be heard above the roaring of the approving, surrounding crowd. "He gets excited and just does stuff."

The crowd was now lustily chanting in unison, their combined voice echoing off the stone walls: "JESUS! JESUS! JESUS! JESUS!"

And Jesus broke free from Peter, holding up both his arms high in the air in the universal gesture of triumph!

Sally knew that Jesus was playing upon the contempt that the common people had for the Temple bureaucracy. The abject hypocrisy and corruption of the Temple Priests, Scribes, and guards was no secret. Sally recognized the masterful manipulation that Jesus achieved that day, not just by giving a speech—but through violent action. His outraged attack on the merchants was burned into the minds of all present. They, in turn, would spread news of it to everyone in the city.

And, yes, Jesus was also clearly inviting the anger of the King, whose main duty to the Roman Emperor was to keep the people calm while extracting every last possible penny in taxes.

Sally was convinced that Jesus knew exactly what he was doing. He was setting the stage for his own highly publicized execution...

—which would then change the course of history!

I can't let him die on that cross!—she concluded.

Sally had the advantage of knowing what he was up to, unlike his bewildered apostles and other followers. She knew that his outrageous claim to destroy and rebuild the great Jewish Temple in three days—loudly proclaimed at his attack on the merchants—was just setting the stage for his own death. His "outrageous" claim would later resonate and amplify his own public execution then supposed resurrection three days later!

If he died in any other way than on the cross...then his movement would be finished.

He'd be just another of many failed, would-be Jewish "Messiahs" lost to history.

And she knew just how and when to do it. Her previous general plan to poison him now solidified into a specific, time-critical attack. He'd never expect it—done at a time and place when he could not resist.

Confident in her plan, Sally allowed Peter to drag both her and Jesus safely out of the shouting, churning mob.

She just had to bide her time.

Chapter 10

ANCIENT ALIENS

Don't be so sad

Just be happy

Throw the switch

Pop the pill

Suck the smoke

Stick in the needle

And don't worry a bit

The future is fantasy

Now is the only reality

Except of course for yesterday

When everything seemed so right

And nothing could go wrong

And you were so sure

And now you regret

Consequences bad

Hoping to fix it all

You start again

With a new Mix...

The Luminary Chronicles, 10:31-37

Sally needed to find her mother, quickly—before the millions of humans were "used", whatever terrible fate that was.

The red light had gone out in the huge storage area. Sally could only navigate her square cannon-craft by its external green lights. But Tommy assured her he knew the way—a precise location amongst the millions of suspended tubes.

Sally floated her spacecraft along carefully, trying to gently nudge aside clusters of tubes to go deeper and deeper into the vast chamber.

In Tommy's database every segment, every cluster, and every tube was specifically designated.

And then they were there—floating in front of a cluster of tubes in which Tommy promised was Sally's mother, Samantha Smith, in time-freeze. But the tubes were fogged over. Sally could not see into them to confirm which one was her mother. And floating up to them created air waves that scrambled them out of order. So Tommy couldn't pinpoint which was the tube they wanted.

They needed to open the entire cluster to find her mother.

"So if we can get them inside—how do we get my Mom out of that tube?" Sally said, struggling to hold the wobbly, deadly craft in place without bumping into and possibly rupturing the tubes.

"Just open up the outer door we came in and scoop them up," Tommy replied casually.

"But…"

"It's easy," he grinned, climbing up in her lap and reaching out to the controls.

"Hey, there tiger," she cautioned him.

But, faster than she could follow, he punched in a series of commands and pulled levers.

The craft reared around to the side, slid precisely up onto the cluster of tubes in question, and engulfed them.

Sally heard a "snap" as a loading panel slid shut, sealing the tubes into the small craft's entrance chamber.

"That was nicely done, Tommy," Sally smiled at him. "How'd you learn to be such a good pilot?"

"It was in one of the databases," he shrugged.

"Then can you hold us steady while I go below and check out the tubes?"

"Sure!"

She went to the exit tunnel, slid down it to the entrance room, and there saw five of the ten-foot long, four-foot wide transparent tubes jumbled on the floor.

The fog in the tubes was clearing.

The people inside were stirring.

Detaching the dangling tubes from their support lines had apparently triggered them to "unfreeze" their occupants.

In one of it Sally saw a white-hooded woman with a stern, thin, wrinkled face.

It was her mother...

"Mommy! Come quick!" Sally heard Tommy crying out to her.

She turned and ran back up to the control room. In the viewscreen, to her horror, she saw that the tubes outside were swaying back and forth!

"Are they opening?" she gasped.

"If they do, the people inside will die!" Tommy said sadly. "There's not enough air out there for them."

"How can we stop it?"

"We'll have to get up to the control room of the Mother Ship and do it by hand. I can't get into the programs anymore from a distance."

"Then take us there!" Sally urgently told him.

And before she could grab onto something, the little boy was leaning for forward, twirling and jumping, handling the oversized controls like a ballerina on a stage.

The ship swooped far up, above the racks of millions of tubes, and merged into a bright yellow light.

"Was this where we were going at first before we escaped, Tommy?" Sally gulped, remembering the yellow light they'd initially been ascending into. "Won't the Aliens who control this giant spaceship get us?"

"There *aren't* any, Mommy," he answered, still fighting with the controls to keep them straight on course through a tunnel of yellow, pulsating light.

"The Aliens are gone?"

"That's right," he answered. "I saw it in the databases. They died-out millions of years ago."

"But then how does this ship...?"

"It's automatic. It just keeps on doing what it started out to do millions of years ago. It goes to where there's an identified 'surplus' in the galaxy and grabs up everything of value. Then it comes back here."

"You mean, to the Galactic Core?"

"Yes."

Sally fell silent, her mouth hanging open in amazement.

Their ship had just emerged into a huge "cockpit" where a *giant, transparent half-dome* covered them—giving them a direct view of the surrounding space!

"It's...magnificent," Sally gasped.

"It's so pretty!" Tommy grinned, clapping his hands together gleefully.

On their viewscreen Sally saw the blackness of space almost entirely filled-in with a dense presentation of *stars* of all sizes and colors imaginable! The largest, nearest ones were mostly reddish—old, dying stars, Sally recalled from astronomy specials she'd seen on TV. And as the gigantic Harvester ship spun slowly on its axis, Sally saw coming into view behind them a HUGE, SHIMMERING SPHERE— with an outer, flattened "accretion disc" of gas and stars streaming towards the huge surface!

"Mommy, it's the..."

"—'*Big, Black Hole*'!" she finished his sentence. "Yes, it's incredible...but shouldn't it be invisible?"

"I think we're looking at what's called the 'event horizon'...that's making the light we can see it by," Tommy hopefully said, screwing up his face in concentration.

"Right," Sally nodded. "Past that point nothing can emerge—but atoms are being torn apart up to that point...producing the light we see."

It was the Monster at the center of our galaxy. It was both fascinating and horrifying, at the same time.

And closest to them off to their right was an *old, red, bloated star*...

And right *beneath* them was a planet—shrouded with orange clouds, with vaguely visible red-looking continents beneath, and strange-looking greenish oceans.

They were in orbit around the planet.

Sally and Tommy looked at each other in astonishment.

"Well," Sally gulped, pausing before resolutely continuing, "first things first. How do we go outside our little square craft to manipulate the Mother Ship's controls?"

She saw, in the big chamber around them, many "stations" similar to the one in their small cannon-ship. Those stations were empty—covered with the same glittering diamond dust as in their small control room.

Clearly, the stations had not been "manned" for many years. If Tommy was accurate, they'd stood silent and unoccupied for *millions* of years!

"The air is too thin for you to breathe out there, Mommy," he said. "But as long as I don't stay too long I can go out and make manual changes. I can exit our entrance panel, quick so not to lose air. The tubes we've got below are still closed so Granny will be ok. Is that ok with you?"

"I don't like you going by yourself."

"Oh, I'll be fine, Mommy," he grinned. "See you in a bit!"

He popped over and kissed her on her cheek before sliding with a happy "*wheeeee!*" down the tunnel.

Then she saw him outside, scampering from panel to panel, kicking and brushing away dust, activating long-dormant controls.

He sure was handy to have around.

And then he was back, panting rapidly.

"Are you ok?" she asked with concern, brushing the clinging diamond dust off of his cute little red jumpsuit.

"Yes, I just need some air," he gasped, gulping like a fish out of water. "I guess I require more oxygen than I thought, after all," he snorted, looking embarrassed at his prior inaccurate prediction. "But I got the Mother Ship to stop trying to open up the tubes in the storage chamber, Mommy. The people in them are safe now, but not for long. I could only get the ship to pause for new orders."

"Orders from where?"

"From someone down on that planet," he pointed.

Indeed, Sally saw a focused, polarized, BLUE LASER BEAM extending from down on the surface up through the orange clouds to intersect with their spaceship!

"So...if it doesn't get more orders—what happens next, do you think?" Sally asked her plucky little android.

His outstretched, pointed arm shifted from pointing at the planet below to what was now off at a distance behind the slowly spinning Harvester ship.

"*That's* where the Mother Ship's going to toss its tubes," he gulped, his big blue eyes stretched wide.

He was pointing to the gleaming accretion disc.

"It's going to throw all the tubes into the Black Hole?" Sally gasped, horrified.

"If it doesn't get new orders, then yes..."

"Well, we'd best have a little talk with whoever is down there!" Sally said, looking again at the foreboding planet.

"And you won't do it without *me*," a stern voice sounded from behind Sally.

Sally whirled around...

"Mom!" Sally grinned, running over to embrace the white-hooded, thin figure.

Sally vaguely noticed that Samantha Smith was holding a big black pistol—as were her four similarly dressed companions climbing up behind her.

"The High Priestess said something like this might happen," Samantha flatly stated, her eyes narrowing. "That's why she asked for volunteers to be 'captured'. But I never expected to see you here, Sally! I thought you were off with your boyfriend David, making more of those evil DE-generators in that so-called 'secret' government research lab under Cheyenne Mountain in Colorado where..."

For a moment Sally was dumbfounded. Things were moving too fast!

"What?" Sally replied, flustered. "He's *not* my boyfriend! He's just my colleague. And what's this about Cheyenne Mountain? I thought that was a moth-balled nuclear attack bunker, left over from the 20th Century's 'cold war'?"

Samantha was rapidly taking inventory of the craft and the viewscreen as she continued to speak.

"The Church has spies in the government, Sally. We know that they're trying to make *Dark Energy Bombs* at Cheyenne Mountain.

And the last briefing I got before letting myself and my squad get caught by the Reapers was that *you* were there helping them in their evil pursuit. DE-missiles will be an *abomination* in the Creator's eyes. Such a hideous offence will bring upon us the full Wrath of God!"

Samantha's intense voice filled Sally with confusion.

"But I didn't... Dave and I only released the specs to the world to do with as they saw fit. And then I was on my way back to visit you from the United Nations when the Alien Fleet descended and I got snatched away to the reptile world...and...?"

"Oh my God—*no!*" Samantha huffed, pushing Sally off from her. "You're speaking nonsense. That never happened. You practically disowned me when I got fed up with how the world was going and I joined the Church of Perpetual Health. You thought that I was stupid for even questioning the use of that evil 'Dark Energy'. We had a big fight! And then you went off to help Dave and the government in their evil pursuits."

"But...there wasn't time for any of that to happen. I don't re-member any of this. It's only been a few days since the aliens at-tacked us and..."

But then again, she recalled the enigma of this Harvester having collected millions of humans in the "few hours" of her time on the Dinosapien Earth...

"Sally, it's been several *years* since the Invasion."

Say what? Years? Really?

Sally distinctly remembered going to the far future—being on Mars when it was destroyed...shooting that oriental woman at the United Nations, Sanako—did it all somehow happen *again?* Was she in one of those "time-loops"? Was there *another* Sally out there?

Was this *really* her Mother?

And how the hell could she have been with Dave at some under-ground military research facility in Colorado? She'd never even been to Cheyenne Mountain!

"Even if that were true, how could you be mad at me for working in the Cheyenne Base trying to find a way to stop the Harvesters?"

"Silly girl, there's more at stake here than just a measly alien inva-sion."

"What?"

"I've already told you what's at stake. Can't you believe me? I'm your mother! The best we can do for humanity's survival is take charge of one of these Harvesters and use its weapons to *stop* the research program deep underneath Cheyenne Mountain!"

"You're not making any sense, Mom."

"That's the mission of me and my squad. We're not here to stop the aliens. Destroying one Harvester won't do that. But the Harvesters *weapons* just might stop the greater problem. So we've got to..."

Sally shook her head in bewilderment, "tuning out" Samantha's shrill warnings.

Was this warrior-priest-lady really her stay-at-home, ordinary mother? But it didn't matter. This Samantha Smith was at least "a" mother of hers, and she was "a" daughter of hers. The two of them were here, together. And they faced a colossal, unknown threat down on the planet's surface.

Whatever the actual time-lineage, though, it was sufficient to confirm a familial relation. After all, according to Tommy, Sally and Samantha's DNA matched up. This was likely as close Sally would get to discover a blood relative 26,000 light-years from Earth!

"Mommy, can I say hello to Granny?" Tommy said, shyly pulling on Sally's pants leg.

Sally was glad to focus on something concrete, reaching down to pat his tousled blond locks.

"You have a *child?*" Samantha gasped, stopping her tirade at this unexpected interruption. She looked down at the cute little boy grinning up at her. "And...*I*...have a grandson? How is this possible?"

"It's a *long* story, Mom," Sally simply stated. Then she turned and climbed back into the oversized control chair of the cannon-craft. "For now, we're 'on the clock'—to save the millions of humans still sleeping out there in their pods. That's our immediate task. We've got a slice of humanity right here under our care. You and your friends better get into seats and hold on tight."

"Where are we going? We need to stay on the Harvester and try to gain control of..." Samantha said as she jutted out her jaw in stern determination for an answer.

"Mom, *I'm* the captain of this ship! Please sit down!"

Samantha Smith had always been a pain of a mother, strict and focused: as in "narrow minded" and dictatorial. Sally found a little satisfaction putting her in her place.

Muttering angrily, Samantha and her companions found seats as ordered.

"We're descending to the planet below to have a little talk with whatever is controlling this Harvester," Sally explained, preparing to steer their smaller craft back to the light tunnel to then locate an exit from the Harvester.

The other, white-hooded women clutched their black pistols tightly. They seemed prepared for action. This was clearly a prepared and eager "hit" squad.

Sally grinned. Regardless of the changes in the timeline, she was *here*...and angry!

Whatever awaited them below was in for a *rude* surprise.

She was coming with an army of *nuns*.

Beware, Aliens below...*beware!*

Ivanna was stunned.

She'd patiently listened to the High Priestess tell her incredible story in silence—resisting the urge to ask many, many questions.

It was completely dark outside. Through the thick glass of the observation window, brilliant stars glittered in the black night sky.

Safe and warm inside, Ivanna felt like she'd been twisted into a pretzel, fired to the ends of the galaxy, then plopped back into her chair a radically different person!

Her mind was ablaze with completely new paradigms and possibilities.

"So what do you think?" The High Priestess asked, sighing. "I won't fault you for not believing a word of my story. In fact, I find it quite fantastic myself. And if I weren't sitting here with you trying to figure a way to stop an alien invasion from outer space, I'd think myself insane as well. But I'm here. So are you. And I hardly think my story is any more incredible than the reality we both face."

The middle-aged woman paused, idly fingering the spiked gold medallion that hung around her neck.

Ivanna took a deep breath, trying to clear her head. With a shaky hand she lifted the cup of hot chocolate to her lips, but then set it back on the end table. The cup was cold.

"Alright then," Ivanna said, "let me see if I have this straight. You say that you are from another Dimension, a parallel-Earth, if you will. You say that you are another version of this planet's Sally. David brought you to my Dimension via a mysterious resonance with your Turtle Tattoo. The both of you fought against different groups of time travelers from the future, interacting with me and Victor along the way in other timelines?"

"That's correct," the High Priestess answered.

"And you say this...*time-war*...is all because of Dark Energy usage—*excess* usage, you say—in this particular Dimension of Earth, which causes the Creator of the Universe to turn his full attention on us, pass judgment on us, and condemn us to extinction just a few years in the future?" Ivanna continued.

"Sadly, that is also true," the middle-aged woman nodded.

"And," Ivanna persisted, "You could have killed Dave to prevent this from happening. But an intelligent giant Snake from yet another doomed Earth-linked Dimension gave you an alternative: to go back in time and re-inhabit your earlier body and try again from within a new timeline?"

"Also correct," Linda agreed.

"And so in this second go-around, you accidently took a detour back to the 12th Century to spend a few years with a remarkable nun—that incidentally prepared you to start take a new name, start a new religion, and become a successful High Priestess warring against excess Dark Energy usage?" Ivanna stated, struggling to come to grips with these fantastic notions.

"It was indeed a remarkable experience," the woman sighed, looking solemn.

"As such, then, you were doing ok stopping the need for DE-generators until the Alien Invaders showed up and threw a monkey wrench into everything?" Ivanna continued.

"It was disappointing," she agreed.

"But, you say, even now there's still time to squash DE over-usage and push off our Day of Judgment until our race is more mature.

However, if we fire the DE-bomb-tipped missiles against the Harvesters, then that massive cosmic blast of concentrated Dark Energy resonating back throughout subspace will guarantee God notices us, judges us, and destroy us? Well now...did I get everything right?" Ivanna skeptically concluded.

The middle-aged woman laughed.

"Well, when put in those terms—it sounds crazy even to *me!*" the High Priestess laughed. Then, more soberly, she continued. "You got the main features correct, Ivanna. So—if you believe my story—the Aliens above us aren't the real problem. They're just a distraction. Our priority isn't saving our civilization. It's saving the entire human species from extinction! I know it's a huge leap of faith, *believe* me. I had a real hard time with this also. But after at least two timeline changes that I know of...it is horribly, chillingly real."

"So...what do we do now, *Sally?*" Ivanna quietly asked, leaning forward in her chair.

Her back hurt. She'd been sitting in one place for far too long.

"You believe me?"

"Well, if you'd told me just one piece of that story then I'd thought you were nuts—and conspired with my two commando friends to put you out of your misery."

"But...?"

"But unless you happen to be a professional science-fiction writer—maybe the best SF writer or all time—then it's just too fantastic and internally consistent to *not* be true."

The High Priestess visibly relaxed in her chair.

"I knew you were a true friend from the first time I met you," Sally said, reaching over and taking the elderly woman's hand in her own.

Ivanna squeezed the woman's hand back. Then she released it, all business.

"So how are we going to stop the launch of those missiles?"

"Not we—*you*, Ivanna," Sally firmly stated.

"Uh...then just how am *I* going to do it?"

"We're going to get you back into the Cheyenne Mountain base, with a bug that will infect their computer systems and freeze those missiles in place."

"Oh, *are* we now?"

"I have a number of other 'Temples' around the world—some with still-functioning super-computers," Sally stated. "And I have the proliferative seedpods of my evolved, intelligent programs right here with me. All you have to do is swallow a pill and they'll move into your blood stream, cross the blood-brain barrier, and infect your brain."

"How marvelous..." Ivanna sarcastically gulped.

"You won't feel a thing," Sally assured her. "Then they'll lie dormant and undetectable in your brain—an incredibly sophisticated biological computer capable of housing them—until you touch any of the computers linked into your base's systems. From there, they'll instantly analyze and migrate into your control network, take it over, and destroy any programs involved in launching those missiles. Thusly we can prevent humanity from engaging the full attention of God! Then we can ride-out this alien 'salvage' operation and try to get humanity back on track."

"Victor will be so disappointed," Ivanna sighed, thinking of the hard work he and many others had put into making the Dark Energy warheads for the missiles.

But, then again, Victor had often told her in private how horrified he was at being forced to do the very thing he'd tried to prevent from happening in the first place—weaponizing concentrated Dark Energy generation!

So maybe he wouldn't be so mad after all, especially when she told him the fantastic story of what was really happening. Oh my, would he ever enjoy learning about new dimensions and timelines! It was right up his 'theoretical physics' alleyway.

"But Sally," Ivanna frowned. "It's impossible to get back into the base. We collapsed the exit tunnel. And even if there were another way to get in, President Swartz would never believe this bizarre story. It's way beyond her capacity to conceive. She's a scientist, yes—but she's a *biologist*, for God's sake!"

The middle-aged Sally again laughed.

"You don't have to be a physicist like your husband or sociologist like yourself or mathematician like me to appreciate 'science-fiction' stories, Ivanna," Sally chortled. But then Ivanna saw her expression turn dead serious. "But you are absolutely right. This is too critical to the survival of the human race to rest upon one person's shoulders, surviving President or not. So you'll just have to go around her. Get to one of the internal computers and touch it. Don't try to explain to anyone what's happening until it's done."

"Alright—but how do I get back in?"

"We'll *make* a new entrance."

"Oh...right...but even if that succeeds—then how will I get my commandos to go along with this? They're determined to keep the base totally protected, sealed shut."

"They will do so voluntarily—since both you and they will be escaping my 'evil' clutches."

"Ahhhhh...." Ivanna nodded. "How clever—you really do make a good High Priestess, Sally."

"Thank you, Professor—coming from you that is indeed a high compliment."

"When do we start?"

"We already have."

"What?"

"Your commandos, I believe, have overcome their 'colleagues'—got the drop on them then tied them up—and are right now taking over the communication array. They are, as we speak, preparing to send a tight burst into your waiting base's hidden antennas to expect their return."

"So that's why you 'allowed' them so generously to keep their weapons and be unguarded in a research facility separate from us?"

"That's correct," Sally nodded. "They are likely informing your President of their plan to grab some of our 'super-guns' and use them to reopen the tunnel back into the base."

"So they think I've gotten 'secret' information out of you to justify my physically returning to the base?"

"It's even better than that..." Sally said, hesitating dramatically.

Ivanna grinned at her theatrics.

"Oh, please tell me, Sally."

"They're going to *capture me* and take me back with you for a proper military 'interrogation'! They think I'm in league with the Aliens above us, with possible knowledge of their weapons and weaknesses."

"But...assuming they'd believe such a lie, wouldn't you going along with that scheme be dangerous to you?"

"I don't care, Ivanna," Sally stated. "I didn't come all this way through space and time to sit safe on Pike's Peak while the world crumbles around me. I'll be the diversion—which they'll focus upon. That'll leave you relatively free to carry out your mission. While I'm being interrogated *you* will stop the true threat."

"If everything goes according to plan...it just might work," Ivanna nodded thoughtfully. "There's a nice mix of intrigue and adventure. Are you sure you're not a Science Fiction writer? I think the President will 'buy' your cover-story. And our military folks will just *love* it—what with all its heroics, spies, and such."

"So it's a 'go'?" Sally asked. "To succeed it needs your complete support. Without it I'm prepared to abort the plan, try something else."

"Yes!" Ivanna strongly agreed.

"Then let's shake on it," Sally said, stretching out her hand which Ivanna again firmly gripped.

"So..." Ivanna pondered, leaning back in her chair, "is there time for a fresh cup of hot chocolate for me—and another tankard of iced tea for you—before my heroic commandos 'rescue' me and 'capture' you, plus snaring a sack of your super-guns?"

"If not, we'll make the time," Sally said, standing up and exiting the room to give instructions to an attending Priestess.

Sally quickly returned with more iced tea plus a fresh, steaming cup of hot chocolate for Ivanna—plus *a large red capsule.*

"Are you sure this won't hurt me?" Ivanna asked, reluctant to let a foreign intelligent "evolved" computer program into her brain.

"No, Professor, you won't feel a thing," Sally said, drinking deeply from her own large glass of iced tea. "Just think of it as powerful sociological medicine—designed to thwart the biggest peril mankind has ever faced."

"Ok..."

Ivanna took a deep breath and swallowed the big pill, washing it down with the delicious hot chocolate.

"Remember, Professor Petrovich," Sally sternly warned her in her best "High Priestess" manner, "The stakes can't be higher. To stop those missiles you must be ready to do *anything!*"

"Anything?"

"If 'plan A' doesn't succeed, then make a Plan B."

That sounded ominous.

Ivanna didn't know if she completely accepted Sally's fantastic story about God's impending condemnation of the human race. But Sally seemed completely sincere. Regardless, it gave Ivanna a valid excuse to try and stop the launch of those awful missiles.

She'd always felt they were a horrible, tragic mistake.

Societies' dependence on using overwhelming force against their enemies could only win temporary victories. The real victories were won through assimilation and transformation. The best solution to their societal problem with God—if it did in fact exist—had to be another alternative, one that neither she nor Sally had yet considered.

What that permanent solution might be, she had no idea. But Ivanna knew that evading God was *not* possible.

After all, Sally was attempting to figuratively *spit in the eye of God!* Ivanna was not a particularly religious person, but she knew enough of cosmological science to recognize how young and naïve the human race must be in the universe.

Perhaps, if asked sweetly, God might yet cut his youngsters a break?

Ivanna wondered if she might yet find a way to help Sally see an even bigger picture.

It *wasn't* too late.

The one advantage of youth—in being a monkey species just down from swinging in the trees—is that there's always more *time!*

But, then again, Ivanna realized she was thinking from the perspective of a human crawling on a tiny speck of rock circling one tiny star out of billions of billions of billions.

She realized that from her perspective a lifespan of a hundred years was a great achievement. But in God's reality her lifespan was likely just a flicker.

Ivanna was again tempted to sincerely and humbly *pray*...

—but that would be admitting defeat.

And she was too proud to let that happen.

"Plan A" had a good chance to succeed.

And there was always the yet unformed "Plan B"...which she was sure would involve physical conflict.

Ah, it's so sad to have a monkey brain, she sighed to herself. *Instead of seeking true Divine Inspiration even I—one of the most educated and "enlightened" of humans—prefer violence.*

It chastened her to realize that put in the wrong situation at the wrong time with the wrong information with the wrong motivations...*anyone* was capable of *anything*, even murder.

Chapter 11

KILLING JESUS

Oh you poor, destroyed man
Hanging there on that bloody cross
Gasping out your last, tortured breaths
For people who don't even know you
Or who jeer and mock you from below
Applauding and cheering your sacrifice
A selfish means to avoid their own guilt
Is it really the Salvation of Mankind
Or just the start of humanity's decline?
Before they could claim their ignorance
But now they've lost that weak defense
Falling on their knees in abject fear
Begging and praying for undeserved mercy
Wanting to be given everything for nothing
Unwilling to move beyond shortsightedness
Still driven by fear, greed, and insecurity
Knowing that they can never be justified
They laugh, jeer, and call for more blood
Killing you they condemned themselves
And insure their ultimate punishment
Not for sin or malice, but for stupidity
Refusing to recognize or even appreciate
That their greatest Enemy was within
And their highest Quest was impossible
To rip out their own bloody hearts

> *And saturate them with Heavenly Light*
> *Migrating to their unsuspecting eyes*
> *Infusing a Divine Blindness...*
> **The Luminary Chronicles, 11:57-63**

Sally knew the end was drawing near.

Nearly two years had passed since Jesus' berserk initial cleansing of the Temple.

As he traveled and preached around Palestine, the cheering crowds grew ever larger. First there were hundreds, then thousands, then tens of thousands in attendance at his rallies. And as his popularity with the people increased to superstar status, so did the hatred directed against him from the established Jewish religious hierarchy.

It culminated in his triumphal return to Jerusalem, riding into the city on the back of a young donkey! It was the fulfilment of an ancient Jewish prophecy: that their King would come to the people as a lowly man of the people, riding "on the colt of a donkey." Expecting the advent of a new Kingdom, huge crowds ran before him spreading their clothes on the road, cutting branches from palm trees to smooth his path, and singing at the top of their voices, the combined *roar* reverberating throughout the city: "PRAISE BE TO THE SON OF DAVID! THE BLESSED ONE COMES IN THE NAME OF GOD! SING HIS PRAISES IN THE HIGHEST HEAVEN!"

Sally, following along behind Jesus in Mary's party, knew that she soon would have to do the unthinkable. To protect the future survival of mankind upon the earth, Jesus could *not* be allowed to die upon the cross. He must die *before* being raised up between heaven and earth!

Yet it was fitting that Jesus complete his triumphal return to Jerusalem. After all, this was where his long downward road had begun: at the Temple. For one last time he would have a furious debate with the Priests, Pharisees, and Sadducees.

Sally knew that Jesus was in essence *daring* his enemies to kill him. He marched with his crowds of adoring thousands straight into his opponents' clutches.

There was no way that the established religious hierarchy could ignore his provocations. Their entire prestige, wealth, and self-identity hung in the balance.

Ostensibly Jesus was returning from his widespread campaign to celebrate the Passover in Jerusalem. This was a Holy time in which the Jewish people yearly celebrated their past deliverance from slavery in Egypt. According to the Torah, the enslaved Jews escaped the Wrath of God upon the Egyptian rulers when they sprinkled the blood of slaughtered lambs upon their doorframes.

Sally found it ironic that she'd been saved in the desert by Jesus' family returning from their exile in Egypt.

But now she regarded the traditional feast with dread.

It marked the end of Jesus' ministry and his own "sacrifice" upon the cross, ushering in the Age of Christianity.

And she'd still not accomplished her obscene mission...

Jesus' last Passover ceremony was a solemn affair. Sally helped the other women serve Jesus and his twelve apostles as the men ate in a secluded upper room. The apostles knew that Jesus was putting his life on the line, confronting his most rabid enemies directly and powerfully at the most "high profile" time of the Jewish year. But Sally knew from the side-conversations she overheard that his disciples figured Jesus would work yet another miracle and escape. She listened intently as he instructed them otherwise, teaching them their final lessons concerning humility, service in his name, and the requirement of atoning sacrifice. When it became apparent that Jesus was speaking of his own fate, his twelve apostles loudly bragged that they would follow him to the bitter end, even if it meant their own deaths as well.

Jesus only sighed, looking at them with compassion in his eyes. Sally knew that *he* knew that they meant well, but didn't yet have the guts to do the hard things. After his death and resurrection, Sally knew that Jesus' followers would be tougher—largely because they'd failed so miserably when Jesus needed them the most. Except for John all his "macho" male followers would run and hide. Sally, cleaning up from the meal, marveled at how Jesus so exquisitely set the stage—for a massive revival of genuine Godliness that would eventually reach to all corners of the globe.

Sally longed to go to him, comfort him.

But he was already in his death mindset.

She had no opportunity to get close to him.

Later that evening, praying with just a few of his closest followers in the Garden of Gethsemane, Sally heard along with the other women that Jesus was captured. The next day he was put on trial and condemned by the Roman puppet, the governor Pontius Pilate, to crucifixion. Sally and the other women stayed as close to him as allowed by the Roman guards. The verdict was cheered by the Priests, Pharisees, Sadducees, and their rabid mob. But before Jesus would be nailed to the cross, he was first to be *scourged*...

Sally stood silently watching, along with Mary and the other women, as Jesus' back was methodically turned into raw hamburger.

Jesus had been first stripped of his clothing and tied to a post. A Roman soldier, expert in the vicious procedure, used a whip composed of several long thongs, each weighted with lead balls. The purpose of the beating was not to inflict welts but to *rip out the flesh*, right up to the point of killing the victim. The soldier was an expert at tearing out flesh, exposing the bowels of the victim, and causing incredible pain and profuse bleeding. Many victims of Roman scourging died. No further punishment was needed.

But in this case the torturer had orders to leave his victim alive, barely...

Sally was sickened by the horror of the proceedings, flinching with each wet "thud" of the heavily weighted "flagrum" as it tore into Jesus' naked back. The ground around the stake upon which Jesus was tied was quickly drenched in blood. He could not contain his terrible suffering—moaning, groaning, and crying-out uncontrollably. It seemed to Sally that the beating went on forever, long after Jesus was effectively unconscious. For lesser offences the Jews whipped their own members forty times. The Romans had no such limitations. They could go on as long as the sadistic practitioner wished.

When it was finally finished, the soldiers dragged Jesus' quivering, brutalized body away to a holding cell in the local prison— awaiting further humiliation and torture at the discretion of Pilate.

Sally wondered where were Jesus' many thousands of devoted followers, particularly those that had joyously celebrated his entrance into Jerusalem. At this brutal show of force by the Roman occupiers, Jesus' many devotees—who'd been wildly chanting his name as he entered Jerusalem just a few days before—melted away back into the city, nowhere to be seen. Sally watched in amazement as even Jesus' closest disciples, his twelve beloved apostles, *ran away.* Their bold claim of following him to the death was revealed to be mere macho bluster.

Only the women remained.

And Sally, as one of them, knew just what she had to do.

"I am going to him," Sally told Mary, gathering up clean towels and a small jug of water. "I will go into the prison and tend his grievous wounds."

"That is brave of you, Sahlee," Mary said, her tired voice trembling from overwhelming grief and exhaustion. "But they will never let you into the prison, particularly to assuage his pain. They *want* him to suffer without reprieve."

"I will bribe my way inside," Sally said, gathering up her gear.

Mary just nodded. Sally knew she was staunch in her loyalty to her son—but realizing she needed to stay away for now, in order to be present supporting him at the actual execution. She could not afford to be arrested or abused by the guards. So Mary allowed Sally to go in her place to the prison.

There, Sally confronted the outside guard.

He was a tough looking, gnarled big man. He had on an armored breastplate and helmet. He stood with crossed, burly arms—with a large sword hanging from a scabbard at his waist. He looked at her with cold, unblinking eyes as if accessing her value as a slut, a slave, or a victim.

"Sir," Sally respectfully addressed him, not meeting his eyes, looking submissively down at the ground. "I am a relative of Jesus, the prisoner who was just scourged. I am here to clean his wounds. Please would you take me to him?"

He laughed.

"Go away!" he ordered in a gruff voice.

"Please, Sir," Sally insisted. "I saw how badly he was beaten, to the point of death. If I do not stop the bleeding, he is sure to die in your care, before he can be crucified. I beg you as a loyal citizen to let me soothe his suffering—and also ensure that you and your loyal fellow soldiers are not punished for his premature death."

His eyes narrowed.

Sally knew that her request was reasonable. Jesus had been scourged far longer than normal. Pilate wanted to make an example of him, so that anyone even thinking of rising up against the Emperor would be chastened. This "King of the Jews" was to be humiliated in the worst possible ways, so that anyone else in the future wanting to rebel against the Roman occupiers would be too terrified to proceed.

The man was reluctantly nodding.

"I could get you in," he grunted. "But other guards inside might not be as kind as me to allow your safe passage to..."

"I will pay you," she stated flatly, taking the "hint." She raised her head to stare unblinkingly back into his cruel eyes.

"What, you a poor little servant girl?" he grimaced. "For me to do what you ask you'd have to be *rich*."

Sally had to hold her ire back, realizing that outwardly she still appeared to be a young teenager—thanks to the massive dose of retroviral immune modulators still coursing throughout her body.

She opened her pile of towels to reveal a concealed pile of glittering *gold coins!* In terms of first century money, it was a fortune.

The guard gasped at the sight of that much gold.

"Do you think this might be enough to recompense you for your favor to me, plus to bribe your fellow guards inside?" she meekly asked.

"Well...perhaps," he said, stroking his stubbly chin with an evil glint in his eye.

"And, Sir, to further reward you for guaranteeing me a whole uninterrupted hour with Jesus—when I exit unharmed my friends will give you an *equal* amount to thank you for my freedom," she innocently smiled up at him.

She was lying. The coins she'd shown him were all that she had. Since she had labored continually now in the first century for thirty-one years—and Mary had paid her all along, not much, but steadily—with few personal expenses she'd managed to accumulate a substantial "nest egg."

Now, she was cashing it all in.

The greed in the man's black eyes practically outshone the glow from the gold coins.

"I will do it—but your friends must be ready with the exit money or I will take my final payment out of *your flesh!*" he brutally spat at her, revealing a mouthful of yellowed, crooked teeth.

Sally pretended to cower.

"Yes, Sir," she nodded repeatedly. "The additional money will be here awaiting my safe exit from the prison after my hour with Jesus. I do appreciate your help, Sir! And I will make sure that the prisoner will survive until he is safely out of your responsibility. And now if you please—would you kindly accompany and guide me...?"

Glancing furtively around at the people out on the street, he grabbed the towel with the concealed coins and hustled her into the prison, motioning for another soldier to take his place at the gate.

As she was led past various other guards—each receiving a small bribe from the first overseer's large stash—she proceeded deeper and deeper into the dark dungeon.

It was so terrible that she almost asked to turn back.

She struggled not to vomit.

It *stank* horrendously from urine, feces, and rotting flesh. *Moans* from tortured prisoners were pervasive in the stale, dank air. Trembling, clawing hands *reached out at her* from cells as the guards hurried her deeper and deeper into the maze. She cringed back from the grasping, filthy digits as their owners alternatively begged her for help or demanded the use of her young body.

And then they were finally at the cell that held Jesus.

It was tiny but secluded—with a thick door keeping him locked up securely. As a high-value political prisoner he was being kept isolated from the other inmates.

"*One* hour, no longer," the last guard curtly snapped at her, unlocking the door and shoving her inside before slamming it shut and locking it behind her. "The Governor is bringing this prisoner back before the people later today," he laughed through the closed door. "Be quick about what you do!"

Only a single, small candle burned within, set upon a holder on a stone shelf—around which buzzed a cloud of flies.

By its dim yellow light Sally saw Jesus.

"Oh, my Lord," she gasped, falling to her knees beside him.

Sally wept.

Jesus lay naked on his chest on the stone floor, his head turned away from her, his arms extended out limply. His long hair was matted with congealed blood. His neck, back, and buttocks were hideously torn and shredded. Hunks of meat hung off his body. Sally could see amongst the gore the glint of white bone, the shattered evidence of broken ribs and a fractured spine. At his waist a coil of bloated, purple intestines protruded. A massive amount of blood was pooled around his body. Buzzing flies busily fed on his raw flesh. The stench was unbearable.

His breathing was shallow and labored.

Clearly, he was dying.

Sally realized that her daring expedition into the prison hadn't been necessary. This man would not live long enough to be further displayed before his enemy's paid-off rabid mob, let alone make it to the crucifixion.

He was already lost to history...just another dissident ruthlessly killed by the Roman occupiers.

Sally realized this must have been what happened in her Dimension, in which Jesus failed to make a continuing impact, lost to history. But here, for some reason, he survived prison to die on the cross. Whatever the difference between the two Dimensions, she had the opportunity to make sure that his life ended in this stinking cell.

Sally knew she had only time to say goodbye—but was resolved to complete the mission that had brought her more than two thousand years into the past.

She tenderly touched one of his savaged shoulders as her tears flowed down her cheeks.

His flesh felt rigid and cold.

She feared he was already dead.

"Sah...lee..." she heard a faint whisper. He struggled to turn his head to look at her, but couldn't.

"I am here, Jesus," she gulped, bringing her tears under control.

"You...should...n-not...have...c-come..." he managed to gasp out, each word a torture. "I...d-don't...want...you...h-hurt..."

She put her towels to the side, took the lid off of her small jug of water, reached into it with her small hand, and pulled out a concealed *sharp knife.*

It was an awful deception...precious water used to hide a murder weapon.

It was hardly the "water of life."

In the dark, dank cell—hearing awful screams and incoherent ravings of other tortured prisoners off at a distance—Sally forced herself to remember her larger mission. Despite what looked like fatal wounds, she must *make absolutely certain* that Jesus never left this cell alive!

She angrily brushed her tears away, clearing her sight to do what must be done.

But, at this moment of truth, Sally unexpectedly found her resolve wavering...

Was this really the right thing to do?

Especially in the face of his terrible condition, did she also need to slit his throat? As it was, he'd die a hero to the people, killed by a savage Roman scourging. If not having a world-wide effect on into the future, he'd at least have brief local fame. For her to execute him with her knife might unleash vile rumors of a "rejected lover's" revenge.

Did she really need to chance besmirching his sterling reputation?

But Sally forced herself to remember that despite his magnificent teachings, his many amazing deeds, and his charismatic presence—Jesus was indeed a radical instigator who threatened not just the social fabric of his own time, but Earth's future societies as well. Sally knew full well—from having seen it with her own two eyes—that the obvious positives of his nascent new religion would paradoxically result in unspeakable horror: the *incineration* of the entire human race at the *Day of Judgment!*

Indeed, even *he* had acknowledged the truth of this inevitable outcome in his apocalyptic preaching.

And yet Jesus was not a monster against whom Sally could easily weld a knife. He was a fellow human being, already weakly writhing in agony. And he was also a kind, loving teacher of Godly Principles. Plus he was the closest thing that Sally ever had to a brother. And, finally, he was a man that she sincerely *loved.*

Did she really *have* to kill him?

Then, suddenly, she saw the answer to her dilemma as a Divine Revelation: a *Vision* seemingly straight from the Almighty!

She resolutely made up her mind.

"You won't have to suffer any longer," she said, steeling her voice. "I am here to grant you mercy."

"*Don't*...d-do it..." he whispered.

"I have to," she calmly stated.

Jesus tried to raise himself on his hands but could not. Instead, he managed to turn his head, exposing his neck to Sally's knife.

"My F-Father does not...need...your h-help..." he grated, helplessly looking up at her.

His face was encrusted with gore and mud. Beneath the clinging filth the flesh of his face was bruised and swollen. Clearly he'd been brutally beaten as well as scourged.

But in the dim, flickering candlelight his *large brown eyes* were the one part of his body unharmed. They opened wide. They revealed an immense sadness, seemingly peering into Sally's soul.

"I believe I am an instrument of God," she whispered back to him, leaning close. "I'm doing what is necessary."

A faint smile touched his swollen mouth.

"Then do...what y-you m-must..." he whispered through cracked, bloody lips. "We will...meet again, my b-beloved Sahlee..."

"I doubt that, my dear friend," she replied, tears again obscuring her vision.

He closed his eyes.

He was unconscious, his ragged breathing slowing precipitously.

He was near death.

Sally leaned in yet closer over his ripped-apart, still massively bleeding back. She carefully positioned her knife at a throbbing neck artery.

Then—in a precise surgical stroke—she sliced it open.

Laying her head firmly down upon his excoriated back, she allowed the blood streaming *from her own neck* to soak into his exposed tissues.

She knew that the huge dose of retroviral immune enhancers still coursing through her body would infect him. Spilled out upon his ravaged back, the active ingredients would easily mingle with his flesh and permeate into his tissues.

"Forgive me, Jesus," she whispered as she strove with one hand to keep the cut wide open and flowing for as long as possible.

It actually didn't hurt that much as she felt her life blood draining out onto the sticky, warming flesh quivering beneath her cheek. It was comforting to know that she was merging her body with his. Indeed, she had finally succeeded in "seducing" him despite his religious convictions to the contrary. Hah! But she was also heartbroken to cause him further suffering—and bitterly angry at herself.

Her last, fading thought was the painful realization that she had failed in her mission.

This "enemy of the State"—Jesus the Nazarene—would recover sufficiently from his scourging to make it to the cross.

She hoped that the brutal guards would be happy, despite losing their promised second installment of gold coins.

After all, they, *un*like her, had done their duty.

"So you're not a follower of Jesus?" Ivanna asked the High Priestess.

They were sitting side-by-side in the school bus as it rocketed through the night sky back in the direction of Colorado Springs.

"We of the CPH 'worship' Science," the High Priestess dully replied, her mouth swollen from being punched in her face.

She held out the spiked gold medallion swinging on its chain around her neck.

"This is what's real to us, the power of the Sun," she sighed. "We reject myths and superstition while still holding up the highest aspirations and values of what we term 'godliness'."

"But Jesus wasn't just a myth," Ivanna continued, probing Sally's religious beliefs.

"Yes, he did exist," she grimly nodded. "But I sometimes wonder if he'd never made a mark on history how much better off we might be."

Sergeant Grant, holding his rifle on Sally from across the short aisle, grunted in anger at her disrespect.

"Oh, I'm sorry, soldier," she politely nodded at him. "Was that offensive to you?"

"Yes, Ma'am, it was," he curtly stated.

"And why is that?"

"Jesus is the Son of God!" he fervently replied. "He came to save the world. He gave up everything—a family, his life, possessions, and money—to die on a cross to save us from our sins. He paid the price for our sins. Without Jesus we would be lost. Saying we'd be better off without Jesus is just crazy."

"So *you* are a Christian?" Sally asked, seeming genuinely interested.

"I am a Catholic," he stated proudly.

"Well, isn't that sweet," she mildly replied, rubbing her swollen jaw. "And are all Catholics as good as you...at hitting women?"

The young soldier glared at her.

"So you believe in a God?" Ivanna asked Sally, hurriedly changing the subject from her commando's "capture" of the High Priestess.

Ivanna was maintaining the pretense that the Major and Sergeant had cleverly, entirely on their own, overcome their guards, snuck back into the Temple by their own cunning, evaded the sleeping Priestesses, cold-clocked the High Priestess, rescued Ivanna, and stolen a basketful of the powerful black guns—because they were such great and clever warriors!

Being typical arrogant men, they had no idea that their "daring escape" was staged.

One of the Priestess was (supposedly) being forced to fly the rocket-powered old school bus back to Colorado Springs.

"Oh, we of the CPH certainly do believe in God," the middle-aged Sally sighed, looking out at nighttime stars as the flying bus dipped lower, descending back toward the World Stadium's crushed remains. "But the true 'God' is far different and greater than the little religions of this world can imagine."

"How so?" Ivanna asked, continuing her "interrogation" so that the two commandos would not expect her of any collusion with the High Priestess.

"The Creator of the Universe is so far above us that to Him we are but specks on specks on specks on specks on specks—you get the idea—far below His regular notice! And His *Standards for Success* of a self-and-God-aware intelligent biological species are more than we could ever hope to achieve, at least in our present state."

"That's just why Jesus is so important," the young Sergeant Grant insisted from across the aisle, emphatically inserting himself back into the conversation. "Jesus sacrificed himself in place of us. He paid the price for *our* sins! That's how we get to go to God even though we are unworthy."

"Grant, just guard the prisoner, would you?" Major Cotrell coolly ordered him, glancing back from where the Major sat with his rifle right behind the Priestess "bus driver".

"Right," the High Priestess continued, ignoring the Major to still address his younger comrade. "And so your religions justify even the most terrible and evil things—raping your own planet for short-term selfish gain, killing those who believe slightly differently from you on religious matters, doing all manner of harm to each other—because your 'sins' will be 'washed away in the blood of the savior'? I tell you, young soldier, that if you just *killed* this Jesus and concentrated instead on being a better person, the world would be far safer *today!*"

"Is that why you made a deal with the Aliens?" Major Cotrell coldly replied from the front of the bus, dragged into the conversation despite his own admonitions. "You think most of us humans are just ugly scum to be wiped away, leaving behind you and your little band of God-hating fanatics?"

"I have made no such deal with the Aliens," Sally insisted.

"Oh, and they leave you alone in your little flying buses and Temples just by accident?" the Major gruffly laughed. "I don't think so! I assure you that you'll spill your guts when we get you back to the base. You might as well save yourself the pain and tell us right now what we want to know."

"I've got nothing more to say on that subject," she coldly replied, fingering her gold medallion while looking out the window.

They were almost down.

Outside there should have been blazing nighttime lights of a vibrant downtown Colorado Springs.

Instead, there were only scattered fires glowing evilly in the dark...

*Very fitting, those fires—*Ivanna sadly thought to herself. *If we actually make it back to the base it'll be so I can just sabotage it. I am myself a destructive force to those I owe the most.*

She didn't want to do it.

But she didn't know what else to do. Despite their invoking a "Plan B" she had no idea what it could be.

"Plan A" must succeed!

Maybe this older Sally was right—they had to hide from God, at least until the human race evolved into something better many millennia in the future. But the young Sergeant was also correct. Jesus was more than just a myth. He was *aspirational*—perhaps too much so. There was no way that any individual human could live up to his radical teachings, his extreme example. And better than offering false hope of empty salvation—is knowledge of one's own glaring faults.

At least then one really knows where one is starting from—what to try and fix.

Yet Ivanna knew that she had to live *down* to the lowest standards of a *traitor!*

And it hurt.

Chapter 12

DEFYING GOD

There are wise old sayings:
"Don't pull on Superman's cape"
And "Don't spit into the wind"
Or "Don't eat the yellow snow"
So why do people so love to swear
Using the Creator's name so cavalierly
As if "God" were only a compliant Robot
There to fulfill our every wish and command
Instead of an unconceivable, unknowable Mystery
Substantiating while validating our very existence
That we see, touch, and feel every moment of the day
Unaware that Energy, Space, and Time remain undefined
The fundamental units considered safely in our control
When in reality we are but lost, ignorant, and stupid
Ants crawling blissfully in our constraining cage
Thinking that all that can be known we can know
That our ultimate Fate is in our own hands
Not at the whim of some unknown "God"
A Deity we can casually ignore
Or (why not?) misdirect...
The Luminary Chronicles, 12:153-158

"Can you get us down to the surface of that planet?" Sally asked Tommy, abruptly realizing that her rudimentary ability to steer the cannon-craft wasn't sufficient to the job.

"Sure!" he laughed, hopping into the oversized control seat as she slid out of it. Then he happily grabbed at knobs and switches, his hands moving faster than Sally could follow.

"How does that child know to...?" Samantha gasped, fixing her stern gaze on the cheerful little boy.

"He's a robot, Mom," Sally said, slipping into another of the big seats beside her mother. "Actually, he's not a metallic beast like those awful Reapers who captured you and the other ladies...but a biological-computational hybrid, an 'android' if you will."

"Why does he call you his mother?"

"Well, in a sense I am—I suppose I created the initial intelligent programs that eventually became his mind."

"You suppose?"

"Just watch the viewscreen," Sally misdirected her. "I think we're in for a real treat."

Tommy expertly steered them back into the yellow tunnel, returning the cannon-ship to the vast storage chamber where the millions of tubes still hung suspended, then to a huge airlock from which they exited into the blackness of outer space.

Far below, the viewscreen showed orange-swirling clouds covering a red continent. Piercing through the clouds to the orbiting, huge Harvester ship was a single, glaring, BRIGHT BLUE LASER BEAM!

It was a beacon.

"*That's* where we're going," Sally said to Tommy, pointing at the laser beam.

"Ok, Mommy," he grinned, his small hands flying amongst the controls, steering the boxy craft to suddenly *plunge* into the orange clouds below them.

"*Wheeeeeeeee!*" he gleefully called-out as they *slammed* into the atmosphere, *blazing fire* springing up all around them as the air was superheated by their passage.

The craft rocked back and forth violently as they plunged ever deeper into the atmosphere.

"The child is going to kill us!" Samantha called-out over the ROAR of their fiery descent.

"Tommy! Can you go slower?" Sally asked him as they were whipped-around in their downward plunge...

—when they suddenly emerged beneath the acrid orange clouds: grandly arching downward instead of plunging, leveling off to then speed across a broken, crater-scared, rocky plain.

Great gashes and canyons stood out on the viewscreen. Nowhere was there any hint of greenery or other evidence of life.

To Sally it looked like the surface of Mars.

"Is that better, Mommy?" Tommy grinned at the controls. "This square spaceship doesn't glide too well."

"You did a great job getting us down," Sally complimented him, although she had new bruises on her body from being slung around so violently during their descent. "Can you land us beside the source of the laser beam that's beaming up into space?"

"Sure!" he said as they approached what appeared to be an *ancient, towering Temple...*

—sporting mile-high transparent columns, of strange spiral shapes that went at odd angles! It was gigantic, the size of a large city on Earth. At the top of the columns was a supported, flat plateau made from the same transparent material.

As they fast approached it, Sally saw on the center of the flat plateau the source of the huge, pulsating blue laser beam: a house-sized, shimmering *blue globe* stuck partially down into the supporting platform.

Sally gasped, undoing her seatbelt to stumble over to where her knapsack lay on the floor.

She pulled out her own blue sphere.

It was *shimmering,* pulsing in tune with the rhythms of the blue laser beamed up into space. Somehow it was linked...

"My lizard friends were prescient—or maybe knowledgeable of whatever aliens await us," she whispered to herself.

She grabbed her own sphere tightly as she scrambled again to her seat and buckled herself back in. Her small sphere spread out a subtle blue light around them all, as if protecting them.

"Hang on Mommy, Granny, and Friends!" Tommy sang-out loudly.

Tommy was bringing them in for a *hard landing...*

—as with a loud BANG they dropped the last few feet in free fall, *bouncing* once before settling jarringly but safely down!

Shaken-up but otherwise unhurt, the women relaxed—looking out the viewscreen at the house-sized blue sphere looming right in front of them.

"Let's go say hello!" Tommy cheerfully exclaimed, hopping from his seat to head for the exit.

"Wait!" Sally ordered him. "We don't even know about the air out there, whether we can..."

"Oh, it's fine," Tommy called back. "It's thick with sulfur—but there's plenty of oxygen."

"What's he saying, Sally?" Samantha suspiciously asked.

"He says it stinks but it won't kill you," she answered. She grabbed her knapsack, depositing the sphere safely back into it. Then she followed the impulsive child down the tunnel to the small cargo hold.

Behind her came the other women.

As the entrance panel pulled to the side, they exited.

The air was indeed hot, thick, and repulsive—like standing next to a belching volcano—but it was breathable. The surface at their feet was perfectly smooth. It was difficult to walk without slipping and falling.

But Tommy raced ahead to the house-sized Sphere—placing his small hands on its upwardly curving surface in awe.

It was similar to Sally's small blue globe, which she again took out of her backpack.

"There's no way to get in!" Tommy said in exasperation, running around its entire circumference.

"I think I know a way," Sally said, lifting up her blue sphere to touch the large one...

—which immediately opened!

Where before there was only a continuous glassy surface, now there was a door-sized circular opening.

It was dark and foreboding.

"Shall we?" Sally grimly invited the others.

"It's why we came here, isn't it?" Samantha affirmed. Her mouth was set in a stern line.

Sally entered into the Sphere, followed by the others.

Inside, it was as if they'd entered another world.

Although the Sphere externally looked no bigger than a small house, inside was a *large valley* filled with *huge, flourishing flowers* of every color imaginable!

The improbable giant garden loomed up above the women's heads.

The air was fresh and clean. A gentle breeze was blowing on their faces. Overhead, what appeared to be a sun much like Earth's hung in a vividly blue sky. Mountains lined the valley, upon which greenery glistened. A few white clouds drifted in the sky.

Strange, gossamer "butterflies" flitted through the huge flowers, each with six-foot wingspans.

"Tommy, where are you?" Sally yelled out, realizing that he wasn't there with her.

"Do not worry about him," a kind, quavering voice pleasantly-replied. "He is quite fine, I assure you."

Walking out of the vast Garden was an *old man* with *long white hair* and a *full beard*. He was dressed in a shimmering white robe. On his feet were golden sandals. He was at least nine feet tall, looming above the humans. He held out large hands in a friendly, beckoning way. His eyes were bright blue.

"Who are you?" Sally gasped, afraid that she already knew, but feeling she had to ask.

"Oh, I am not God," he chuckled good-naturedly, indicating for Sally and the others to follow him. "I am merely your humble host. Come! I have refreshments for you at my house. I'm sure that you and your companions would be much more comfortable chatting with me there. Please, follow me."

So-saying, he turned and led them along a path through the Glorious Garden to a plain, wooden house.

Inside, on a table, were laid out what appeared to be fresh bread, jams to put on the bread, and tankards filled with a frothy, golden beverage.

"It is just a snack for you fine ladies," he graciously indicated for them to sit on human-sized chairs, handing a knife to Sally as he sat upon a large chair to the side. "Please, eat! Spread the jams on the bread. It's all fresh-baked. The drink is similar to your honey-flavored wines, I think, though containing no ethanol—suitable to your religious dictates. I made it after reading your minds. Is the meal acceptable?"

Samantha suspiciously tasted one of the mugs then smiled in appreciation.

"It is delicious," Sally's mother reluctantly admitted, sitting down at the table while the others did the same. Sally sliced off hunks of the still-warm bread and passed it around.

But she regarded the frothy golden drink with suspicion. She was parched and dearly wanted to chug several tankards. But she held back, enduring the thirst.

"If any of you would like to freshen up, the bathroom is over there," the Giant pointed to a doorway at the back of the room. "It is multiple-usage for several people at once, so don't hesitate to take care of your bodily needs. There are as many stations within as needed. Otherwise, please eat up!"

Soon they'd all gone to the bathroom, ate, and drunk their fill.

Sally didn't realize it had been so long since she'd had anything to eat or drink. She was famished. And the food, plain as it was, tasted wonderful.

She even allowed herself sips of the golden drink, enough to slack her thirst, but no more.

"So what brings you here to the Center of the Galaxy?" the kindly Giant asked them, setting his large elbows on the table and resting his chin upon his hands.

His large blue eyes were kind, piercing, and *hypnotic!*

Sally shook her head, just barely able to pull her eyes away from his overpowering gaze.

"We're trying to save our fellow humans who are trapped inside the Harvester spaceship orbiting above," she briefly explained. "But since it seems you can read our minds, you probably already know that, so why do you ask?"

The white-haired Giant laughed gently.

"Of course I know," he nodded, acknowledging her insight. "But it would be rude of me to presume. Also, your unformed thoughts are chaotic. It is difficult for me to relate to your level of immaturity. It even gives me a mild headache. You often think totally opposite things at the same moment, at war with yourselves from within. I haven't seen such a primitive race in many millennia. You must have really pissed-off God to be marked for salvage so early in your development."

Sally was taken-aback.

How could she deal with a Being that knew her mind—her very mental makeup—before she could even speak her thoughts?

"Oh, quite easily," he answered her unspoken question. "How do you communicate with your pet dog or cat? They are beneath your level of intelligence, yet you get along with them just fine. In like manner I confer with you."

"So to you we are just *pets?*" Samantha suddenly huffed back at him. "Ladies, show him we mean business!"

The Priestesses all pulled out their guns, pointed straight at the Giant's large head...

—when each of the guns instantly turning into *a bouquet of pink flowers!*

"Ah, hah, hah!" he merrily laughed, his big-muscled arms wrapped about his upper chest as he rocked back and forth in his large chair. "You *are* an irritating, but amusing species, aren't you? Pulling guns on your host? My, but you are a fearful, ungrateful species. You'd think my generous gifts would convince you I meant you no harm. Do you not realize I can kill you all with a wave of my hand? Instead, I welcomed you into my home."

Sally felt embarrassed for her mother and the other women.

"I'm sorry," Sally apologized to the Giant. "We don't mean to be rude. We are far from our home. We're nervous, seeking answers."

"Ah, then please continue," he smiled graciously. "And since you are comforted by your little toys, you may have them back."

The flowers instantly turned back into black pistols, which the women with Sally hesitantly lowered. Then they tucked the guns back into the holsters at their waists.

"That's better," the Giant nodded. "Now, Sally—since you are the leader—please ask me your questions."

She was suddenly very scared. This Being was not God, but certainly possessed god-like powers. If she and her companions—not-to-mention the millions in the pods above—were to survive...she'd have to summon up all her wits.

But the other women seemed to be sagging, their eyes closing. Did they eat too much? Or...were they under the influence of a drug?

Sally was glad she'd only sipped the golden drink.

"I take it that the form you inhabit isn't your actual body?" she quietly asked.

"I took this image from your minds, a mythological construct to which you'd give initial deference," he nodded.

"So other races have appeared here in orbit, descending down to meet you?"

"Many—of various shape and sizes, that..."

"So why did you bother to talk to them?" Sally interrupted him, trying to rattle him. "Why not just *dump them directly* into the Black Hole?"

The Giant again good-naturedly laughed.

The other women had their heads on the tabletop, apparently about to fall asleep.

"In my far-distant youth I was what you'd call a xeno-biologist. I actively traveled to other stars, discovered lifeforms on different planets, and then brought them here for display."

"So...this is a cosmic zoo?"

"Oh, that was long ago," he sighed. "That was when I and my people here were still alive."

"You—and your people—are *dead?*"

"We...*moved on*...billions of your years in the past," he kindly smiled at Sally. "I am only an interactive image that they left behind to ease the passage of sacrificial lower lifeforms. Of course that was long ago. I am far more than that now. But you need not worry your little heads...merely *obey* me!"

At that chilling revelation, Samantha's head snapped up. She sharply rapped her companions so they sat up as well.

"Ah, your little buddies are awake," the Giant smiled benignly.

But his big blue eyes now had a hint of *red* in them.

Samantha and her fellow nuns were growing uneasy. Sally saw that they increasingly saw the Giant as their enemy. If they provoked him again she had no idea of how he might react.

"Would it be alright if my companions went outside to enjoy your beautiful garden?" Sally suddenly asked.

"Perhaps that would be easier for all of us," the Giant agreed, as with a wave of his hand they vanished from the table.

"Now it's just between you and me," he said, the genial smile fading.

She saw red flashes of *intense fire* in his eyes!

"You know me?" Sally softly asked.

"I recognize you—as one favored by the Creator to be a *Fulcrum of Time*—a Time-Twister! Around you Time flows unpredictably. I've encountered only a few of you in my travels throughout the Galaxy. And every time I've met one of you, trouble inevitably follows. Even when I kill you, you reappear in another form. I don't know why the Creator has seeded his Creation with such as you—but I suspect it gives Him some type of pleasure. Or could it be to chasten beings such as myself?"

"I...don't think...I'm anything special...?"

"And you do *not* in any way chasten me!" the Giant roared as he suddenly morphed into a *fire-breathing Dragon*—complete with armored scales, huge talons, poison-dripping teeth, and a long lashing tail.

"*Fear* me!" the Dragon shouted.

Sally sat stock-still, staring defiantly at it.

Then he instantly switched back into his previous, friendlier looking form.

"See?" the Giant mildly asked. "You didn't even flinch. Your companions would have cowered in terror! But your brain, Sally, is constructed far differently from theirs. I am delighted to make your acquaintance!"

He grinned at her.

"How is my brain different?" she suspiciously asked, not sure if she could believe anything he was telling her.

"You see beyond the immediate circumstance. Your mind calculates like one of your earthly chess-masters, seeing countless permutations forward. But your Vision is not limited to movements of game-pieces on a two-dimensional board. No, you are able to see in *five dimensions* at once: up, down, width, time, and parallel worlds. You possess a marvelous gift from the Creator."

"So...does that grant me particular favor in your eyes as well?" she hesitantly explored.

"I suppose it does," he leered at her, revealing a perfect set of gleaming-white teeth. "Perhaps I could be your 'magic-genie' to grant you a wish. Would you like that, youngling?"

She kept perfectly still, refusing to play his game, whatever it was...

"Wonderful!" he exclaimed, clapping his big hands together with a "BOOM" that rattled the house.

Outside, Sally could faintly hear her companions shouting for her in alarm—at what they thought was an explosion coming from inside of the now-locked house.

"I don't see what...?" Sally began, frowning.

He *floated* up into the air above the table, now clad in a golden genie suit with a blue turban on his head!

A gleaming oil-lamp sat on the table, ready to be rubbed...

"See? I'm a genie! What's your first wish?"

"Just tell me what the Harvester is going to do with my fellow humans," she quietly asked him, ignoring the theatrics.

"Oh, you're no fun," he snorted as with a "pop" the genie-form vanished and he again sat at the table.

But this time he was not a god-like figure anymore.

Instead, he was a *green, moist, tentacle-sporting creature* with spider-like eyes scattered around several lumpy appendages. Red filters that looked like layered gills fluttered periodically, sucking in air.

"This is my true form—at least many millennia ago when my people swam the green seas of this now-dead world," a raspy voice emanated from several membranous orbs. "I show it to nobody. You are the first to see me as I was. It is a token of respect, you *Twister of Time*."

"Thank you so much for the honor," Sally said, trying to sound respectful in addressing the revolting, mutated octopus-like creature.

"I think in some ways you might actually be my equal," his voice sputtered.

Sally stood up ramrod-straight at the table, trying to emulate her tough mother.

"*Why* does the Harvester want to throw my people into the Black Hole?" Sally relentlessly continued, reaching into her knapsack to lift up her own small *blue sphere* that she'd brought with her—setting it carefully on the tabletop between her and the pulsating, dripping creature.

The gelatinous creature cringed backward.

It was in a panic, seemingly *fearing* her small sphere...

"*Answer* me!" she demanded.

"Revenge!" he cried-out in obvious pain. "The Creator doomed my people to be gentrified into racial senescence. So we scoop up His *outcasts* to flavor a defiantly *perverse* new Universe—one made in *our* image, *not* His!"

"A...*new*...Universe?" she queried as the blue sphere in her hands began ominously glowing *bright red*.

"Your scientists know of it," the hideous creature sputtered. "It's the pinpoint '*White Hole*' that eventually can emerge from Black Holes as a new 'Big Bang'—to form, outside our present fabric of space/time, a completely different and fresh Universe! It's all part of the Creator's vast 'Multi-Verse', don't you know? But instead of us meekly allowing our Creator to do whatever He wants, we 'adulterate' the mix. I, along with other Remnants of ancient departed races here at the Galactic Core, have been doing this for eons. And when our galaxy's Black Hole finally births its new Universe, it will be as *we* have dictated, not God. You and your stupid little comrades—particularly that crude thing you call a mother—are *perfectly flawed* for our needs."

Sally was stunned.

They were stirring-in the "rejects" of this Universe to *poke* their collective finger in *God's* Eye! Really?

And these ungrateful, spiteful, ancient 'remnants' were using *Homo sapiens* as one of their "flawed" pawns in their perverse Galactic Game.

Sally felt adrift, helpless, and lost. What could she do against such an all-powerful Entity?

She might as well give up, surrender, and allow herself and her comrades to get tossed into the Black Hole.

But the ancient aliens wanted to do this awful thing not just to "humanity"—but to Sally's mother, *Samantha*.

Sally's eyes narrowed in rage.

This "remnant" just made his crazy scheme *personal*.

"But," Sally queried, rigidly controlling her emotions while carefully diverting the Creature's attention. "I thought that everything going into a Black Hole would be crushed to subatomic particles—any information thereby lost forever. There'd be nothing left to affect anything that squirted out as a 'White Hole'!"

As if in illustration, a couple spurts of greenish, slimy liquid splashed up from the orifices of the creature.

Sally wiped stinging droplets off her arm, shuddering.

"It *flavors* the mix of the plasma," the creature hissed at her. "It's beyond your limited comprehension. Come back in several hundred million years and you might understand—much as did the ancient race that gave you that sphere!"

"You fear it, don't you?"

"I shall *destroy* it by..."

Sally saw a roiling *red light* JUMP from the sphere in her hands— latching onto the alien octopus and *strangling* its "throat."

The creature *screamed* in pain!

Her startled gaze softened.

"I'm sorry," Sally insisted, even now unwilling to hurt this ancient though disgusting creature. "I didn't know."

Still kicking and writhing, the red light *dragged* him kicking and sputtering into the depths of the sphere!

Then all was silent.

The sphere had returned to its faint blue color.

"Sally, are you alright?" said Samantha as she fearfully entered the room. "We were locked out, but now..."

"I *couldn't* know what my sphere would do," she mused, still amazed at what had just happened. "It wasn't in my mind—so the Remnant couldn't see it."

Indeed, her friendly Dinosapiens had given her far more than just a holographic sphere-projector.

They must have known what she might encounter.

Sally's grateful musings were interrupted by a *rumbling* as a violent quake *jarred* the floor beneath them!

"Let's get out of here!" Sally urgently gasped, dropping the again peacefully glowing sphere back into her knapsack.

She raced out of the rapidly crumbling house, the others right behind her.

Holding a wide, yellow flower, Tommy trotted up next to Sally.

"Did you have fun with the Monster?" he cheerfully asked.

She glared at him.

"Why didn't you tell me what we were facing?" she snapped at him.

"I couldn't," he gulped as he continued skipping along beside her. "He wouldn't let me."

He hung his head sadly.

"It's ok," she said, gasping for air as she raced along, looking back to make sure the others were keeping up.

All around them, the entire manufactured world was *falling to pieces...*

—as with a great "roar" the mountains collapsed! The wondrous giant Flowers were *snapped* at their stalks and turned to dust. The blue sky above them *fractured*—with orange, acidic "rain" drops spattering down and burning their skin.

"There's the exit!" Sally yelled as she spotted a black circle suspended a few feet up off the now-festering "soil".

And it was rapidly closing.

Sally and her friends just managed to dive through before it shrank to a dot and vanished behind them.

Then they ran for the black, square cannon-ship—dashing through and into its safe interior as the entrance panel to the small cargo hold slammed shut.

"Get us out of here!" she yelled to Tommy as she felt the entire craft *sliding* at an angle to the side...

But Tommy had already scampered up the tunnel to the control room and was frantically working the controls. Sally and the rest of the women emerged behind him, jumping into the oversized seats, and engaging their seatbelts.

The craft *leapt upward* into the air and *shot* through the acrid orange clouds above—as Sally peered intently at the viewscreen.

Looking down from a high vantage point, Sally saw the towering Temple-like structure *collapsing*—then vanishing into the blue laser beam, *imploding* with a huge EXPLOSION on the planet's surface!

Above them, coming rapidly into view, was the immense, orbiting rectangular Harvester.

"We made it back!" Sally gasped as their ship zipped up to its side and carefully slid into the waiting, opened airlock.

"What now, Mommy?" Tommy asked as the big door closed, sealing them safely back inside, protecting them from the vacuum of outer space.

"We're taking *control*," she stated fiercely, holding her knapsack tight in her grasp. "I have a feeling that the Mother Ship will obey your commands now, Tommy. We've got its Master as our prisoner."

"What happened in there after we were thrown out?" Samantha demanded. "What did you find out?"

"More than you want to know."

"The High Priestess didn't send us just to be morale boosters," Sally's mother insisted.

"Oh, Mom," Sally said, reaching over to pat her mother's liver-spotted hand. "A morale booster was just what I needed. I'll tell you and the other ladies all about it. But for now we've got to get away. We can't chance other ancient aliens taking control of the ship and tossing us into the Black Hole!"

It didn't take long to get the Harvester out of orbit around the dead planet.

Then Tommy engaged the ship's interstellar drive.

Later, their cannon-ship safely back in the vast half-orb control center of the Harvester, Sally sat looking out at the *roiling kaleidoscope* of Subspace!

The others had found corners to curl up on the floor to sleep. They were exhausted, using each other's legs and arms as pillows.

Sally could not sleep. She sat in the oversized control chair, pondering.

How could she possibly defy God? Tricking that ancient creature was one thing, but the Creator of their Universe—and perhaps the Lord of many other Universes?

It was a mindboggling thought.

And what did that evil creature mean that she was a "Twister of Time"? Could that really be true? And if so, what did it mean?

Regardless of the future, though, they were going home. The millions of "harvested" humans sleeping peacefully in their tubes were safe. And that, for now, was good enough.

Ivanna exited the school bus hastily, realizing that at any moment those awful Reaper robots might attack them!

The Priestess who had been driving the flying bus suddenly dashed away into the surrounding darkness.

"Let her go," the Major ordered Grant, who was poised to sprint after her. "We don't need her anymore."

The High Priestess didn't seem concerned about anything, walking confidently beside Ivanna, her white-hooded head held high.

"Kill anything that moves," the Major instructed Sergeant Grant.

"Yes, Sir!" the young soldier replied eagerly.

Major Cotrell held his assault rifle at-ready as did the Sergeant. Slung over Cotrell's back was a sack containing a dozen of the powerful black guns they'd stolen off the Priestesses back at the Temple.

"Why don't you just *stun* whoever we meet with one of those electricity guns?" Ivanna asked as she slipped in behind the Major. "Wouldn't that be quieter and more humane?"

"We don't know what charge is left in these guns. We may need all of them to burn through the rock blocking the escape tunnel."

"But I thought the tunnel was collapsed?" Ivanna said as she ducked under a fallen column as they carefully climbed down into the sub-basement levels once again.

Behind Ivanna, the High Priestess said nothing.

Sergeant Grant brought up the rear.

"Only the last length of it is filled with rock," he curtly replied. "If we can melt out the plug, then we've got a clear shot to making it back inside the base."

"It's a good thing that the Priestesses didn't know there only remained a plug," Ivanna grimly nodded. "They would have opened it up themselves. They wanted to shut down our Dark Energy research and stop us from launching the DE-bombs."

She knew she had to maintain her cover as a rescued participant. There couldn't be a hint of suspicion until she laid a hand on one of the Base computers.

"I guess they're not as smart as they think they are," the Major answered, not realizing that her ready recollections were to prevent him from suspecting that *she* was now the "Trojan horse" for infiltrating and shutting down the base operations!

"You don't know what you are doing," the High Priestess sadly grated from behind Ivanna. "You'll doom the whole world with your evil..."

"Nothing's been able to slow down those damn Harvesters!" the Major irritably snapped back at her. "If we take out a few of them, maybe they'll call it a day and just leave."

"And maybe cookies will rain down from heaven!" Sally snarled back at him. "Our best strategy against them is appeasement. If we just give them what they want, then maybe..."

Sergeant Grant struck her sharply in the back of her white-hooded head with the butt of his assault rifle.

"*Ow!*" she complained as she continued climbing over the debris following Ivanna. "What did you do that for, young man?"

"I didn't hit you that hard," he replied. "But you should shut up. I know what you're doing."

"And what's that?" she shot back at him.

"You're trying to get us talking and debating so that your 'nuns' can hear us, pinpoint our location, and ambush us."

"You are a stupid young man," she growled back at him. "You hit a lady, twice! And you claim to follow a loving Jesus? What is this world coming to?"

"Everybody please keep quiet," the Major ordered from the front of their creeping line. "You're correct, Sergeant—that nun pilot who escaped is probably right now calling in reinforcements to stop us from getting back into the base. So keep a watch on our rear. They'll probably come at us from behind."

As if on cue, laser blasts suddenly "ZAPPED" around them!

The beams stirred up a cloud of dust but didn't hit anyone.

Grant swung around and let loose a barrage of bullets, hurting Ivanna's ears from their *"BRAPPPP"* sound.

"Quickly, now—we're making a dash for it," the Major said, grabbing Ivanna by her hand and pulling her along.

They ran through open spaces, ducking and dodging around fallen beams and crushed cars—finding places to get into the lower levels, ever watchful for another attack.

And then they were back where they'd originally entered the smashed Stadium's lower levels. They proceeded cautiously forward, only seeing by the dim light of the Major's small flashlight.

Ivana looked for the body of that heroic young lady, Sergeant Murphy, who'd initially collapsed the tunnel sealing it against infiltration by the enemy.

Her body wasn't there. But one isolated bloody *foot* lay on the floor.

Ivanna fought the urge to vomit.

"They scavenged her uniform, equipment, and flesh," the Major whispered to Ivanna. "Damn cannibals, it's hard to see how even in the present circumstance that people can sink so low."

"We're not all that high to start with," Sally sadly replied.

"Zeke, guard our backs," the Major ordered him.

The Staff Sergeant retreated back into the dimly seen columns, his rifle at-ready.

"I can help," Ivanna offered, reaching for the extra rifle that had originally been Murphy's.

"Fine," Major Cotrell said, unslinging the rifle from his shoulder and handing it to her. The black skin of his face was dripping with sweat. In the dim light the whites of his eyes glared against his dark skin. "But you concentrate on guarding our prisoner. Zeke and I will take care of any combat."

Ivanna nodded, nudging Sally in her side with the tip of the gun— guiding her to move back and crouch with Ivanna behind Zeke.

Ivanna realized how hot and stuffy it was. She didn't trust her reactions. She knew that Sally could bolt and escape at any moment and she'd be too slow to stop her. But, then again, that wasn't the plan.

"Fire in the hole!" the Major called over to them.

He had the sack of guns at his feet. He'd set the first one to its highest output, five stars, and had it pointed straight at the mound of rock and dirt that spilled from the collapsed tunnel entrance...

KAWHOOOMMMMMMMM!

Ivanna crouched lower from the spray of hot pebbles and steam erupting from the boulder pile as THE MAJOR'S GUN INCINERATED THE PILE OF ROCKS—then sputtered to a stop.

"That's it for that gun," he coughed in the swirling smoke. "Here's the next one..."

KWWWWWIIIIINNNNNNNGNGGGGGGG!

And so it continued for what seemed to Ivanna an eternity.

Then the Major slid down next to her, panting, his face pitted with cuts from the exploding rocks that had sliced into his flesh.

"That's it," he gasped. "It took the charges of all but one of the guns we liberated from those Priestesses, but the tunnel's open. Let's move, *fast!*"

"We've got to wait a minute," Ivanna cautioned him. "The tunnel's glowing red-hot! It'll cook us if we try to enter..."

"You're right," the Major nodded. "We'll give a minute."

"No sign of any opposition yet, Major," the Staff Sergeant reported, peering intensely into the cluttered darkness of the sub-basement level.

"Good," he replied. "Maybe that nun pilot didn't make it back to her people yet for reinforcements. The laser attack when we entered could have just been that nun."

Or, more likely, she made sure that neither the Priestesses nor any marauders came to disturb them while the tunnel was being re-opened—Ivanna thought to herself. *And she prodded us along with blasts from her gun, making sure we had a sense of urgency.*

"Ok, it's cooled. It's not glowing red anymore. Let's move!"

Ivanna, with the support of the Major, staggered into the still-steaming opening followed by the High Priestess who was nudged onward by Zeke.

Ivanna still held the heavy assault rifle.

A few hundred yards into the tunnel the Major turned back.

"What are you doing?" Ivanna asked, concerned.

"We're not leaving it open for our enemies to follow along behind us," he calmly stated, grimacing as he made careful adjustments on the one still-charged black gun.

An ominous "*huuuummmmmm*" sounded from it, growing steadily louder.

"What did you do?"

"Closed-down the aperture of the muzzle..."

He handed the small flashlight to Sergeant Grant, who grimly took it.

"Major Cotrell!" Ivanna said, reaching over to grip his arm tightly.

He gently loosened her grip.

"It's going to explode," he calmly stated. "I've got to go. Once I get it into position I'll try to make it back."

"I'll get the women back to the base, regardless," Zeke reported.

The Major was rapidly running in the direction they'd just come...

"Thank you!" Ivanna called out to the Major as he vanished into the swirling smoke and steam.

"Run!" the Major yelled from the darkness. "*Run fast!*"

Already exhausted from their descent into the guts of the Stadium, Ivanna conjured up every last bit of strength as she sprinted alongside the High Priestess, Zeke bringing up the rear...

—as the tunnel behind them EXPLODED into an onrushing *cloud of fire, smoke, and hurtling rock!*

And then it was over.

Ivanna found herself covered with a layer of broken rock and dirt. Weakly she dug herself out of the debris from the explosion.

She coughed uncontrollably in the thick, swirling smoke. Her rifle had been knocked from her hands. Where was it?

"Are you alright?"

The High Priestess stood above her, holding the assault rifle in her hands.

With her free hand, Sally reached down and helped Ivanna to her feet, before handing her the rifle.

"Here, *you're* the captor and *I'm* your prisoner," Sally matter-of-factly stated. "I'm sure we won't have to walk for long. The Presi-

dent's surely got a rescue team coming for us as we speak, having detected that second explosion."

"B-but, where's the Major and Z-Zeke?" Ivanna stammered, just
barely able to stand, accepting back the heavy assault rifle.

The Staff Sergeant lay off to the side, motionless.

"A rock caught him in the back of his head," Sally sighed. "His
skull's crushed. Too bad—he was a nice young man. I enjoyed our
verbal jesting. It's good the Major collapsed the entrance. That over-
loaded gun fused the rocks together, making it impossible for our
weapons to cut through again. Your President will think the base is
safely sealed. Her guard will be down. Your men did a service to
their species. When it's appropriate, we will honor them."

Ivanna wiped away tears from her eyes, thinking of the sacrifice
the two men had just made. But Sally didn't look too concerned. Her
words, in fact, sounded insincere—as if she were point-blank *lying* to
Ivanna. She also looked *angry*, as if her plan wasn't going like she
wanted. To Ivanna the High Priestess was a general calmly executing
a difficult and complex plan, noting "acceptable" loses and inevitable-
but-temporary reversals. Whatever, Ivanna had seen enough of war
for a lifetime.

She either wanted to live out the rest of her life sitting beside the
water-reserve pool in the subterranean hideout—or deal a final blow,
no matter how futile, to the enemy with the *ten DE-tipped missiles!*

Either option would do.

She no longer cared about tricking God to save the human race.

She just wanted a modicum of peace.

Chapter 13

REVENGE

How sweet it is
Releasing that pent-up rage
Upon the head of a hated enemy
Causing them incredible pain and grief
So well-deserved by them for injustices
Perpetuated upon you and your loved ones
Best served hot and spicy, with great gusto
Getting up in their faces, howling your rage
Stuffing it down their gagging throats
Watching them cry and beg for mercy
Yet giving them nothing but hate
Such a feeling of great joy
If only it weren't so brief
Fleeting outrage
Left in tears
Lost...

The Luminary Chronicles, 13:137-140

Ivanna lay on a hospital bed, exhausted.

They'd immediately taken her there for medical evaluation after the rescue team found her and the High Priestess staggering along the dark tunnel. Ivanna was quickly cleaned up, bandaged, and rehydrated with an intravenous line. But she could not even stand up. Every muscle in her body was limp.

Maybe she *was* 83 years old after all...

"Ivanna, *darling!*" came a welcome voice.

It was Victor, hurrying into her room.

"They just told me. I rushed right over. How could you do such a thing—going out of the base on a dangerous commando raid?" he gushed at her, alternatively looking relieved and angry.

She weakly laughed, reaching up to grasp his liver-spotted hand.

She was shocked. He looked much older since she'd seen him last, just a few short days ago. He was stooped where he should have stood tall. His distinguished mass of vibrant white hair lay limply to the sides of his head where it should have jumped out. Where he should have been smooth-shaven he had unsightly stubble. And where his blue eyes normally sparkled with vitality and curiosity, they were dull and weary-looking.

"*You* do what you have to do," she sighed. "And I do what I have to do."

Behind him came the President of the United States, Julia Swartz.

She also had aged considerably in Ivanna's brief absence: her grey hair now streaked with white, her pert nose red and runny, her dark eyebrows faded, and the wrinkles of her face deeper and more prominent than before.

Ivanna knew it was just normal grooming taking a low priority, but the President's appearance was nonetheless shocking.

"I'm glad you both are here," Swartz said, sinking into a chair beside Ivanna's bed. "The scientists say they are ready to launch the missiles. I've managed to get them to delay until your return. Thank God you're back, Ivanna. I was afraid—after the tunnel collapsed—that you were dead."

"I came close," Ivanna gulped. "But some irreplaceable soldiers gave their lives to get me back safely."

"I'm so sorry," Julia sincerely said. "But for now, I need to know—did you discover anything of value on the outside?"

Ignoring the President, Victor "dramatically" climbed stiffly up upon the bed and lay down square against Ivanna, snuggling close.

"Don't listen to that shrew, my dear," he wearily instructed her. "You rest with me. We'll deal with Madam President later when you are good and ready."

Grateful for his protective presence, Ivanna felt her eyes closing as if heavy weights were pushing down on her eyelids.

She heard—seemingly off at a distance—the President loudly protesting. But Victor's warmth encouraged her to acknowledge her physical, mental, and spiritual exhaustion.

She sank into a dreamless sleep.

Sally, the *High Priestess* of the *Church of Perpetual Health,* did not have the luxury of deciding when to confront her accusers.

She sat on a hard chair, her hands handcuffed behind her back, with her few possessions laid out on a white plastic table in front of her. Her outer robe, hood, medallion, and contents of her pockets lay on the table.

She sat in her underwear—white shorts and T-shirt, which was rather chilly for her in the cool room. It was a featureless, closed room. A large mirror covered most of one wall. It was obviously a one-way mirror with people on the other side observing her every move.

In the room, it was just Sally and an interrogator.

"Tell us what this is!" the hard-faced woman ordered her, holding up the spike-adorned golden medallion.

Sally sighed deeply.

"I've already told you a dozen times."

"Then tell us again!" the woman snapped at her.

The woman was in a plain black pant suit, with no military insignia. But her hair was in a military style, cut short. Her eyes were brown. Her racial heritage was indeterminate, perhaps a mixture of Japanese and Latino. But she was certainly military intelligence, using time-honored interrogation techniques.

One of those techniques was brutally boring repetition.

"It's a medallion that symbolizes my religion," Sally replied yet again, "representing the healing power and energy of the sun that shines down upon all of us."

"What does it do?"

"It hangs around my neck!"

Sally's head was snapped back as the woman sharply slapped her on her cheek.

"Do you really have to do that?" Sally objected, wincing at the pain in her swollen jaw. "I already got hit there by Sergeant Grant..."

"Who is *dead* because of you!"

"—and which I deeply regret. But it wasn't my fault. In fact, it was he that kidnapped me. I was just being a good hostess to your people."

"You held them prisoner!"

"No," Sally calmly replied. "I *rescued* him and the others of your spy mission from marauders. If I hadn't intervened, those animals would have killed and *eaten* Ivanna and her companions. And I'm still trying to be helpful to you, despite your uncouth behavior. I ask again to speak to your President. I have critically important news for her concerning the Harvester ships, so you need to..."

Sally was slapped again, this time even harder.

"Auuugggghhh," Sally grated, starting to get angry.

She'd been there for too long. Surely Ivanna had sufficient time already to get to a computer terminal. But nothing was happening. Sally knew she had to hold out as long as necessary. Perhaps Ivanna was restrained or unable to move. She'd undergone a lot for an elderly woman. All Sally could do was keep the focus on herself, let Ivanna have the time to make her move...

—or just take the initiative herself.

Any good General always has a plan "B".

But it would be bloody. Sally didn't want that. She much preferred a bloodless "coup".

"Tell me what you know and I'll convey it to the President," the woman ordered Sally.

"You are a silly person who I could not trust to accurately portray the gravity of the situation," Sally spat back at her. "So until I speak directly with the President, face-to-face, I have nothing further to say!"

At that the door to the room opened and *President Schwartz* abruptly walked in, flanked by two security guards. She carried a full glass of water. The male and female guards, both armed with pistols, stood back against the wall.

The President carefully placed the glass of water in front of Sally before sitting opposite her.

"You can go," Schwartz said to the interrogator, who immediately departed.

President Schwartz nodded to one of the soldiers who came over, lifted the glass of water to Sally's parched lips, and allowed her a few quick sips.

"Once you cooperate with us," the man said, his steely eyes boring into Sally's, "you can have the full glass."

"So you have information for me?" the President curtly asked Sally.

"Why is Ivanna not here?" Sally replied, evading the direct confrontation. The sips of water only increased her deep thirst, making her angry instead of "cooperative."

"She is resting peacefully, sound asleep," Schwartz answered. "But I require your information right now. Whatever it is, please tell me!"

"I'd rather have Ivanna here to verify parts of what I have to tell you. Some of it is rather incredible."

"She is not available. I repeat: please tell me now! I will decide for myself what to believe or disregard."

"Well..." Sally sighed. "I'd hoped to do this later, but I suppose I can move up my timetable?"

"Do what?" the President suspiciously replied, the guards at the back of the room moving closer to the table...

"Have a good nap!" Sally smiled, between her teeth emitting a high-pitched whistle.

Instantly, from the tips of the spikes ringing the Medallion, *gas under pressure* hissed out into the room.

"I..."

"No...!"

"Stop the..."

And just that quickly they were unconscious, the President with her head lolling on the tabletop, spilling over the glass of water—the two guards collapsed upon the floor.

"Ah...you weren't injected with the antidote to the nerve toxin?" Sally pretend-sadly asked. "I'm so sorry!"

Sally looked ruefully at the puddle of water on the table. Oh well, plenty of time to slack her thirst later.

Outside, an *alarm* began blaring!

Sally sprang up from the chair, turned around, grabbed the medallion with her hands that were still secured behind her back, and spun—CRASHING the still-hissing heavy metal plaque through the mirrored observation window.

As broken glass crashed onto the floor—Sally prancing backward to avoid it—the occupants of the observation room slumped to the floor, likewise unconscious.

Stepping carefully through the shards of broken window into the observation room, Sally jammed her tied hands to one side, searched the pockets of her once-interrogator, found the key to the handcuffs, and managed to remove them from her hands. She quickly stripped a jumpsuit off one of the unconscious guards and slipped it onto herself. It was baggy but it made her feel more comfortable than parading around in her underwear.

"That's much better," Sally said, rubbing her chaffed wrists. "Now let's get a few more true-believers in here."

She snapped down the inside heavy lock to the observation room's door, grabbed the medallion up from where it lay on the floor, and then hopped back through the broken-out window. There, she snapped down the inside locks on the interrogation room as well.

As pounding started on the outside of the door, she carefully laid the medallion flat on the floor, pushed in several of the spikes in a specific sequence, and stepped back.

The miniaturized Dark Energy generator secreted inside caused a wavering black globe to appear above the table.

From the mini-portal jumped a gun-toting Priestess, then another, then another...

—who fired a coordinated, *crackling*, penetrating ELECTRICAL BLAST through the door.

The pounding outside was instantly silenced.

"Thank you, ladies," Sally said as she walked over, unlocked, and then opened the door.

A dozen armed guards lay unconscious outside in a heap.

"Bring the President," she ordered as more and more Priestesses kept coming through the mini-portal orb hanging suspended above the table.

Then it flickered out, depleted.

"It took six months to load my medallion, but it was worth it," Sally noted to the gathered Priestesses. "For whatever reason, our stealth viruses didn't work. So we're going to have to take the base by force."

The priestesses grabbed the unconscious Swartz up by both her arms and hauled her through the door, carrying her along beside Sally.

"And to answer your unspoken question, my dear President," Sally said to the woman whose head lolled to the side, "it's not Dark Energy itself that's the problem. It's unrestrained, excessive usage—as with your world-busting bombs!"

"Where to now?" Sally's chief lieutenant asked.

"Let's go destroy some missiles," Sally growled, accepting a black pistol handed to her by one of her followers.

Victor jerked upright on the hospital bed beside Ivanna, hearing the siren wailing in the distance.

"Ivanna! Wake up! We've got to go!" he urgently yelled at her, shaking her shoulder.

"Wha...what's happening?" she said, groggily opening her eyes.

He jerked her up off the hospital bed, yanked out her intravenous line, and pressed gauss onto the bleeding vein.

"Hold that in place," he said, levering her over into a wheelchair resting conveniently beside the bed.

"What's that noise?" she said, grimacing at the siren's wails.

"It's a base-wide emergency siren, calling everyone to their duty stations," he said, wheeling her rapidly out of the room, into an elevator, and to an underground tunnel that led towards the main research dome.

Behind him they both heard loud *booms* and *rattlings* of energy guns and rifles firing back and forth at each other.

"Sally!" she gasped, realizing what was happening.

"Sally?" Victor asked, confused, breathing heavily while rapidly pushing the wheelchair along. "Do you mean Sally Smith? Dave kidnapped her from the research facility here right before the invasion. Is she still alive?"

"No, Victor, I'm talking about the *other* Sally!"

"What other Sally?"

"Oh, it's terribly confusing," she gasped, holding on tight to the wheelchair's arms, amazed that her elderly husband could push her along so fast. "But the *High Priestess* of the *Church of Perpetual Health*—that middle-aged 'Linda Powers' woman who came back with me from the surface—is really another Sally from a different dimension."

"A different what?" he gasped, panting heavily as he ran behind, pushing the wheelchair.

"*Dimension*, dear. And she says we shouldn't launch the missiles—that it will precipitate a *much* worse situation!"

Victor could see the end of the tunnel coming up. If he could just keep from having a heart attack they might just make it before the blast doors slammed shut.

"What could be...worse...than...an Alien Invasion?" he gasped, completely out of breath.

"She says it brings the Day of Judgment from God—*Armageddon*, Victor—the end of all humanity."

Victor pushed the wheelchair through the end of the tunnel just as a heavy, solid-steel blast door *slammed* down behind them!

He collapsed on the floor beside the wheelchair, barely able to breathe, his head spinning.

"And...you...believe her?" he gasped, starting to get his breath back.

"I—think that I do."

"Darling Ivanna," he said, grabbing onto the arm of the wheelchair and dragging himself up, "that woman, whoever she truly is, is nothing more than a religious fanatic. She hates science! And so she hates Dark Energy just because it is a new scientific achievement."

"But if she has a valid reason..."

"She has no reason, Ivanna!" Victor barked at her in exasperation, "She and her crazy Church say so at every turn! They claim that Dark Energy is evil. It is *not* evil. It is just a part of our Universe that we don't yet fully understand. Her fear comes from ignorance. And her excuse sounds completely irrational also—just more religious nonsense."

Armed soldiers were running up to them. He gratefully let the soldiers help him to stand up—supporting him as he staggered away toward the missile control center.

"I suppose," Victor heard Ivanna's faint voice behind him as other personnel helped her out of the wheelchair. He knew she was in good hands. They would take her to a dress-out room for entering the clean facilities, where she'd get a warm gown.

He walked shakily into the missile launch control room, putting Ivanna out of his mind to focus on the immediate crisis. Technicians were busily working at various screens. The atmosphere was tense. Victor checked with several of the technicians, assessing the condition of the missiles.

A four-star general strode up to Victor. It was General Walker, a small man who communicated great authority just by his ramrod-straight stance. He had cold grey eyes, short white hair, and a soft voice that nevertheless caused anyone of lower rank to snap to attention.

And he held a pistol in his right hand, ready to take on any invaders.

"What's the situation?" he asked.

"Everything's ready," Victor reported. "The automatic targeting is online. As soon as the missiles break out of the atmosphere, the multiple warheads will separate and head for their targets. We should catch the Harvesters totally unprepared. If we're lucky and everything works, our DE-bombs should completely destroy a *hundred* of the alien spaceships. It'll *light up* the blackness of outer space!"

"Did you talk to the President?" the General pointedly asked.

"I didn't get the chance."

An aide came running up to the General, listening intently on an intra-base cellphone.

"They've got the President!" the aide excitedly reported. "Our troops are holding them back on the other side of the base, but they're close to breaking out. Our defenses are muting the resonance frequencies of their energy weapons, giving us a chance. But our bullets aren't comparable to... "

"Then that settles it," the General calmly stated. "If the President is compromised then we can't wait on her orders. It falls to me to make the decision."

Victor stumbled back against a wall as a huge "THUD" marked the fall of the missile blast doors into place outside in the cavern proper.

"Now that the blast doors are down the intruders won't be able to destroy the missiles with their energy weapons," the General approvingly noted. "Those barriers were meant to protect the base from the launch—but they'll also protect the missiles from attack. That gives us at least a few minutes. How long will it take to get them off their pads?"

Victor did a rapid calculation in his head.

"It's a minimum of twenty minutes...maybe a bit longer," he replied.

"Then do it."

"Yes, General, I'll direct the operation."

"Good. We've had enough political nonsense. It's high time that we *smoked* those alien bastards in orbit!"

Victor ran over to the computer consoles, informing the technicians and other personnel that the launch of all ten missiles was a "Go!"

He vaguely noted Ivanna walking out of the dress-out station, clothed in plain blue coveralls. With her streaming, blond-dyed hair, she looked quite fetching.

But she also looked worried.

As she walked towards the computer terminals, an *arm outstretched toward them* as if to touch them—a soldier gently steered her away to sit over to the side, safely out of the way.

Victor knew he should go check on her health, both physical and mental—but he was just too busy.

The countdown had begun.

Sally felt the *wrenching, twisting unreality* of popping out of subspace. There on the viewscreen—hanging beautifully against the blackness of outer space—was Earth.

It was a precious, beautiful pearl. It shone against the black, star-speckled backdrop: a sphere of vibrant blue and white. It was only a tiny part of a finite fraction of Creation—but it was Sally's home.

And they were *hurtling at a fantastic speed* toward the small marble that grew visibly larger!

"Shouldn't we be slowing down?" Samantha asked Sally as she and the other women sat buckled into their seats in the cannon-craft.

Their small ship was sitting inside the huge central control room of the Harvester. The clear dome above the control consoles pointed forward along their path through the solar system—providing an uninterrupted view of what was in front of them.

The cratered, dead moon loomed off to the side.

They were rapidly *zooming* into the ever-growing Earth!

"Tommy!" Sally spoke into a microphone-like protrusion that amplified her voice outside the cannon-craft. "Are we going into orbit?"

She saw the little boy who sat out in the thin air of the control room shaking his bushy head in the *negative*.

"*Tommy!*" Sally urgently ordered him. "Slow us down! Swing us into orbit!"

He just sat at the control station in the center of the Harvester control room, doing nothing.

"Why is the boy not responding to you?" Samantha gasped, realizing that they were about to crash full-tilt into the planet.

"Oh, that would be *me!*" a squeaky, little voice sounded from within Sally's knapsack.

"What?" Sally gasped, looking down at the knapsack at her feet.

The blue sphere rolled out upon the floor...CRACKED WIDE OPEN—and out of the shattered globe stepped a miniature *Satan!*

The little red figurine had tiny horns, a cute little forked tail, a wicked grin, glaringly yellow eyes, and a tiny pitchfork.

"Did you really think your primitive prison could contain me?" the high-pitched voice cackled. "I just pretended to let it grab me. *I'm* in control here! I'm taking my revenge on all you stupid humans. I'm *crashing* you into your home world!"

"Then you'll die with us!" Sally yelled, trying to *stomp* on the scampering creature but missing.

"Kill it! Kill it!" Samantha shouted, aiming her gun down at it...

—as it *skittered* about the cannon-ship's small control room, *hopping* up on the central console, *dashing and leaping* from wall to floor to perch, *jeering* at them upon the black box, then *zipping* under their feet.

"We can't get a clear shot!" one of Samantha's soldiers yelled.

"What about now?" the tiny figure shouted as it suddenly GREW into a ten-foot tall giant!

"Ah, hah, hah!" it laughed, throwing its horned head back, revealing green, poison-dripping fangs. "There's nothing you can do! Prepare to die!"

The High Priestess slumped back against a blood-splattered wall.

Despite the element of surprise and the superior weapons of her nuns, the soldiers were beating them back.

Bullets may be primitive, but they are effective destructive projectiles.

Sally had one in her shoulder, which had shattered bones therein—causing her excruciating pain.

"The blast-shield is lowered around the missiles," Sally's lieutenant reported as she crawled up beside the High Priestess. "It's made to stop a nuclear blast. Even if we overcome the soldiers firing at us, it'll take several hours for us to melt through."

"And we don't have that long," Sally groaned, looking reprovingly at the red blood dribbling down her own arm.

"Should we retreat back to the mini-portal?" the woman breathlessly queried as Sally simultaneously heard *bursts* of assault rifles firing *barrages of bullets* into the fortified positions of the nuns. "If we discharge our guns into the medallion we might be able to re-open the depleted portal and escape!"

"Joan, once those missiles launch we've lost everything," Sally grated through clenched teeth. "It won't matter if we're trapped in the mountain or out on our mountaintop. The remaining Harvesters will destroy everything of value left on the surface. And then God's Wrath will descend upon us."

The situation looked hopeless. Perhaps they should just surrender to the military?

"So what can we do?" the woman asked, not in fear but determination.

"We've got one last chance," the High Priestess mused. Yes, there was still a chance. "Plan A" could still occur. Sally still had her "ace in the hole"! They couldn't give up. "Ivanna's in there. If we can just distract the other defenders long enough for her to reach a computer terminal, then we may still prevent this catastrophe. Tell the others we're going to *charge* across the open area at the soldiers!"

Sally shakily levered herself up, holding her black pistol before her at-ready.

"But Your Highness—that's suicide," Joan realistically observed.

"Not necessarily," Sally said, grabbing President Schwartz by her hair and dragging her up beside her.

Sally *slung* the groggy politician around to *plaster* her right onto her chest—holding her firmly there as a shield.

Sally's good arm held the woman tightly onto her—as her other bloodied, weakened arm held her black pistol firmly against Swartz' skull.

"Don't fire! We're coming out!" Sally yelled, hearing the withering rifle fire slow. "I've got your president! I'm willing to make a deal!"

The bullets stopped raining down around her.

"As soon as we're close enough to overcome them," Sally whispered to Joan, "we'll charge their missile control dome. The blast walls there are thinner. And even if we don't breach them, it may give Ivanna a chance to make it to one of the computers."

As soon as the siren sounded off, all the personnel on this side of the base other than defending soldiers had retreated. Sally knew Ivanna had to be in one of the Domes, liking at the control Dome with her husband Victor.

"I'll pass the word along," Joan said, slinking off behind piled-up debris.

"What...what's happening?" President Schwartz gasped, blinking, rapidly regaining her faculties.

"Be a good girl and maybe you'll live to see tomorrow!" Sally grated in her ear. Sally cruelly shoved her forward, but still keeping her firmly plastered to her chest.

"We...we can t-talk about..."

"Don't give me an excuse to wreak my revenge upon you for two millennia of weak governance that got us into this mess in the first place!"

"What...are you...s-saying?"

"Don't talk—*walk!*" Sally viciously ordered her.

Together, they stepped out into the open—just as the *Turtle Tattoo* on Sally's wounded left arm began to *glow!*

"Tommy, if you can't stop us—can you set our GPS earth coordinates for where we impact?" Sally yelled out to him, ducking under the swipe of the long, swinging pitchfork.

On her wrist, superimposed over her Turtle Tattoo, Sally saw a *set of numbers.*

She didn't know the exact location it indicated, but could guess. She'd used GPS coordinates often in stashing her intelligent "pods" around the world.

It agreed with what her Mother had been trying to tell her earlier!

"Yes...Mommy," he mechanically replied over the speakers in the cannon-craft.

She rapidly read the numbers out to him as the Nuns zeroed in on the looming Satan-figure and together *fired* their black pistols!

The control room was filled with a *crackling force-field* that totally *encased* the still-laughing satanic giant!

For the moment it was immobilized, helpless...

—as Sally lurched across the room, snatched up the black box, bounded down the short tunnel to the exit panel, hit the release, jumped through holding her breath, ran into the large central control dome, raced over to Tommy, and SLAMMED the box down on top of him, covering him completely.

That should stop him from obeying any more orders from the Alien Entity!

But it was too little, too late.

Sally looked up to see Earth filling the viewscreen.

As they hit the atmosphere, a huge wall of fire BLAZED up to cover the spectacular view of the expanding continent of North America.

The congregated cluster of nuns suddenly broke their "surrender" of hands-held-high and snapped their pistols forward, *firing in unison* at the missile control dome!

"Hah!" Sally grinned, thrown off her feet by the resultant concussion. "Take *that!*"

The President was crawling weakly away.

A returning barrage of rifle bullets ripped through both Sally and the President, leaving them lying head-to-head on the rocky floor.

They were both mortally wounded.

"Why...?" Julia gasped.

"Why not? Sally grinned, coughing up bright red blood.

If Ivanna could just reach a terminal, that would validate their sacrifice.

The combined force ROCKED the entire dome on its foundations, throwing everyone inside to the floor.

"The exit tubes in the cavern's ceilings are open!" Victor yelled over to the General. "The missiles are lit!"

Outside, Victor could hear the unmistakable *RUMBLE* of ten IC-BMs firing their rockets.

Suddenly Ivanna jumped out of her chair and ran for the nearest computer—her arm held out straight, palm up and fingers spread wide...

—as General Walker whipped up his gun and *shot her* through her chest!

She crumpled just feet from the computer terminal, her arm still outstretched—inches away.

"No!" Victor screamed, jumping up to run over beside his dead wife and cradle her head in his arms. "*Why* did you do that?" he cried-out to the General.

"She was compromised...trying to do something to stop the launch," the old soldier moaned, limply dropping the gun beside him onto the floor. "Dear God...what have we come to?" he asked no one in particular, looking up dazedly at the disintegrating ceiling of their control dome.

Out in the central cavern, a dying Sally saw the red blaze of incomprehensible heat melting the blast shield as the tall missiles behind *slowly rose up* off their launch pads!

She saw that the exit shafts above had opened.

"We've lost," Sally whispered in utter defeat. Around her mangled body determined nuns continued fighting against the defending soldiers.

But their cause was doomed.

Sally saw her white-hooded nuns mowed down by the withering rifle fire. But the few surviving women kept up their concentrated fire upon the control dome, shattering its blast walls, imploding it upon all those within.

"Is your 'God' happy...High Priestess?" the President, lying crumpled next to Sally, spitefully laughed.

"He was blissfully ignorant of our many failures," Sally sighed back at the President, allowing her heavy eyelids to slip shut, "but no longer."

The *heavy vibration* in the flooring beneath Sally's broken body told her that the missiles were rising up into their launch tubes—about to carry their massive DE-bombs up into orbit.

The Dark Energy discharge from their detonations would be enormous.

Hello God—here we are! Come judge us as You will...

The gigantic, five-mile-long Harvester spaceship—traveling at the speed of a comet, three hundred miles per second—SLAMMED through the thin atmosphere and directly into the surface of Earth.

Cheyenne Mountain, the epicenter of the impact, *vanished* in the resultant explosion—completely incinerated...

—as a *huge column* of vaporized ejectus rose up into space...

—and a *blast wave* of super-heated air swept out in all directions from the impact site, instantly killing anyone in its path for hundreds of miles around...

—leaving behind a deep, *bubbling crater* more than fifty miles across: encompassing what had been Cheyenne Mountain, Pike's Peak, and the nearby town of Colorado Springs.

"*What the hell?*" Dave gasped, feeling the entire earth *shudder* beneath his feet.

He looked up from the dead bodies of a squad of nuns he and Arthur had just ambushed, at a *curtain of fire* rising past the horizon.

"That's not good," Arthur shakily observed, reaching up to adjust his dark eyeglasses against the glare. "I think we better get into the shelters, fast!"

He dropped the dead nun whose pockets he'd been riffling through to see if she had more pistols hidden away.

Dave saw that his partner's normally sunburnt complexion was *ashen white!*

"Is that a nuclear explosion?" Dave asked, still frozen in place.

"Worse...a *lot* worse!" Arthur said, grabbing Dave by his shoulder and jerking him towards a nearby sewer cover that was set into the street, which led immediately underground.

"How...what...?" Dave gasped again, stumbling along beside Arthur as they lurched up to the round iron cover, lifting it out to "clank" it over to the side.

Dave heard an *ominous rumbling* off in the distance which was fast approaching. He glimpsed a *blazing, red line* stretching from horizon to horizon growing taller and ever closer!

"That's the other half of my plan to stop the Harvesters that's come to ruin," Arthur moaned, grief-stricken.

"What?" Dave asked again, totally bewildered.

But Arthur just grabbed Dave's arm again, jerking him down through the opening. Then Arthur dragged him stumbling into the stinking darkness...

—as a *firestorm* of raging heat shot past on the streets above, sending a fireball down through the sewer opening after Dave and Arthur!

They both fell flat into the fetid sludge of the sewer, covering their heads.

Dave felt searing heat on the back of his head and arms for a few seconds that, mercifully, quickly abated.

"Jesus Christ!" he gasped, lifting up his singed head. "What the hell *was* that?"

"Just a portent of even worse things to come," Arthur dejectedly replied, sitting up in the sludge and burying his head into his arms. "unless, of course, we finish our work."

"So it was the Harvester spaceships?" Dave gulped, wiping gobs of stinking, seared sewage off his face. "They threw something else at us?"

"Something else, yes," Arthur said, his face twisted in anger in the faint red glow of the raging fires outside. The intense flames were shining through the distant sewer opening, "something to try and stop us from punching-up our Dark Energy planetary shield!"

"Then we'd better keep at it," Dave said while resolutely pushing himself up to his feet. "We're close to getting enough DE-generators shielded across the world to fire-up an energy barrier to protect Earth."

"Yes..." Arthur nodded, seemingly gathering his wits back about him, "we can still succeed."

"Of course we can," Dave angrily asserted. "We're not stopped. We're almost there!"

Arthur's grimace slowly changed into a small grin.

"Yes...we're almost there," he agreed, standing up to clap Dave on his back with a big, wet, filthy hand.

"I'm ALIVE!" he screamed up into the raging inferno.

Rising out of the settling column of ejectus in Colorado he was a *glowing hundred-foot tall Giant!*

Instead of destroying him, the vast energy released by the Harvester smashing into Earth only fueled his further reanimation.

The Satanic Demon reached up to the skies with massive talons and *SCREAMED* in *delight!*

"This is going to be *fun!*" he bellowed-out into the maelstrom surrounding him, "My eons-long exile is over! I will make this little planet my *playground!*"

The towering figure *leapt up into the sky* and ascended through the super-heated stratosphere towards his still-intact orbiting fleet of Harvesters.

Not only would the remaining wretched "humans" be gathered for flavoring the coming, new Universe—he'd *breed* them for eons into the future on his planet at the Galactic Core. They'd join his own private herd of abysmally failed intelligences, tweaked and tortured at his own pleasure. They'd help his "private stock" of cosmic rejects get *revenge* upon a negligent, inattentive God!

LET THERE BE PAIN!—he yelled-out wordlessly into the airless expanse of space.

He drifted up to a Harvester whose huge entrance airlock doors soundless opened to greet him.

This was so much more enjoyable than passively waiting to interrogate new arrivals at the Galactic Core.

If that "Sally" human were still alive, he'd *thank* her! He'd been imprisoned in his ancient Palace, allowed only to supervise his massive fleet of Harvesters. But she'd brought the means of his escape.

Now she was just random atoms blasted up into space.

He felt a mild twinge of regret.   For a pitifully lower lifeform, he had found her mildly amusing. Too bad there were none like her left alive on this planet. From afar he'd kept careful track of them. After all, they were his deadliest enemies, these "time-twisters." He was just glad they were finally gone.

But Earth was an even-poorer place with no "Sally" remaining. The Sally of this dimension died in the crash of the Harvester. The original Sally from the other Earth dimension who'd transformed herself into a "High Priestess" was simultaneously incinerated inside Cheyenne Mountain. And the replacement Sally from this new time-line had already gotten herself squashed in an imploding museum.

The "Girl with the Turtle Tattoo" had been unique, beloved by the Creator. But now she was dead. Good riddance!

His victory over God was almost complete.

Chapter 14

REGRET

Icy snowballs

Warming fireplaces

Cheerful greetings

Comforting hugs

Prancing puppies

Bouncing babies

Moved beyond and gone

Are quickly forgotten

But never lost

Tweaking memories

Of better times

Unappreciated until

When left behind...

The Luminary Chronicles, 14:68-72

Dave sat dejectedly beside a heater, warming his numb hands.

Icicles hung from his full beard. His eyebrows were frosted over. His long hair was matted in place.

He'd just come in from a scavenging run out into the burned-over remains of the frozen D.C. streets above.

There wasn't much left to find up there.

The past few months had been terrible. What seemed right around the corner moved increasingly into the future: concealment of a sufficient number of DE-generators worldwide to use in creating a continuously sustained planetary energy shield. And the worse thing was that the main "snag" preventing it from happening was that damned *Church of Perpetual Health!* At every turn, its CPH fanatical

Priestesses infiltrated, hunted, and attacked the Rebels—destroying the rebels' precious hidden generators.

Dave *hated* them!

And although the work continued, his heart wasn't in it.

He still felt the loss of Sally as a punch in his gut delivered fresh each morning when he woke up. It was his "breakfast" of regret. He knew that the "Sally" of this timeline hadn't even liked him—in fact was disdainful of being called his "girlfriend"—but he had a *connection* to her, damn it! ...a connection that was now forever lost.

This must be what an identical twin felt when losing his or her twin, no matter how much they loved or hated each other. It felt like a piece of his own body was chopped off: his legs, his arms, his tongue, or whatever—crippling him permanently.

He was now lesser than he was before.

And the desperate situation on Earth was even worse after the Harvester spaceship crashed onto the planet. How or why it occurred, no one knew. But the results were horrific. The entire planet was in a full-blown "nuclear winter."

The first wave of decimating firestorms gave way to muddy, blackened "snow" that drifted constantly down everywhere. Huge glaciers of burnt and frozen waste piled up. The massive ejectus from the impact site—plus the soot of the vast fires that initially raged across the planet—blocked sunlight from reaching Earth's surface. Food production, already at a minimum, was now nonexistent. Without the sun's energy, plants could not grow. Farm animals and even fish in the ocean were dying off at extinction rates.

Without crops or meat animals, what remained of the human population was rapidly starving to death.

It made for "slim-pickings" for the still-prowling Reaper Robots. But the relentless robots kept up their determined scavenger hunt. If anything, they seemed even more eager to find and capture humans—as if the Harvester crash set back their "quota"!

If Dave and the rest of the surviving Resistance didn't get their "planetary shield" up before long there'd be nothing left to protect.

Dave was certain humanity would survive. It might take a hundred years—or even a thousand—but *Homo sapiens* would reemerge upon a warming planet, crawling out of its few remaining pockets to repopulate the earth.

And it wasn't like they had zero energy. They still had their Dark Energy generators—many now running continuously due to the "donation" of a large number of CPH weapons to slay the robots. Yes, many an isolated, trapped Reaper "lost its head" at the point of those CPH laser-guns, to safely conceal yet another compact DE-generator from orbital detection.

Having a source of unlimited energy gave humanity the possible means of avoiding extinction. Large hydroponic tanks, powered by the DE-generators, were growing the food that Dave and his small army of fighters needed to survive.

But to achieve this Dave now had blood on his hands—a *lot* of blood!

Was it worth it?

He'd personally killed hundreds of the fierce, female nuns. He didn't mind defending himself against the predatory gangs of lawless marauders or vicious cannibals—slaughtering them without remorse—but the nuns had principles, conviction, and their own sense of honor.

Even though the Resistance and the Church were now bitter enemies—waging savage war on each other—Dave knew that the female religious fanatics weren't sub-humans or criminals.

In other circumstances, they might have been close allies. But the Priestesses attacked the Resistance fighters with religious zeal—invading the Rebel's camps and slaughtering everyone!

To the Church of Perpetual Health, Dave and his comrades were hated heretics leading mankind on an evil, perverse path—to be stopped at any cost.

Yes, the CPH and Resistance were slaughtering each other. But the rebels were slowly winning. Final victory over the nuns edged ever closer. Dave knew he should be elated. But he was weary beyond belief—convinced that Sally would have *hated* him for his ruthless actions.

But the Priestesses made it clear that they were not going to give up their guns without a fight—especially to assist generation of the much-despised, "evil" Dark Energy. Back in their "heydays" the CPH

spent billions manufacturing their exclusive medications, accumula-
tor generators, and energy-weapons. Now they were ruthlessly wielding those stockpiled devices in a fight to the death.

Since CPH jealously guarded their possessions from the so-called
"heretics"—Dave, Arthur, and the rest of the Resistance just had to
take the guns!

He had many nightmares of the killings he'd personally partici-
pated in these past few months.

"Penny for your thoughts?" Arthur smiled at Dave as the burly,
still dark eyeglasses-wearing ex-FBI Agent came and sat down next to
Dave.

"I'm just worried about our 'final' assault on the headquarters of
the Church," Dave frowned, not wanting to talk.

But Arthur persisted, pressing him.

"Why so? We've generated enough fuel to get several attack and
transport helicopters into the air. They're museum pieces, haven't
been flown in decades, but we've got them working. The Church
won't know what hit them. In one fell swoop we'll end the war, unite
the surviving humans, get the planetary Shield up—and take the war
to our real enemies, the Aliens up in orbit!"

"Uh...right," Dave listlessly replied, still warming his freezing
hands at the glowing heater, just having returned from the iced-over
surface above. "That's the Plan, I guess..."

"Then why are you so down?" Arthur asked, putting a big arm
across Dave's shivering shoulders.

"I...just wonder...if it's a war worth fighting."

"What? Of course it is! No matter the nuclear winter that's out
there, once we get our DE-generators in place across the planet we
can resurrect the entire world. Things '*look the worst right before the
dawn*'! There's '*a silver lining behind each cloud*'! The '*sun will
come out tomorrow*'! And '*tomorrow, tomorrow, I love ya tomorrow*'! Hah! Now ain't that the spirit of us ornery humans?"

"I suppose..."

Dave couldn't shake his gloom, looking down at the floor dejectedly.

"You still miss her, don't you?" Arthur commiserated, withdrawing his big arm.

"I'm past that," Dave lied, looking away. "I wasn't ever her boy-friend. She was just a pain, one that's gone now. We could still use her mathematical genius, but we're getting by ok."

His voice trailed off as they were interrupted.

A fighter came up to the heater dragging a battered nun behind him.

He tossed her onto the floor at their feet.

"What's this?" Arthur asked, standing up to glare down at the handcuffed, bloodied woman. She looked half-frozen to death.

"Our patrol caught her spying on us," he said. "She didn't have a gun for us to 'liberate', but she did have *this!*"

He held up her snow-encrusted, sun-medallion.

"So? They all wear one of those damn things," Arthur frowned.

"—that do *this?*" the man said, pushing it in at its center. "We saw her using it."

A holographic image sprang up, emanating from within the Me-dallion.

It was a three-dimensional, projected image of a smiling older lady, her white hood pushed back from her head, cheerfully issuing instructions. She held in her hands a big black bible. She had long grey hair. Her eyes were twinkling and full of life.

"...death of our beloved High Priestess didn't stop us," the little voice from the petite image rang-out confidently. "Our Holy War con-tinues! It's true that our energy-gathering guns are weakened—this Satan-spawned weather is terrible. We are suffering terribly. But we must persist. *Find* Dave King and bring him in *alive!* Here is the lat-est picture we have of him. That is your number-one objective. I will convert him from the error of his ways. And then, when the so-called Resistance sees their Leader recant his misconceptions, we humans will unite! All Dark Energy usage will cease. And we will wait out the evil Reapers. The aliens will soon depart, thinking they have de-stroyed this world, sufficiently plundered. But from the ashes, my friends, God will bring us back. Remember the teachings of our dear Lord, Jesus Christ, when He said in the Holy Bible that..."

The man touched the Medallion again, shutting off the replay of the recorded holographic presentation.

"It goes on like that for a long time," he gruffly stated. "Lots of sermonizing—but I thought you might want to know that now they've targeted David as their 'number one' objective."

"Yes, well done Henry," Arthur said, taking the Medallion from him.

Arthur took out his black pistol, tightened the ray aperture, and stuck the tip of the nozzle against the shivering nun's head.

Defiantly, she struggled up to her knees.

"You have ten seconds to tell us the exact location of your head-quarters in Jerusalem before I execute you," Arthur coldly warned her. "Tell us what we want to know and we'll let you live."

"What...as a sex slave?" she defiantly coughed back. She struggled to stay up on her knees rather than collapse back onto her face.

"Better that than dead," Henry spat at her. "But don't worry, girl. We won't abuse you. We're not fanatical crazies, like you. You'll just work for us instead of some stupid Church, that's all. So be smart, kid. Do like the General says. Tell us what we want to know!"

Yes, Dave saw she was only a kid, perhaps no more than twelve years old.

"...six...five...four...three..." Arthur kept counting.

"*Wait!*" Dave said, pushing the gun to the side.

He'd been so zoned-out that he'd not even realized what he was seeing in that holo-projection!

"That woman on the holoscan?" Dave said, gently taking the girl's face in his hands as he still sat there on the floor in front of the heater.

"Y-yes?" she said. Her green-blue eyes reminded him of Sally. For a moment she became a person and not just a vicious enemy.

"Who is she?"

"What?"

"What's her name?"

"Uhm...she's...the new High Priestess...?"

"No, her *real* name!" Dave insisted.

"I...don't know..."

Arthur pointed the gun again at her head, gently pushing Dave's hands away from the girl.

"Go ahead and kill me!" she sobbed. "I don't know anything. I was just looking for your Leader. I thought I saw him go down a sewer opening..."

"—and did you report that to anyone?" Arthur queried.

She clamped her mouth shut, refusing to answer.

Arthur fired a focused laser burst *through her head!* The intense light momentarily spewed from her eyes, ears, and mouth. To the startled Dave she looked like a Halloween jack-o'-lantern.

She slumped over onto her side, her brain fried to a crisp.

"*What* did you do that for?" Dave yelled at Arthur, jumping up to his feet. "I was *questioning* her!"

"She didn't know anything else," he shrugged. "And we've got too many mouths to feed down here already."

Dave turned and angrily walked away, fuming.

He didn't need the girl's confirmation. He knew the name of the new High Priestess. It was "Jean King"—his own *mother!* She'd been "resurrected" from metastasized breast cancer as the first scientific "miracle" of the new religion. After the disappearance and presumed death of their original leader, Linda Powers, the Church of Perpetual Health apparently had *appointed her* as their new High Priestess!

"Hey, I'm sorry, Dave," Arthur said, rushing up from behind. "You know that we have to be ruthless. We've executed thousands of those stupid nuns. They're totally brainwashed. Keeping them alive just puts deadly enemies in our midst. You know we can't take them as long-term prisoners. Why are you so upset?"

Dave felt a reluctance to admit his connection to the new High Priestess. And Arthur was correct—he himself had done the same as Arthur, and even worse.

"It's just that if we knew the exact location of the CPH headquarters in Jerusalem, our raid will have a much better chance of success—before the Harvesters decide to take a bead on us!"

"Yes, that's true..."

"And maybe that girl knew of others who knew something—who we could capture and interrogate."

"Well...that's a longshot...but maybe..."

"And what the hell is this that you are making major decisions without consulting me first?" Dave angrily added. "I thought that *I* was the 'Great Leader' of this world-wide Resistance?"

"Uhm...of course you are, David...I just..."

"You weren't thinking!" Dave shouted at him, fixing the man with a fierce glare. "We're still facing Aliens in orbit above us. We've got to use our brainpower together or we've got no chance!"

"Right...you're right...I apologize," Arthur answered, seemingly contrite.

"Good... So how long is it until we leave?" Dave asked. He was glad to have a "safety-valve" to vent his frustrations—but not happy to risk angering his long-time ally and friend.

"Tomorrow morning we leave on the first leg of the journey," Arthur replied. "We're fueled and packed."

"And are our bases ready to resupply and refuel us along the path?"

"They say they are."

"If we can't take off from even one of the intermediate destinations, then all this will be for nothing."

"That's true. But we're prepared. We'll be ok."

Behind Dave he heard people dragging the limp body of the young woman away. Presumably her remains would be deposited at a distance from the concealed entrances to their underground D.C. headquarters. He had a passing thought to give the young nun a decent burial—but brushed it aside. She was dead. She didn't need his kindness. Those still living needed his full attention.

"So we're all 'prepared' in Canada? Greenland? Iceland? Norway? Spain? Italy? And Turkey?" he snapped at Arthur.

"They've all reported in—fuel supplies are waiting for us. But I still don't like you insisting on going personally, David. That's an awful long flight without alerting the Harvesters to our presence. You don't need to personally direct the final raid on the CPH. Why not just order the local Resistance to head up the attack and you monitor what happens from here?"

Dave growled under his breath.

"Arthur, I *have* to go on this mission."

"Well..."

"So it's decided," Dave firmly stated, turning away.

He was throwing the dice—all or nothing. If they could destroy CPH's command center, then the remaining pockets of Priestesses would scatter. The Resistance could concentrate on concealing more DE-generators—instead of defending themselves against other humans!

But Dave knew it was his *own mother* who was leading the fight against him. What would he do when he finally came face-to-face with her? Would he hug her? Would he kiss her? Would he lecture her? Or would he shoot her as dead as Arthur had that young nun?

He had no idea.

Rising out of hidden hangers into the gloomy morning air, sitting strapped into a front seat of the helicopter, Dave was certain he was never going to see Washington D.C. again.

It was now a perpetual, gloomy twilight. He was glad to leave. That which once was the thriving center of governance for the United States of America was now just a snowed-over, burnt-out husk. It looked no different than a thousand other decimated, frozen metropolitan disaster areas. And the persistent black soot-clouds above, through which little light filtered, was incredibly depressing.

Dave missed the sunlight.

"Operation is nominal," the pilot beside Dave reported. "It's been a long time since this craft was airborne, but so far so good."

Dave nodded back at him.

For once, the relentlessly cheerful Arthur had nothing to say, buckled into a jump seat in the back of the transport chopper with other fighters. Dave, still angry with him over his execution of the young nun, didn't even look back at him.

He just wondered if they could make it halfway around the world.

And why was he *really* doing this? Was it to take charge of the final push against the CPH? Or was it merely a death wish—to be killed heroically in battle instead of from ignoble suicide?

He knew that if this went on much longer he'd just take one of the nuns' super-guns and boil his own brains.

The stress, demands, cold, and horrors of the wars against humans and aliens alike—was getting too much for Dave to bear.

Plus there were the many unanswered questions. Why did that Harvester crash into the Earth, triggering a Nuclear Winter? Where was his Sally from the previous timeline? Was his prior life even real or just a delusion from being hit on the head? Were his jumbled memories of George turning into a talking dinosaur a nightmare or real? And what about George telling him the world would end because of his inventions? Was that the present Apocalypse...or something even worse?

Dave didn't know and was too tired to try to figure it all out. If he made it to Jerusalem, fine. If he didn't—fine! The world had grown so dark, so savage, and so empty he'd be glad to leave it *all* behind, not just the District of Columbia.

"We'll be flying really low," the pilot barked at Dave over the roar of the helicopter blades. "Hopefully we can get out of D.C. before any Aliens spot us."

Dave nodded absently.

He and a small squad of his best, heavily armed fighters were flying in a U.S. Army CH-21 Vietnam War-era transport helicopter. This and the other three helicopters in their contingent had survived the initial alien bombardment by being in long-term subterranean storage beneath the Smithsonian Air and Space Museum.

Yes, they were museum pieces—but still functional. At least, that's what Dave and the other fighters hoped. Indeed, they were betting their lives on it.

Beside the two transport choppers, alongside them flew two newer assault helicopters, heavily armed. They'd apparently been in the process of being decommissioned for display, cut short by the alien invasion. They were Boeing AH-64 Apache attack helicopters, each with a two-man crew. They had night vision systems, a 30 mm chain gun, and four hellfire missiles each.

Against the alien swarm-crafts, they'd have little-to-no hope of survival. But against fellow human forces, they'd be devastating. They just might be the edge that the Resistance forces need to prevail against the heavily defended world headquarters of the CPH in Jerusalem.

The Resistance technicians had outfitted each of the four helicopters with extra fuel tanks. But still, attempting to go halfway around the world, there'd be many refueling stops along the way.

Each helicopter had a shielded DE-generator installed to use as a last resort for energy-production. The helicopters weren't originally equipped to run on electricity, but small ion-blasters fitted to the blades could keep them spinning at a low speed.

But that was only for extreme emergencies. Since the robot-head shields weren't globes, any rocking of the helicopters would send off the normally downward radiation of the DE-generators to the sides. They'd be picked off in minutes the higher-patrolling alien attack ships.

But they might have to risk using the ion drives.

It was going to be a long journey.

They'd be flying at just a few hundred feet off the ground to evade detection by the Aliens. Another danger was the air "quality." A continual rain of heavy soot and junk made for poor visibility and sluggish rotation of the blades. However, that same perpetual, gloomy drizzle helped hide the helicopters from the high-orbiting Harvesters.

Dave wished those damn Aliens would just go away!

But, no, the number of raids by Reaper-laden transport crafts to the surface of the planet after the "accident" that destroyed Earth's climate did not decrease, but actually increased.

It was like the Reapers needed every last human they could find.

Any humans roaming out on the surface had a high chance of being picked up by a robot, bundled into a transport craft, and lifted up into orbit to be stashed into one of the Harvesters.

After finishing off the CPH, Dave was eager to take on the Alien Armada. He just needed to get a sufficient number of shielded DE-generators linked-up across the world. And then, with a global force field protecting the planet, Dave could concentrate on producing DE-*bombs!*

Where the military failed, he knew he could succeed. Yes he knew that was the reason why his prior incarnation escaped from the military research facility in Cheyenne Mountain—or so he was told by Arthur. But now Dave was a much different person.

Now, he had an insatiable *blood lust!* He wanted every single one of those implacable Aliens orbiting high above Earth's surface not only to die, but to *suffer!*

If he could just get the global network of DE-generators linked up—then everything was going to change.

But the first step was to decimate and destroy the crazy, fanatical CPH, whether his mother liked it or not.

The trip up across the remainder of the United States to Canada was uneventful.

They had to make several stops for quick refueling. But that wasn't difficult. Helicopters were constructed for landing wherever, under adverse conditions. They communicated with the ground Resistance units by quick bursts, mimicking RF static. Touching down, fighters swarmed out of underground caves, warrens, and basements—to resupply the choppers and get them back flying in minimal turnaround time.

Once, a whole squad of nuns attacked just as they landed. The fanatical nuns were beaten back with relentless assault rifle fire. The ambush caused only minor damage to one of the rotors, which was quickly repaired. Dave wondered if the timing of the attack was just coincidental—or did the CPH know they were coming?

If the CPH was tracking their progress, the nuns could bolster their defenses in Jerusalem.

It was not a pretty thought.

They might go halfway around the world just to fly into an ambush!

The total distance they had to travel to reach the Holy City was somewhere between seven and eight thousand miles, depending upon the route they took. Flying at a cruising speed of around 100 miles per hour, it would take them a minimum of three to four days, assuming they could flew constantly with no stops.

That was the quickest scenario. But it still allowed the new High Priestess plenty of time to fortify the CPH headquarters in Jerusalem against hellfire missiles. Worrying about the future, though, was pointless. They'd handle it when they got there. But for now, Dave was "lulled" into a fitful sleep by the uneven *throbbing* of the whirling rotor blades.

They spent a night in Halifax, Nova Scotia before attempting to transverse the Atlantic. The landscape was blanketed by heavy snow. The harbor, once home to thousands of large and small craft, was empty— filled instead with ominous, bobbing icebergs.

The global nuclear winter was accelerating.

The planet was freezing.

From Nova Scotia the small party of helicopters ventured out over the North Atlantic. There they encountered a fierce storm, which tossed their little helicopters around like toothpicks. Since they were flying only a few hundred feet above the towering, white-capped waves, it was incredibly dangerous. Unfortunately, one of the two Apache attack helicopters was caught in a downdraft and sucked straight into a towering wave.

It vanished beneath the churning waters without a trace.

The survivors in the still-flying helicopters were even more solemn than before—and bitterly determined to complete their mission—when they managed to barely limp into Greenland.

They spent the night there, licking their wounds.

Then they flew on to Iceland. And from there the plan was to attempt a long flight to Scotland. So they filled their extra tanks to capacity plus packed every square inch of available space with spare fuel containers.

The three lonely helicopters lifted up from the snow-covered airport in Reykjavik and headed out over the ocean, fighting a thick blizzard. Flying low was much too hazardous, especially after the loss of the Apache. So they took the chance of flying higher, at 5,000 feet. They were above the worst of the low-lying storm, but risked detection by prowling alien cannon-ships.

Indeed, one of the two CH-21 transports momentarily flew into a clear patch of sky and was immediately targeted by a patrolling cannon-craft. A *brilliant red laser* streaked down from much higher up in the sky, instantly exploding the craft.

Dave watched helplessly as the disintegrated remains fell into underlying clouds.

The two remaining craft swung deeper into the cloud bank, dropping lower toward the turbulent ocean's surface.

They escaped the prowling alien craft, but were devastated emotionally—knowing their comrades in the doomed transport had no chance. They were just shot out of the sky. One moment they were flying along, cramped and bored—and the next moment they were dead.

They will be avenged!—Dave shouted inside his own head.

His blood-lust was at a fever pitch, stoked by their extended inaction stuck in the transport helicopter.

But they still had a long stretch of dangerous ocean to transverse before he'd have any chance to spill the blood of their enemies—whether human or alien! Indeed, they just barely stayed aloft with ion-power after their regular fuel was exhausted—finally fluttering feebly down into Elgin, Scotland.

Dave and his men were as drained as their fuel...cold and exhausted from the long, perilous journey across the Atlantic.

They landed at the Elgin Cathedral, a magnificent sandstone monument of medieval architecture. They heavily dropped onto a snow-filled, empty courtyard, landing with a jarring "thud." Local fighters came running out from under the high arches, dragging fuel containers.

"Is King 'ere?" one shouted, looking up at the fogged-over windows.

"I'm here!" Dave said, climbing stiffly out and jumping down upon the packed snow.

He beat his arms against the bitter cold, trying to stay alert. His body wanted him to go off with the local guerilla fighters to their hidden base and get twenty hours of sleep. But he knew they had to keep going.

"We've bin waiting fur ye a lang time, Dauvit!" the man cheerfully called-out, coming over to shake his hand.

Both he and Dave were clad in thick overcoats, wearing heavy gloves, with snow goggles covering their eyes. A putrid, dark snow was continually drifting down from the dark sky, making it hard even to see each other.

In addition, an icy wind was blasting in off the ocean, making it difficult to hear anything.

Plus, Dave had trouble understanding the man's thick Scottish accent. But he caught the jist of it.

"Whit speirins fae Jerusalem?" the man asked, shouting into Dave's ear.

Dave yelled back: "We've gotten a few good bursts from our people in Jerusalem. Our fighters are congregating near the Temple Mount. We think the 'CPH' headquarters are somewhere in the surrounding catacombs. Have you heard anything from here?"

"Th' Italians captured twa nuns," the man shouted back. "Under torture thay claimed th' headquarters is a freish excavation directly under th' Temple Mount, neane o' th' older, natural catacombs!"

"That's very helpful!" Dave yelled back. "Thank you! We've got to leave!"

"God speed tae ye—murdurr a' they damn nuns!"

"We'll try!" Dave yelled against the bitter wind, climbing back into the door of the chopper.

They lifted off laboriously, barely escaping being slung sideways against one of the high spires of the skeletal cathedral's ruins by the powerful wind.

Their next stop was outside London, then near Paris, then Rome, then Athens, then Izir Turkey, then the island of Cyprus, then Beirut Lebanon—and then, at last, the Holy City of *Jerusalem*.

They'd made it.

He was bone weary and could barely keep his eyes open, but elated none-the-same.

It was time to *kill* a whole boatload of nuns!

Dave was *eager* to get about the task.

At this point in his long journey he had zero regrets.

Chapter 15

THE HOLY LAND

Jesus walked these flagstones
And other religious Founders
Kings, Emperors, and Priests
Making a few rocky hills Sacred
To be fought over viciously
Soaking the streets in red blood
A perpetual orgy of slaughter
Self-righteous Warriors certain
Of the nobility of their actions
Raping, pillaging, killing everyone
Who dared to question or pursue
Another Way different from theirs
Automatically condemned Heathens
Or worse yet, the vile Heretics
Worthy only of extermination
That God might be appeased
And grant to the proud Victors
Glory, Honor, and Wealth
Freedom from nagging Guilt
Doing, always, what is "right"!

The Luminary Chronicles, 15:89-94

Jean King sat in a comfortable armchair at the head of a long conference table, looking at her chief lieutenants.

On the tabletop in front of her lay a big, black Bible.

"Tea?" she graciously asked, arising to lift up a steaming porcelain tea kettle by its handle.

The white-hooded women at the table all nodded in unison.

It was a new ritual, imposed by the High Priestess. She felt that even in the midst of bitter conflict, there was no need to be uncivilized.

Every war meeting started with tea.

A young servant girl passed out cups. Each contained a dry teabag. The Priestesses accepted their cups with a silent prayer of thanks.

Then Jean walked from one to the next, pouring hot water into their cups.

It was a ritual passed on from the hallowed, martyred Sally—the "water of life," shared by everyone. To the rank and file plus the world at large, she'd been the imperial "Linda Powers." But to her closest friends and followers she'd revealed her inner beauty as their beloved "Sally."

The brief ceremony symbolized that in the *Church of Perpetual Health*, no one would ever go thirsty!

Jean then walked back and sat at the head of the conference table.

But as they sat sipping their cups—where the hot water leached caffeine-laden brown clouds from the precious teabags—a darker cloud hung above them.

The evil "Resistance" was poised to launch a huge attack.

"Brownies?" Jean politely asked.

Again, they all nodded in unison.

The High Priestess lifted up a tray of small, finger-food-sized fresh-baked brownies, handing it to the nearest woman to pass around.

Dutifully, they each took one, holding it until they were all served—then together nibbling ritualistically.

The ceremony ended. Jean instantly was all-business.

"Have they landed?" she asked.

"Yes, Mother," one of them replied, standing up. She unfolded a dusty map of Jerusalem to stick it up with pins on a poster-board off to the side of the conference table.

"So where are they?"

"They landed on Mount Zion, Mother," the woman said, placing a big red pin onto the elevated site located near the Temple Mount and the Western Wall. "Their helicopters are being refueled as we speak. They still have one Apache, with its four hellfire missiles in place. The other was lost in the ocean. Plus they have one surviving transport helicopter."

"Is my son still alive?" Jean asked, deep concern showing on her drawn face.

"We believe he is," another woman stated, in fact I'm getting an image now from our observers."

She stood up to project a live transmission from her cellphone onto a blank, white wall. There, standing beside a dark helicopter whose blades were still slowly turning, was the image of a heavily jacketed, brown-bearded man.

He was standing talking with the local Resistance commander—a tough-looking, wiry, white-bearded old man.

"That's him. That's Davey!" Jean grinned, pointing to the younger man. "Oh, thank the Lord! He's come back to me at last. We can finally resolve this silly war."

"It would be much easier just to kill him and his comrades," another woman at the table, a tough-looking older woman, complained. "They're out in the open—the Leader, his chief enforcer, and the local commander. Your Highness, they're *vulnerable*."

"*No*, Gracie!" Jean peevishly yelled back at her. "There will be no killing today!"

Jean was standing, her mouth pressed into a thin line, with *fire* in her eyes.

Then she visibly calmed herself, reaching up to stroke her long, grey hair as she walked over to the hanging map.

Even though she still required it of all her Priestesses, she hated having the Hood upon her own head. It was a sign of her "new" order after Sally's death. Hers was a kinder, gentler administration. She was determined not to be just a mysterious hooded ruler, but a true 'Mother'!

Jean viewed her flock as unruly children—who needed firm discipline and direction, yes, but also love.

"You will flank them at the *Mitchell and Ha Tkuma Gardens*," Jean said, pointing out the locations with a finger. "But don't attack unless defending yourselves," she ordered. "Merely keep in place, surrounding and containing their fighters. It won't be long before peace will reign not only over us in Jerusalem, the Holy City of God—but across the entire planet."

The hooded women looked at each other with concern. It was obvious to Jean they were not convinced by her grand rhetoric. They'd been at war with the Resistance fighters for far too long. Too much blood was spilt. Too many of their Sisters were dead because of brutal attacks from the Rebels.

And they'd been brainwashed to kill their fellow humans without hesitation.

"There will be a *sign from above*," Jean confidently stated, smiling benignly at them. "You will see. It only takes a mature, loving Mother's touch to tame even the most savage of beasts. Undeniable proof will convince even the most cynical critic amongst you—which you will see *today*."

The women sat silently at the table, dutifully staring forward.

"Keep Faith, my dears," Jean said as she returned to her armchair and sipped at her cooling cup of tea, *"dismissed."*

One by one they filed out...

—until only Gracie was left, Jean's chief lieutenant.

"Mother," she politely addressed Jean. "I still think this is a mistake—we can't trust..."

"I've already accomplished what everyone else thought was impossible, haven't I?" Jean snapped. Her benevolent expression instantly transformed into fierce conviction.

"Yes...our transmissions over the last remaining satellites were received—but it could be a ploy."

"It is evidence that things have *changed*," Jean firmly stated, setting her now-empty cup off to the side. "After the supposed 'end of the world' when our dear Mother Sally was martyred, *both* sides were chastened. It was the *Will of God* that Armageddon end not with fire but *Ice*. So in this frozen world we have a *choice*: we can continue senseless conflict or *reconcile*."

"But Mother Sally was crystal clear on..."

"She was a *fanatic*, Gracie," Jean abruptly interrupted her. "She was on a mindless *Crusade* against Dark Energy. She *didn't* have our best interests at heart! And look what it brought us, dear Gracie—only misery and death. The pitifully few remaining humans on our beloved planet are clawing themselves to pieces! But our new alliance promises to fix Earth's climate, let us survivors live in peace, and eventually elevate us to our rightful place in the Galactic Community. Can you deny this is *God's Will?* Our Lord and Savior Jesus Christ Himself in the Holy Bible showed that mankind would be given a second chance after the Apocalypse, did He not?"

Jean grinned broadly, reveling in the glorious vision.

But her chief deputy didn't seem convinced...

"It...all sounds wonderful," Gracie gulped, "But..."

"Today, in this place, a *Summit* of the best and finest human fighters remaining on Earth will join together," Jean smiled, walking over to Gracie to place her hands on the thin woman's shoulders. "The leadership of the two remaining world-wide institutions will meet here in the Holy City. I repeat—have *Faith*, dear Gracie. It's going to work out fine. It says so right in the Bible."

She loudly "thumped" her hand down upon the big black book sitting on the table.

"I...I...hope so..."

"Don't 'hope'," Jean sternly commanded her, "*believe!*"

"I...believe," Gracie repeated, visibly overwhelmed by the iron conviction of her High Priestess.

"Good," Jean gently replied. She patted Gracie on her shoulder, "now you *get my Son* and bring him to me!"

"Yes, Mother," the woman sharply nodded, turning and quickly leaving the room.

Jean looked up at the ceiling.

On it, she'd had her Priestesses paint a replica of Michelangelo's depiction of God touching Adam and imparting to him the spark of Life—exactly as it looked upon the ceiling of the Sistine Chapel in the Vatican before it was destroyed in the initial alien bombardment.

This is what it's all about—she thought to herself, looking up at the strong hand of God poised to touch the limp, lifeless hand of Adam. *It's not about inevitable death, but the Divine Act of Creation!*

Jean King was convinced that Earth was not just an empty stellar husk to be pillaged for its few remaining goodies. That nonsense about the unrestricted use of Dark Energy bringing down the wrath of God was just plain stupid. The Bible didn't say anything about Dark Energy. Yes, Armageddon was now clearly upon mankind—but the Righteous *would* be saved to dwell on a *new* Earth, in a new *Kingdom of God!*

Of this Jean had no doubt. And she was in the process of making it happen.

She was certain that her beloved Jesus would be proud of her.

Dave was checking his solar-powered laptop for any short-range transmissions. He should be beneath the ground now, headed for the hidden base and some much-needed sleep. But as "The Leader" he needed to be on top of everything before giving-in to his exhaustion.

"Damn laptop," he muttered.

The battery hardly ever charged up fully in the nuclear winter, but outside the 'copter in the open there was enough diffuse light for it barely to get the laptop working. Dave wanted an immediate broadband survey of the immediate area. Sometimes he could get an early indication of enemy activity, particularly lurking ambushes as nuns communicated on shortwave bands.

Then he heard an ominous noise and looked up...

—and saw a *black rectangular spacecraft* fully five miles long descending from the roiling brown clouds above!

"Oh, hell," he gulped, horrified.

Its *throbbing, heavy vibration* jarred Dave's teeth.

Dave was frozen in place, immobilized by *deja vu*...

A Mother Ship had descended out of orbit only once before in Dave's experience. It was at the alien incineration of Edmond, Oklahoma. That was when he and his comrades were thrown into the time tunnel...

—and here it was happening again!

Was it coming to finish that which, by unknown forces, was thwarted before?

"Come *on*, David!" Arthur said, grabbing Dave by his arm and dragging him toward a tunnel leading below the surface of Mount Zion. "Commander M'Sheekha just left for the base below. There's only one cart left. We've got to get out of here!"

Dave snapped his laptop closed and stuck it back into his backpack.

"No!" Dave protested, trying to jerk free. "I've got to see what happens. Eashoa will wait for us below. We've got to get our choppers before..."

As if hearing him, the Apache helicopter behind Dave suddenly lifted off, its pilot taking the initiative—rapidly rising toward the descending behemoth above, and then *firing its four hellfire missiles!*

They streaked up toward the gigantic spaceship...

—bursting futilely into *little red flares* against the Harvester's surrounding force-field...

—as a wide, dazzling LASER BEAM suddenly blasted from the huge craft overhead, dead-straight at the nearby Temple Mount!

The resultant EXPLOSION knocked Dave off his feet.

A more focused beam flashed down straight at Dave and Anderson. The grounded transport chopper took the brunt of the blow, partially protecting the two men. But it was destroyed.

The Apache attack helicopter, apparently of little concern to the Harvester, was *flung* by the blast through the sky. To Dave it looked like a toy thrown from the hands of a giant child. It tumbled end-over-end in the sky, disappearing in the maelstrom beyond the Temple Mount.

Dave noted dejectedly the path of its floundering descent...their one military asset against the Aliens was *gone.*

"Oh, hell," Dave groaned.

He continued to watch in horror as the continuous, sizzling red beam continued *slicing through* the snow-covered mound, reducing the Temple Mount to a lump of molten lava.

"Mom?" Dave gasped.

Arthur pulled him into the tunnel as the Harvester methodically pulverized selected, still-protruding surface features of the City of Jerusalem.

"We've got to get deep down into the catacombs if we're going to survive the bombardment," Arthur said, pulling Dave onto a golf cart that then swooped downward into a long, descending tunnel.

Around Dave the walls of the tunnel were trembling, as *shock waves* continued permeating through the limestone rock around him.

The jarring "thuds" hurt Dave's ears.

"The Aliens must have been tracking us from the start," Arthur sighed dejectedly beside Dave on the careening cart, shaking his head in resignation. "Here we thought we were pulling a fast one on them—and they were waiting for us! They probably wanted our main forces together in one location—so they could squash us all once and forever more."

"Not us," Dave grudgingly yet gratefully observed, "it's the Church!"

"What do you...?" Arthur began.

"We came here to destroy the CPH, didn't we?"

"Yes...?"

"That Harvester's done a better job than we could ever hope to manage with our small, dispersed army," Dave said. He looked up at the shuddering ceiling of the limestone tunnel as they sped deeper into the bowels of the mountain. "If the headquarters of the CPH was truly located beneath the Temple Mount—as we suspected—then it's now gone. The aliens have actually *helped* us. With the CPH leadership destroyed, their nuns all across the world will just fade away into the background. The CPH can no longer stop us from *linking together* our hidden DE-generators!"

"You mean...?"

"We've *won*, Arthur!" Dave intensely said, grabbing Arthur's shoulder in a tight grip as they continued swooping down the tunnel in their cart. "It's now *inevitable* that our planetary, Dark Energy shield will appear around Earth! And then we'll take our fight to the Reaper robots that are cut-off from their support system, stranded down here on the surface. We'll take back our planet!"

"Praise God!" Arthur intensely whispered, taking his dark eyeglasses off and holding them in his hands.

Rocking back and forth in the rapidly descending cart, Dave was caught by surprise. He looked into *black pits* where Arthur's eyes should have been. And *diamond, glittering patterns* swooped up from the hypnotic depths, snaring Dave!

Before he could resist he was sucked into Arthur's empty eye sockets. He squirmed mightily, trying to break free.

But there was no escape.

Jean King was caught by surprise.

She had not expected *Satan* to come knocking at her door...

But there he was!

He was stooped over, fully ten feet tall—twelve feet if you counted the long pointed horns growing from his big bald head. His scaly skin was a fiery red. He had long yellow hair covering his groin and butt like a goatish kilt. His "feet" were large hoofs. From the upper crack of his butt a long, reptilian tail protruded, twitching excitedly back and forth.

"May I come in?" he respectfully requested.

His eyes glowed—*hot yellow!*

"Can I stop you?" she disdainfully replied.

"No," he admitted as he squeezed through the opening into the conference room, sitting nonchalantly on the floor and leaning casually back against a wall.

"So you're the Alien I've been communicating with?" she said, sitting back down in her armchair.

"I am, indeed," he grinned, revealing a mouthful of long pointed teeth.

"And you honor our agreement by *destroying the Temple Mount?*" she yelled at him, trying to understand this terrible apparition sitting calmly in front of her, taking up half the room.

"I'm only doing what God dictates," he cryptically shrugged, reaching over to pick up one of the remaining brownies.

He eyed the treat doubtfully then popped it into his mouth.

He chewed it thoughtfully.

His red face lit up with pleasure!

"I doubt that!" she angrily replied, crossing her arms and staring accusingly at the Demon. "We had a deal!"

"Yes, one that I tested," he grinned. "It's lucky for you that your headquarters is actually deep underneath the 'Church of the Holy Sepulchre' instead of the Mount—as you *misdirected* both me and your human enemies—here where your Jesus is said to have been buried more than 2,000 of your years ago," he wickedly grinned. "We actually *spared* this site in our bombardment, knowing that you were hiding deep in catacombs beneath its ruins instead of where you mis-directed us."

"I wasn't going to risk our whole operation by giving you our exact location," she coldly stated, "and it seems I was quite correct in doing so. How did you find me?"

The sitting, giant Demon shrugged. "I have technology that's good at locating any planetary target, particularly one that uses radio waves such as your few still-working cellphones. My Armada just needed a knowledgeable agent, me, to fine-tune the location mechanism. I've actually only recently arrived here at your planet."

"How very nice for you," she sardonically replied. "But God will *not* allow you to..."

"You mean this 'Jesus' person?" he interrupted her.

"You know of Jesus?" she guardedly asked.

He casually speared another brownie with a talon protruding from one of his fingers, popping it into his wide mouth.

"I do indeed," he cryptically replied. "And I've studied up on your world's religious literature," he evilly grinned as he loudly chewed on his treat. "Your Jesus' teachings in that Bible over there on the table describe the end of your world—remarkably accurate! In fact, his ac-counts gave me as much pleasure as do your little cakes. So in honor of your revered 'Messiah' I dressed the part of his main Adversary. Did I get it right?" he added, seemingly concerned that his appear-ance was correct.

"You see yourself as the Devil?" Jean said, her icy voice showing her revulsion.

"I don't 'see' myself," he laughed, theatrically snorting out two puffs of black smoke from his large, flared nostrils. "I *am* the 'Devil' of your world."

"What do you mean?" Jean replied, growing even more fearful.

The Alien jerked up to his feet, *smashing* the ceiling upward with the motion of his head—while flinging out his powerful arms to *crush* the walls back behind him!

In the hallway outside of the ripped-apart wall Jean saw a *pile of dismembered, bloodied corpses*—her dead Priestesses.

Gracie's severed head sat unblinkingly upon the top of the heap, staring accusingly at Jean.

"I AM THE SERPANT IN THE GARDEN!" he *screeched* joyfully. His voice was an amplified, thudding trumpet vibrating the walls. "I AM THE INQUISTOR OF HUMANITY, THE TEMPTOR, THE PRINCE OF DEMONS, THE UNCLEAN SPIRIT, THE AUTHOR OF EVIL, THE MURDERER, THE FATHER OF LIES, THE PRINCE OF DARKNESS, THE RAMPAGING BEAST, THE ANGEL OF THE ABYSS, AND THE GREAT DEVOURING DRAGON!"

Jean sucked in her breath, appalled.

"Isn't that exactly how your 'Book' describes me?" the Alien laughed, sinking down to sit again with his back to the remains of the shattered wall.

"We were supposed to have a deal," Jean angrily repeated. "You were going to *go away* if we helped you fill your cargo requirements. You were going to *leave behind* us Righteous people, in peace—while *carting away* all the evil sinners!"

The Alien laughed.

"Haven't you read your own Book?" he seemingly innocently asked, pointing to the thick black Bible still lying undisturbed on the table.

"What do you mean?"

"Isn't there a passage which says '*There is none righteous, no not one*'?"

"Well..."

"And so I will indeed uphold my end of the agreement," he cackled, then *screeched* again, his amplified voice almost breaking Jean's eardrums: "I WILL TAKE *ALL* THE SINNERS—LEAVING BEHIND *ALL* THE 'RIGHTEOUS'...which means that *not one single human* remains behind, including *yourself*—you stupid little animal!"

Jean found herself defenseless against this evil, powerful Creature.

"But," she desperately tried to protest: "*Jesus* makes the unrighteous righteous and..."

"Oh?" he laughed again, stopping her weak defense. He flicked out his long, forked tongue in disdain. "And just where *is* this 'Jesus'?"

Jean felt tears trickling down her cheeks.

Here at what she'd thought was her greatest victory in forging a truce with the Aliens—that became her greatest trial and defeat, she stood alone.

"Nowhere..." she admitted, defeated.

She slumped into her chair, burying her head in her arms.

Jean's worst nightmare was made manifest. She was abandoned by Jesus. Instead of Him, she was now a servant of Satan.

Chapter 16

MOONBEAMS

Don't cry, little bunny

Lost without your Mommy

It's true that wolves are prowling

But the night is not so dark

If you lift your head up to the sky

And drink in those cool moonbeams

Flooding into your big, wide eyes

A connection from you to the Cosmos

A backhanded greeting from the Sun

There to guide your faltering hops

Instilling you with hopeful direction

From the dangers of open spaces

Into the shelter of your family

Huddled safe in a warm hollow...

The Luminary Chronicles, 16:383-386

Dave stood upon the surface of the moon, clutching his backpack in his arms.

Surrounding him were gray craters, stark black shadows, and a star-sprinkled horizon.

Above him floated the round orb of Earth—but no longer a bright pearl, rather a muddy marble.

"It's ugly, isn't it?" Arthur sighed, staring sadly up at the dirt-colored ejectus and smoke-clouds that completely shrouded the planet.

The FBI Agent's black eyeglasses were back in place, hiding his empty eye sockets.

"How is this possible?" Dave gasped, feeling gingerly around him.

A *clear transparent bubble* surrounded both him and Arthur—that pushed outward from the pressure of Dave's hands but didn't break. It was protecting them from the airless, frozen surface of the moon!

"Just watch..." Arthur stated.

A cloud of little dots were approaching the moon from the Earth, growing larger and larger. Each of the many dots was illuminated and outlined by a pulsating, blue light.

The dots resolved into a fleet of giant Harvester ships.

"They're looking to escape Earth's gravity-well before triggering their subspace drives," Arthur mildly observed, staring at them as they zipped past and behind the moon.

"What's happening?" Dave asked Arthur, totally confused.

"They got what they wanted," he shrugged. "Now they're rats deserting a sinking ship...looking to jump into an even larger sinking ship—delivering what's left of humanity into a *bottomless black pit.*"

"Jesus Christ..." Dave gasped in shock. "That sounds an awful like *hell.*"

He still didn't know what was happening. Was this a nightmare, a delusion, or real? The last thing he remembered was trying to escape the Harvester's blasting laser means, hurtling down the tunnel deeper beneath Mount Zion. And he'd looked into *Arthur's eyes...*

"Yep, it'll be hell for any survivors," Anderson sadly stated, "and even worse for anyone left on the planet."

A *strange haze* was growing against the blackness of space behind the fleeing Harvester spaceships.

It was growing brighter...and *redder.*

In the direction of the sun, Dave saw a *roiling mass of bristling red fire*...growing ever larger and nearer!

"It's the End of the World," Arthur quietly stated, his big hand shaking as he put it up to his mouth in awe. "God is sending a *gigantic plasma cloud* from a *solar super-storm* to sterilize the surface of the Earth."

"*God* is destroying the entire world?" Dave gasped, "But why?"

Agent Anderson ignored the question.

"At last it's finally happening—with no reprieve," he grinned. "There won't be any more hopping backward. There won't be any further 'alternate timelines.' At last it's happening for *real*."

In shock, Dave looked at his friend uncomprehendingly. It was obvious to him that Arthur wasn't just an ex-FBI Agent who loved to wear dark eyeglasses.

Dave realized that his past memories were correct—Anderson *did* harbor an intelligent, evolved computer program in his brain.

And "alternate timelines"...Dave's prior life *did* happen!

"Yep," Arthur answered Dave's unspoken question. "I'm not just a person who happened to befriend you to fight the Aliens. I'm a *time-traveler* from a future that no longer exists. I was sent back in time to *facilitate* the unrestrained usage of Dark Energy—and stop those who opposed it—knowing full-well that such a Cosmic Flare would attract the full scrutiny and Judgment of *God Himself*."

"Say what?" Dave gasped. "You mean our planetary shield? Is this what we're seeing right now...in the *future?*"

Anderson nodded.

"It lit up the cosmos, David. It flared like a light bulb in the Universe. And it attracted the *full attention* of God!"

"But...our planetary shield will protect the Earth, right? Didn't it stop those Aliens and send them packing? Won't it also keep out that approaching plasma cloud?"

"Oh, Dave—you are so trusting," Arthur shook his head sadly. "The Harvester ships just punched holes into our so-called 'planetary shield.' Yes, it took them weeks to figure out a way to do it—but they got through. Your pitifully weak 'shield' in the long run was *worthless*. And, also, it *will* stop the sun's super-storm ejectus—maybe for a few seconds. After that, the Earth's entire surface will be incinerated, shield or no shield."

"Arthur, *no!*" Dave groaned, grabbing his beefy friend and shaking him. "This can't be true. Tell me this is a hallucination or a nightmare!"

"Nope! Sorry, buddy. It's all true," Arthur grinned, brushing off Dave's hands to then hop up and down with unrestrained glee. His feet "crunched" into the caked lunar dust at his feet. "And along the way—in *several* timelines, in fact—I did get attached to you, David.

So now that it's finally happening, I wanted you here with me to appreciate it."

"You're *enjoying* this?" Dave said, not believing his ears or the
evidence of his own eyes.

Yes, Arthur had an expression of *pure joy* on his face!

"We've been...only glancing peripherally...noticed before by our
dear Creator...but now—it's the *magnificence* of our Creator finally
turned *full-force* upon us!" Arthur yelled up rapturously at the reddening sky.

"To *destroy* us?" Dave disbelievingly gasped.

"That doesn't matter, Dave—don't you see?" Arthur earnestly replied. "We are basking in the direct Presence of the Creator of the
Universe. It's glorious! It's our greatest Honor. *His Will* be done,
amen! *Hallelujah!*"

For a moment Dave gaped wordlessly at the deliriously celebrat-
ing, dancing Agent.

"You're completely *nuts!*" he screamed at the Agent. "Get me out
of here. Send me back to Earth!"

"Oh, David," Arthur sighed, his eyes fixated on the *roiling cloud
of plasma* engulfing the Earth, hiding the planet from view, relentlessly expanding—and then headed straight for the moon. "Fate is a
terrible and beautiful thing. Our heroic, though losing, *struggle*—
against both our own terrible sins and our impending doom—is what
is most-pleasing to our Lord. Everything dies. This whole entire
Universe will die. But it's our fighting against the inevitable that's a
sweet aroma, our most-worthy sacrifice, to our awesome God!"

"Oh, that's fine theology—I suppose," Dave grated, looking at the
approaching, blazing maelstrom in fear, "but I prefer to keep going
rather than stopping. Send us back!"

"You want to go back to your hopeless, futile life—than, in a short
while, to yet again witness the magnificent End of the World?" Arthur
seriously asked.

"*Yes!*"

"Well, you do still have a year left."

"A year? That's all?"

"Yes. This is happening one year ahead in your future, Dave. I
thought you should know about it. Now that it is finalized, its course

set, I show it to you as a courtesy. Not many people can mark the date of their own deaths. So enjoy the time that remains to you when..."

"No! That's not enough time!" Dave urgently interrupted him. "Can't we ask God to hold off for a while—say a thousand years or so?"

"I'm sorry, Dave. We're just not that important."

The horrific panorama of craters and black shadows reddening under the approaching plasma cloud began to *fade*...

"Come with me!" Dave shouted at Arthur, reaching out for him.

But Arthur was taking off his black eyeglasses to stare up sightlessly at the glaring expanse of fire-filled outer space, a look of sheer wonderment on his eyeless face.

The black pits of his eyes were filled with swirling diamond patterns....

—which reached out to again suck Dave in...

"Goodbye, my friend," Arthur said, smiling rapturously.

And Dave suddenly found himself back in the rapidly descending, racing cart...

But Arthur was gone.

And Dave, drained of energy, felt himself slumping forward, lulled by the rocking of the small vehicle.

His heavy eyelids drooped. His bone-weary muscles relaxed.

He clutched his backpack in his lap as if it were a dear baby, laying his head down on its rough fabric...

—and fell into an exhausted, dreamless slumber.

Jean King stood on shaky legs on top of what was left of Mount Zion.

It was night.

Behind her was a square, black spaceship, settled into the muddy snow.

Standing beside her was Satan.

He brought me here to see with my own two eyes what his Power accomplished—Jean moaned to herself.

Beside them was the wreckage of a melted-down helicopter. A small opening in the ground remained of the escape-hatch her son and others used to creep into their hidey-holes.

Above them Jean saw a full moon shining down through a slit in the dark, roiling clouds. It briefly lit up the scene in a garish white glow.

The Harvester had cut that slit in the thick clouds through which the moon shone, at the direction of the Demon. It was just another demonstration of his overwhelming Power.

"I do *so* enjoy your little world," the Demon grinned, revealing sharpened rows of pointed teeth, "enough to gobble it up!—especially after I've thoroughly 'tenderized' it."

Where Jean should have observed a proud, ancient city set upon rolling hills—there were only ruins amidst gaping craters quickly being covered by freezing snow drifting down from the ever-present black clouds above.

Looming over everything was the gigantic Harvester, which floated beneath the clouds in the turbulent night sky. It was an overwhelming Force dominating the tiny fighters scampering-about below.

And swarming across the ruined streets and slopes of Jerusalem were thousands of the robotic Reapers, snatching up any exposed human survivors.

In the silvery moonlight, Jean could hear their distant screams and cries.

Each one cut her to the heart.

"There's nothing much left here for you to take," Jean numbly observed, shivering.

She had on her thick, hooded jacket, but it wasn't enough to keep out the pervasive cold.

As much as she disliked it, the white hood was up over her head. The dirty snow falling on her was like frozen mud—clinging and smearing her normally impeccably clean clothing.

She felt that her innermost soul was being soiled.

"Oh, there's plenty of good stuff still beneath the surface," the Demon chortled, pacing on the now-flattened mountaintop, leaving deep hoof prints in the snow. "You *Homo sapiens* love to dive into holes, as did your rat-like evolutionary ancestors. Below us are the remnants of your human enemies. You son is amongst them, is he not?"

"How do you know so much about us?"

"My surveillance is pervasive. After all, I'm 'Satan,' aren't I?"

"You're not omnipotent."

"Oh?"

"You need me to help you dig the few survivors out, right?"

"Yes!" he happily stated, letting his blazing yellow eyes focus on her trembling, smaller form. "Their little burrows are too tight and deep for the Reapers to go down and pull them out. So you must entice them to come out voluntarily. I'll send your image and words out on every frequency across your planet. Wherever they have a receiver, they'll see or hear you."

Jean fought back tears, trying to understand.

"Why do you care so much about us? You've looted all our material resources. What's so special about harvesting our flesh? Do you *eat* us?"

He grinned widely, exposing his knife-sharp teeth.

"Ah, hah, *hah!*" he bellowed out into the frozen expanse around them. "In a sense I will. They are a foul 'flavoring' essential to a magnificent 'meal' I'm preparing at the center of the Galaxy."

"I could offer some spicy herbs instead?"

"Not the same!" he snapped. "And it's not just quality—it's quantity. To make a real impact I need as many of you disgusting creatures as possible."

"If you say so," Jean sourly whispered.

"Just do your part," the Demon growled. "Draw them out of their filthy rat-holes."

"What should I say?" she dully complied, unable to feel the tips of her fingers or nose in the bitter cold.

"Tell them you negotiated a truce," the Demon hissed at her. "Tell them that that those who 'turn themselves in' will be given safe sanctuary. Tell them that the 'invaders' will transport them to a safe place on your planet where a colony will be allowed to continue past the Harvest."

"But you told me you were taking *everyone*, including *me!*" she soberly reflected.

He grinned evilly.

"I *lied*," he laughed good-naturedly. "It sapped your will to resist, did it not? But now I offer you a *true* measure of hope."

She ducked her head down into her coat, closing her eyes.

Jesus prayed to God for help, apparently against temptations from this very same Satanic Alien! In response, the Savior received supernatural strength to battle the Creature. But all she'd gotten from God was silence. Was God testing her? She dearly wanted to believe it was a test—just as she'd ordered the now-dead Gracie to do—but found she just didn't have the heart.

Satan lied to her before. He was probably lying now.

Her world was dead, her faith squashed, and she herself would soon would be snuffed-out as well.

"I have no reason to cooperate," she whispered, lowering her head even more, trying to block out the horrific scene around her. "Just kill me and be done with it."

She felt a hard, hot arm slide across her shoulders.

The fetid breath of the Demon blew beneath her hood and into her nose as he leaned close above her.

The foul stench made her gag.

"But I *like* you, 'Mother'," he leered. "The idea of leaving a colony behind makes perfect sense, doesn't it? And I will do exactly that— perhaps located where your Brazil once was—with *you*, dear lady, *in charge* of it! What do you say? Isn't that interesting? You can be the 'mother' of the survivors, making them obey all your little religious dictates. Now tell me the truth—doesn't that cheer you up?"

She suspiciously looked up into the glowing yellow eyes hanging seductively right above her.

The Demon was playing her, like a cat toying with a mouse.

She involuntarily shuddered.

"Why would you do that?" she suspiciously asked.

The Demon's chest heaved, seemingly in sympathy to Jean—the large red scales expanding to accommodate the sucked-in air. Its long red tail "tenderly" curled itself around one of Jean's trembling legs.

It felt like a snake.

"Well, my dear 'High Priestess', we want to *keep* coming back here!" he dramatically snorted at her, covering her head in puffs of black smoke from his flared nostrils. "You *Homo sapiens* are delight-fully and exquisitely evil. There's none as wicked or as disgusting as you in the whole Cosmos. You are self-aware and God-aware, yet still behave as ignorant, selfish animals. You haven't progressed beyond your monkey origins. You are evolutionarily, mentally, and spiritual-ly stunted. On the Cosmic Scale of intelligence you are imbecilic! It's *wonderful!*"

"That's just not true," she weakly protested.

"Really?" the Demon snorted. "You slaughter each other without compunction—raping, killing, and stealing. You wage savage and endless war on each other. You shoot and kill innocent people, even women and children. And the worst pillagers of all are those that claim to follow God. Hah! There are no fiercer savages than your own 'holy' Priestesses. You're all *deliciously* evil, far more than me! At least I'm honest in my endeavors while you delude yourselves, thinking you are 'righteous,' doing 'God's Will.' It's marvelous irony!"

The Demon shrilly laughed, apparently enjoying his tirade.

"But that's not everyone," Jean feebly tried to debate with him.

"You poison and pollute your own planet," the Satanic figure con-tinued, undeterred. "You cover the planet in your own stinking wastes. You kill your oceans. You adulterate your atmosphere. You drive countless other species into extinction. You reproduce without limit—not even considering the effect upon those very offspring themselves. You enslave each other. You abuse each other. For the sake of a momentary surge of pleasure many of you live your lives self-enslaved to tiny addictive chemical compounds. You poison and destroy your own bodies with your daily foods, just because they 'taste good'. Shall I continue? There's much, much more evidence of your species' depravity!"

Jean had no defense. Everything he said was true.

"So—why not just *kill* us if we really are so hideous?"

"Because what you are, despicably filthy intelligent creatures, is *exactly* what I need for my higher purposes!" the Demon reassured her, slapping a hot hand onto her exposed cheek. "I want a *surviving* colony of yours to *breed* and *continue* to proliferate. The seed-colony will repopulate your planet. And in another century or millennium or tens of thousands of your years—I will return for a *fresh* batch of you marvelously decadent, disgusting miscreants."

She grimaced, hurt by his cutting accusations. Yet her inward guilt attested to his condemnations. After all, had not even *she* supported and perpetuated the present War against her own kind, even against her own son? To do that travesty only required experiencing a small taste of sweet Revenge—plus a thin rationale of labelling others as "heretics"—to turn even her, the so-called 'High Priestess,' into a vicious murderess!

But...if given more time...perhaps, was there still hope? Might humanity somehow find the strength of character to right its course, to strengthen its moral fiber, and rise above its genetic imperatives?

—*especially* if she and her beloved Bible were at its helm?

Was God offering her a last chance to redeem herself?

"Maybe...maybe," she muttered to herself, her abject dejection hardening into firm resolve.

If all of humanity was "harvested" then that was the end. But if— even as a breeding colony—a few could survive...did that not justify *whatever*...no matter the lies or sacrifices necessary...to reach that goal?

Jean looked out again, from under her concealing hood, at the awful destruction of the Holy City. The full moon was fast being hidden by the closing gap in the roiling clouds above. The silvery field of snowy ruins was fading into darkness.

"I'll do it," she whispered.

"Good," Satan grinned, steering her back to the landing craft.

Inside, he put her into a waiting chair.

"I've a recorder and transmitter right here," he cheerfully explained. "When you are ready, just say whatever words come to mind—knowing you are ensuring the survival of your race. And I won't even prompt you. In fact, I'll leave you to yourself," he soothed her, stepping outside and closing the door of the craft behind him.

He grinned up at the roiling dark sky.

Of course he *wasn't* returning in eons for a few measly extra little humans. When the remaining humans were coaxed out of their hiding holes across the planet he'd have almost *ten million* of them tucked away into his orbiting Harvesters. In effect he'd have replaced all those lost when that pesky Sally crashed her loaded Harvester into the Earth.

It would make for a sufficiently-*vile* spiritual taste to his brewing new Universe...

—perversely influencing *new* Laws of Nature...

—making it a place where God would never go, recoiling in *disgust* from even entering therein!

And in that new Universe his ancient race would freely regenerate—and reign supreme.

Dave was jarred awake as the cart *slammed* to a stop!

For a moment he thought he was still on the surface of the moon, standing beside Arthur as the super-heated plasma cloud streamed down upon the craters...

But, no, it was just the white light of a lonely LED flashlight sitting up on a ledge.

"Where's Anderson?" a voice asked as several people grabbed his arms and helped him out of the askew cart.

"Arthur?" Dave said, blinking in the bright light from the lamp. He...he's gone," he stated flatly, jerking away from the supporting arms.

"Gone?" an elderly voice said, apparently not understanding.

"He didn't make it," Dave growled at the person while painfully stretching his limbs. Why was he so stiff? How long was he on the moon? How long had he been riding in the runaway cart?

He felt like he'd been rolling downward into the bowels of the Earth for hours. And yet his wristwatch showed it'd only been a few minutes. What the bloody hell?

"Oh, that's terrible," the grizzled, white-whiskered man said, shaking his head sadly.

It was the local *Commander* of the Jerusalem Resistance Forces, Eashoa M'Sheekha. He had a large black patch securely held in place over his right eye by a black elastic band running over his forehead and around his head.

Dave focused on him for the first time: seeing infinite sadness in Eashoa's one brown eye. His white hair and beard were long and stringy. Physically he looked old and frail. But his craggy face radiated powerful determination.

"He died doing what he wanted," Dave sighed, still not understanding the amazing events of the last few minutes.

"He was my dear friend," the Commander continued. "It's such a tragedy he didn't live to hear the good news that..."

"What good news?" Dave asked. Other personnel were leading him down another tunnel towards a well-hidden, deep command post.

"It's the global shield, Dr. King!" a young woman excitedly stated, running up to him.

The Shield! There was still time!

If we don't use it to light up the Earth—then maybe we can yet avoid Arthur's hideous ending!

"...is up and running!" the whiskered Commander excitedly finished the young woman's statement. He clapped his hands together in emphasis. His one good, brown eye was stretched-wide with happiness.

"What? Already? Really?" Dave gasped.

"When that Harvester melted-down the Temple Mount, the CHP 'nuns' around the world just gave up," the old man laughed. "And when *we* sent out word of what happened, *our* people across the world got the missing remaining generators up and running in record time. We achieved 'critical mass'! And now it's working just like you said it would, Dr. King. The protective grid just now snapped into place around the entire Earth. The Harvesters are locked out. We've won! It's a massive demonstration of the harnessed power of Dark Energy—and *everything* which that entails. Arthur would have been so happy."

Dumbfounded, Dave let the elderly man lead him over to a computer console where he could see a simulation for himself.

He saw on the screen a pulsating, blue glow surrounding the Earth—with thousands of small rectangles trying vainly to punch-through!

"We're receiving transmitted impulses from the planetary shield back through the DE-generator net," the woman excitedly related to

Dave. "We now have a good idea of the distribution and activity of the orbiting fleet."

"Even their communications to the Reaper robots are blocked," the Commander noted. "They're completely cut off from the orbiting fleet. If that one Harvester hadn't descended down above us we'd have blocked them out completely. If we can somehow take out the Harvester above Jerusalem then we'll finally have won-back control over our own planet."

"And if we're lucky, the Harvester above us may not even know what's happened in orbit," the woman added. "When it tries to ascend back into space it could crash straight into the barrier. It might even destroy itself."

To the hundreds of Rebels in the room, it was a miracle.

All around Dave, people were dancing in the isles of the control center—cheering, hugging, and crying-out with happiness!

But Dave was silent.

He knew that the reprieve was only temporary. The Aliens would quickly find a way to breach the barrier. And in *just one year*...total global disaster.

"Isn't it wonderful?" the young lady who'd first greeted him grinned.

She spontaneously grabbed him around his neck and hugged him.

"Oh, Dr. King, forgive me," she breathlessly smiled, "I'm Devorah Scheinman—one of your communication technicians."

"Oh, nice to meet you," Dave gave the rote answer, while feeling more dejected than he'd ever felt in his whole life.

As the short-haired girl danced away, Dave looked up at the high, rocky ceiling. The long tunnel from the surface had delivered him deep inside one of the subterranean chambers of "Solomon's Quarries" beneath Jerusalem. Here it was that large blocks of limestone had been cut out to build the Jewish Temple above. Indeed, Jerusalem was honeycombed with caves, cisterns, aqueducts, caverns, and connecting tunnels. Some, historically, were used for storing or transporting precious, scarce water—others for hiding from enemies, and still others for mining construction materials.

The Resistance, however, used the existing, extensive subterranean network to hide their operations deep under the streets of Jerusalem. Cables led up to hidden, hardened communication arrays. From there, the entire world-wide fight against the Aliens was coordinated. It was second only in its complexity and reach to the Washington D.C. Resistance headquarters.

But Dave didn't care anymore.

He wearily pushed himself up and walked away from the mass of computers and control tables, still clutching his backpack.

"Dr. King, where do you think you are going?" the elderly Commander M'Sheekha asked him, following along as Dave retreated from the chamber.

"Don't know...don't care," Dave shrugged, trudging toward the closest, dark, upward-leading tunnel.

"But...?"

"I'm *resigning* as the so-called 'Leader' of the rebellion—I've had enough," he said, starting to trudge up the tunnel. "Get someone else to do it."

"But...who will we choose to...?"

"*You* do it," Dave said, slinging his backpack over his shoulder while picking up an assault rifle hanging on a rack. "I did my part. I got the DE-network up. That's it. I quit. I'm out of here."

"Me...but...?"

"Get the hell away from me!" Dave angrily ordered the concerned old man. "If you don't want the job, then give it to someone else. I don't care anymore."

Devorah suddenly came running over, having heard Dave's shout.

"Dr. King, Dr. King!" she urgently called out to him.

"*What?*" he snapped-back at her.

"You'll want to see this! It's your Mother," she said, pointing at a nearby computer screen.

"She's still alive?" Dave said, pausing in his departure. He reluctantly walked over to the screen.

Yes, it was indeed Jean King, his mother...saying something about a colony the Aliens had agreed to set-aside, if only the remaining humans would just go to the surface and surrender. She'd negotiated a deal to allow the few remaining humans on the surface to gather together and survive. The Harvester hovering over Jerusalem, beneath the high planetary shield, would supposedly transport them to that site. The High Priestess asserted that the Aliens were making this deal to leave behind a functioning critical mass of humans who would repopulate Earth.

At some time in the far future the Aliens would return for another Harvest. But in the interim the surviving colony would be unmolested. Rather than die scattered about the polluted, freezing surface they'd have immediate food and support at the CPH-governed colony in Brazil. Jean promised that the Alien-sanctioned CPH rule would be "just" and "benign." All past conflict would be forgiven. They'd be one big loving community!

A loud debate broke out among the personnel, some arguing in favor of the deal while others doubting the Aliens' sincerity. A few suggested they use the situation to get "ringers" onto the Jerusalem Harvester. This might be their chance to take up by surprise, seal their final victory over the Alien Mother Ships.

Dave grinned, then started chuckling, and then broke out into loud "guffaws"!

The surrounding crowd of Resistance fighters gradually quieted, turning to look at their "leader" in disbelief.

"It doesn't matter!" Dave shouted to them before abruptly turning away. "None of this matters. It's over. It's done."

Leaving behind the whole shocked crew, he turned his back on them and walked into an upward-slanting tunnel.

He didn't know where it led to, didn't care.

He was *finished*.

Sally was gone. Instead of protecting the tattered remnants of the human race, the planetary shield was bringing upon the Earth the *Wrath of God*. And to add even further insult to injury—*his mother* had apparently *defected* to the Alien invaders. The solar super-storm would incinerate humans in the "colony" as easily as those scattered about the surface of Earth.

Nothing mattered anymore.

The moon could never again seduce him with its bewitchingly-alluring moonlight. For Dave, there was only the dismal black of un-caring outer space. For many hideous sins, Dave knew he and the human race was forever *damned*!

But was that really so bad?

No more struggling.   No more fighting or killing.   No more slaughtering young, brainwashed nuns.

Convicted of his own personal sins, Dave was walking out into the Nuclear Winter to die.

Chapter 17

<u>DAMNATION</u>

There is a certain freedom
In knowing you are forever damned
Released from the burden of Righteousness
Everything becomes an inevitable decline
No longer the struggle to climb The Path
You can turn and happily relish the slide
Even enjoying the increasing speed
As you hurtle down, out of control
On an eternal, wicked rollercoaster
A speeding train traveling ever faster
Descending downward into hot Hell
How horrible, however, to discover
A challenge to your peace of mind
Grabbing you by your throat
Swinging you around in a circle
And forcing you to grab the Edge
Slowing your downward fall
As you begin again, yet again,
Scrabbling painfully upward...
Cursed Conscience driving you
Cursed Love compelling you
To spit in the face of Death!
The Luminary Chronicles, 17:47-52

265

In the freezing snow, Dave sat perched on the side of a large, rectangular fallen tower. His backpack hung heavy from his shoulder, his assault rifle in his lap.

Once-upon-a-time the fallen tower he was sitting on must have been a grand architectural structure.

Now, it was just a long jumble of smashed stones.

It was no longer night. But it wasn't daytime either. It was something in between—fitting for the end of the world.

Dave closed his eyes. He was oblivious to the biting wind, the steadily falling muddy snow, and the nearby prowling Reaper robots.

He was freezing to death...but he didn't care.

"Come here to pray?" an elderly, slightly quavering voice interrupted Dave's depression.

Dave opened his eyes, irritated.

He saw *Commander Eashoa M'Sheekha* climbing up to "plop" down beside him on the raised edge of the fallen tower.

"Not really," Dave replied sourly.

The Commander swung his legs over the edge of the tower, leaning nonchalantly back.

Eashoa, like Dave, wore no hood. The continually falling muddy snow made a type of cap upon the glaringly white hair of his head. Large bags hung beneath his one revealed brown eye. His skin, once wrinkled leather, was pale and limp, hanging in folds. His white mustache and beard were tattered, matted, and twisting in the blasting, icy wind.

"You are sitting on what used to be the Minaret of the *Mosque of Omar*," the old man calmly observed. "It was built back in the 12th Century—and often used for the Muslim 'call to prayer.'"

"It just happened to be here when I stopped," Dave listlessly replied. "I don't do much praying anymore."

"You're not a believer?"

"Just *what the hell* are you doing here?" Dave snorted, ignoring Eashoa's question. "I didn't ask you to follow me."

Dave peevishly set his rifle aside to hitch his thick overcoat up closer around his neck. The assault rifle lay to the side of him, rapidly being covered up by the perpetually falling dirty snow.

"They don't need me at the headquarters either, Dr. King," the old man wryly shrugged.

"You didn't take over for me?" Dave asked, mildly interested.

"I told Devorah—that girl you met—to take the job," he sighed. "As you said, it doesn't matter. So why not give the 'C' team a chance to get into the game? It's the 'final inning' with no chance to win, isn't it?"

Dave grimaced at the old man, who seemed to know more than he should.

Dave realized he knew next to nothing about this old man. All he knew was the name—Eashoa M'Sheekha—likely a Jewish retired military man who'd formed-up the local Resistance chapter.

Why did the old man walk out? Why did he follow Dave? Why had he casually turned over command of the Resistance to a lowly technician?

Despite his deep depression, Dave was mildly curious.

"But...it's not easy to command an army or keep up a global network of Dark Energy Generators or to orchestrate a strategy against the army of Reaper Robots that remains here on the surface," Dave noted. "It's hardly a job for a young girl, no matter how talented. Besides, she told me she was just a communications technician."

"Yes, but with a lot of practical combat experience..."

"It takes a General, not a private!"

"Then go back in there and do it yourself," the old man mildly admonished Dave. "I've got my radio with me—I'll tell them you're unhappy with my last orders and are coming back to set things right."

He lifted a slim, cellphone-looking device from his jacket pocket.

"Put it back," Dave said, shaking his head in the negative, "I've made my decision. But still, Commandeer—putting a young girl in charge? Really?"

"I've known young girls in my time who could work miracles," Eashoa quietly stated.

Dave shook his head sadly, his attention attracted to a large, ancient fresco peeking up out of the ugly, muddy snow below the fallen tower.

He made out a naked chest and arms, hands outspread as if be-seeching the heavens—and a sad but serene, brown-bearded head. There peering up out of the muddy snow was the face of Jesus!

"Well...talk about people falling down in their duties—*he* sure let us down, didn't he?" Dave laughed, kicking a hard icicle toward the fresco.

The icicle bounced off the two-dimensional face, leaving a big dent behind.

Jesus was now missing his nose.

"He predicted all of this, don't you know—the end of the world?" Eashoa said. His old quavering voice sounded small against the sav-age, whistling wind. "But people didn't believe him. And then they didn't follow his teachings, either. If they'd really done so, then may-be God would not judge mankind so harshly. Perhaps He'd give them more time to get their act together."

"More time...?" Dave frowned.

"Jesus talked like his 'second coming' and 'day of judgment' was right around the corner. Instead, the deadline was extended by more than two millennia."

"Uh, right," Dave nodded. "I guess that's more than enough time for mankind to come to its senses, come to think of it."

"It's just sad," Eashoa continued. "He gave them everything they needed. But they repeatedly rejected His beautiful gifts."

Dave frowned, looking at Commander M'Sheekha more closely. He'd only briefly talked with him previously over their encrypted-bursts, long-range RF-net. He didn't know the man at all. And now they were sitting together in the frozen wasteland of the destroyed City of Jerusalem while "clomping" Alien Robots prowled through the snow-covered rubble just out of sight.

The one-eyed man looked to be at least a hundred years old.

"Just how old are you, anyway?" Dave asked.

The wrinkled old man laughed—pausing to cough uncontrollably before answering.

"Sorry about that," he said, hunkering lower into his ragged, thin field jacket. "I used to have a powerful immune system—never got sick. Now, I'm fading fast...lost an eye to a Reaper's tentacle...can't grow that back, can I? And, oh yes, my age... Well, Dr. King, to tell you the truth, I don't actually remember. I've lost track."

Huh. Lost track? Well, why not—time was different now. There was *AI*, "After Invasion"...and *BI*, "Before Invasion." Everything else was just lost memories and unfulfilled fantasies.

"Look...Commander...I appreciate your concern, but..."

"Call me Eashoa, Dr. King."

"Uh, ok—and you can call me 'Dave'—it's been nice to talk with you, but this isn't necessary. You're obviously sick. Please just go back to the base. There's no sense in both of us freezing to death out here."

"I'm doing what I want to do, David. Don't worry about me."

Funny old coot...calling him by his given name, "David"—but it had a nice ring to it, sort of like when Arthur did the same.

Dave slowly looked him over as they both sat in the icy wind being turned into muddy snow-men.

Then Dave reached a shaking hand into the pocket of his overcoat and withdrew a crumpled Snickers candy bar.

He tore off the tattered wrapping, letting it flutter away on the biting wind, handing half to Eashoa.

"I've been saving that for a happy day," Dave laughed, biting into the nuts and caramel. The frozen nuts were so hard they almost cracked his teeth. "Since this is my last day, I'm declaring *Victory* and beating a hasty retreat. Sorry it couldn't be a bottle of celebratory, warming Champagne."

"I don't drink. This is great," Eashoa said, accepting the other half.

"Me neither," Dave admitted. "I always thought I had to keep my senses sharp, in total control all the time. Now...I might take up the habit. Hey, thanks for the company."

Eashoa nibbled at the half-bar delicately, even reverently.

"It's been a long time since I've had one of these treats," the Commander nodded thankfully. "It's one of the things I most enjoyed in the modern world—packaged candy. When I was growing up, a sweet treat was fresh fruit. Around here, we always had plenty of figs, pomegranates, oranges, dates, mangos—especially tasty when dipped into a mug of local honey."

"No more fresh fruits," Dave sighed, shivering in the dark nuclear winter. He quickly polished off his half of the candy bar, "and *never* will be again."

The old man looked out over the shattered, apocalyptic landscape.

"Well, there's always *some* hope," he grinned, slyly winking at Dave. "Except, of course when…"

Dave snatched up his rifle and *fired a burst* right across the Commander's white-bearded face, causing him to duck!

The bullets passed so close that they *creased* the black patch over the Commander's right eye.

But behind Eashoa, *a towering Reaper* crashed down and tumbled off to the side…

—its tentacles *convulsing wildly;* before finally dropping limp upon the brown snow!

"I got it right through one of its eye-lenses," Dave said with satisfaction as Eashoa shakily straightened back up. "My stream of bullets smashed its 'brain'. Hah! I learned that little trick after dissecting a number of those ugly heads. Maybe that's *payback* for the one that took *your* eye, huh?"

The old man laughed wryly.

"We'd better hide," Eashoa said. He was now all business. He peered furtively around. "Taking out that Reaper's going to bring a hundred more upon us in seconds."

"Where can we go?"

"Follow me!"

And so they crept away. Eashoa ducked underneath a huge, fallen stone column, Dave right behind him. They moved out of the freezing wind into a warmer, secluded chamber.

Eashoa grabbed something out of the darkness and lit it with a match.

Dave saw him hold up an oil lamp.

"I'll get us to a safe spot," the Commander whispered to Dave as they both heard just outside their hiding place the "CLOMP, CLOMP, CLOMP" of hordes of fast-approaching Reapers. The robots were making strange "whistling" and "clicking" noises as they excitedly "talked" to each other.

Dave was slightly amused. Even the Reapers were suffering from the terrible weather conditions. They were falling back on verbal signals. Damn! The whole world was falling to pieces.

But still not really caring what happened, Dave mechanically followed Eashoa lower into the ruins. They climbed through narrow openings downward into the intermeshed debris of tumbled-over columns and arches.

"Look, this is all just a waste of..." Dave started to protest, his half-frozen limbs rebelling at the difficult descent.

"We can talk more when we're safe," Eashoa whispered back up at hum, "shushing" him.

Dave kept quiet for a bit, then frowned.

"Just where are we?" Dave sullenly asked as they continued their descent away from the dangerous surface.

"This is what's left of the *Church of the Holy Sepulcher*," Eashoa quietly replied. "It was crushed in the initial bombardment when the aliens descended upon us. Lucky for us the Harvester up there skipped this section of Jerusalem with its recent laser blasts. There are a few open areas inside the ruins where we can hide."

"You know this place?"

"Oh, yes," the Commander replied, lithely leading Dave through narrow twists and openings, ever deeper, "I practically grew up here. It was impressive when intact—though unnecessary and wasteful."

"What do you mean?" Dave answered, getting more interested despite his continuing depression. He struggled to keep up with the dim, wavering light from the swinging lamp held by the spry old man.

"Well, David," Commander M'Sheekha replied back over his shoulder, "this is a monument to what Christianity became—a sad and magnificently hollowed-out *mockery* of its Founder."

Dave ruefully nodded to himself in agreement.

"Oh, you mean like being an official hierarchy, a political structure, a set of rules and regulations, a monument to wealth and power, a web of rituals and ceremonies—instead of being what Jesus meant his true Church to be: a source of joy, empowerment, and spiritual growth?"

Up ahead, M'Sheekha was silent for a moment as he continued leading them deeper into the ruins.

Then, in apparent appreciation, the old man gruffly repeated his prior question: "So are you a Christian, David? You seem to know your stuff—and with a keen insight."

Dave both laughed and sighed at the same time.

"I was raised in a small, conservative, protestant church...where its flaws—as compared to the Jesus I thought I saw in the Bible—were many."

"So were you ever able to do anything about it?" Eashoa carefully asked as they slowed, crawling through a particularly-dangerous, unstable section.

"I tried...but what can you do?" Dave said. "I gave a few lectures on how the church should elevate Jesus above Tradition—even wrote a book I self-published on the subject—but they didn't want to hear such 'liberal' ideas. After all, their main self-identification was to be 'conservatives' rather than them being disciples of Jesus."

Dave heard Eashoa sigh deeply in sympathy.

"What happened?"

"Oh, the same thing that happens to all 'trouble-makers' who buck the system—they silenced me, marginalized me, and when I still wouldn't shut up...they in essence kicked me out. Actually, I just walked away, but it was the same effect."

"So sad," the Commander replied. "Careful David—if you push too hard on that beam it'll fall and crush you."

"Thanks," Dave answered, as he gingerly twisted his whole body along a cold rock floor, not touching the rotten beam above, dragging his assault rifle behind him. "But after that I learned to keep my mouth shut. People love their traditions, despite their rhetoric to the contrary. Push too hard against the 'God-ordained' man-made Rules and you get ostracized or worse."

Eashoa wryly laughed.

"Yes, I know that from my own experiences," the Commander agreed. "Trying to change society can even get you killed."

"That's just what happened to our dear, long-departed Jesus—wasn't it?" Dave said.

Suddenly Dave jerked backward.

There, right in front of him, were the smashed *skeletal remains* of several men and women.

By the flickering oil lamp, the empty sockets of their skulls were ominous, looking *accusingly* at Dave. They reminded him of Arthur's black eye-pits—both dead and alive at the same time.

"Don't mind them," the Commander called back to Dave from further down in the ruins. "They died when the Aliens first attacked. Now they're just heaps of bones inside of what remains of their clothes. 'Empty suits' you could call them."

Dave squirmed past, trying not to touch the tattered remains of the desiccated corpses.

"We're almost there," Eashoa cheerfully called back.

And Dave finally slid out of the fallen jumble into a relatively-open space.

"We're here, David. We'll be safe for a while," Eashoa said, setting the oil lamp to the side on the stone floor.

"And just where are we?" Dave said, looking around. He was breathing hard from their laborious descent into the bowels of the smashed cathedral.

They were in a lower level of the ruins, inside a cave. Set off from a small central chamber were a couple slots carved into the rock walls. On the floor to the side Dave saw drainage grates.

"Well, Dr. King, allow me to officially welcome you to the '*Tomb of Joseph of Arimathea.*' It's a burial cave dating from the time of Jesus," Eashoa said, himself looking ancient and ethereal by the dim, flickering light of the oil lamp.

"You mean, where...?"

"Yes, this is one of the places that later church officials designated as where Jesus' body was buried following his crucifixion."

"I thought that it was in a garden, with a big boulder covering the entrance where..."

"That was twenty-some centuries ago, David. Lots of things change in two millennia," the old man patiently observed.

"Yah, I guess so," Dave said, sitting down on the cold rock floor.

The old man wearily sat next to Dave.

"I never before had the chance to come to Palestine," Dave sighed. "It's nice, now at the very last, to be here in Jesus' actual tomb. I always appreciated the Radical Principles that Jesus brought to the world. I just couldn't understand why the official churches hardly ever lived up to those principles—often even working at odds to them—or so it seemed to me. Even the many so-called 'Christian' preachers I heard hardly ever talked about Jesus and his teachings."

"Sad, sad—but true," the old man sighed, leaning back against the stone wall. "They turned Jesus from a great, challenging Teacher into a comfortable Icon. He became a symbol around which they could build *their* church. Perhaps some of his teachings permeated society to good effect. But the biggest benefits were left on the table."

"Of course his best teachings were impossible," Dave shrugged.

"Yes, impossible for mere humans to fully achieve," Eashoa agreed.

"So they were aspirational," Dave concluded. "Still, though, you'd think that his followers would make them their priorities instead of focusing on weakening, defanging, and deflecting them."

"The 'take-home' message was simple enough."

"That's true...totally love God and pass on that same love to their fellow humans."

"That's well-said, David."

"I didn't say it," Dave sighed, "Jesus did—when his enemies tried to get him into a no-win debate asking him which of the Ten Commandments was most important. Instead he said the *number one* priority was to love God with all one's heart, soul, and mind."

"And the *second* priority of a follower of Jesus was like unto the first: to love one's neighbor as one's own self."

"Jesus' summation of Moses' famous Ten Commandments—not one rule put above another rule but a 'state-of-being' inside one's own *heart*," Dave sighed. "That's really hard."

Eashoa laughed. "Yes, not just 'name the number of a rule,' *one-to-ten!*"

"And he cut to the heart of their hypocrisy...claiming they were the greatest students of the Jewish Law while utterly forgetting the *intent* of the Godly rules," Dave replied.

Eashoa nodded knowingly.

"Both of those top priorities are so simple to state yet so incredibly difficult to truly accomplish."

"That is so true. No wonder I hardly ever heard preachers dealing with either subject."

"Instead of the incredibly hard task of enthroning Jesus in their hearts, they buried Him safely away in a cold tomb in a giant Cathedral constructed by men," Eashoa smiled, gesturing outward, indicating the cave they sat within.

"That's just what I've seen all my life," Dave sadly but emphatically agreed. "Jesus urged the complacent, selfish public to become *uncomfortable*—to *dare* to attempt that which is dangerous, difficult, and complicated. But instead they insisted on making him into the 'Comfortable' Jesus who 'required' only that which was safe, easy, and simple. I'm not at all a 'Christian' but I sure as hell am a follower of *Jesus*. The *real* Jesus was worthy of being followed."

Eashoa smiled gently, appearing to recognize a real friend.

"So, my dear Dr. King, mankind will be damned not because of their vile excesses but because of their lack of imagination: their disdain of adventure, their fear of true growth, and their demonization of Godly Creativity," Eashoa softly answered. "I'm speaking of what matters most of course, not just science and material achievement. I'm speaking collectively of the heart, soul, and mind."

Dave frowned. He held his shivering arms close over his chest.

"That's so true, Commander. I hadn't thought of it like that. But you hit the nail on the head. You've really turned Jesus teachings from the negatives that preachers love to hammer on...into the *positives* that can lift people up with true joy. Are you sure you're Jewish and not Christian?"

"Oh, I'm a lifetime Jew, David. I just have an uncommon historical knowledge of the first century. Much of that time-period is shrouded in ignorance and mystery. But one thing I know for sure— Jesus didn't come to beat people down. He came to lift people up."

Dave shook his head in weary exasperation.

"But why couldn't more people believe that? Just think of the brutal evil of the Crusades, of the Inquisition, of intra-Christian persecution and wars, of the Salaam witch trials, of the church-sanctioned subjugation of women, of persecution of scientists, of..."

The old man sighed deeply, raising a wrinkled hand to stop Dave's tirade.

"They Christian religions did some good. Undeniably many worthy acts were done in the name of Jesus. The 'big ideas' existed in society at least as Ideals. He did have an effect, just not near what was possible if his followers had fully embraced the intent of his teachings."

"I still can't understand religious people casually screwing people not of their particular faith."

Eashoa reached up to scratch underneath his eye patch.

"It's much more satisfying and easy to tear people down than build people up. Even a scoundrel can feel 'big' if he cuts everyone around him off at the knees. Suddenly he's the tallest person around even though he's not done anything of true worth."

"So it's intellectual and spiritual *laziness?*"

"Yes."

"Then we *deserve* to be condemned."

"Seems that way..."

"But surely there are exceptions?" Dave mused.

"Individually, yes there are exceptional people who at least try to adopt the full teachings of Jesus, whether they follow his religion or not. As a species, though, the human race when put under stress is still stuck in its monkey genetic priorities."

"Of course it's hard to rise above one's own innate boundaries," Dave admitted. "That is...to be the devil's advocate."

Eashoa "snorted" in reply, the harsh noise echoing around the small rock chamber.

"Satan does not require a human advocate."

"I apologize," Dave gulped. He was suddenly aware he was out of his religious and intellectual depth. "My brain's getting fuzzy."

Eashoa laughed kindly.

"You are, indeed, an unusual disciple of Jesus, my friend," the old man smiled. "I wish there could be more like you."

For some unknown reason, that deeply warmed Dave's heart. Where before he was ready to sit in the cold and freeze to death he now felt a twinge of...if not hope, then perhaps companionship.

"So do you think Jesus was really buried here?" Dave said, squirming on the hard stone beneath his butt.

The old man, lit by dim yellow light, shrugged. Simultaneous he smiled, crinkled the many wrinkles at the corner of his large, brown eye.

"Who knows? That was such a long time ago..."

"But *we* don't have much more time, Eashoa, do we?" Dave sadly stated more than asked.

"Yes, the Aliens have got us by the 'short hairs' that's for sure," the old man sighed, laying his rifle to the side.

"And it's not just the Aliens threatening us," Dave quietly stated. "Arthur...showed me...something amazing...and horrifying!"

"Oh?" the Commander said, lifting up his still-dark eyebrows, causing his forehead to furrow like a well-plowed field.

His one good eye seemed to *glitter* in anticipation.

Dave decided he could trust this old, hardened, Jewish soldier.

"The world is going to be destroyed by *God*—not theoretically in ages to come, but just *one year* from now in the future."

"Destroy the world?"

"Yes! It's the real *Judgment Day*—and we fail! God stops Mankind dead in its tracks! Aliens or not, humanity is at the end of the line."

The old man just sat there, looking steadily at Dave.

All around them was silence. They were far enough below the surface that no patter of snow, no distant explosions, and no "CLOMPING" of robotic feet could reach them.

"The Alien invasion is just a salvage operation of an already sinking ship."

"You...really believe this?" Eashoa asked.

"I saw it with my own eyes...from the surface of the moon."

"You were on the moon?" the old man asked, seemingly skeptical.

"*Arthur* took me there—and he stayed! He told me, there on the moon, that we were a year in the future. That's when a solar superstorm's plasma cloud sent by God *destroys* Earth's surface, oceans, atmosphere—*everything!* I saw it happen with my own eyes! It was the most horrible thing I've ever seen. I'd like to believe it was some sort of hallucination, but I can't. I don't know how or why, but it was real. And then he sent me back here to...well...enjoy life, I guess, uhm..."

Dave's voice trailed off. He sighed deeply, closing his eyes and leaning back. He knew it sounded crazy, but he didn't care. It was just nice to unburden his soul to a sympathetic ear.

Plus, he was glad not to be climbing down through the dangerous ruins of the Church of the Holy Sepulcher. This was a nice place to sit and die. He'd eaten his last bit of food, the candy bar. So he could let hypothermia grab hold, as he'd tried before Eashoa interrupted his death-spiral—and let his spirit drift away. It could be a painless, peaceful ending.

Except...

"But I still don't see how God could just *erase* us from the Universe," Dave frowned into the quiet of the tomb, still trying to wrap his head around it.

"You think you are the Crown of Creation?" the Commander quietly asked.

"Well, sure...aren't we?"

Eashoa laughed.

"Oh, David—and you a scientist?" the old man snorted in derision. "Just how many 'earth'-type intelligent species do you think exist in the Universe?"

"Well..." Dave mused. "I guess if there are trillions of Galaxies, each with billions of stars—and even if there were only one intelligent species per Galaxy, which is a ridiculously-small guess—then..."

"Then earth's *Homo sapiens* are just one of many self-and-God-aware Intelligent Races throughout our one Galaxy, let alone the Universe!" the old man concluded. "Our whole civilization is like one ant in a large colony amongst thousands of colonies. Yet we think that we are irreplaceable."

"Not true?" Dave said.

"That 20th Century scientific giant, Carl Sagan, had it right—one of billions or even trillions," Eashoa stoically said, his old voice quavering. "And yet..."

"And yet?" Dave prodded him.

"There *is* something special about *Homo sapiens*—something that would be missed in the Universe, despite humanity's many atrocious flaws. So you say God has had enough of us?"

Dave snorted in disgust: "We're cosmic *toast*."

Then he sighed deeply.

"I guess I just fundamentally don't blame God," Dave shrugged. "Even many of Jesus' closest 'followers' today *choose* to 'overlook' his

Radical Principles. As you said, they turn Jesus into a comfortable Icon. And beyond Jesus, many so-called, 'dedicated' followers of God—of whatever religion—turn the Supreme Being into a compliant Idol that 'approves' their worst desires and activities. It's disgusting. *We* are disgusting. I can see why God would Judge us unworthy and burn us up."

"So we all fail Judgment Day?" the old man quietly asked.

"Apparently so..."

He didn't really care if the Commander believed him or not. It was just nice to say the words out loud. Dave knew it all sounded crazy. But, on the other hand, it made a certain amount of perverse sense.

As if reacting to Dave's total surrender, Eashoa hopped up defiantly to his feet.

Fortunately the small cave was large enough that they could stand crouched-over.

"Then I have something to show you, Dr. King!" Commander M'Sheekha stated intensely. He lithely moved over to one of the hewn-out slots in the stone. "I'm going to need your help here."

"Say what?" Dave said, listlessly crawling over behind him.

"I'll need your rifle—I don't want to risk breaking mine."

"What?"

"Just give it to me!" the old man snapped.

Not understanding, but too tired to care—Dave passed his assault rifle up to the old man who was stooped over, halfway into one of the inset, empty burial chambers.

A loud "BANG, BANG, BANG" sounded as Eashoa started hammering on the stone at the far end of the cavity with the butt of the rifle.

After what seemed to Dave to be a long while, the Commander passed the rifle back out to Dave. Its stock was battered and twisted. Dave hoped the rifle would still fire, but doubted it.

"Well, I guess I'll have to use my own rifle also," Eashoa sighed. "It's my favorite weapon. I hoped to not have to risk messing it up. But, no matter—like you said, one year in the future and we're all toast anyway. Right?"

Wordlessly, Dave passed the other rifle up to him.

After another full hour of banging, Eashoa finally gave a *shout* of triumph!

Dave heard a loud "crash" at the back of the burial slot as the wall fell outward into yet another, more-deeply hidden chamber.

The loud noise jarred Dave from the semi-stupor he'd been slipping into.

Also, a musty, *acrid* smell suddenly filled the outer chamber.

Dave put a hand over his nose, grimacing.

"Give me a hand!" Eashoa yelled back, laboriously backing out while carefully dragging something along with him. Dave reached up past the man to grab on, feeling *crumbling fabric*...what?

And then it was laid out right before Dave on the floor.

By the dim light of the oil lamp, Dave saw a tightly-wrapped *mummy*.

"What *is* that thing?" Dave gasped.

"Help me unwrap it," the Commander grated, starting on one arm. "Careful. It's delicate!"

Dave crawled to the other side of the mummy, doing as ordered.

With difficulty he began peeling back ancient fabric off one finger of the mummy's small hand...

—then *jerked* away from it!

The finger was *warm*.

Jean King stood with Satan on the bridge of the Harvester as the huge spaceship rose up into the sky.

They were delivering their initial load of surrendered nuns to the fleet in orbit around the Earth.

Upon Jean's broadcast order, the local nuns dutifully crawled out of their hiding places and surrendered to the closest Reaper robots.

If anything, they were obedient to the point of stupidity.

Thousands of Jean's best fighters, gathered together in Jerusalem to defend their headquarters, were quickly collected. They were delivered by the prowling robots to the hovering Mother Ship within which Jean and the Demon resided. There, the unconscious nuns were "tubed" and assembled into hanging "pods." Jean was sickened by the whole procedure.

She numbly watched through the observation dome as her Harvester zipped upward through thick roiling layers of muddy clouds...then into clear sky beyond, where stars shone unobscured.

She knew full well that her people *weren't* being stored for eventual delivery to a breeding-"colony" as the Demon promised.

She also knew that she was Satan's complaint pawn—outwardly meekly doing his bidding, believing his lies and dutifully making broadcasts.

But in reality she was making *plans...*

—when their giant spacecraft suddenly SMASHED into an *invisible barrier!*

Jean was thrown to the floor, stunned.

Above her, the horned red Demon *SCREAMED!*

"What...what happened?" she gasped.

It grabbed her up by her neck, swinging her around in the air!

"Did *you* do this? Is this your *trickery?*" he demanded.

Despite her hands desperately hanging onto his hot, scaly claws—she couldn't breathe or speak. Her neck was being crushed!

He disdainfully released her, dropping her with a "thud" to the floor, turning away in disgust to study his instruments.

She dragged herself up to her feet, nursing her bruises, and staggered over to the transparent dome to press her hands against it, peering intently into the outside atmosphere.

Then she saw it.

A faint *blue-glowing barrier* hung above them—separating their Harvester from the higher stratosphere and the even-higher orbiting Harvester fleet!

"So, you kept me occupied gathering up your pitiful little Priestesses—while your son and his so-called 'Resistance Fighters' put up a virtually invisible planetary Dark Energy shield?" the monster behind her accused her. "I should *crush* your skull!"

"G-go a-ahead," she choked-out, barely able to speak.

Indeed, the Resistance had outwitted her. They'd succeeded in setting off a COSMIC FLARE that would attract God's full attention and bring on Judgment Day. She should have been shocked and angry. However, she felt unexpectedly happy. Having set in motion the incineration of the Earth's surface, the present Aliens were just annoying irritants.

The scavenging Aliens just didn't matter anymore.

"But you'd like that, wouldn't you?" he said, clattering over to her on his hard hoofs which sounded like hammers striking the floor.

He reached with a long claw to lift her chin so she was looking up into his yellow-glowing eyes.

"You are going to convince your son and his fighters to *give up* and *join* the 'colony'!" he *roared* at her.

"I'll d-do no s-such thing," she whispered harshly, her throat almost crushed. "The p-previous High Priestess h-hated Dark Energy and fought a w-war over its usage—but I see n-now she was *w-wrong*."

"I can overcome the Barrier..." he stated menacingly, his long red tongue flicking out to lick her forehead.

She grimaced, his saliva stinging like acid—trying to jerk backward against the inwardly curved observation dome.

"—but doing so will take time," he concluded. "So I'd rather have your little rat-compatriots shut it down themselves. You *know* them, 'Mother' Jean King. What will it take to convince them to do so *voluntarily*?"

"Something that y-you're not c-capable of that's..." she glared back at him.

He grabbed her head, stopping her in midsentence. He bent his own face downward, and plastered her up next to his own hot red cheek.

"Oh...oh...I see...*yes!*" he laughed. "My, what *fun!* We make a great team, Mother King. We will indeed tell your little tunnel-rats *exactly* what they want to hear."

"You...can read...my thoughts?"

"Oh, it's jumbled. Your little brain is chaotic. But I've caught the drift well enough."

As he ordered the Harvester to descend back into the putrid clouds below, Jean heard his cackling laughter ringing throughout the control chamber.

Her eyes were tightly closed.

Her head and throat hurt terribly.

She slumped to the floor, barely conscious. The Demon had reached into her head and taken what he wanted. She felt like she'd been raped, not physically—but mentally and spiritually.

Oh, he was going to *pay* for what he'd done to her and her planet.

Her prior dismay was fast dissipating.

She was getting *angry*...

Judgment Day coming or not, her "motherly" instincts were ablaze. And it wasn't just to protect her blindly-obedient nuns—it was now her son, mankind, and the entire planet.

Also she was buoyed-up by a lifetime Faith in the Holy Bible.

After all, Satan—after being unchained and loosed upon the earth as detailed in the book of Revelation in the Bible—was finally thrown, by God, into the lake of burning fire.

She was convinced that he would, without fail, *burn* in hell forever!

But, first, she had to play along with him, concealing her deepest thoughts...for just a while longer.

Chapter 18

<u>THE OBELISK</u>

Waiting outside of Time

Is more than just an empty Void

Where the spirits await their fates

But a clustering of random possibilities

Centered upon a vast, living column of Light

Extending through the whole Multiverse

Binding everything loosely together

A conduit to the inconceivable

A place where Angels play

Giving active homage

To that which is

Yet beyond...

The Luminary Chronicles, 18:74-76

Once Dave figured out how to catch an edge of each strip of the ancient, overlapped fabric, he found he could peel it off rapidly.

But there were many layers sticking together.

Underneath, though, Dave caught glimpses of green on one arm right below the fabric—obviously rotted flesh, yet with no stink or odor?

I didn't know that they could preserve these mummies this well— Dave absently thought to himself. *The flesh is still warm and supple, but rotted—a putrid green!*

"So just what is this mummy...and how'd you know it was here?

Eashoa sighed deeply.

"*I* did this—long ago," the old man said as he worked across from Dave, carefully unraveling each deeper layer of the fabric on his side of the mummy. "I didn't know what else to do. I couldn't allow the body to stay buried in the normal fashion."

Dave frowned up at the muttering old man while still working diligently on his half of the wrappings.

"What do you mean?" Dave asked, completely confused by the Commander's cryptic words.

"Left where it was initially buried it would have been badly damaged by natural earth-movements and biological processes," Eashoa quietly explained. "So I brought it here and hid it in this secret chamber. The hardest part was keeping fresh air out—too many fungi and bacteria. Even a tiny stream of replenished micro-organisms would have consumed the flesh, given enough time."

Dave was too befuddled to worry why they were busily unwrapping an apparently recently mummified body. He was just content to follow the Commander's lead.

Dave shrugged.

He had a feeling it would all work out. Dave noted that the old Commander exuded a peculiar calming effect on all those around him.

"So I sealed the stone using the techniques of the time," Commander M'Sheekha continued talking. "I replenished it periodically with better methods. In that way, I preserved what by rights should have dissolved into dust long ago. I probably shouldn't have intervened—but I just couldn't let it crumble into dust."

By the dim light of the flickering oil lamp, Dave saw they were down to the last layer.

"I'll take it from here," Eashoa M'Sheekha said, motioning for Dave to move back.

The air in the tomb was getting thick. Dave's head was spinning. He felt sick. Everything seemed unreal. Could this really be happening?

Dave squirmed back over beside a fallen stone archway, resting his arms up on the curve of the rocks, with his back to it.

"We've got to be careful not to tear the skin," Eashoa said, leaning close over the body. His movements obscured the mummy from Dave's view as he delicately pulled the last layers up and laid them to the side with the rest of the piled-up, crumbling bandages.

And there partially revealed—as the old man leaned back—was the *naked body* of a young woman.

The Commander took off his thin field jacket and laid it carefully over the chest and upper legs of the motionless, well-preserved body.

He reached over and moved the oil lamp closer.

Then he laid a time-weathered old hand tenderly upon her forehead...

—when the girl's eyes *opened*, staring up blankly into the face of Commander M'Sheekha!

Dave was frozen in place, transfixed.

"E-Eashoa?" a thin, dry sound came from her lips.

"I told you, Sahlee—we would meet again," he softly replied, bunching up some of the fabric to place it tenderly behind her head. "But you need not try to speak our ancient languages. English will do fine. You remember it, don't you?"

She nodded weakly.

Dave didn't know if he could believe his eyes.

But there was no doubting the truth.

It was Sally.

She had those same luminously green, large eyes. She had her long, fluffy red-brown hair. And on her wrist—which he had mistaken for rotting flesh—was the bright-green Turtle Tattoo.

And it was *glowing*.

Devorah Scheinman sat at the computer terminal, not believing what she was seeing.

Others were clustered around, likewise dumbfounded.

On the screen, *Dr. David King* was urgently instructing the Resistance fighters to surrender! And standing right behind him, with her aged hands flat on his shoulders, was the current *High Priestess*.

"...my mission, unknown to my comrades in Jerusalem, was to contact the Aliens and see if they were serious. I'd previously received a secret message from them. They were offering lasting peace," Dave patiently explained. "The Aliens claimed that my mother at the CPH received a similar overture. Of course I was skeptical. But now, having met with both my mother and the Aliens, I'm convinced their offer is genuine."

Devorah was greatly disturbed by his appearance. The last time she'd seen him he was a haggard middle aged man leaving to go out inexplicably into a filthy blizzard. But now he looked young and well-kept. His beard was neatly trimmed, his mustache well-brushed, his longish brown hair tied back neatly with a rubber band behind his head.

He just didn't look like a grizzled fighter who'd been struggling in terrible conditions for years.

He looked "pre-invasion", like a well-coiffed *politician*.

"...skeptical at first that they were going to leave a remnant of humanity at peace in a well-supplied colony. But, as you see from these pictures, the Brazil site is exactly that, plus..."

As he continued talking, images appeared on the computer screen of green hills, agricultural fields, farm animals, and thriving forest areas—all protected beneath a large blue energy dome.

"—which will be expanded as we arrive with our compact DE-generators to add to the existing shield," he noted. "You brave Resistance fighters have achieved a planet-wide, diffuse barrier that is only temporarily preventing additional Harvesters from descending out of orbit. This may give us a short reprieve, but provides little long-term advantage. Instead, we need these generators shoring up and expanding the dome protecting the Brazilian colony against Nuclear Winter. This is..."

As he continued talking, Devorah shook her close-cropped head in confusion.

"The nuns bought into the offer," she stated to those cluttered around her, frowning. "They're surrendering in droves. But they were never fighting against the Aliens. They were fighting against *us* for being supposed heretics. How could Dr. King just give up like this?"

A man with a ragged uniform, sporting the Israeli army insignia of a Colonel, sighed: "Well, he walked out on us, didn't he? Maybe he saw a better path, Devorah. We're just hanging on by our fingernails. We've no real prospect for success other than denying the invaders their last few human victims."

Another, older oriental-looking woman quietly observed: "He says the Aliens established this Brazil colony, supplying it with everything they initially needed to get up and running. I don't know about the rest of you, but I'm tired of this fight. We're living like animals in burrows. Our planet's been ruined—it'll be centuries before we can live on the surface on our own. If there's really a thriving colony, why not join it?"

"But why would the Aliens who haven't even bothered to talk to us before, want to now leave us in peace with a fresh new start?" a younger fighter asked.

"Wait, he's addressing that very point," another man said, "shushing" the others.

"...suspicious of their motives," the clean-cut image of the fresh-faced Dave on the screen continued. "They want to return periodically to 'harvest' more of us! But they can't do that if the nuclear winter kills us all off. So to them, this isn't charity—it's a *breeding* colony for their future needs."

There were horrified "gasps" throughout the chamber... "What? That's awful! We'll never consent to such barbarism! We're not animals to be bred and then slaughtered!"

"Yes, that's awful, isn't it?" the reasonable, rational Dave on the screen serenely continued. "You're probably reacting just as I did—with horror! But when I inquired further, I quickly discovered that the Aliens will not return for at least another thousand years—perhaps *tens* of thousands of years. So instead of us few survivors dying-off in the near future, we'll have a long reprieve."

Devorah was skeptical, loudly shouting at the screen: "But *how* can we believe them?"

Others of the assembled fighters were nodding in agreement.

"...how can we believe that claim?" Dave was asking on the screen, mirroring her concerns. "Well, I've looked at their star charts. Traveling at near the speed of light, roughly a thousand years is the minimum time required for them to go to their star then return—assuming no 'down' time at their planet, which likely will occur. So they'll be away from Earth for at least a thousand years."

A star chart showed up on the screen. A red box marked a particular star nearer to the center of the Milky Way from Earth's green-boxed position out on one of the spiral arms.

"So my recommendation to our units around the world," Dave on the screen continued, "is to unhook your DE-generators from the grid and bring them with you up to the surface. Transport crafts await you, *not* the Reaper Robots. These ships will take you directly to the Brazil colony where I will await your arrival."

"This is too convenient," Devorah shook her head. "Nothing we've seen yet from the Aliens supports such charity to us."

Again, as if hearing her words, the figure on the screen kept speaking...

"—and this is not kindness from the Aliens. It is a practical decision on their part to help us survive until they make another run at us. But a lot can happen in a thousand years. By the time they get around to checking on us again we may be knocking on *their* door. As they claim to be millions of years advanced beyond us, this doesn't concern them. But it sure makes me hopeful. I, for one, am going to take this chance and run with it."

Many in the control room were looking conflicted, uncertain.

A babble of voices broke out debating what they'd seen...

—that is until someone noticed that the hands resting lightly on Dave's shoulders had changed their configuration. Now, the High Priestess' hands were no longer flat. Indeed, each hand had curled-under four fingers, leaving the middle finger of each hand sticking out at the camera.

All the humans watching it knew exactly the message that the white-hooded woman standing behind the seated Dr. King was sending: the universal sign for "Screw you!" In fact, it was a *double* screw-you!

"This is our chance for a reprieve, to rebuild our world," the 'Dave' on the viewscreen urgently continued—as the High Priestess behind him nodded in agreement while steadily maintaining both of her "one finger salutes." "Yes, we're not defeating the invaders—but that could never happen anyway. We've slowed them down, but can't stop them! In this way, we have a partial victory—plus many years to regroup and advance technologically before they eventually return. Perhaps in that distant future we'll not be mere biological scum to be harvested, but actual partners. So I'm choosing the best option available to us. I hope you do the same. Please unhook your DE-generators from the grid and come up to the surface. Do it now!"

Then the screen went blank.

"So...what do you think?" the Colonel asked Devorah. "Do we send out an order to surrender, despite that obvious warning from the High Priestess—and give up our shielded DE-generators, causing the Global Shield to shut down?"

She shook her head firmly in the negative.

"That wasn't Dr. King," she simply stated.

"What?"

"He didn't give the covert authentication codes," she flatly stated, her voice grim.

"Could he have forgotten?" the Colonel wondered, frowning.

"On a world-wide announcement of such magnitude?" the young girl asked, "Never! Whoever or whatever was talking to us, it *wasn't* our Resistance Leader."

"So we...?"

"Send out the message to keep decapitating the Reapers—getting more DE-generators obscured and continually running—and thereby strengthening the Global Shield. For now the shield is preventing the orbiting Harvesters from descending, but we don't know how long it will keep them off Earth's surface. That simulation of Dr. King was correct that the Planetary Shield is just a temporary measure. But we can keep shoring it up, maybe until they get tired and leave!"

The Colonel nodded in agreement.

"I'll get the encrypted burst sent out immediately."

The older woman beside Devorah patted her shoulder sympathetically with a chubby hand.

"I know that was hard for you," the chubby lady said, slumping into a chair beside the young lady.

"It was a tempting offer," Devorah replied. Then, after a long pause, she intensely concluded: "But it was *exactly* what we wanted to hear! My Jewish Faith doesn't prepare me to accept gifts from conquerors—rather, to expect *poison pills*."

The chubby oriental lady grimly nodded: "Yes, there's an old Chinese saying from my own ancestors...'*Beware suspicious folks bearing gifts.*' Our enemies are *not* our friends."

The Colonel returned, rubbing thoughtfully at his big bald head with one hand.

"We've sent out the orders—but what about Dr. King? If that was him, he's now a traitor!"

"It *wasn't* him," Devorah confidently stated yet again. "He's likely still in Jerusalem, in need of our help."

"But he walked away from us...?"

"—and we're *not* walking away from him! He created the DE-generators and figured out a way to link them together to stop the invasion in its tracks. He gave us the means to resist and we're *not* abandoning him," she firmly stated. "Those Aliens are so rattled that they're beaming out slick propaganda. Send out search squads. Commander M'Sheekha went out to find him. They both could be in trouble. Get our people back!" she yelled.

The Jerusalem Resistance Fighters jumped to obey her order.

She was, indeed, an excellent pick to be the interim Commander.

Dave was struggling in the cramped, unstable jumble deep beneath the ruined Cathedral.

To better maneuver, he'd left behind his rifle and backpack with Eashoa.

He was trying to remove usable clothes from the skeletal corpses they'd passed on their way down to the tomb. It was difficult. Not only were the human remains jammed together under an array of huge stones and building materials, but broken bones thrust through most of the clothes like spears.

One set of clothes seemed fairly intact—a tough red jumpsuit. It was hard to remove from under a crumbled pile of masonry, but with persistence Dave worked it free.

Eventually, Dave managed to pull out enough pieces of still-intact clothing to offer them to a naked young girl...*Sally!*

Dave still couldn't believe it was true.

Yet somehow, a version of Sally was down there in the tomb with the old man. He could hear them talking at a distance below him, but not well enough to make out their words.

And in response to his bewildered questions, Commander M'Sheekha simply said he'd explain later, choosing to concentrate on slowly rehydrating the girl—who, yes, now appeared to be in her late teens—with calibrated sips of water from his canteen. She kept deliriously begging for more. But that one canteen was all the clean water they had. It needed to last for a while.

Dave ached for her to recover—to be safe, warm, and with plenty of water to slack her terrible thirst!

And most of all he never wanted to leave her side.

But Eashoa had sent Dave off to find clothes for Sally in the ruins of the smashed Church of the Holy Sepulchre.

After her revival she was disoriented, weak. But she was rapidly gaining strength. It appeared that whatever she'd done to convert herself into a young teenaged girl, the fresh air hitting her body triggered an amazing recuperation!

Likely being in a sealed, near-airless tomb chamber had somehow contributed to her long-term "suspended animation."

And as Dave crawled back down towards the tomb, dragging an armful of soiled, torn clothes, he began to make out their words.

Eashoa was explaining everything that had happened since the Alien Invasion—bringing the reanimated Sally up to date.

As Dave crawled out into the open space, Sally weakly rose to her feet, tottered over to him, and *flung* her arms around him.

"Dave..." she whispered in a gravelly, but still-girlish voice in his ear, "It's *so* good to see you again! I've *missed* you."

She was still dressed only in Eashoa's thin field jacket.

Dave hugged her through the fabric, feeling her warm body pressed up against him—smelling the acrid musk of her hair, still with pieces of crumbling fabric stuck into it.

He didn't know whether to kiss her or run screaming away from a zombie corpse!

He decided to kiss her on her cheek.

She giggled like a little girl.

If this wasn't "his" Sally—she was close enough. Maybe he still wasn't her "boyfriend", but perhaps "friend" was a good start.

"I got some clothes for you to try on—not the latest fashions, of course—but maybe better than nothing?"

"Thank you so much, Dave," she grinned at him before wobbling away to a corner to try them on, slipping out of the field jacket.

Dave averted his eyes from her naked young body, wearily stumbling over to the Commander who was peering intently at the small screen on his pocket-receiver.

"You better take a look at this, Dr. King," he said, handing it to him.

It was nice of Eashoa to address him by his academic title. Few ever offered him that token respect. He knew he should correct the Commander and insist on him using Dave's first name. After all, they'd already given each other permission to be informal. But he was just too exhausted mentally and physically to care that much. Besides, keeping things strictly formal was appropriate around a near-naked teenager.

So Dave sat down and looked at the small screen. He was astonished to see an image of *himself*—calmly and coolly *betraying* the entire Resistance effort!

"Why that's...that's...total *crap!*" Dave exclaimed in horror.

"Yes, it certainly is," Eashoa agreed, taking the receiver back and returning it to his pocket.

"We've got to contact our people here, tell them it's a fake!"

"There's no need for that, David," the Commander answered, looking vaguely out into the distance. "The Aliens pulling this trick didn't know about our covert authentication codes—none of our fighters will believe it. Plus, a denial's already been sent out by the Jerusalem fighters, so we don't have to risk revealing our presence to the Aliens by trying to contact headquarters. Also, that's actually not our biggest problem. We've got a *much* more serious situation to address."

"What could be *more* serious?" Dave frowned, weakly sitting down next to the Commander on the cold rocks.

"You remember how you told me that Arthur took you a year into the future to witness the incineration of the earth?"

"Yes?"

"Well, that's *not* the timetable anymore."

"Say what?"

"It's not a year away."

"It's...*nearer?*"

The Commander sighed deeply, looking up with his one good eye at the close rocky ceiling of the Tomb.

"It's one week from now."

Dave sat in stunned silence. One week? The End of the World was coming in *one week?* Just seven days from now? But...that meant there was no reason to do anything! Arthur said that there was no "rewinding" of time. *Fate* was going to be fulfilled. This was it!

"But Eashoa, how could you possibly know this?"

The wrinkled old man reached up and lifted away his eye patch.

Dave looked into an empty, dark socket where *glittering, diamond-patterns* spun hypnotically.

Dave gasped in disbelief.

"You...you...?"

"I told you Arthur was my dear friend," he calmly stated as he lowered the black patch into place. "He recruited me to help in his effort to attract the full attention of God. You see, Dave, I don't fear God. Just like Arthur, I *want* to get the Creator's attention focused back upon Earth. It's been diverted for far too long."

"But...how do you know the timing?"

"The intelligent computer super-programs implanted by Arthur into my brain—that a future Sally originally designed—can sense changes in the time-stream, David," the Commander simply stated. "So believe me that Judgment Day is one week from today—and that the human race has already been found wanting. I wish it were otherwise, but *God's Will* be done."

"But...if that's true," Dave whispered, hearing his voice reverberate in the rocky tomb, "then why...?" he pointed over to Sally who was busily putting on the last pieces of outer garments.

"What pleases the Lord of Creation most, my friend," the old man said in a quavering voice, "is struggle against insurmountable odds. And that girl there...the *Girl with the Turtle Tattoo*...represents, if nothing else, a colossal and heroic *struggle*. I did not know if she could be revived—but I wanted to give her the chance to be here, with us, at the very last."

Sally walked back over and sat down next to Dave.

She was clothed in the torn but wearable red jumpsuit, a long-sleeved flannel shirt under it, black boots, and a thick winter jacket on top.

She was recovered, back to her petite, chirpy self.

"What did I miss?" she smiled at Dave and Eashoa.

She tossed an unused long overcoat over to Eashoa, which he gratefully accepted to put over his returned thin field jacket.

Dave snorted.

"Oh, just that the Commander here is in league with time-travelers, has one of your super-smart implants in his brain, and has predicted the end of the world one week from today," Dave answered nonchalantly.

Sally didn't even blink in surprise.

Instead, she wryly *grinned.*

"*And*...he's Jesus," she added quietly but firmly, "who I dearly love."

This was Dave's turn to illogically not look surprised. But it wasn't because he understood her words. It was because her words just didn't make any sense. She was back to being an indecipherable puzzle, as per "normal."

"Jesus?" Dave dumbly repeated. "And...you *love* him? Say what?"

"Don't *you* love Jesus?" she asked, apparently teasing him.

"What...? No! I m-mean...sure—b-but...*Jesus?*" he stammered, totally confused.

"Oh, I suppose you don't speak fluid ancient Aramaic, do you?" she cheerfully quipped at him.

"I'm afraid not..." he shrugged, bewildered.

"Well, Dave," she said, taking on an affected lecturing tone to him, "in ancient Aramaic the word *Eashoa* means 'The Life-Giver' and *M'sheekha* means 'The Anointed One.' In our modern English those words together translate to 'Jesus Christ.'"

Across from Dave, the cross-legged-sitting old Commander shrugged like it was no big deal.

"Wait...but...isn't Jesus supposed to be up in heaven or some-thing?" Dave gaped at the old man.

"Well, yes," he admitted. "But you see I had this—as you just now heard alluded to—*intimate* relationship...with a certain young girl."

Sally grinned good-naturedly.

"—and I was put on what you'd term 'probation' to roam the surface of Earth for a few eons or so."

"You say...a 'relationship'?" Dave gaped again, looking back and forth from the old man to the young girl.

"Not to worry your romantic head, David," Eashoa shrugged. "It wasn't physical—yet it was also far *more*. You see, Sally went back in time to stop me from favorably influencing future societies. She wanted to prevent ensuing freedoms which would allow excessive Dark Energy usage in this Dimension. So the clever little girl *tempted* me. And I...well...I sort of *gave in* at the very last, not that I had much choice in the matter. As I'm sure you know, once her mind is made up our Sahlee can be very persuasive."

Dave didn't know what to believe. This old man, who looked a hundred years old, certainly *thought* he was Jesus. And the newly reanimated Sally agreed with him. She certainly had strong feelings for him. But that would mean...?

"So you're—*not* perfect?"

The Commander threw his head back and laughed heartily, his "guffaws" echoing about the tomb.

"Oh my, that's one of the painful myths I've had to endure hearing for over two thousand years now," he sadly sighed. "My dear young man, 'perfection' is in the eye of the beholder, is it not? I just *struggle* the same as you—in the face of terrible odds and painful trials. I try to do the best I can. Who can ask for more from us mere humans?"

"*God*, apparently," Dave cuttingly replied. "Isn't the human race being condemned to oblivion in just one week from now for *failing* to be perfect?"

"Yes, that's partially true," the Commander sighed again, leaning back and looking up at the ceiling. "But by every measure you can come up with, Mankind as a whole *has* abysmally *failed*. Yes, as we discussed previously, there are a few notable exceptions—but the Creator is quite justified to erase your malignant species, if that be His conclusion."

Dave shook his head in bewilderment. This was all too incredible! Eashoa was Jesus? Sally was back from the grave? The world was ending in just a week?

It was too much to wrap his mind around.

"So what can we do about it?" Dave asked, deciding to just accept Eashoa's fantastic story on faith. "Since you apparently have Divine Knowledge plus time-traveling skills plus a super-smart intelligent computer sitting in your brain, tell us! How do we subvert the *Will of God?*"

Eashoa nonchalantly shrugged.

But Sally leaned forward as she sat cross-legged beside Dave, the oil lamp's single flickering flame highlighting her intense expression.

"We go *back in time* again—and *stop* the Alien Invasion!" she fervently concluded. "That's apparently the seminal event which in this timeline pushes up Judgment Day. Without the resultant *global shield* lighting up the earth—then Armageddon will be postponed for years if not centuries on into the future!"

"But Sally," Dave protested, "Arthur told me on the moon in the future that this time there'd be no going back. He said that this was the final destruction—that there were no more timelines to delay the inevitable."

She frowned, considering Dave's words.

"But then again..." Eashoa began.

"Yes?" Dave suspiciously asked.

"Our dear friend Arthur is no more," he sadly but accurately observed.

"What do you mean?" Dave asked.

"It was a year in the future you stood with him on the surface of the moon, right?"

"Yes...but...oh, I *see*," Dave gasped, his eyes stretching wide in realization. "That future no longer exists! If Judgment Day is in one week, then the Moon and Earth of a year in the future are *gone*. We're *already* into a new timeline. Arthur was *wrong*—and it was the cause of his own death."

"So it is possible," Sally grinned, her green eyes wide with excitement. "But Jesus—you said you *wanted* to attract God's attention. But now you don't?"

He shrugged. "Now, a hundred years from now, a thousand years, a million years—it's going to happen, whatever we do. But...it's just so much *fun* playing with you little creatures down here—especially with you, dear Sahlee. I know it's selfish of me, but I wouldn't mind having a few more years or centuries to..."

"Great!" Sally broke in, clapping her hands together in emphasis. "So we go back and stop the invaders in their tracks! But then, *how* do we go back in time? When it happened to me before, it was always outside my control—except, of course, when I used my future Martian Obelisk. But the 'crash landing' into the desert destroyed it—and nearly me as well."

"Uh...'Jesus'!" Dave said, loudly *snapping* his own fingers in emphasis.

"Please, just call me Eashoa," the old man answered. "That's been my name for a long time now. Whenever you or Sahlee say 'Jesus' you conjure up an image burnished and elaborated over the centuries. That's not me. And you need not snap your fingers to get my attention...wait! I'm physically over a hundred years old and getting hard of hearing—so, yes, snap your fingers all you wish," he laughed.

"Ok, then...Eashoa," Dave tried again. "But can't you like, you know...work miracles? Can't *you* just snap *your* fingers and send us back in time?"

Jesus sighed, his head sadly hanging down. "I'm sorry friends, 'probation', remember? I don't have any super-powers. I'm just like you...a mere lowly human. Yes, I'm an extremely long-lived human thanks to a gift from Sally of her retroviral immune-enhancement treatment—but other than that, I'm quite ordinary."

So, he really did think he was Jesus—yet couldn't work any miracles. How convenient! Actually, did he perhaps find and mummify Dave's "Sally" from the other timeline—as Dave and his friends huddled during the first Alien bombardment? If she had access to Optimmune that alone could explain her dormant state leading to reanimation. If so, her "mummification" was *recent*—and Eashoa was having delusions of grandeur jiving with some fantastic delusions by Sally...?

After all, many people over the ages claimed to be the returned Messiah—yet could present zero tangible proof.

If only the Commander *were* the real Jesus, then He could negotiate not just with the Aliens, but with God Himself!

But, whatever he was, he was indeed a valued friend deserving at least to be humored—and Sally's *real* "boyfriend."

But the Aliens were stone-cold reality.

"So we're stuck?" Dave grimaced. "But it's not in our nature to just give up, Eashoa. We 'ordinary' humans fight to the last breath. We may be despicable scum, but we're *mean* and *persistent* scum!"

"Well...*Sally* may know a way," Eashoa gently suggested.

She perked up at the encouragement from Eashoa. Her eyes narrowed as she concentrated, remembering back—back to the 12th Century...

"You mean that *tunnel?*"

"It took an incredible, accumulated amount of energy to achieve."

"Yes, over fourteen years of it, released from my gun in one gigantic blast. And it made a time-conduit that sent me over 900 years back into the future!"

"Uhm, will someone please clue me in as to what we're talking about?" Dave asked.

"And we've got over *two thousand years* of accumulation...if we can still find it!" Sally yelled. She jumped up and hopped around the small tomb, barely containing her excitement. "It should have more than enough stored energy to blast us back into the past!"

"Sally! Please tell me what...?" Dave implored her.

"I took one of my *accumulator-guns* back with me to the 1st Century—but then I couldn't find it," Sally grinned widely, spontaneously hugging Dave before releasing him.

This was the solution. She *knew* it!

"If it survived the trip," she continued excitedly, "—and I've no reason to think it didn't—then that gun has been sucking-in energy for over two millennia!"

"Well if energy is the problem, then why not just use one of our DE-generators?" Dave reasonably asked. "Now that we have them hidden from detection by the Harvesters, we've got them running constantly. They tap into virtually unlimited energy from subspace."

Dave had a good point. But Sally knew just having a powerful energy source wasn't enough to break the time barrier.

"I don't know—but somehow it's not the same. Maybe it has to do with the concentration of the delivered energy. Or maybe the waveform...or some sort of interaction with my Tattoo?" Sally shrugged, stopping her random hopping to sit back down beside Dave. Her mind was racing a mile a minute. Presumably her brain was catching up after her 2,000-year "nap"?

"But it doesn't seem random," Dave frowned as he stared at her Turtle Tattoo on her wrist. Yes, he saw it also. It was glowing enough to warm her skin. "There are things going on here that are beyond just rational manipulations of energy."

"Yes, I guess we're like little kids playing with an oven," Sally shrugged. "Is the stove running the oven powered by electricity or gas or microwaves? Each energy source has different characteristics and can do different things. But in the end, the kid only knows she puts in dough and it comes out cookies that..."

"—are exquisitely dependent upon the kid's own efforts," Dave nodded in agreement.

Sally's mind was whirling. It was great to be thinking again! Jesus was so kind to preserve her in the buried tomb, allowing the Optimmune remaining in her system a chance to reanimate her body. It was like she was reborn!

Truly, Jesus was a good friend.

"That's a brilliant illustration, Sally," Dave congratulated her. "Even I—with a Ph.D. in physics—don't know the real nature of each of the fundamental components of the Universe. We scientists are still children playing with a blast furnace. I like your analogy of kids baking cookies. It's a quite tasty illustration!"

She nodded gratefully. It was nice to be back with Dave again. He always "got" her, even when they were fighting with each other.

"Alright then, we agree we need your two-thousand-year-old gun. But where is it?" Dave asked her.

She frowned, realizing the enormity of what she was proposing.

"It's...somewhere in the Wilderness of Judea, alongside the Dead Sea. I think if I saw the same configuration of mountains—like *fangs* sticking up out of the desert—we could find the *Obelisk*."

"And just what is this 'Obelisk'?" Dave asked.

That's right. He didn't know.

"It powered my trip that started fifty years from now in the future in the original timeline, back to the 1st Century," Sally stated matter-of-factly, summarizing up a huge achievement in just a few words.

She realized she was giving Dave a lot to digest, so offered a better explanation: "It's a Martian device made by a long-vanished race that my scientists and I managed to convert into our very own Time Machine—to take me where *I* wanted!"

Dave looked skeptical. Sally realized he didn't know she was the "original" Sally from the other Dimension who became a High Priestess in this Dimension, grew old on Mars, then took a massive dose of Optimmune that turned her into a child as she traveled back to the first century.

But there wasn't time to catch him up-to-date. He'd just have to keep up. Whatever incarnation of Dave King he was, he still had a brilliant mind attuned to the uncanny and so-called "impossible."

"So instead of this unpredictable bouncing-around...?"

"I figured out how to do it myself," Sally grinned. "I'm a certified mathematical genius, right? In my previous life I had billions of dollars to hire experts such as you in Physics and every other discipline. With the artifact from the ancient Martians I figured out the theoretical formulas for tapping into a whole *new* form of energy!"

"*Another* energy?" Dave gasped.

"Yes—the fabric of Time itself: *Time Energy!*" she laughed.

Dave looked intrigued. Despite their desperate situation, Sally knew he'd find the subject fascinating.

"And the Obelisk was supposed to harvest it as it went back in time," Sally continued, "to give me complete control over the entire world of the first century."

"That's incredible," Dave said, stunned by the implications. "But, Martians?" he prodded her.

"It's a long story," She sighed. "But..."

"But?" Dave repeated.

"But it crashed into the Wilderness of Judea," she sighed, remembering that terrible struggle. "I barely made it from there to the shore of the Dead Sea, where a two-year-old Jesus and his family came upon me, rescuing me. The Obelisk is useless. I think I broke

it. The insides—as much as I could see—looked fused. But my gun
should be there...somewhere nearby..."

"So this Obelisk should stick out like sore thumb?" Dave asked.
"And then we just hunt in the sand around it for the gun?"

"I'm afraid it's not that easy," she sighed, wishing it were so.
"Even as I was leaving it behind to walk all night through the hills to
get to what I thought was a good water source, it was being buried by
the blowing sand. And my gun is somewhere near to it. Just thinking
about that terrible trip makes me *thirsty*. I'm dry as a *mummy!*"

A terrible thirst threatened to overwhelm her. It wasn't just their
present dehydrated situation in the tomb, but a lifetime of going
thirsty!

"Ok," Dave said. "But how do we get there in less than a week—
across this frozen terrain—without the Aliens snatching us up?"

"It's way too far to walk," Sally said, pushing the burning thirst
away. "And from what Eashoa told me, the surface roads are blown
up, blocked by ruins, or snowed over."

Sally saw Eashoa get a far-away look in his brown eye as he absently stroked his thin white beard with one hand.

"That's right where my old friend 'John the Baptist' did a lot of his
preaching," Jesus mused. "If we *could* get there, I'm familiar with the
whole territory—and could narrow down the search for your 'fangs'."

Sally felt Dave's strong hand grip her smaller one.

"I think I know where we might find a ride," Dave confidently
nodded. "It's not certain. I may be wrong. But if it's still there, we
have to hurry!"

Sally was encouraged. Dave could be annoyingly irritating at
times. But when he had a tangible objective in sight he latched onto it
like a bulldog.

Apparently Eashoa felt the same.

"Alright, David," the old man nodded, hopping spryly up to his
feet while grabbing up the oil lamp. "Lead the way. You don't mind
me calling you 'David', do you? It's a common Biblical name that just
slips off my tongue. We're close enough, the three of us, that I probably should call you by your intimate derivative, 'Dave.'"

"Of course not, Je...I mean Eashoa. Whatever happens, it's a privilege and honor for me and Sally to be your team members. You call

me whatever suits you the best. My mother named me after the David in the Bible, anyway. So that's really my given name."

Sally smiled. She reached over to grasp her old friend's hand as
he took Dave's other hand.

For a moment they all stood hand-in-hand in a circle.

"All for one—and one for all," Dave grinned at them both.

"Agreed!" Eashoa smiled, giving Sally a squeeze of her hand.

"Yes," Sally nodded firmly.

Then Dave released her hand. She was glad he did so. She'd felt
an electric spark between the two of them. But this wasn't the time
for rekindling old feelings. This was the time for *action!*

"But we may need a diversion to get there across this Reaper-
infested city," Dave said, frowning.

Sally liked Dave this way—focused and determined.

Eashoa pulled out his small radio unit.

"I'll send a quick, encrypted text-burst to headquarters. They
likely have squads already out searching for us. I'll briefly tell them
what we're attempting—just enough for them to know where we're
going—and that we need a *powerful* distraction."

"Great, Eashoa," Dave nodded, picking up his assault rifle. "That's
even better than me trying to use my laptop to send a signal. Do it—
and then follow *me!*"

Sally laughed, knowing he was joking.

He was telling *Jesus* to "follow *him.*" Hah!

She glanced at Eashoa, hoping he'd not get angry.

But Eashoa was laughing good-naturedly. He also liked a good
joke. He was just like Sally remembered him from the first century,
only a lot older—wrinkled, leathery, with white hair and a black
eyepatch.

But he was still great.

It's just like that old "praise song" of Dave's Mother's church—
Sally thought to herself, *Jesus was "just alright!"*

Even if it turned out they truly had only a week to live, Sally knew
deep in her reanimated mummified bones that it was *good* to be alive.

Chapter 19

A TOSS OF THE DICE

Yep, you should...
"Know when to hold them
Know when to fold them
And when to walk away"
An old, familiar tune
Claiming skill at gambling
Not so much technical aspects
But the sense, the skill, the art
Displayed as a certain cunning
In the face of incomplete data
Taking an educated guess
At filling in the empty blanks
And then that last, desperate leap
Not knowing where you will land
Or even if you will land at all
Perhaps into a deep, black pit
Or reaching a convenient ledge
Snagged onto by its extreme edge
From there to live yet another day
Thankful that this time you survived
Where it was equally plausible
That you missed and died.

The Luminary Chronicles, 19:103-107

Satan dragged Jean King up from the floor where she'd been crumpled. He plastered her face onto one of the viewscreens.

"*What* does this mean?" he yelled at her.

The High Priestess was exhausted and weak. The Demon had given her a small room containing just a toilet as her "quarters". She "slept" curled up in a ball in the corner of the room. He seemed to forget that she, unlike him, was a biological entity requiring extensive physiological support.

Instead of tending to her needs he dragged her around from place to place like a pet on a leash, preferring to keep a close watch on her.

But he'd not given her any food or drink for over a day now. And she wasn't going to give him the satisfaction of begging for sustenance.

"What—this writing here?" she replied weakly, straining to see and make sense of the symbols zipping across the screen.

"It was encrypted! It is a burst from your son and other companions! The Harvester intercepted it! Tell me what it means! Tell me now!"

Jean was terrified by the screaming, raging monster. But she also felt a grim satisfaction. She and her son were driving him *insane*.

The Demon didn't seem so concerned about being trapped on the Earth's surface by the global DE-shield. Instead, he was outraged that an "inferior" species dared to defy him!

She peered closely at the screen, seeing words, and then reading them out loud: "*Attack Harvester. Have plan to stop invasion. Need time.*"

She paused, considering. Maybe David and whoever else with him weren't as helpless or compliant as the Demon assumed. They needed time.

"I...suppose it means what it says," Jean shrugged.

"And *what* is that?" the Demon yelled so loudly it hurt Jean's ears—before *slamming* his big fist onto the console right in front of her face, crumpling it!

Jean cringed backward.

"Well...obviously...they have a secret weapon that they mean to use against this spacecraft," she said. "They've got you trapped here close to the surface, where they can reach you easily—and are looking to *destroy* this Harvester."

"But they should be surrendering!" he yelled, green poison dripping from around his bared sharp teeth.

"Well," Jean replied, sagging back to the floor, "they and the other Resistance fighters obviously saw through your illusion—and are redoubling their efforts against you to..."

"They will pay dearly!" the Demon roared, flinging his clawed hands up into the air while throwing his horned head backward.

"If...I may suggest," Jean stated, struggling to keep conscious and sharp, "you might want to do a 'strategic' retreat to a different location. Perhaps if you actually went to Brazil and started preparations there for the 'colony' then..."

"I will find them and annihilate them!" he screamed into the control room, dragging her along behind him as he headed over to another, intact console. "And why can't you stand up on your own?"

"I need food...drink..."

"You little biological creatures are so pitiful, so helpless," he growled again as he manipulated control knobs and activated scanners. He had stopped yelling, immersed in his search. "Return to your room! I'll have suitable sustenance manufactured and delivered there. I need to keep your pitifully insignificant body alive, for now. Go!"

Jean dragged herself up and staggered away, but not before carefully noting the sequence of movements he'd done at the controls...as she'd been doing for some time.

"Poor Davey," she whispered to herself. "I hope he's doing better than me."

Dave, Eashoa, and Sally were creeping through the snow-covered ruins of Jerusalem.

They'd managed to avoid prowling Reapers, whose numbers were much decreased from the day before. Doubtless there were slimpickings of stray humans on the surface of the decimated, burneddown, iced-over, and re-bombarded Holy City.

Dave and his companions were slowly approaching the side of the ancient Mount of Olives.

It was getting dark. Even during the day, little light filtered through the roiling dark clouds above. Now that it was evening it was especially hard for Dave to see their way forward.

Also, a spooky, frigid fog swirled around them.

"*There* it is," Dave excitedly whispered, pointing ahead.

Looming above them out of the mists, Dave vaguely made-out a huge tomb set-into and protected within a large rectangular alcove. It was all hewn out of solid rock. Its top was a pyramid. Beneath that was a columned rectangle. Beneath that were large stone steps. And at its bottom, obscured by muddy snow, was an opening.

"What is it?" Sally asked, pointing at the huge structure.

Eashoa answered: "It's '*The Tomb of Zechariah*'—a monument attributed to a Prophet who was stoned to death for pointing out the sins of his people. You may remember this from the Bible?"

"I'm afraid I'm not well acquainted with your Holy Book," Sally responded.

"It was one of the Old Testament Prophets," Dave offered, leading them forward...

—where right in front of the tomb, appearing out of the thick mists, tilted on the slope of the ground but seemingly still intact, was the *Apache Attack Helicopter!*

It was just where Dave had anticipated, judged from its angle of decline when it was blown out of the sky by the descending Harvester.

Dave and Eashoa approached it cautiously, their rifles held at-ready.

"Be careful!" Sally called softly from behind them.

But there was no need to be hesitant. Both swing-up window-hatches on the right side of the craft were ripped off, lying crumpled to the side in the snow. There was no sign of the pilot and gunner.

"The Reapers got our men," Dave angrily spat, lowering his gun in bitter dejection. "I thought they might have survived the crash... But even though the helicopter is intact, we've got no way to fly the damn thing!"

"Is it fueled?" Eashoa asked, stepping up on a rung to peer into the upper, pilot's seat.

"I think so," Dave said. "They were refueling it when the Harvest-er appeared."

"Good," Eashoa answered, pulling himself up into the pilot's seat and strapping in. "*I* can fly it."

"Really?" Dave asked, feeling gingerly at the cold surface, brushing away clinging snow. Then he likewise pulled himself up into the lower, open gunner's seat.

He put his backpack at his feet.

"I studied them extensively, along with all the other armament systems that the U.S. kindly sold to Israel," the old man sitting behind and above Dave curtly answered. "I was too elderly to be approved to fly one, of course—but I'm quite familiar with the controls and weapons systems."

"No, not *that*..." Dave hastily amended his statement. "I mean *you* were in the *Israeli* military?"

Eashoa chuckled.

Dave heard him up behind him clicking through a pre-flight sequence.

The engine caught, sputtered, and then ROARED loudly...the big long blades starting to turn.

"You didn't know that Jesus was *Jewish?*" Eashoa yelled over the noise from the rotors.

Dave grimaced, realizing that he wasn't thinking straight. Too much had happened in the last few days. He was exhausted, mentally as well as physically.

"So where do *I* sit?"

It was Sally, hopping up on the siding to peer into the two tight cockpits.

"Well..." Dave gulped. "Since we're the two with rifles, maybe you should just stay here safe while we..."

She reached in and grabbed Dave by his longish brown hair, jerking his head painfully to the side.

"*You* can stay behind while *I* and Eashoa go look for my 2,000 year-old gun!" she ordered him.

"There's room for you both in the gunner's seat if you jam in closely," Eashoa reasonably replied from above them. "After all, Sahlee, you're still a slender teenaged girl. What about it, Dave?"

"Well, I..." Dave started to reply—when Sally suddenly pulled herself up and forced herself in right next to him! They were cheek-to-cheek.

"Better...see if we can get this seatbelt...around both of us," Dave struggled, trying to get both ends around the two of them.

"You guys ready?" the Commander called down to them. "Headquarters knows what we're doing. I just sent them off a burst. We're ready to go!"

"Uhm, well..." Dave tried to answer as he just managed to "snap" the buckle into place—at its furthest-extended position, around him and Sally.

"Hey, stop squashing me!" Sally complained as he shifted his position and they ended up hugging each other, face-to-face.

Actually, Dave didn't mind it all that much.

She was an intoxicatingly attractive "teenaged" girl.

The rotors were turning rapidly!

—and, so-configured, they rose up into the mists.

"Ah, *there* they are!" Satan grinned happily.

Jean was back by his side. She'd had a short break to get a nap plus eat and drink the "sustenance" that robots brought her.

It was a gooey, grey paste plus a tube filled with a faintly yellow liquid.

It tasted like eating grease and drinking urine.

But it *was* nourishing, refreshing her starved body.

And her head was much clearer.

"Witness the *demise* of your enemy, High Priestess!" he cackled as his claws twisted the controls to reveal an infrared false image on a viewscreen—against the muddy snow and ruins of Jerusalem—a single low-flying helicopter. "Your turncoat son is in that winged craft. I traced that burst-transmission to it. He killed many of your Priestesses and thinks he can threaten me. But he is about to die!"

"Do what you must, Satan," Jean King replied demurely. She was sitting dejectedly at another of the Harvester control terminals.

"Yes! My Will be done! They are trying to escape but I will incinerate them!" he grinned toothily, his yellow eyes stretched wide in glee—his long tail twitching back and forth, his twelve-feet-tall body stretched up straight in anticipation!

A crosshairs appeared on the screen.

Carefully, he centered it exactly on the tiny little helicopter.

"Now then, no more threat to me or to my new Universe!" he muttered with deep satisfaction.

He pressed a blue button to activate the five-mile-long spacecraft's main, gigantic laser weapon...

Sally was the first to notice they were no longer flying by themselves in the snowy, dark sky.

"We've got company," she gasped in Dave's ear, looking up through the windshield.

Actually, Sally and Dave were in a torrent of icy wind that blasted in through the empty hatches on the right side of the helicopter.

Dave looked up. Hovering close above them he saw the *gigantic rectangular, shimmering-blue spacecraft.* Mashed up against Sally he was helpless to fire their 30-mm chain gun, not that it could do much against the massive energy shield of the Harvester.

Not even Hellfire missiles had made a dent in that force-field.

"I have night vision on!" Eashoa yelled to Dave and Sally against the roar of the freezing wind. "I'm going down as low as I dare! We'll try to evade them!"

"Fat chance...we're toast!" Dave yelled back. He decided to hug Sally close instead of keeping on trying to squirm away. "I'm sorry we never got the time to know each other better," he said in her ear.

"Me too," she answered back.

—as a *BRILLIANT BLAST* of *INTENSELY-WHITE LIGHT* suddenly flared around them, filling up the cockpit with intense heat...

—and then disappeared.

Momentarily blinded, Dave blinked his eyes in disbelief.

"We're still alive...?" he gasped. "How is that possible?"

Above him he saw the huge spacecraft—which was no longer glowing blue.

Instead, it was *dark* and obviously *lumbering* in the sky.

Satan pressed the firing button again.

Nothing...

—and yet again!

Nothing at all happened. After the initial flicker, it was dead!

His eyes narrowed to slits. He looked over at Jean.

She smiled sweetly back to him, sitting confidently at her control console.

"*What* have you done?" he seethed at her.

She looked at him for a moment in a gentle, maternal fashion before answering.

"Well—you vile creature—I've deactivated your weapons and defensive shield," she replied. "Also, your steering mechanisms are frozen shut."

"You've been *watching* me," he said with grudging respect. "I underestimated you, High Priestess."

"Yes," she agreed as she serenely watched a BOLT OF PURE-WHITE ENERGY flashing up from the ground!

Caught with its shields down, the Harvester suffered a lethal blow—the entire five-mile-long spaceship flung around in the air, throwing both Satan and Jean to the floor.

"No!" the Demon shouted. "No! No! No!"

"Yes," Jean grinned smugly. "They're discharging their DE-generators at you. My old friend Sally told me this was possible. It destroys their generators, but without your shields—it *kills* you dead!"

He jumped up from the floor to grab her in his hot claws.

"*Not* before I make you *suffer!*" he shouted at her.

—as two more BLAZING-WHITE ENERGY COLUMNS struck, *blasting* though the entire bulk of the Harvester, *tearing* out huge chunks—and sending the entire spacecraft spinning like a top down toward Jerusalem!

Like a rag doll, Jean was thrown up against the inside of the spinning clear globe.

As Jean lost consciousness, looking into the control chamber, she had the satisfying sight of Satan with both paws to each side of its red head, staring at the up-rushing Earth—*helpless!*

"Not again!" he howled in defeat.

"Wow...your Resistance fighters really did it!" Sally gasped into Dave's ear as the gigantic spacecraft spun past, barely missing them.

"We're not safe yet!" Eashoa called to them.

He revved up the engine, slanted the craft forward, and accelerated rapidly.

Looking behind them out the intact windscreen Dave watched the Harvester—as if in slow motion—*crash* into the city of Jerusalem!

The huge spacecraft crumpled like an accordion as it hit.

And then a GIGANTIC EXPLOSION lit up the entire stormy sky in *blood-red* as what remained of Jerusalem was simultaneously crushed and consumed in a raging inferno!

The helicopter was tossed about like a butterfly in a hurricane.

Debris from the explosion savagely *hammered* the helicopter.

And as Dave held Sally tightly he felt her *shudder*, hit by shrapnel through the opened hatchway to their side.

Dave felt hot blood running over his hands.

"Sally?" he whispered in her ear.

But she did not respond.

Chapter 20

IN THE WILDERNESS OF JUDEA

You'd think once is enough
But, no, terrible defeats reoccur
Recovering from that bout with cancer
Makes the reappearance the more horrible
Sure, all that crap about "growing in strength"
You can take "character development" and toss it
Back to where it belongs on the junk heap of history
Wishing one had less character and much more success
The Evil Unholy Trinity laughing its guts out with glee
Mother Nature, Lady Luck, and Human Frailty
Repeating your worst nightmare endlessly
Waiting at any moment to attack brutally
Yet even in the worst circumstances
It's "one foot after the other"
Knowing that we tried
Makes all the difference
Giving a type of satisfaction
That we were not finally overcome
Until the desert sands swallowed us...
In the unrelenting, wet Wilderness of Life.
The Luminary Chronicles, 20:48-52

The helicopter ran out of fuel somewhere in the Wilderness of Judea, alongside the Dead Sea.

They fluttered to a bumpy landing.

315

It was morning—not that you'd know it from the perpetual gloom of the Nuclear Winter. Also, it was freezing. A light snow drifted down around them. The Dead Sea looked even deader and more sluggish than normal.

Sally was laid out on Eashoa's overcoat, ashen-faced.

She'd lost a lot of blood. But they had her stabilized, her wounds bound up with gauze that they'd found in a small first-aid kit.

"Do you think she'll live?" Dave asked the Commander, his voice trembling.

Eashoa looked at Sally's motionless body.

"After what she's gone through, to die on the shore of the Dead Sea seems...incongruent," Commander M'Sheekha sadly stated. "But without competent medical care..."

His voice trailed off.

Even the normally bright Turtle Tattoo on her wrist was fading.

Her red-clothed legs stuck out from beneath her thick coat like limp sticks.

The Commander wearily sat with his back against the sleek, grey shell of the spent Apache attack helicopter.

It was banged up badly. One of the rotor blades was twisted. They were lucky they'd gotten as far as they did.

"Do you think we're anywhere near the Obelisk?" Dave asked, still hovering over Sally.

"Hard to tell, David," Eashoa answered. "Our GPS system isn't working. The Aliens destroyed most of our orbiting satellites long ago. So I was just flying in the dark night 'by the seat of my pants,' so to speak. However, I was relying on my extensive knowledge of this territory, so..."

"Yes?"

"I still remember how far my family took me along the Dead Sea before we encountered that strange kid lying unconscious and dying on the seashore...and this is fairly close to that spot."

"How can you tell?" Dave asked, looking around at the bleak, gloomy low hills covered with deep, muddy snow.

Eashoa shrugged, nervously stroking his long white whiskers. "It's just a feeling."

"Well *that's* certainly *not* just a feeling," Dave said, pointing excitedly down at Sally.

The green Turtle Tattoo on her wrist was faintly glowing. And even more than that, it was waxing and waning!

Eashoa slid over by her, tenderly holding her thin arm in his big hands and pointing the wrist out over the sluggish waves of the Dead Sea.

The light on Sally's wrist faded to nothing.

"Alright then, the other direction?" the Commander said, carefully swinging her limp arm around...

The faint light grew brighter, the pulsation quickening!

"It's pointing us to it," Dave concluded eagerly. "Grab up what supplies you can find, Eashoa. Load them in my backpack. I'll carry Sally if you'll carry the rifles."

"Let's do it," the Commander resolutely said, squaring his shoulders and narrowing his one brown eye in determination. He reached up to adjust his black eyepatch. "We've come all this way—what are a few more miles?"

In just a few minutes they were trudging away from the lonely, broken helicopter...into the snow-bound Wilderness of Judea.

Sally finally regained consciousness as the dim light of the sun—filtered through the dark clouds above—was fading away.

It was evening. She lay on the ground on a blanket, beside a small fire. Beside her on the blanket were a canteen and a beat-up assault rifle.

"W-where are w-we?" she stammered.

"Sally! You're awake!" she heard someone exclaim happily.

She tried to look around. But it was difficult trying to move her head. In her field of vision she saw nothing but rolling hills covered with muddy snow.

A brown-bearded, tired-looking face leaned down into her field of vision.

"You were hit by pieces of the exploding Harvester," Dave said to her. "You lost a great deal of blood before we could stabilize your wounds. I was afraid we were going to lose you. But it looks like you're healing."

As she struggled to sit up, Dave put a supporting arm behind her back.

"W-where's Eashoa?" she asked, blearily looking around in a sudden panic.

"He's fine," he answered her. "He's off scouting. I found some snow-covered brush and managed to get it burning. Try to get warm."

"D-did we m-make it all the way to the O-Obelisk?" she gasped, feeling stronger by the minute.

"We found the two sharp peaks you mentioned," Dave said, letting her sit up on her own. "But there's no trace of the Obelisk. If what you said is true, it's been buried under the desert sands for two millennia, plus another thick layer of snow on top of that from our Nuclear Winter. Your Turtle Tattoo led us to this point, but then stopped glowing. I tried using my laptop to get an electromagnetic signal, but there's nothing. If the Obelisk is down there, it's completely inert."

Sally looked at her wrist.

She couldn't even see the tattoo. Just as Dave had said, it wasn't glowing. Her arm was spattered-over with the still-falling, muddy snowflakes.

"C-can I h-have some w-water?" she said, looking about the campsite.

She was consumed with a fierce thirst. She didn't even have enough saliva left to lick her dry, cracked lips.

Dave put the canteen to her mouth.

"Don't drink too much," Dave sadly said. "There wasn't time for the helicopter to get restocked after we arrived at Jerusalem. We only have this one partially filled canteen of clean water, and no food. I'd give you melted snow but I already tried tasting it—it's toxic. Just a few drops made me sick to my stomach. We'll be lucky to survive here for even a few days. But hopefully that'll be enough to search this local area. After Judgment Day hits, though, it won't matter how thirsty any of us are when..."

His voice trailed off in exhaustion and despair.

Sally drank a few sips before turning her parched lips away. She was still desperately thirsty, but felt better. Her side hurt where she'd been hit with the shrapnel, but those persistent retroviral systems in her blood were still doing their job, fixing her up. Yay!

Though her vision was still blurry, she felt stronger. In a few days she might be healed, back to her normal perky self. That is, if they had a few more days...

"Thanks," she gasped.

But the icy, whistling wind seemed *ominous* to Sally. She had a sinking feeling that they *didn't* have several days to do a leisurely search.

And she was right...

—as a bright red LASER BURST lit up the hills and a *football field-wide, sizzling beam* burned the landscape!

"It's the Aliens," Sally groaned, looking up to see a square, black craft floating down out of the clouds, fast-approaching their position.

Sally felt Dave grab her up and rush her into the gathering darkness, his hanging backpack banging against her side...

—as behind them, *another laser blast*, more focused than the first, *incinerated* their camp, their campfire, their supplies, and Dave's assault rifle.

"Damn it!" Dave swore, ducking under a protective ledge on one of the close-by rocky hills. "I think my rifle was broken, but now it's completely destroyed. I thought we were *rid* of those monsters up there."

"They m-must have escaped the H-Harvester...before it c-crashed," Sally whispered back to him...

—as yet another *sizzling laser-strike* swept over the hills around them.

Sally winced as Dave scrunched in as far as he could go under the ledge, pushing against and protecting Sally with his own body.

Hot steam swept over them as the thick layers of snow outside were instantly *vaporized!*

Sally clamped her eyes tightly shut against the blistering steam. Then she gingerly opened them. And she couldn't believe what she saw. Off at a short distance—revealed beneath the evaporated snow and blown-away sand...Sally saw the unmistakable red, flat side of the *OBELISK!*

It was *glowing red*, apparently *re-activated* by absorbing the laser energy that just swept over its top.

"DR. DAVID KING," an amplified, menacing voice reverberated over the hills from the descending spacecraft. "I HAVE YOUR MOTHER, THE 'HIGH PRIESTESS' JEAN KING. SHE SAYS YOU ARE THE ONE WHO MADE IT POSSIBLE FOR THESE FEEBLE HUMANS TO TRAP ME ON YOUR MISERABLE LITTLE PLANET. I ADMIT IT WAS CLEVER OF YOU TO BOTTLE UP MY FLEET IN HIGH ORBIT. I INVITE YOU TO JOIN ME. COME TO ME AND DO MY BIDDING AND I WILL LET YOUR MOTHER LIVE. RESIST ME...AND SHE DIES!"

A loud *"thrumming"* hurt Sally's ears as the square spacecraft with its protruding cannon floated down towards the surface.

With a loud "THUD" it settled at an angle upon the rocky slope of a nearby hill.

Yellow lights flared up along its top, brilliantly illuminating the surrounding landscape.

A large flat panel slid to the side and out stepped what to Sally's eyes appeared to be a tall, red *Demon*—dragging a limp nun.

"I TAKE THE IMAGE OF YOUR GREATEST OPPONENT!" the Demon's still-amplified voice boomed across the stark landscape. "I AM THE STUFF OF YOUR NIGHTMARES! I AM THE ABSOLUTE RULER OF THE UNDERWORLD. I AM A POWER THAT SUCCESSFULLY OPPOSES YOUR GOD. I AM THE DEVOURER OF YOUR SOULS. I AM YOUR *TRUE* 'GOD' THAT YOU ALREADY SERVE EVERY TIME YOU FAIL TO BE 'GODLY'. I AM THE END OF YOUR STUPID REBELLION. I AM YOUR TRUE FRIEND, NOT THIS ALOOF 'GOD' THAT SEEKS TO DESTROY YOU. I MEAN TO TAKE YOU TO A NEW PLACE WHERE YOU CAN SERVE A MAGNIFICENT PURPOSE. I GIVE YOU A DESTINY FAR GREATER THAN YOU CAN CONCEIVE. COME TO ME AND BE TRULY FULFILLED!"

Dave cringed, trying to hide both himself and Sally from this fearful apparition.

"That Alien sure talks a lot," Dave whispered to her. "You stay safely hidden and I'll go distract him. Maybe I'll *debate* with him— talk *him* to death!"

He started to stand up but she pulled him back beneath the ledge.

"No, Dave," she whispered back. "We c-can't stand up to him! You stay and..."

"I take up your challenge!" an equally determined voice answered the Demon—as *Eashoa* stepped out from behind a dune, striding forward purposely.

"And just who are you?" the Demon grinned evilly at the approaching old man. He casually dropped Jean to the ground and took a few steps forward, his hoofs ringing on now-revealed hard rocks. "You are not Dr. King. Why should I bother with you?"

"Because you have no choice!" the old Commander shouted, suddenly lifting up his beat-up assault rifle and aiming it straight at the twelve-foot-tall, towering Demon.

"Ah, hah, *hah!*" Satan laughed. "I see from the little minds around me that your rifle is damaged beyond repair. You are trying to *bluff* me, old man. That gun is just a prop in the drama of your utter destruction. It is amusing. It'd be a true *miracle* if you could successfully resist me."

"And just maybe I have some 'juice' left that you don't know about!" Eashoa yelled back at him, holding the battered weapon close as he pulled the trigger...

—letting loose a *barrage* of bullets!

"I've learned a lot about repairing broken guns over the last few centuries!" Eashoa shouted over the ROAR of his assault rifle.

Sally cringed back from the "*breeeeppppp*" of the savage discharge.

The noise was strangely comforting, reminding her of a long-lost friend...

What *had* happened to her little lost dinosaur pet, anyway?

The Demon was hit numerous times, *smashed* to the ground—its red chest *vibrating* from the impacts, its arms *flailing*-about and its tail *whipping* in a violent half-circle!

Then it crumpled to the sand, motionless.

"And I know a little about 'miracles'," Eashoa sneered, walking cautiously up to the limp creature. Contemptuously, he prodded its side with a black boot then walked over to help Jean King up to her feet.

She looked shocked but very much alive.

"What's happening?" she said, blinking. "And who are you?" she said to the Commander.

"I am a friend," he gallantly replied, bowing deeply. "You are safe now, dear lady."

"Go to your mother," Sally urged Dave. "I'm ok."

Leaving Sally behind under the safety of the ledge, Dave dashed out across the muddy sand, slipping and sliding, to leap over the body of the fallen Demon and grab up the nun in a warm hug!

"Mom! You're alive!" he grinned at her. "And I'll bet it was *you* that made the Harvester vulnerable, causing it to crash back in Jerusalem, saving us."

"Well," she smiled, seemingly flustered. "A mother does what she can to protect her children."

"Very touching!" the Demon said as it levered itself back to its feet. He casually batted the Commander's rifle off to the side. "You thought your little projectiles could stop me? I'm not a biological being!"

"So you dare to return here after you were soundly vanquished?" the old man asked, seemingly unperturbed—still standing defiantly in front of the rising Demon.

"Well, I'm not up to my usual strength, that's true," the horned Demon laughed at Eashoa as it rose onto its hoofs. "But even as a projection of my true self, I'm a *hundred times stronger* than an old man like you."

It stretched up to its full height, disdainfully looking down upon the cluster of three little humans.

Sally's rapt attention was suddenly diverted...

Over there by the protruding Obelisk she spotted a *glint of deep black* poking up out of the sand.

"You *are* persistent, aren't you, my old adversary?" Eashoa stated, calmly stepping in front of Jean and her son, protecting them from the Creature.

"Do I know you?" the Demon questioned, leaning closer to focus his bright yellow eyes down upon the elderly soldier.

The glaring floodlights from the spacecraft lit the entire scene in an eerie glow. Sally was transfixed by the drama. It was like she was watching an intense Broadway play, the actors standing stark and vivid up upon a brightly lit stage.

"Oh, you know me," Eashoa said, his one big brown eye staring unblinkingly up into the Creature's malignant gaze.

Likewise keeping one eye on what was happening by the landed spacecraft, Sally roused herself from the transfixing spectacle. She began crawling silently and inconspicuously across the wet sand...

She hoped her red jumpsuit squirming along behind its back wouldn't attract the Creature's peripheral attention.

"*Well* now," the Demon gleefully laughed, its long forked tongue flicking out as if in anticipation of a tasty banquet, "if it isn't my ancient foe the *Son of God!* I didn't recognize you, what with you being so old and feeble. On how many worlds throughout this wide Galaxy have we battled?"

"Too many to count," the Commander stated.

"—and, it appears, I've finally *won!*" the Creature snorted, two puffs of black smoke coming from its flared nostrils. "I see you've lost your supernatural powers. You're just a weak little human now, aren't you *Jesus*—left to repair broken guns with your own two little hands? What happened to you? Did your Daddy get mad at you and cut you off? Have you been a *bad* little boy?"

"Jesus?" Jean King gasped, looking at the old man with awe. "Is it really you?"

"Hi, Jean," he nodded to her. "You've done well, my child. You never lost faith in me. And I never lost faith in you."

"Oh, my God!" she cried, falling to her knees.

Sally kept crawling. That black glint was getting closer...

"This is *so* touching," the Demon laughed again. "But it doesn't change the fact that you, Jesus, are a *pitiful shadow* of what you once were."

"And you don't look so good yourself, Satan," Eashoa replied.

Sally noted he deliberately kept the Creature's attention focused upon himself as behind the Demon's back she kept on crawling!

"Well, I admit that your precious little humans have—only temporarily though, mind you—cut me off from my major energy-sources," the Demon impatiently replied. "For the moment I'm not my usual omnipotent self. But I'm certainly powerful enough to squash all of you little..."

"Stop!" Sally suddenly yelled at him from across the sands.

She was weakly standing, aiming with both her hands the *black gun!*

But the gun didn't seem real. It was *pulsating*, as if it were simultaneously part of this and some other reality.

She thought it might be red hot. But, instead, it felt *slick*— greased by an unknown dimensional lubricant...

—all ready to loose in one immense blast an incredible, two millennia-accumulated bolt of sheer ENERGY!

Sally suddenly realized it hadn't just been accumulating common diffuse terrestrial energy for the last 2,000 years. It had also accumulated *TIME* ENERGY when it fell backward with her across two millennia!

This was an immensely powerful weapon.

"Careful, there, young lady," Satan cautioned her as he spun around. He extended a chastening paw in her direction, apparently recognizing the extreme danger. "You might *hurt* someone with that gun—in particular, your boyfriend, his mother, and your decrepit religious mentor. If you fire on me, *they* will be incinerated as well."

"If we are all to die, then I'm damn well taking you with us!" Sally growled. She kept the gun aimed straight at the Demon. "I think you know this is a special gun—one that might even kill you! Let my friends come to me and then we'll talk."

"Talk?" the Demon threw his head back and laughed, "What about—'*everything*'?" he sneered. "I'm not interested."

Before Sally could respond to his taunt the Demon suddenly leapt *a hundred feet* up in the air and off to the side, landing on a hill where he *jumped* yet again...

Sally tried to keep him in her gun sights.

But he was too fast—skittering away into the surrounding dark hills faster than she could follow.

Just like that, they were alone.

Sally dropped to her knees in the wet sand. The gun felt like it weighed a ton in her hands.

"I think I can fly the cannon ship," Jean quickly interjected as Sally felt Eashoa's strong hand gently helping her back to her feet. "We can use it to try and escape Earth's Judgment Day. I assume you can bring down the global shield if you want?" she asked her son.

"You know about Judgment Day?"

"Why, of course, Davey," she shrugged. "It's in the Bible isn't it?"

"Sure, but..."

"—and Sally told me all about it as well," Jean gravely added.

"I did?" Sally said as she staggered up to them, the heavy black gun hanging unfired from her hands.

"Oh, not you, dear—the *other* Sally."

"*Which* Sally?" Sally asked.

"My good friend, of course—the first High Priestess."

"She was a Sally too?" Dave asked, confused.

"She was different from the Sally who was with you when you announced the discovery of DE-generators at the United Nations," Eashoa tried to explain to him.

"What happened to her?" Dave asked. "She vanished when I and my other friends disappeared."

"She saved us from the initial incursion by the Demon—dying when their Harvester slammed into the earth, which triggered the Nuclear Winter," the old man continued. "She turned out to be an amazing incarnation of Sally. Her legacy, unfortunately, is a mixed bag."

"So the Sally that got killed by the falling debris in the American Art Museum...?" Dave asked.

"Yes, she was also a different Sally," Eashoa replied. "I know it's confusing. Even I from my broader timeline-change-sensing 'perspective', find it hard to keep up. This is indeed an entertaining planet, Dimension, and timeline."

"So there have been *four* of me?" Sally asked the old man, marveling at the strange twists of fate she'd somehow triggered.

"I'm afraid so, my dear Sahlee," Eashoa gently replied, reverting to his personal pronunciation of her name.

"And which one, again, are *you*?" Dave asked, concerned, peering intently at the pert, teenaged girl in front of him.

"I'm the *original!*" Sally asserted, stomping her girlish feet into the sand in emphasis. "Indeed, despite present appearance, I'm nearly a hundred years old."

"Oh...well...how about that?" Dave gulped, "But, what about *me?*"

"Well, I suppose that you're—*not* the original, I'm afraid," she sighed regretfully, but then hastened to add, "however, you're quite indistinguishable—an excellent 'Dave'!"

"Well, then," Dave frowned. "I suppose that's some consolation. Then since we've got it all sorted out should we...?"

"NO YOU DON'T!" a *huge, booming voice* above them rocked them back on their heels.

It was Satan.

But now instead of being a mere twelve feet tall...he was a *thousand* feet tall—with the red *Obelisk* held casually in one of his clawed hands!

They stared up in disbelief.

The towering Demon above them contemptuously tossed the Obelisk away...spinning it up into the sky to vanish into the roiling, black clouds!

"THANK YOU FOR BRINGING ME HERE. YOUR TIME-TRAVEL DEVICE WASN'T DEAD AFTER ALL. IT STILL HAD STORED WITHIN ITS DAMAGED MATRIX VAST AMOUNTS OF TIME-ENERGY GATHERED IN ITS TRAVELS. SO I SUCKED IT DRY, REGAINING MY FULL POWERS," he laughed, placing his giant paws upon his goatish gargantuan hips. "AND NOW I'M GOING TO SQUASH YOU LITTLE BUGS *FLAT!*"

He lifted up one gigantic black hoof, poising it high above Sally, Dave, Jean, and Eashoa...

"I don't think so!" the old man shouted back. "Look above you, Satan! Can you defeat that?"

The gigantic creature looked skyward.

It let out a terrible *scream* that rocked the hills around Sally!

She saw above the towering giant—radiating down through the thick, nighttime clouds—an *ominous red glow*...

"It's Judgment Day!" Eashoa yelled up at him again. "It's advanced yet again because of the massive DE-explosions you provoked in Jerusalem! And now it's centered on you, attracted by the Obelisk's energy! You can't escape! You're still trapped here on this planet's surface! God is sending you straight to Hell, you wicked Beast!"

"Then I'm taking you putrid insects *with* me!" the Demon yelled back at them as he lowered his gigantic hoof...

—as Sally jerked up her inter-dimensional gun and pulled the trigger...

—and the hoof was fractured into three parts as the *bolt of pure-white ENERGY* went up through it...continuing on through his leg, through his torso, through his head, up through the Dark Energy planetary shield, and off into the far reaches of outer space.

The Satanic figure *shattered* into a thousand pieces.

The biggest piece, the major part of one hoof, *SLAMMED* down onto the cannon spacecraft, *crushing* it before bouncing off to the side and coming to a rest against a low hill.

All around them, other fragments of the gigantic Satan-figure were raining down...

But in the middle of the hundred-foot-high hoof fragment leaning against the nearby slope Sally saw a large *swirling, black hole.*

"That's a *portal,*" Sally informed the rest. She pointed with the steaming-hot gun that she still held in her hands.

It was a *fifty foot-high glittering, black-diamond maelstrom...*

"But where does it go?" Dave asked, his voice trembling.

"Does it matter, Son?" Jean said. "I think my Sally—the real High Priestess—would tell us to 'go'!"

"It's our escape," Dave nodded. "Judgment Day will hit us in minutes if not seconds. Come on, everybody!"

"Stop!" Sally ordered them, standing her ground between them and the hoof fragment, *pointing* the gun directly at them!

"What?" Dave frantically asked. "What the hell are you doing, Sally? We've got to get out of here!"

Sally still held the gun rigidly aimed straight at them.

"Maybe we should just end it here," Sally said as pieces of the shattered Satan kept crashing onto the rocks and sand all around them. "Do we really want this merry-go-round to continue? Do we want to go through this time-cycling again—then on and on and on?"

"We've got to find a way to *survive!*" Dave yelled back over the loud "thudding" of the still-falling Satan-fragments. "This can't be the end of humanity. We've got to do what we planned—go back in time and stop the Alien invasion. That will push off Judgment Day again, giving our species more time to evolve. If we can just hold off God long enough then maybe we can..."

"And what do *you* say, Jesus?" Sally asked her old friend, interrupting Dave.

Then she slowly lowered the gun. She stepped over and took his well-weathered hand in her own.

His ancient face crinkled up into a wry smile.

"I think that we should trust in God," he simply stated.

"Me too," Jean King added, reverently taking Eashoa's other arm in her own.

"Then that's it," Sally said, nodding to Jean and the Commander as she slipped the gun into her waistband. "We're staying. What about you, Dave?"

Dave, in apparent agony, looked from Sally to the steadily shrinking Portal and then back again.

He was clearly torn between their friendship and the prospect of escaping yet again...

As he struggled, Sally became aware that her arm hurt.

Glancing down, she saw that that pesky *Turtle Tattoo* was glowing brighter than she'd ever seen it before! It felt like it was burning through her wrist. It was certainly telling her to go—go *now!*

To hell with the damn thing!

She ignored the fierce pain, shoving her left wrist beneath her right armpit.

Dave sighed deeply, stepping over to hug Sally tightly.

Her left arm slipped back to her side, the fierce pain in her wrist fading away.

She felt his warm breath on her neck.

"It's better to be with you for a few more minutes, than to live an eternity without you," he whispered in her ear. "I'm staying too."

"Then we're going to have to fight!" Eashoa yelled, running over to snatch up his assault rifle.

Sally looked around in fear.   The demon-fragments that had crashed into the sandy hills around them were *reforming*...

Each of them became a smaller *replica of the Demon!*

They ranged from a few inches high to dozens of feet tall...

—each of whom the moment they formed up began *screaming* together in high-pitched rage...

—and they were all walking towards the still-glistening, swirling *Portal*...

"If those Creatures get sent back in time they'll make Earth a bulwark in their plan to defy God, preventing DE-usage—and torturing humanity at their leisure for eons into the future!" Eashoa yelled at the others over the wailing of the Demon-clones. "We've got to defend the Portal long enough for it to completely shut down!"

Sally ran with the others toward the Portal.

Then they turned around, standing firmly right in front of it, facing-down the swarm of approaching satanic figures.

"We can't stop them with just one rifle and my nearly-depleted gun," Sally calmly observed. "That won't give us enough time to..."

"Hi, Mommy!" a cheerful voice sounded from down around their legs.

Startled, Sally looked down to see *Tommy!*

"I brought some friends with me," he chortled. "I hope you don't mind!"

Behind her she heard a loud "*stomping*"....

—as she pushed her comrades off to the side and a HERD OF TOWERING DINOSAURS came thundering out of the Portal!

Long-necked, seventy-ton *Sauroposidons* were smashing and trampling the Satan figures.   T-rex-like, *spined Acrocanthosaurus* top-predators were biting Satans in half or swallowing them in one gulp!   "Thunder-thighs" *Brontomerus mcintoshi* were kicking the Demons into pieces!   And *Pterodactyls* with twenty-foot wingspans were swooping down to spear stray, scampering-away Satans!

Above them the reddening glow was *consuming* the clouds, *blazing* across the sky!

The landscape took on a shimmering, *melting* quality—like a painting straight from Salvador Dali.

"Let's keep them on the run!" the Commander yelled, advancing with his gun blazing at the Demons that survived the initial dinosaur assault.

But the gun went silent...

"I'm out of ammo!" Eashoa yelled at Dave, who swung his backpack around to yank out a clip and toss it to him.

"Thanks!" Eashoa called back as he slapped it into place and kept blasting away.

And at Eashoa's elbow happily pointing out the stray little Demon trying to sneak past was Jean King.

Together the unlikely theological duo charged ahead, relentlessly driving back the remaining demons.

"Shoot them, Jesus—*shoot* them!" Jean chortled.

—as Tommy dashed out from behind Sally again..."*Surprise!*" he happily yelled up at them.

"*Breeeeep!*" a familiar reptilian face honked loudly as it hopped up in front of Sally and Dave.

It was the ostrich-sized small dinosaur "Breep."

"Breep, *there* you are!" Dave laughed, hugging him around his long, sinewy neck.

"Hey, boy, it's good to see you," Sally said, joining Dave in the spontaneous hug...

—as with a *kick* of its powerful legs it *leapt* through the closing Portal...

—taking Sally and Dave with him.

Chapter 21

TIME ENOUGH

In between the Here and the Now

Rests an eternity of contemplation

Where a thousand years is like a day

And each day is like a thousand years

Lost so often in the hectic press of life

Consumed by momentary imperatives

Forgotten pursing fleeting pleasures

But still ours to reach out and claim

Should we have the guts to do so

Expanding sight, taste, smell, and feel

Hearing angel chimes in empty space

Not as mere meditation or nothingness

But a rich tapestry of what's possible

And beyond that to what's impossible

Vividly seen as new colors and images

There in the expanse of our own minds

Made undeniably solid and real...

The Luminary Chronicles, 21:1-5

Dave was facedown, lying upon thick grass.

The many green blades tickled his face. He smelled fresh air. He saw an orange bug crawling on rich brown dirt at the tip of his nose. He felt his backpack pushing down on his torso. Wherever he was, he at least still had his supplies and laptop. He slowly lifted up his head and looked around at a verdant, vibrant valley.

Shakily rising to his feet, he found himself in the center of a grassy meadow on a mountain slope.

The sky above his head was deep blue. Surrounding taller mountains rose majestically high into the sky. A sparkling, white-water river ran through the center of the valley. And spread out into a misty haze before him were all manner of living creatures. Some he recognized. Others looked strange, bizarre...

"*Dave!*" he heard a happy shout behind him.

Expecting to see Sally he spun around... But all he saw was a thin young man running toward him. The man had a scraggly goatee, longish greasy hair, and numerous tattoos covering his arms. He wore a plain white T-shirt over torn jeans.

And on the left side of his face was a *black tattoo of a cobra*, etched from his forehead to his throat.

"Snake!" Dave gasped, remembering the "hippy" boyfriend—or tattoo artist—of Sally's.

He almost knocked Dave down, hurtling into him and hugging him tightly.

"Uh...but aren't you supposed to be dead?" Dave said, allowing the man's thin hands to thump him happily on his back. "I went to your funeral—is that it, then? Am *I* dead? Are we in heaven?"

"I'm so glad that you made it, dude!" Snake grinned widely into Dave's face. "Naw, we ain't dead. This ain't heaven, but it's close! I just pretended to get killed. And I been keepin' an eye out for ya!"

"Uhm...'made it'...what do you mean?" Dave asked, only now realizing that his legs were trembling. He felt totally drained of energy. He stumbled, almost falling.

And the mountains seemed to be spinning around him.

"Oh, sorry, dude," Snake said, helping Dave to sit back down on the grassy meadow. He kindly lifted the heavy backpack off of Dave's shoulder and set it to the side. "I've forgot how traumatic the trip is. Man, that's a *long* ways to travel, fer sure! You need some water, maybe a sandwich?"

"So...did I...did *we*...make it to the past?" Dave said, swallowing hard and forcing his head to stop spinning. "Are we before the Alien invasion? Is there still time to stop them?"

Snake put an arm around Dave's trembling shoulders, helping him to steady himself.

"No, man," Snake said, shaking his head in denial. "You failed, dude—but I guess that's what God wants, huh? As long as we kin stay livin' then that's not so bad, right?"

Dave pushed off Snake's arm and looked straight up at the intensely blue sky. A strange-looking bird with *four* wings leisurely flapped past. And across his legs, a *three-foot-long* "centipede" was crawling. He almost panicked at the weirdness. But around him in the meadow, small clusters of blue and white flowers waved cheerfully, calming him.

"Snake—assuming for the moment that both of us are really alive—just where *are* we? Were we transported through the Portal to another planet? Is this...one of those parallel Dimensions that George told me about? Or are we deep in the past before humans appeared?"

Snake took in a long breath of the fresh air, smiling benignly. He looked a bit frustrated—as if he'd like to smoke some weed, but couldn't find any.

"You *did* it man!" Snake congratulated Dave, giving him a friendly slap on his leg. "You did what I and the others were *hoping* you could do."

"I still don't understand," Dave said as he watched the three-foot long "centipede" creature leisurely crawl off his leg back into the long grass. A soothing, cool breeze blew across Dave's face. Despite his intense weariness and tension, he felt himself relaxing.

"Snake, what's..." he looked from the centipede back to his younger friend—who was now *gone!*

And in his place was a twenty-foot-long, thick-bodied, rainbow-colored, *actual* giant snake!

It fixated Dave with mesmerizing, golden spheres that were flecked with red. A black slit went up through the center of each of the eyes.

Dave heard a gentle, telepathic voice in his head.

"*We're the ones who were guiding Sally all this time,*" the Voice spoke in Dave's head. "*We're an ancient race of intelligent reptiles from one of Earth's parallel dimensions. Sally was special. There are only a few like her in the Universe. She was beloved by God—*

given the chance to alter timelines. She didn't know any of this, of course, but we knew and chose to help her."

"But to transmute your form, communicate with me by telepathy? I can deal with you being intelligent reptiles. But how can you...?"

"We are also Martians."

"What?"

"We made the Obelisk that resulted in the overthrow of Satan," Snake stated casually.

"What?" Dave repeated dumbly.

"Did it not seem a stretch that Time Energy would focus the Day of Judgment's fire's upon that evil Creature?"

"Well, I really didn't have time to..."

"We were already ancient when we escaped Mar's deteriorating surface conditions through the Obelisk into a parallel Earth dimension."

"But that was in..."

"Yes, Earth's distant past—from which point on we developed even further."

"So you knew all about...?"

"Oh yes, Dave," the Voice calmly agreed. *"We knew of God's impending Wrath. But still, we could see no way to avoid God's collective Judgment upon the Earth. Next to God, we were—and are—nothing. But then, toward the end, we detected something wonderful...a human girl blessed by God to be a fulcrum around which Time itself could bend: a 'Time-Twister'!"*

"So...you...?"

The rainbow head of the giant Snake waved back and forth in apparent glee.

"We gave her a cute little Turtle Tattoo with which we could interface—and tried to help her make good choices," the Voice continued in Dave's mind. *"We tried to guide her in her...pivots! And somehow those pivots always led back to you. She and you were connected, somehow."*

"Yes...I felt it..."

"And we hoped that Sally might go back in time and change things, so that our Great Creator would be tempted to take pity on

our unworthy timelines—and allow at least a few of us to continue forward upon the Earth."

"But...that *didn't* happen. Judgment Day *hit* us...I think," Dave gulped, his throat feeling dry. "Maybe I could have that glass of water now?"

"Let's go over to the little stream," Snake said, his long thick body flowing smoothly across the grass.

Dave stood up shakily. He put his backpack on, and followed the intelligent reptile—then gratefully slumped to his knees beside a small, burbling, mountain stream. He cupped his hands into the water and brought it to his lips. It was delicious.

Refreshed, he turned back to the giant, intelligent snake.

"The last thing I remember was being dragged into the Portal," Dave said, feeling warm sunlight streaming through the tree leaves above him. A warm breeze caressed his face.

"Yes," the Voice agreed as Snake nodded his large head, his forked tongue rapidly flicking in-and-out. *"But it wasn't just there. All through the various Dimensions the Portal also opened. And though it appeared in each Dimension only briefly, a number of Earth's Intelligent Creatures were allowed to come here."*

"So is this Earth?" Dave asked again.

"Yes."

"But...*when?*"

"Well, Dave..." the Voice in Dave's head dramatically paused. *"You are one billion years in your future!"*

Dave looked at the telepathic Snake uncomprehendingly.

"Did you say a *billion* years—in the *future?*" Dave gasped, his eyes stretched wide. "But...that's *way* past Judgment Day! Oh my God..."

The big snake curled itself into an overlapping circle, positioning its big head on top, staring at Dave with its large orange eyes before answering.

"Yes, the Earth in all its parallel Dimensions was destroyed," the Voice sadly stated. *"But life survived at the bottom of the deep oceans—mostly single-cell amoeba and bacteria. But that was sufficient."*

Dave nodded, understanding.

"*Over the next many millions of years an atmosphere returned,*" the mental Voice continued. "*Comet strikes from the traumatized, scrambled solar system brought in fresh water. Gradually, multicellular life again developed and evolved further. No truly intelligent God-and-Self-aware intelligent races have yet re-evolved on this New Earth, leaving plenty of room for us. The sun's more swollen and redder than before, but we have a new home here—where, hopefully, we intelligent beings from the distant past can finally strive together to be truly wiser and more Godly.*"

Dave struggled to take this in as he stood beside the small creek.

"But...*can* we learn the lessons of our terrible mistakes—or are we doomed to repeat the past?" Dave mused.

"*We don't know,*" the Voice answered. "*But now we have the chance to try.*"

"So where is Sally?" Dave asked, weakly walking from the stream back into the lush meadow. "We were pulled into the Portal together. Did she land somewhere nearby?"

The giant snake hung his head, not looking at Dave.

"I said—where *is* she?" Dave asked more intently, stepping over to lift up the big snakehead and look it square in one of its large orange eyes.

"*We don't know,*" the Voice admitted sadly. "*When only our reptilian species made it across we assumed that maybe you and she— the last two humans—were sent backward in time to do what you'd intended, stop the Alien invasion. And the arrival of us travelers from the past was scattered out, even up to this present moment.*"

"But...you say...?"

"*Only you came through,*" Snake sighed inside Dave's head. "*Sally may be once again in the distant past vainly fighting to stop unalterable Fate...again and again—fighting the Aliens or lost in the time-stream—we just don't know.*"

Dave patted Snake on his scaly head and turned away, wobbling back into the flowery field. He sat in the middle of the waving grass, facing away from Snake. It was an awful lot to take in all at once.

He was the only human left.

It was going to be a lonely existence. Sure there was a giant talking snake, other creatures from other timelines, and a whole host of newly evolved animals.

But there was no Sally.

He hid his face in his arms.

He didn't want Snake to see him cry.

Chapter 22

<u>NEW EARTH</u>

All the apocalyptic Holy Writings
Teach of a "New Earth" where the Righteous reign
In a pure land where sin and filth does not exist
Where, unsoiled by original sin, man can thrive
What a magnificently impossible dream
Humans with their genetic imperatives
Scratching, biting, and fighting
Caught up in being the Fittest
Requiring that others must die
For the Dominant to Survive
A chaotic existence driven by chance
Environmental Imperatives ruling progress
Where all creatures compete in a ruthless game
And the unfit get eaten while the "fit" compulsively breed
Chained to the dictates of physics, biology, and psychology
Anything different but a momentary fancy
Of those that were not content
To surrender to their Creator
But live out their remaining existence
Contemplating the gap between what is desired
And what there must be...
Unless?

The Luminary Chronicles, 22:1-5

Dave found great intellectual challenge and satisfaction interacting with the intelligent dinosaurs and reptiles who'd escaped from the past by traveling a billion years into the future.

Dave was delighted to discover that George and his wife Alice made it across. The Portal opened in the Dinosapien city where Sally #2 had gone with George and his wife Alice—such that they and many of their species escaped Judgment Day.

They told him what Sally #2 heroically did to save their people from the Harvester. So Dave missed his brave Sally even more.

They filled in the blanks with further trans-dimensional observations—telling him how his Sally prevented the alien Satan from arriving unhindered from the Galactic Core, losing her own life in the process. What an amazing girl she was, in all her several incarnations! Her selfless sacrifice was what made it possible for God to allow a few to continue beyond Judgment Day.

In Snake's Dimension, they'd been long hoping for and expecting the reprieve. So when the Portal appeared, they were ready. Most of their small remaining number of ancient, intelligent Martian reptiles quickly made it across.

In a few other reptilian dimensions some individuals also escaped through the briefly opened Portal.

Dave—a life-long amateur herpetologist in addition to being a physicist—was fascinated with their various cultures and wonderful scientific achievements. Plus they exhibited endless patience towards him.

They viewed him as the last relic of a failed, primitive biological experiment.

On one hand he was insulted to be looked down upon, pitied for his "flaws."

On the other hand he was grateful for their acceptance since he knew full well that he and his species were the *cause* of Judgment Day descending upon all the variations of Earth!

So Dave stoically bore the shame. Indeed, it was because of *him* that the nonhuman civilizations—including most of their individuals living at Judgment Day—were incinerated a billion years in the past.

And yet despite his notoriety Dave could have happily stayed on with them, content to be a mammalian freak-show "rock star".

As long as he was the *last* survivor of *Homo sapiens* he was unique, an object of interest, not at all a *threat*.

But he did not want their acclaim or pity.

Neither did he want their perks.

The Dinosapiens and snake-people were collaboratively building *starships*—powered by (what else?) Dark Energy! He could have joined the science teams building the engines, or even applied to be a crewmember. But he had no thought of leaving Earth.

Also, he did not choose to live in the thriving dinosaur or reptilian cities.

Instead—though he visited them from time-to-time, particularly George and Alice—he opted to spend most of his time in a small hut that he built for himself in the woods near the elevated mouth of the valley.

And, as several years passed by, he traveled away from the valley less and less.

It was peaceful for Dave there, all by himself. Food was plentiful. There were fruits and nuts in the forest. He was now, by choice, a vegetarian. He didn't have the heart to kill any of the many strange and wondrous, newly evolved animals. So the critters in the valley accepted him without fear, becoming his friends.

The Dinosapiens kindly provided him with a variety of forged tools—including picks and shovels. So he started several plots of farmed land, where he grew his own vegetables. The Dinosapiens brought with them seeds from a billion years ago, so he had real potatoes, corn, beans, tomatoes, and carrots. It was more than enough for his modest dietary needs.

Snake at first visited him often, but then less and less. Snake had always been fascinated with a reptilian version of the "Star Trek" novels. He was now training to be a crewmember on the first interstellar mission.

Dave wished him all the best, but preferred to remain secluded in his own little slice of New Earth, withdrawing into himself.

He stopped trimming his beard and hair, becoming more and more a wild "mountain man" in form as well as function.

He took care of his own simple needs and began to compose songs, playing on a crude guitar he built for himself.

And each day he walked down from his hut through the forest to that stream where he'd taken his first drink of water upon arriving in the future—and from there to stroll out into the lush meadow.

But now it was getting to be fall. The green leaves of the trees in the forest were turning yellow, brown, and red. Many of the "birds" that filled the sky were migrating away in big flocks.

They were intent on their journey. Some of them were particularly aggressive, even predatory. Dave was especially careful of the big black ones with the red, curved beaks. He'd seen them descend upon flocks of smaller birds and tear them to shreds before gobbling up their remains. He was glad for them to migrate out of the valley!

This was not an idyllic "garden of Eden" where the animals all got along with each other. Evolution was still at play, granting survival only to the fittest.

Involuntarily, Dave shuddered.

It was chilly enough for Dave to wear his jacket—getting threadbare, but still functional.

In spite of the pervasive presence of fierce, implacable Mother Nature, Dave still found the verdant valley wonderful—still vividly recalling the terrible Nuclear Winter he'd suffered through so long ago!

He shuddered again, remembering that awful time when the sky was a continuous muddy dark, when little sunlight made it to the surface, and green plant life disappeared.

How had he survived then—and why did mankind bring that horrendous end upon itself? He often meditated on the ills and sins of mankind—working it over and over in his mind.

Surely humanity could have avoided being condemned! *Jesus*, they had no excuse! And yes, they even had the *real* Jesus to point them the Way.

So why was the *Homo sapiens* species so abysmally *stupid?*

And, yes—perhaps that *was* their ultimate Sin which doomed them in God's eyes—a voluntary, *deliberate* stupidity!

Dave laughed to himself.

Maybe that was why God allowed him to pass over to New Earth— as a "visual aid" to remind the other intelligent races what could happen if they got too "big for their britches."

The last survivor of a *malignant* intelligent species...

But then Dave's musings were interrupted by a *crashing* and *stomping* out in the woods!

He was instantly on his guard.

Yes there were top predators on this new world, such as the cooperative flocks of four-winged black birds—but none so large as to threaten Dave.

At least, that'd been true for the past several years he'd been there...

Was there perhaps a larger predator in the woods he'd not yet encountered?

Maybe he should return to his safe hut until he found out what was out *rampaging* through the forest?

But, no—the *tearing* and *ripping* sounds faded off into the distance. Whatever unknown predator was out there in the woods had departed.

So Dave walked on out into the meadow, just as he'd done hundreds of times before...

—and saw there lying prone in the grass, face-down, and *shivering*...Sally.

He ran over to her and gently helped her to roll over, to gaze up unbelievingly at the blue sky with her wide-opened green eyes.

She was still clad in her bright-red, tattered jumpsuit. The warm coat she'd had on before entering the Portal was gone, likely ripped-away.

The black super-gun that had opened up the Portal was securely tucked into her waistband.

And turned up to the sky on her wrist was the green Turtle Tattoo, its bright glow slowly fading away.

"Is...is that you, Dave?" she whispered. Her bright green eyes were wide and confused.

"Yes, it's me, Sally."

"But...you're so—*hairy!*"

He laughed, absently stroking his long shaggy beard while flipping back the long bangs hanging down past his shoulders.

"It's been a long time since we got knocked through the Portal."

"W-where's B-Breep?" she frowned, starting to look around her to each side.

"I think he's out exploring the woods," Dave grinned widely, realizing what it was that he'd heard earlier thrashing through the forest.

"What...in the w-woods? Just w-where are we, Dave?"

"It's a long story," he smiled at her, helping her to wobbly get up to her feet. "The short version is we were *thrown* past Judgment Day a *billion* years into the future! I got here first. I thought you were lost. You or Breep never arrived. For years I've been the last human. But now you're here also! And there's plenty of time for me to tell you all the details of my future and past adventures. In fact, I'm even writing a book about it."

He put a hand to her arm, steadying on to stand upright on the green grass.

"A b-book?" she asked, shivering in the cool breeze. He whipped off his jacket and draped it around her tattered corpse-clothing.

She looked suitably stunned by his revelations to her.

"Yep, I'm writing on my solar-powered laptop which I cleverly managed to bring along with me, tucked into my backpack," he excitedly chattered away. "It's quite poetic and artistic. Lots of fun to write! In fact I actually *sing* each of the chapters. Hah! I initially thought it was just something to amuse me and keep me from jumping off a cliff or something. But I now see that it's maybe a cautionary tale for future human generations. Well, that's presumptuous of me, of course, since they'd have to come from the two of us and..."

"But I'm n-not your..." she automatically began to chide him, then stopped, weakly shrugging. "Well, m-maybe I am..." she ruefully smiled at him.

Dave giddily contemplated the idea of making children.

The Dinosapiens and Martians wouldn't like it. In fact, they'd probably forbid it.

But they were just dumb reptiles. Humans were meant to rule! He'd find a way to deal with them when the time came.

He helped her take a few faltering steps. She looked around in amazement, luxuriating in the beautiful magnificence of the valley.

"How do you live here?"

"Oh, I built a hut. It's actually quite nice. You'll like it."

"You know how to build a hut?"

He laughed. "Yes, I know that plus a bunch more about surviving in the wilderness. But if you don't like it, Sally, there are cities we could go to."

"Cities? But you said you were the last human?"

"Some of our lizard friends came along with us."

"Oh...then it really is up to us to keep the human species going?"

He grinned again.

"Yep! And our descendants should know about their past," he mused as he walked slowly along with Sally through the meadow, "and maybe avoid making the same mistakes. Also, I think if our fellow dino-reptilian survivors see us safely contained, then mankind—this time around—will have help."

"H-help?" she asked, curious.

"Our 'friends'," he answered, "all together on one New Earth, at last. I think the human race will greatly benefit from being with races much older and wiser than us. We'll have a chance to do things over again, but right this time. That is, if we're smart instead of stupid."

"C-can we truly...be s-smart?" Sally hesitantly queried. Dave was pleased to see her quick mind starting to process the incredible changes she'd just experienced. "I mean...are we even c-capable?"

"We've already accomplished a lot Sally," Dave softly replied. "And that's when we were often at odds to each other. Together—united in purpose—we've got considerable brainpower."

"That's true..."

"And our genetics *do* give us powerful advantages along with the obvious negatives."

"You m-mean we f-find a w-way..."

"—to survive," Dave firmly concluded. "I don't think that's an imperative we should allow to be suppressed. We will do anything to keep on going, even dream of how to do the impossible!"

They walked together through the rustling grass in silence for a moment, just enjoying each other's company.

"What...d-do you...c-call it?" she seriously asked as she wavered unsteadily along, Dave reaching out again to support her elbow.

"My book? Its title?"

"It w-will have to be s-subtle."

"I hadn't thought of a title yet—I've been so busy dissecting and searching for the essence behind our incredible misadventures."

"T-titles are c-critically important," she knowingly stated.

Dave remembered she'd started her own, unique Church with its own impressive, compellingly descriptive title.

"Yes, it should be motivational but without invoking an obvious plot scary to our nonhuman friends."

He looked up at the deep blue sky, at the shimmering sunshine glancing off golden leaves, and out over the swirling white of the central, cascading mountain river.

The sun's unobscured light was incredibly beautiful. It provided undiluted warmth, energy, and insight.

"I think..." he replied thoughtfully, "I'll call it 'The Luminary Chronicles'."

"Nice name," she nodded. "Could I p-please have some w-water?"

He steered her over to the nearby, gurgling stream.

"As much as you want," he grinned, "—as much as you want!"

THE END

[continued in: *The Girl Who Danced With Snakes*]

Thank you for reading!

Dear reader,

I hope you enjoyed **The Girl Who Tempted God**. I was fascinated re-searching what scholars speculate about the "unknown years" of the young Jesus—then extrapolating forward into a distant, improbable fu-ture. The sequel to this book, **The Girl Who Danced with Snakes**, begins with Dave and Sally in what looks like a far-future Garden of Eden. But as with any lush garden, there are always snakes lurking...which con-spire to separate the two lovers forever.

I hope you are intrigued by the sequel's deadly central question: "To truly love must you drink poison?" Even a vile Socrates shudders at the answer.

Finally, I need to ask you for a favor. If you enjoyed this book and would like to encourage others to read it, **a review written by you** on the Am-azon page for this book would be greatly helpful. It's hard to get re-views nowadays and your support will be very important to both me and other readers. If you'd like to do so, I sincerely thank you in ad-vance for your time and effort. It can be as long or short as you wish.

Thanks again for reading my **Girl with the Turtle Tattoo** books and ex-periencing with me the thrill of historical exploration and extrapolation.

Sincerely,

Dan Lyle

About the Author:

Daniel Basil Lyle holds a Ph.D. in Biology, is a lifelong amateur herpetologist, taught medical immunology at a University, completed a career in cell biology research, lectures on how to apply theological and psychological principles in practical ways, and has a strong interest in all aspects of cosmology and physics. From a small kid he was fascinated with dinosaurs. As such, he has always lived with exotic creatures, including harmless snakes, all housed in his own homemade habitats. Some of his tame pet pythons and anacondas ranged up to twelve feet in length. He is the author of over thirty books, many of which are religious in nature. His writings go beyond the ordinary, exposing deeper aspects of life. His books are meant to be fun, conversational, and helpful. His various works are available at LylePublishing.com and Amazon.com. The "Girl with the Turtle Tattoo" science fiction series was inspired by paintings done by his mother, movies adapting Stieg Larsson's crime novels, and various men and women sporting spectacular body-art tattoos. The author hopes that you, the reader, find his characters spontaneous, quirky, surprising, and even thought-provoking—just as did he!

www.ingramcontent.com/pod-product-compliance
Lightning Source LLC
Chambersburg PA
CBHW070531260626
47161CB00002B/331